St. Petersburg

ST. PETE

by Andrey Biely

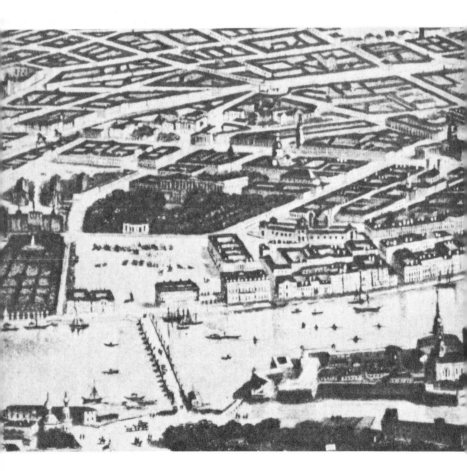

GROVE PRESS INC.

RSBURG

Translated with an Introduction by JOHN COURNOS

Foreword by GEORGE REAVEY

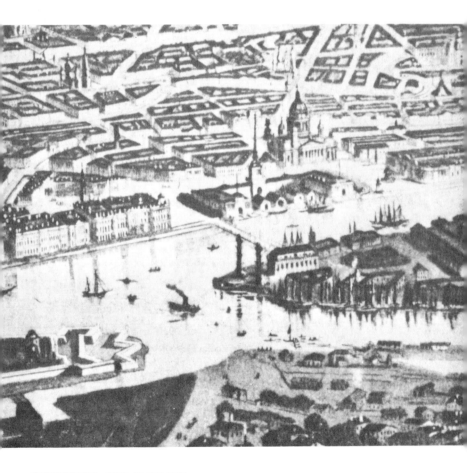

NEW YORK

Grove Press wishes to express its appreciation for the editorial help of George Reavey.

First Evergreen Edition 1959
Tenth Printing 1981
ISBN: 0-394-17237-X
Grove Press ISBN: 0-8021-4355-5
Library of Congress Catalog Card Number: 59-5417

Typeset by The Polyglot Press

MANUFACTURED IN THE UNITED STATES OF AMERICA
DISTRIBUTED BY RANDOM HOUSE, INC.
GROVE PRESS, INC., 196 WEST HOUSTON STREET,
NEW YORK, NEW YORK 10014

To

Isabel Satterthwaite

FOREWORD

St. Petersburg is the first of Andrey Biely's novels to be published
in English. It is an extraordinary novel conceived on many levels
and deliberately constructed to produce an impression of chaos and
nightmare. The plot however is fundamentally simple: it is a father-
son situation in which the father represents traditional bureaucracy
and the son a hostile, but rather confused, anti-traditional, nihilistic
revolutionary element. The action is compressed into little more
than two days in a particular city—St. Petersburg. The planned,
rectilinear city with its anonymous crowds and brewing revolutionary
events (1905) is a very important element and indeed a sort of
historical character, symbolized by the statue of the Bronze Horseman. The geometry of Petersburg as well as its bureaucracy is precise
and Western in plan, but underneath there is a seething, atavistic
Asiatic turmoil which threatens to upset the established order. It
is a city of strange shadows ("the biology of the· shadow has not
yet been studied"); of "insomnia, cigarettes, and alcohol"; a city
whose order is on the verge of an abyss; a city where secret agents
lurk in the dark and a monstrous agent-provocateur "with lips that
resembled slices of salmon—the yellowish kind" looms mysteriously
behind a whole network of shadowy events. It is a city in the grip
of nervous expectation, cataclysmic foreboding and a fatal urge to
destruction. This urge is exemplified in Nikolaï Ableukhov (the son)
and his bomb in a sardine tin—the bomb that ticks relentlessly
through the major part of the novel. The bomb explodes in the end
—a double symbol of a national and a family tragedy—but achieves
no complete destruction. The novel might well have been called
"The Last Days of St. Petersburg." It gives us a most vivid picture

of the nerve-wracked atmosphere during the last days of the two-century-old Petrine city before the Revolution.

St. Petersburg is certainly a major work of the twentieth century; but the reader must accustom himself to Biely's nervous style, his deliberately broken, many-layered narrative, and his abstract treatment of character, concentrating on the external, physical detail, gesture and typical utterance. In form and style, Biely certainly broke with the nineteenth-century tradition of the novel, and erected in Russian literature an original monument of his own which, as a result of many external circumstances, has not yet received sufficient attention or appraisal either in Russia or in Western Europe.

Andrey Biely began to write when he was at school and at the University of Moscow. His first important contribution was made between 1902 and 1909, when he published his four *Symphonies*, three books of poetry (*Gold in Azure, Ashes,* and *The Urn*), and a number of essays mainly concerned with his attempt to make of Symbolism a new *Weltanschauung.* The *Symphonies—Northern Heroic, Dramatic, The Return, The Cup of Snow-storms*—already contain the musical principle and pattern he was to develop further in his later prose. They also marked a sharp break with traditional prose, and stressed his prophetic vision and poetic ecstasy.

Biely's period of major prose began in 1908-09 with the novel *The Silver Dove*, originally intended to be the first volume in a trilogy entitled *East and West. St. Petersburg* (1910-11), the second novel, broke away from the original design and must be regarded as an independent work. The trilogy as such was never completed. However, *The Silver Dove* is also a novel of major literary importance from the point of stylistic innovation and influence.

In Switzerland, Biely next wrote *Kotik Letayev* (1915-16), in which he described his early childhood from the dark chaos of the womb to the age of five. This work is full of the most extraordinary symbolism and applied parallels; its structure is derived from music and is complicated; the unordered images of the earlier life gradually give way to rational interpretation at the "Renaissance stage" at the age of five. In 1922 Biely published a sequel to this, *The Crime of Kotik Letayev.* During his last decade he was working on a sequence of novels under the general title of *Moscow.* Three of these novels were published: *The Moscow Eccentric* (1926), *Moscow Under the Blow* (1926), and *Masks* (1932). The remainder of his work can be divided among poetry, short stories, memoirs, and theoretical, philosophical and critical pieces. In all he published some fifty volumes.

Taking into consideration the differences of background and individual character and style, it is possible to establish a parallel between Biely's work and that of James Joyce. Both writers, the Russian and the Irish, born within two years of each other, were to exercise the same tremendous impact on the creative prose of their languages. In places, their verbal innovations are almost identical; in others, their angle of vision and their interests are as remote from each other as the Wall of Hadrian from the Wall of China. They are both immersed in and preoccupied with the problems of memory and the distortion of time. In both writers musical principles are active, but in the work of Biely this is expressed more abstractly and mathematically. Throughout his work, one becomes more and more aware of a structural pattern not only as the whole, but as the part: in the paragraph, the sentence, and the phrase; and it is clear that Biely's pattern, less varied than Joyce's, is based on a principle of verbal point-counterpoint which he discovered and applied with increasing precision throughout his work.

But where Biely and Joyce meet on larger common ground is in their attitude to, and place in, the use of the prose language and the structure of the novel in their respective cultures. In reality, the cultural and historical moment was the same, because both writers were faced with the problems and consequences of the maturity and breakdown of old forms and attitudes—Romanticism, Realism, Naturalism. The novel had reached what seemed to be an apogee in the nineteenth century, but by the 1890's, a new spirit was felt both in Europe and in Russia—of music and of Symbolism. Both Biely and Joyce embody some aspects of this new spirit, and they both use it in varying ways to propound a new esthetic, to explore and enrich the resources of their languages, and to transform the pattern of the novel.

Both writers are monuments in their particular spheres, and their influence is as profound as it is widespread. Although the full impact of Andrey Biely's work was complicated and then vitiated by the nature of the Russian Revolution or, rather, its ideological developments, which ran counter to the spirit of Biely's work, it is impossible to suppress or ignore the work of writers like him, like Joyce —or like Boris Pasternak today. Biely's novels have not been reprinted in the Soviet Union since 1935, and his memory has been treated with derision and contempt by such Communist Party leaders as Zhdanov (1946) and by lesser bureaucrats. But the work of human genius, unless completely obliterated, has a vitality and force that can overcome such immediate obstacles.

GEORGE REAVEY

INTRODUCTION

The place is St. Petersburg, the time the eventful year 1905, the year of the disastrous war with Japan, of strikes, of terror, of "abortive revolution," of the conspiratorial acts of the still unexposed agent-provocateur Azev, who worked for both the revolutionaries and the secret police, betraying one to the other, of Pobedonostzev, the powerful reactionary who controlled a weak Tsar and an immense nation which reached from the frontiers of Germany to the Pacific.

Such is the contemporary background, such the personages, from which Andrey Biely weaves his comprehensive story, rich with obsessive excitement. It is a literary feat of coordination, of the deft fitting together of a host of facts, occurrences, implications, thoughts, emotions and associations past and present, into a coherent whole, leaving in the reader the impression of having experienced a whole epoch of time. The mood of chaos this novel conveys is curiously consonant with the temper of our own time. In this sense it is prophetic.

It was that hardened practitioner of fiction, Arnold Bennett, who, in choosing the world's twelve best novels, put at least ten Russian works on his list. Tolstoy's *War and Peace* is acknowledged by many to be the world's greatest novel. Somerset Maugham, in agreeing with this judgment, added the comment that the novel also presented a philosophy of history, and that this addition suffered by comparison with the rest which comprised a narrative of the lives of human beings, individuals reacting to one another and to events.

St. Petersburg, first published in 1913, and here presented in English for the first time, is also a novel which Bennett or Maugham might well have selected among the world's fictional masterpieces, had it been available in translation. What is important is that here, too, in this strangely obsessive book, we have a philosophy of history —that is, of Russian history. Yet there is a difference, a vital difference. Andrey Biely does not, as does Tolstoy, present this philosophy in chunks of solid informational prose which might be published as, indeed, extracts from Tolstoy's masterpiece were once published as the factual story of the Napoleonic campaign in Russia, wholly dissociated from the fictional narrative.

You could not, on the other hand, if you wished, dissociate Biely's philosophy from the characters he has drawn. You are interested in these characters as in real beings in real life; yet, in a very large measure, they are symbols of the results of historical processes which have made them what they are. Like Dostoevsky, who did not write history or philosophy, Andrey Biely could say: "I philosophize like a poet." That is to say, his characters are alive, in a very specific sense, by virtue of being emotional, infinitely human, rooted in life itself; palpitating crystallizations of *homo sapiens* which stand for something in the background in which they appear. In Flaubert's phrase his people are individuals who "rise to the dignity of types." There is an avoidance of all didacticism. Even as Dostoevsky practiced psychoanalysis in his fiction long before Freud appeared on the scene, long before there was even any terminology for exploring the subconscious, his discoveries springing from the intuition of genius and receiving spontaneous (poetical) form, so also does Andrey Biely endow his people with qualities which are integral to their particular being, yet at the same time subtly implicative of larger issues and larger meanings, without once allowing his narrative to degenerate into a thesis. "Local color" would be a weak term for the atmosphere with which the author invests St. Petersburg, which plays an important role as a character, no less than the human beings who grope among its all-pervading vast shadows like souls fascinated by their appointed tasks and unable to escape from the narrow orbits into which the fates have placed them. The city possesses them, as it may be expected to possess the reader, held as it were by a hypnosis we attribute to dreams.

Indeed, Biely could not have laid the plot he has devised in any other city. In this novel, his masterpiece, he has written a work which plumbs the Russian spirit with a current significance for the West which no reader should miss. And it is no mere coincidence that Dostoevsky before Biely chose his backgrounds primarily in St.

Petersburg, a city of granite deliberately built on the miasmic
swamps along the Neva, "a window on Europe" provided by Peter
the Great, a figure meaningfully commemorated generations later by
Russia's supreme poet, Alexander Pushkin, in his masterpiece, *The
Bronze Horseman*, which takes its title from a colossal statue in
St. Petersburg, of the great Tsar astride a rearing horse, a statue
which plays its part in this novel. The Russian metropolis dominates
both authors in a very essential way.

What is Russia? There is an attempt here to answer the question
asked today. What has become of "the Russian soul" the non-Russian
writers used to prate about in pre-World War I days? The great
Russian poet, Alexander Blok, who too has close kinship with Biely,
wrote in 1918:

> *Russia is a Sphinx! Exultant and afflicted,*
> *Drenched in blackest blood,*
> *She gazes, gazes, gazes into you,*
> *Yes, with hatred, and with love!*

Russia, Blok pleads, had saved Europe from the Mongols by assuming the great burden of the invasion by Genghis Khan. "Yes," he
asserts, "we are Asiatics, with slant and avaricious eyes . . ." And
if the West refuses Russia's proferred love, then we shall "turn
toward you our ugly Asiatic mugs." And was it not Dostoevsky who
advised Russia to face East instead of West? Atavism? It was
Dostoevsky, too, who harped on the duality of the Russian individual,
and now Biely goes a step farther and attributes this duality, a sort
of split personality, to the Russian psyche in general.

This native acknowledgment of Tartar blood in the Russian is a
circumstance that figures in an essential way in Biely's novel. The
two leading characters, the Ableukhovs—father and son—are described definitely as of Mongol descent. The Ableukhovs, bureaucrat
father and terrorist son, though superficially Europeans, are Oriental
at the core. In them extremes meet. In ostensibly Western surround-
ings, thanks to Peter the Great, there develops a combustible energy,
ultimately nihilistic, and wholly destructive—it might be said, mutually destructive. In short, if we would believe Biely, we must inevitably accept Napoleon's dictum: "Scratch a Russian, and you
will find a Tartar."

For roots of this novel we must return to Peter the Great and
his bold attempt to take the Tartar out of the Russian. We speak

of the Iron Curtain today as if it were something new. Before Peter a far more impenetrable curtain separated Russia from Europe. The humanism of the Renaissance had passed Russia by. Anti-foreign feeling was strong. Indeed, when a band of Elizabethan merchant-adventurers first penetrated Russia from the North they came upon a monastery in which, in a painting of the Last Judgment, the righteous, all Russians, were shown on one side; the sinners, on the other side, were all foreigners!

With a mighty will and stern vigor Peter was resolved to change all this. Having studied the shipyards in Britain and Holland, and seduced by the sights he had witnessed abroad, and having mixed in Moscow with the progressive foreigners in the "German Quarter," he made a round of his Court and with his own hands snipped off the proud beards of the backward reluctant *boyars*; impotently they submitted to the indignity. (He could not as easily trim their hearts.) He also saw to it that these same *boyars* should stick their ornate shirts inside their trousers instead of having them, peasant-wise, flapping outside. Perhaps by now we may detect a deeper meaning than we might otherwise in Kipling's seemingly superficial witticism: "The Russian is a charming fellow until he tucks his shirt in." (The younger Ableukhov's predilection for a Tartar skullcap and furnishings at home should be noted.)

Apropos of Peter's "reforms," Thomas Masaryk recalls—and it is worth repeating here for the record—Peter the Great and his worthy Prime Minister Menshikov conversing. "Seating themselves at the table and drawing a line across the center of it, each of them took a louse (his own) and, having placed the insects on the table, they laid bets with one another which louse would first crawl as far as the line . . ." (Have not the milder jests of the elder Ableukhov, a power in Russia, something in common with this?)

And so, inevitably, we always return to that incongruity, Peter's city, "the window on Europe." He built the city on the European plan. Wide avenues—prospects they have been named—crisscross, on the rectilinear, gridiron principle, more like those of American cities than anything in Europe. Italian architects were hired to line these prospects with beautiful buildings in European style, making the city one of the finest modern capitals in the world and the particular joy of the elder Ableukhov's heart. The churches, to be sure, and the picturesque little chapels, all lit with candles, along the Nevsky Prospect, which looked so uncomfortably out of place when I saw them during the Fall and Winter of 1917-18, were anomalies;

yet the perpetually lighted candles and the thronging visitors revealed the Russian heart to be divided between the iconoclasts and the devout.

What is significant is that "the window on Europe" was really what it purported to be: a window on the West, a window for European cultural, political, and economic breezes to enter; a window for European scientists, authors, and artists to crawl through. Are we surprised to learn that Catherine the Great should carry on a voluminous correspondence with that great European radical Voltaire while traditionally utilizing the Cossack knout on peasants and refractory subjects?

Incidentally through that same "window on Europe" there crawled in one Karl Marx, squeezing through with that bulky tome *Das Kapital* and the briefer *Manifesto*, whose influence and works so deeply incensed the elder Ableukhov, while his son had made the rash promise to his fellow revolutionaries to do his bit to bring these documents into action, scarcely realizing at first that he would be called upon to commit parricide.

That "window on Europe" had indeed created a clash in the Russian heart, a duality of temperament, on which the anti-Westerner Dostoevsky had incessantly harped. Andrey Biely takes up this duality where the author of *The Possessed* left off. And the city itself, the vast Russian metropolis, becomes a basic character as alive and as portentous as the individuals who inhabit it and, in this novel, symbolize it.

St. Petersburg has been compared to James Joyce's *Ulysses*, which Biely's novel preceded by several years. Both compress the action of their narratives, both use something of the stream-of-consciousness method, both employ a variety of techniques, both describe sharply divergent characters, present flashbacks and memory associations, newspaper reports, and thoughts and emotions which overlap and interplay. In Joyce's novel it is Dublin; in Biely's, mist-enveloped St. Petersburg, in which people strut about like shadows in a dream-play. There is the impact of middle-class gentry and the proletariat, the impact of metropolitan St. Petersburg on the left bank of the Neva and less impressive, less elegant Vasilyevsky island on the opposite bank, inhabited by the workers, the revolutionaries, and the malcontents, who awakened such horror in the elder Ableukhov, who regarded them as enemies of the Russian people. They were the people who circulated lampoons about him, and cartoons revealing him with oversize ears. The turbulent surface and sublife of the city are reflected in their characters; all in all this novel possesses a many-dimensional quality. The physical scope is infinitely greater than that of *Ulysses*, for the city flings its shadow over all Russia, and, in a more limited measure, offers a critical commentary on Western civilization, of which, in a sense, it is something of a victim.

This is not the place to define the individual characters. Yet it should be pointed out that few figures in fiction symbolizing evil can surpass Lippanchenko, who is doubtless modeled on Azev, a figure at once sinister and nuanced, rivaling Bosola in *The Duchess of Malfi* and Svidrigalov in *Crime and Punishment*.

This novel is a vast fantasy, at times like a nightmare, realistically constituted as it is for the most part of the stuff of daily life, yet all of it built up like a piece of music, with a motif of terror, oddly mixed with humor, running through and holding the diverse fragments together in a form at once symphonic and subtly hypnotic. Several of Biely's earlier works indeed took the form of prose *Symphonies—First, Second, Third* and *Fourth*—realistic in substance and as often as not tolerant of the vernacular. The same elements have been carried over into the longer and weightier pattern of *St. Petersburg*, which despite its length and diversity of characters and moods is neither rambling nor disconnected. Its structure is always indivisible, inextricably put together, and is deliberately conceived and executed. Shall we say it is a work so finely planned to the slightest detail that its integrity is maintained by some magic in the art of precarious equilibrium?

It must be insisted, however, that though this novel, in the words of that penetrating critic, D. S. Mirsky, reveals Russian nihilism in its two forms—"the formalism of the St. Petersburg bureaucracy with the rationalism of revolutionaries . . . represented as the melting-point of the devastating rationalism of the West with the destructive forces of the Mongol steppe"—it always remains on the plane of imaginative fiction. Its philosophy of Russian history—on this point Mirsky agrees—never degenerates into a dissertation. The suspense is terrific as the reader follows the course of events revolving around a bomb (in a sardine tin) with which young Ableukhov has been assigned to kill his own father. The excitement deepens in intensity as the moment approaches when the clockwork mechanism, ticking away toward its appointed end, must willynilly explode. Yet within these few hours the reader is present during vast movements of history and moments which seem like eternities.

This book, then, is that rare thing: an idea successfully integrated in fiction, and as inseparable from it as a living body from its blood. The author has devised a method and a prose commensurate with the content: stylistic rhythms—happily unobtrusive—expressive of vigorous action and profound thought.

Andrey Biely ("White") is a pseudonym for Boris Nikolaevich Bugayev. He was born in Moscow in 1880, the same year as the poet Alexander Blok, with whom he was closely connected. His father, N. V. Bugayev, was a famous mathematician and professor at Moscow University, from whom Biely acquired his first interest in mathematics. His mother, thirty years younger than her husband, was beautiful and volatile. The circle of friends that visited the Bugayev home influenced Biely from an early age: he gained a deep interest in Russian poets from the scholar and educator, L. I. Polivanov; he met M. S. Solovyev and his brother Vladimir, an eminent mystic whose teachings greatly impressed the young man; many of the founders and leaders of the Russian Symbolist movement became acquainted with him.

After eight years at the University of Moscow he took degrees in mathematics and philosophy, and then spent some months traveling in Belgium and France, meeting Wedekind, Jaurès, and other Western intellectuals. His first writings were regarded by the professorial class as "decadent," but such discriminating writers and critics of the Symbolist movement as Valery Bryusov and Merezhkovsky at once saw his potential abilities.

Like the other Symbolists of the period, in 1905 Biely was inspired by the Revolution to which he attached mystical significance. At last losing faith in revolutionary achievements, he devoted himself to his writing, winning his first considerable notice in 1909 with *The Silver Dove*, a long novel in a humorous Gogolian vein which was to exercise much influence on the creative writers of his day.

In 1910, Biely went abroad again, to Italy, Sicily, Tunisia, Egypt and Palestine, a trip that contributed some of the visual images in the final pages of *St. Petersburg*. The following year he married Asya Turgenev, and in 1912 became involved with the anthroposophism of Rudolf Steiner, in whose strange mystical establishment at Basel the couple lived for a few years. It was during these years that he wrote *St. Petersburg*.

Returning to Russia in 1916 on the eve of the Revolution, Biely was saved by it from military service. At first warmly sympathetic to the Bolsheviks, a sympathy he shared with Blok (author of the famous *The Twelve*), he, like Blok, was soon disillusioned by them and sought solace in the idea of a mystic renaissance in Russia, and became the pivot of this movement which prospered even in the face of Bolshevik opposition. Proletarian poets flocked to him for instruction in their art.

After the death of Alexander Blok, in 1921 Biely felt the need to leave Russia. He spent two years in Berlin, where he became the center of the Russian literary émigrés. But unable to find a basis for his creativity there, he returned in 1923 to Russia, compelled by the deep roots of his work, and by his ideas of a great future Russian culture.

After 1930 he found himself in an increasingly isolated position among the new Stalinist generation. He died in 1934 at the age of fifty-three.

It is customary to make acknowledgments for kindness and courtesy in the appearance of a literary work. The translator owes a great debt to Eugene Somoff and his wife Elena Konstantinovna for first introducing him to Biely, and in particular for presenting him early during the First World War with a copy of the first Russian edition. Secondly, and foremost, he is obligated to his friend, Prince Dmitry Svyatopolk Mirsky ("Damn my title!" he once wrote the translator), for pointing out to him the essential beauties of Biely's novel during a weekend with me at Oxford. This is but a slight token to his memory. He was a great man and a lovable one, and a good friend. He is the author of the best history of Russian literature in any language, a work written in English. Against the advice of his best friends, he went back to Russia in 1932, feeling that his rightful place was in his homeland, but during the so-called Trotskyite purge in the Stalinist regime, he was, at the instigation of envious literary hacks, sent to a Siberian concentration camp and eventually died in an agony of madness to which he had been driven by the sufferings imposed upon him. Thirdly, I want to thank my wife Helen, who read *St. Petersburg* in my translation and could not put it down for excess of intense excitement induced by the quality in the novel which Mirsky properly called "obsessive."

JOHN COURNOS

PROLOGUE

Your Excellencies, Your Lordships, Your Honors, Citizens!

What is our Russian Empire?

Our Russian Empire is a geographical entity, part of a well-known planet. This Russian Empire comprises in the first place Great Russia, Little Russia, White Russia, and Red Russia; in the second, the Kingdoms of Georgia, Poland, Kazan, and Astrakhan; in the third place. . . . Well, etc., etc., etc.

Our Russian Empire consists of a multitude of cities: capital, provincial, district, and autonomous cities; and furthermore, of a metropolis, and the mother of all Russian cities.

The metropolis is Moscow; Kiev is the mother of Russian cities.

Petersburg, Saint Petersburg, or Peter (it is all one), is also part of the Russian Empire. And the Tsar-City, the City of Constantine (or, as it has been called, Constantinople) belongs to it by right of heritage. But we shall not dwell on this.

We shall dwell largely on Petersburg: call it Saint Petersburg or Peter (it is all one). By virtue of the same reasoning, the Nevsky Prospect is a Petersburg prospect.

The Nevsky Prospect possesses an impressive quality: it consists of a vast expanse for the circulation of the public; numbered houses restrict it—this makes it easier to find any home we may want. The Nevsky Prospect, like any prospect, is a public prospect; that is, a prospect for the circulation of the public (not of air, to be sure); the houses, which line it and shape its frontiers, are what give it substance—h'm . . . yes . . . for the public. In the evening, the Nevsky Prospect is lighted by electricity. By day the Prospect needs no illumination.

The Nevsky Prospect is rectilinear (speaking among ourselves), because it is a European prospect; every European prospect is not simply a prospect, but (as I have already pointed out) a prospect is European, because h'm . . . yes . . .

That is why the Nevsky Prospect is a rectilinear prospect.

The Nevsky Prospect is an important prospect in the capital city. It is not altogether Russian. Other Russian cities offer little more than piles of little wooden houses.

Petersburg differs impressively from them all.

If you insist on affirming an uncouth legend that Moscow has a population of a million and a half souls, then you will have to admit that the real capital should be Moscow, because only capitals have a population of a million and a half; in the provincial cities there are no such populations—there never were and never shall be. If you believe this uncouth legend, then Petersburg is not the capital.

If Petersburg is not the capital, then there is no Petersburg. Then its existence is merely imaginary.

But Petersburg is not merely imaginary; it can be located on maps—in the shape of concentric circles and a black dot in the middle; and this mathematical dot, which has no defined measurement, proclaims energetically that it exists: from this dot comes the impetuous surge of words which makes the pages of a book; and from this point circulars rapidly spread.

CHAPTER ONE

There was a dreadful time, we keep
Still freshly on our memories painted;
And you, my friends, shall be acquainted
By me with all that history:
A grievous record it will be.

—Pushkin

1

Apollon Apollonovich Ableukhov came of very good stock: Adam was his ancestor. A later and more important ancestor of his in the same honored line was Shem, the forefather of the Semitic, Hessitic, and red-skinned races.

At this point, we can transfer our attention to ancestors of a less remote epoch.

These more recent ancestors had spent their lives among the Kirghiz-Kaisatsk hordes whence, during the reign of the Empress Anne, one Ameer Ab-Lai, great-grandfather of the Senator who, on his conversion to Christianity, received the name of Andrey and the surname of Ukhov, had bravely entered the Russian service. The name of Ab-Lai-Ukhov was later abbreviated to Ableukhov.

This particular Ableukhov was the progenitor of all the later generations of the Ableukhovs.

A lackey attired in gray trimmed with gold galloon was dusting the writing desk with a feather-duster when a chef's white cap was thrust through the open door.

"Is the master up?" the cook inquired.

"He's rubbing himself with eau-de-cologne and he'll be wanting his coffee soon."

"The postman said there was a letter from Spain. The letter has a Spanish stamp."

"Permit me to remark, it'd be better for you not to poke your nose into matters that don't concern you!"

The chef's head suddenly vanished. Apollon Apollonovich Ableukhov strode into the study.

Apollon Apollonovich's attention was arrested by a pencil on the desk. Apollon Apollonovich instantly decided to give a refined form to the pointed end of the pencil. He stepped quickly to the desk and seized . . . a paperweight which in deep meditation he turned for a long time this way and that.

His distraction was due to a profound thought that had suddenly struck him; at an unseasonable moment it had rapidly unfolded and pursued its runaway course.

Apollon Apollonovich began quickly to jot down his fleeting thoughts. This accomplished, he thought: "It's time for the office." He entered the dining room to have his coffee.

Then cautiously and with curious persistence, he began to question the old lackey:

"Is Nikolai Apollonovich up yet?"

"By no means. He's still in bed."

With a dissatisfied gesture, Apollon Apollonovich went on rubbing the bridge of his nose.

"Eh . . . eh, tell me . . . when Nikolai Apollonovich, so to speak . . ."

But without finishing his question he promptly helped himself to more coffee and glanced at his watch.

It was exactly half-past nine.

Every morning the Senator asked the same question about Nikolai Apollonovich. And every morning he frowned at his own question.

Nikolai Apollonovich was the Senator's son.

2

Russia knew the Senator for the superior quality of his circumstantial speeches; subtly these speeches spread and led in certain quarters to the rejection of certain requests. With Ableukhov's investiture in the responsible post of department head, the Ninth Department became inactive. Apollon Apollonovich carried on an obstinate feud with this Department by means of official papers and, where need be, of speeches promoting the importation into Russia of American binders and files, to which the Ninth Department had been opposed.

Apollon Apollonovich was the head of a department of some magnitude: the department of . . . what's its name?

If we compare the dry and wholly insignificant figure of our esteemed personage with the measureless immensity of the mechanisms he directed, we might pause in naïve astonishment; and, indeed, everyone was astonished at the outburst of mental energy which poured from this skull box in the face of the resistance provoked across the length and breadth of all Russia.

The Senator had only just attained his sixty-eighth year. In moments of exultation, his pale face resembled the gray paperweight which in a relaxed moment he had handled a short while ago. Indeed his face was like papier-mâché. His stony Senatorial eyes, sunken within deep round hollows of a dark green hue, seemed larger and bluer.

Apollon Apollonovich was not a bit perturbed when he contemplated his quite green ears which had been immensely magnified on the blood-red banner of revolutionary Russia. Thus he had been lately portrayed on the title page of a vulgar comic journal, one of those "Judaic" papers with red covers which circulated in those days with astonishing rapidity and in ever-increasing numbers on the swarming prospects.

3

A cuckoo clock cuckooed on a wall of the oak-paneled dining room. Apollon Apollonovich sat before his porcelain cup, breaking off pieces of crust from a roll; as he sipped his coffee, he joked with the lackey:

"Semenich, who is the most honored of men?"

"I suppose, Apollon Apollonovich, no one is more honored than a Privy Councilor."

Apollon Apollonovich smiled broadly:

"You're mistaken—it's the chimneysweep."

The lackey, who already knew the answer to the riddle, also knew that he must not divulge it.

"Why do you think so? I hope I may venture to ask, sir?"

"Well, Semenich, everyone must make way for a Privy Councilor . . ."

"I suppose that's right."

"But even a Privy Councilor must make way for the chimney-sweep. The chimneysweep would soil him, you see."

"That's a fact, to be sure, sir."

"Yes, that's the way it is. There's only one service even more honored . . ."

After a pause, he would add:

"It's the man who cleans the water-closet."

"Pfuh . . ."

There was a gurgle of coffee being swallowed.

"That reminds me, Apollon Apollonovich, once when Anna Petrovna . . ."

At the last word, the gray-haired lackey stopped short.

"The gray coat, sir?"

"Yes, the gray."

"Which gloves, sir?"

"The suede."

"I hope you don't mind waiting, Your Excellency. The suede gloves are in the chiffonier: shelf B-North-East."

Apollon Apollonovich had only once intervened in the petty details of his domestic life; he had revised the domestic inventory. Order was established in the household: all the shelves and the sub-shelves were lettered and named. The shelves were lettered A, B, C, while the four walls of the shelves were named after the four points of the compass.

After putting his spectacles away, Apollon Apollonovich had made a list in his small, meticulous script: spectacles, Shelf B and N.E., i.e., North-East. His valet was given a copy of this list.

The world's storms flowed noiselessly through this lacquered house; yet they flowed and flowed fatally.

4

A long-legged bronze graced the table. The lampshade of delicate violet-rose that topped it no longer sparkled. Our age has lost the secret of cunningly wrought colors. The glass and its fine design had been dimmed by time.

From every angle, the greenish surfaces of the gilt-framed pier-glasses swallowed the drawing room; a gold-cheeked cupid crowned each of them with a wing; a small mother-of-pearl table sparkled.

Apollon Apollonovich, placing his hand on a cut-crystal handle, flung open the door with a rapid gesture; his steps sounded on the small gleaming squares of the parquet floor; from all sides little heaps of porcelain trifles leaped into sight—Apollon Apollonovich had brought these trifles from Venice thirty years before, when he had visited that city with his wife, Anna Petrovna. The memory of the misty lagoon, the gondola, and the arias sobbing in the distance, flitted inopportunely through the Senator's head.

At once he transferred his glance to the grand piano.

Leaves of incrusted bronze gleamed on its yellow lacquered cover; and again—oh, irksome memory!—Apollon Apollonovich remembered a certain white night in Petersburg. The river flowed past the windows; the moon was high; and a roulade of Chopin's thundered; he could remember distinctly Anna Petrovna playing Chopin (not Schumann).

Leaves of mother-of-pearl and bronze incrustations sparkled on the tiny boxes and little shelves on the walls. Apollon Apollonovich seated himself in an Empire armchair on whose pale azure satin seat there was a woven pattern of wreaths. He snatched at a packet of unsealed letters from a small Chinese tray; his bald head bent over the envelopes.

He opened the envelopes. Here was an ordinary one, the stamp crookedly affixed. He mumbled to himself:

"So, so, very well . . .

"A petition . . .

"Another petition, and still another . . ."

In due course, later, he would attend to it . . .

He came to an envelope of heavy paper with a monogram and a seal.

"H'm . . . Count Dubleve. . . . What's he up to now? . . . H'm . . ."

Count Dubleve was the head of the Ninth Department.

Then he came across a pale rose envelope. The Senator's hand trembled: he recognized the handwriting. He stared at the Spanish stamp, but made no move to open the envelope.

"But the money was surely sent?" he thought. "Yes, the money will be sent!" he added.

And thinking that he had extracted a stub of a pencil from his waistcoat pocket when it was actually a tiny nail brush, Apollon Apollonovich prepared to make a note . . .

"Yes?"

"The carriage is waiting, Your Excellency."

Apollon Apollonovich raised his bald head and strode from the room.

David's painting, *Distribution des aigles par Napoléon premier*, in a reduced copy hung over the grand piano. The picture represented the great Emperor in a chaplet and a purple and ermine mantle.

A total absence of rugs imparted to the reception room an air of cold magnificence. The parquet floor gleamed; if the sun 'had lighted upon it even for an instant, one would have involuntarily blinked one's eyes.

Senator Ableukhov had elevated his preference for coolness to a principle and now he based his whole life upon it.

This principle was personified in the master of the house, in his statues, in his servants, even in the dark brown-yellow bulldog who spent his life somewhere near the kitchen. In this house, everyone lived in a state of diffidence and embarrassment; everyone was in awe of the parquet floor, the paintings and the statues, smiled timidly and held his breath; everyone scraped and bowed, and wrung his cold fingers in fits of sterile officiousness.

Since the departure of Anna Petrovna, the reception room had remained silent, and the lid of the grand piano had been lowered; roulades thundered no more.

When Apollon Apollonovich descended into the vestibule, his gray-haired valet accompanied him, glancing at his master's honorable ears. Apollon Apollonovich was fingering a snuffbox—the gift of a Minister.

Apollon Apollonovich paused at the foot of the stairs, seeking the appropriate word:

"What, generally, does he do? What does he do?" he asked.

"? . . ."
"I'm referring to Nikolai Apollonovich."
"Nothing in particular, Your Excellency. He just greets us . . ."
"And what else?"
"He shuts himself in and reads books."
"Books, eh? What else?"
"He paces up and down his rooms."
"So that's it? . . . And how?"
"In his dressing-gown, sir."
"Quite. . . . And what else?"
"Yesterday he was expecting someone . . ."
"Whom?"
"A costumer, sir."
"What sort of costumer?"
"A costumer . . ."

Apollon Apollonovich rubbed the bridge of his nose: a gleam of intelligence illuminated his face, which suddenly looked patriarchal.
"Have you ever had a sty?" he asked.
"No, Your Excellency, I've never been troubled that way."
"And you were brought up on a farm?"
"Yes, Your Excelleney."
"And you kept no pigs?"
Apollon Apollonovich chortled.

5

The sleet poured down upon the streets and prospects, the pavements and roofs.
It also poured down upon the pedestrians, rewarding them with the grippe. It defied upturned collars, penetrated to the body, and afflicted equally the high school boy, the college student, the official, the army officer, and the nondescript pedestrian.
The nondescript pedestrian glanced about him sadly. He stared at the prospect; he circulated in an infinity of prospects without a murmur—in a stream of those like himself—amid the rumble and the clamor, listening to the voice of automobile roulades.

At last he stumbled on to the embankment, where all seemed to
end: the call of the roulade and the nondescript pedestrian.

Far off, appearing more remote than they really were, the islands
crouched apprehensively; and their buildings crouched too. It
seemed that the waters might fall and submerge them at that instant
in the deep and greenish mist; and in the fog, the Nikolayevsky
Bridge quaked and thundered above this green, turbid atmosphere.

On that misty morning the doors of the yellow house facing the
Neva were flung wide open. A carriage drawn by a pair of spirited
gray horses pulled up before the entrance. A lackey with gold
galloon rushed out and gave directions to the driver. The gray
horses started forward and pulled up the carriage. On the door was
a coat of arms: a unicorn goring a knight.

A dashing police officer who was passing by suddenly grew dumb
and drew himself up like a yardstick when he saw Apollon Apollonovich Ableukhov in a gray overcoat and a tall black cylinder hat
on his head, gray-faced as always, quickly run out of the entrance
and rush even more quickly to the footboard of the carriage, pulling
on a suede glove as he hurried.

Apollon Apollonovich Ableukhov cast a lightning, absentminded
glance at the officer, the carriage, the driver, at the big black
bridge, at the expanses of the Neva, through whose mists loomed
the faint outlines of the many chimneys in the distance where
Vasilyevsky Island seemed to shrink in fear.

The gray-haired lackey quickly slammed the carriage door. Impetuously the carriage sped into the fog; the police officer glanced
over his shoulder into the dirtyish fog, where the carriage had so
impetuously fled; he sighed and walked away; the lackey also
glanced in the same direction: at the expanses of the Neva, through
whose mists loomed the faint outlines of the many chimneys in the
distance where Vasilyevsky Island seemed to shrink in fear.

6

Hanging, as it were, above the dense mist, there first appeared
the indeterminate shape of St. Isaac's which, as the carriage sped

onward, gradually descended earthward; then out of the mist
emerged the equestrian statue of the Emperor Nicholas and, at its
foot, a grenadier of Nicholas's day with a shaggy bearskin on his
head.

The carriage now sped along the Nevsky.

Apollon Apollonovich Ableukhov rocked on the velvet cushions
of his seat. Four small perpendicular walls sheltered him from
the filth of the street. These walls protected him from pedestrians
and from the damp red covers of the vulgar periodicals which were
flaunted at street corners.

System and symmetry soothed the Senator's nerves: his nerves
were constantly set on edge by the ups and downs of his domestic
affairs as well as by the futile rotation of the governmental wheel.

His taste was distinguished by harmonious simplicity.

Above all, he loved the rectilinear prospect. This prospect reminded him of life flowing between two vital points.

Here the houses in measured cubes merged into a single, sys-
tematic, five-storied row.

Exultation filled the Senator's soul when the line of the Nevsky
was cut by the lacquered cube of his carriage: here numbered
houses came into view; and here the public circulated; here, from
there, far, far away, on clear days, dazzlingly gleamed: the gold
needle-like spire, the clouds, the red glowing sunset; there, from
there, on foggy days, one could see nothing, no one.

There were the Neva and the islands. Very likely in those remote
days when the tall roofs, and the masts, and the spires rose up out
of the moss-grown marshes, piercing with their tips the foul, greenish fog—

—the Flying Dutchman had come winging on his shadowy
sails emerging from the leaden expanses of the Baltic and
German seas, and had brought into being here, in Petersburg, by means of illusion, his misty lands and had given
the name of islands to this surge of gathered clouds.

Apollon Apollonovich disliked the islands. The inhabitants of
the islands were uncouth factory workers who, in the early morning,
poured in multitudinous swarms toward the many-chimneyed factories. They were certainly numbered in the population of the

Empire; their census had been taken like the census of those who dwelled on this side of the Neva.

Apollon Apollonovich disliked having to think about the islands: they should be crushed out of existence!

As he peered meditatively into the boundless mists, this mighty official, who was confined within the dark cube of his carriage, suddenly expanded in all directions and soared above it all; a desire was born in him that the carriage should speed forward, that prospect after prospect should rush to meet him, that the entire surface of the planet should be embraced, as in the coils of a serpent, by blackish-gray cubes of houses; that the entire earth, prospect-bound, should in her linear cosmic rotation intersect infinity on the rectilinear principle; that the network of parallel prospects, intersected by a network of other prospects, should expand and cover the world abysses with square and cubical planes: a square to an inhabitant, in order that . . .

After the straight line, the square was the figure which soothed the Senator above all symmetries.

Now and again, he surrendered to a kind of aimless contemplation of pyramids, triangles, parallelepipeds, cubes, and trapeziums.

In the center of his dark velvet-upholstered cube, Apollon Apollonovich prolonged his enjoyment of the small four-cornered walls. Apollon Apollonovich had been born for solitary confinement; it was his love of governmental planimetry that had invested him in the polyhedron of his responsible post.

The wet slippery prospect was intersected by another wet prospect at a ninety-degree angle; a policeman stood at the point of intersection.

Precisely the same kind of houses rose here, and the same kind of gray human streams flowed by, and the same greenish-yellow fog hovered in the air.

Parallel with the running prospect was another running prospect with the same row of boxes, the same system of numeration, and the same clouds.

There is an infinity about the running prospects, and an infinity about the running intersecting shadows. Petersburg, as a whole, represents a sum to infinity of the prospect, elevated to the Nth degree.

Beyond Petersburg, there is nothing.

7

It was the last day of September.

On Vasilyevsky Island, in the depth of the Seventeenth Line, an enormous gray house peered out of the fog. A dirtyish stairway led to the upper floors; there were doors and doors; one of these opened.

A stranger with a tiny black mustache appeared on the threshold.

A bundle, neither small nor large, dangled rhythmically from his hand; a dirty napkin with a red border of molting pheasants served as the outer covering.

The stairway was dark, strewn with cucumber peelings and trodden cabbage leaves. The stranger slipped on a leaf.

With one hand he quickly grasped the handrail; the other, which held the bundle, cut a zigzag. It was obvious that the stranger was anxious to preserve the bundle from any untoward accident, that he wished to prevent it striking the stone step; acrobatic agility was evident in the movement of his elbow.

When the stranger encountered the house porter, who was mounting the stairs with an armful of wood, he betrayed a deeper solicitude for the fate of his bundle, lest it become entangled with a log.

Downstairs the stranger saw a black cat which, with uplifted tail, ran across his path; it made his heart thump and his face turn pale.

At this instant his movements resembled those of a young lady.

Such movements are indeed characteristic of some of our contemporaries who are worn out by insomnia. The stranger suffered from insomnia; there were hints of it in his room, which reeked of tobacco smoke, and in the bluish tinge of the sensitive skin of his face.

The stranger entered the court, a tiny asphalt square, dwarfed on all four sides by a five-storied, many-windowed pile. In the middle of the courtyard there were stacks of damp firewood; and through the gates one could see a section of the windswept Seventeenth Line.

Oh, Lines! You preserve the memory of Peter's city: Petersburg.

In a remote age, Peter had drawn these parallel lines. Now they were grown over, here with granite, there with a stone barrier or a wooden fence. The line drawn by Peter has been transformed into the line of a later age—that of Catherine, a line rounded with a sweep of colonnades.

Between these vast edifices, a few small houses of Peter's age still remained: here was a timber house; there, a house overgrown with vines; farther, a blue one-storied house with a gaudy sign "Restaurant" whence issued motley odors to assail one's nostrils: here it smelled of sea salt, herring, hawsers, leather jackets, pipe tobacco, and tarpaulin.

Oh, Lines!

How they have changed: how the grim days have changed them!

The stranger suddenly remembered: how, on summer evenings in the old days, he used to see a little old woman sitting and munching at the window of that small lustrous house; since last August, this window had been closed; and in September he had observed a coffin being carried into the house.

He thought that life was becoming increasingly expensive; it was difficult for working people to make ends meet; and there was Petersburg, threatening with its arrow-like prospects and its horde of stone giants.

Beyond loomed Petersburg; there, out of a surge of clouds, buildings peered; there, it seemed, some cold and malignant spirit blew his vaporous breath; there out of battling chaos he fixed his stony stare, his skull and ears projecting out of the fog.

Immersed in these thoughts, the stranger clenched a fist in his pocket; and then he suddenly thought of the falling leaves.

He knew it all by heart. For many, these falling leaves were the last leaves. The stranger became a bluish shadow.

Shadows swarmed across the bridge; the stranger's dark shadow was one of them.

From this shadow's hand a bundle dangled rhythmically, a bundle neither small nor large.

8

The venerable Senator maintained some contact with the swarming crowd by means of wires, both telegraphic and telephonic. For him, the stream of shadows moved on like a stream of tranquil tidings. Apollon Apollonovich was thinking of the stars; as he rocked on a black cushion he computed the energy conferred by Saturn.

Suddenly—his face wrinkled in a frown and the muscles of his face twitched; his eyes rolled feverishly and turned blue; his hands clutched at his chest. His body lurched backward; his cylinder hat, striking the back of the carriage, fell on his knees . . .

The unaccountability of the action was not conducive to any rational explanation; the Senator's code of rules had not foreseen this . . .

As Apollon Apollonovich contemplated the passing silhouettes he likened them to shining dots; one of these dots, slipping from its orbit and assuming the form of an immense blood-red sphere, bore down upon him with dazzling speed:—

—among a mass of bowler hats on a street corner he perceived a pair of eyes: the eyes expressed the inadmissible: they had recognized the Senator; and, having recognized him, they had expressed rage: they had dilated, lighted up, and flashed lightning.

When he delved later into the details of this incident Apollon Apollonovich accepted rather than remembered the fact that the derelict had held a bundle in his hand.

Hemmed in by a flow of droshkies his carriage had paused at a street crossing. A stream of nondescript citizens had crowded against the Senator's carriage, destroying the illusion that he, Apollon Apollonovich, as he sped along the Nevsky, was fleeing a million miles away from the human myriapod. Distressed, Apollon Apollonovich moved closer to the carriage window. Then he caught sight of the derelict. Later, as he recalled his face, he tried to classify its owner in one of the many established categories.

At that moment the stranger's eyes had dilated, lighted up, and flashed lightning.

As he leaned against the wall of the carriage Apollon Apollonovich peered through the dirtyish tufts of mist and saw those eyes and all their play of emotion. His heart began to thump and expand, and he became aware of the blood-red sphere which was ready to explode.

Apollon Apollonovich suffered from an enlarged heart.

Automatically, he replaced the cylinder on his head, pressed his hand against his galloping heart, and gave himself up to his beloved contemplaton of cubes, in order that he might give a proper account to himself of what had happened.

The horses came to a halt. A policeman gave the salute. Through the window of the vestibule beneath the bearded caryatid, which supported the tiny balcony, Apollon Apollonovich saw the now familiar scene: the gleaming bronze heavy-headed mace and the dark cocked hat fallen upon a human shoulder: the octogenarian doorman had fallen asleep over *The Stock Exchange Gazette.* It had been like that yesterday and the day before.

For the last five years, he had slept like this. He would die like this . . .

Five years had passed since Apollon Apollonovch had first arrived in his carriage to rule the Department. During that time a few things had happened. China had been in turmoil, and Port Arthur had fallen.

The doors swung open. The bronze mace sounded its knocks. Fresh from the carriage, Apollon Apollonovich glanced round the vestibule.

"Your Excellency. . . . Please be seated. . . . You're all out of breath . . ."

"Don't fuss. You're running about like a little boy."

"Would you like a glass of water, sir?"

Tiny furrows creased the face of the eminent man: "Now tell me, my good man, who is the husband of the countess?"

"Which countess, may I ask?"

"Any countess, to be sure."

"?"

"The decanter!"

"He-he-he-he . . ."

9

The stranger drifted on amid the slowly moving throngs. More accurately, he fled in confusion from the street crossing where he had been pressed against the carriage, where he had glimpsed the notorious ear and the cylinder hat.

He had seen that ear before!

He broke into flight.

Intersecting columns of conversation, he snatched at fragments of it.

"Do you know?" he heard on the right. The rest was lost.

Then he heard:

"They're getting ready . . ."

"What, to throw a . . ."

"At whom?"

The stranger strained to hear. He thought one of the pair had said, "Able . . ."

Did they say "Ableukhov?"

The stranger stood still, shaken by what he had heard. Their words came back to him: "They're getting ready . . ." "To throw a . . ."

He listened to others, and tried to fathom the fragmented words.

Provocation was on a spree along the Nevsky. Provocation gave new meaning to words overheard. Provocation had its seat in the stranger's soul.

Oh, Russian people!

You are becoming the shadows of fleeting mists, of mists that have always swept in from the Baltic. Into these mists guns have been pointed.

At twelve o'clock, a dull discharge from a gun gave voice to Petersburg, the magnificent capital of the Empire, rending the mists asunder and dispersing the shadows.

The young stranger's shadow alone remained unshaken by the discharge and did not fall apart as he completed his flight toward the Neva unhindered.

Then suddenly he raised his eyes and found two poorly dressed girl students gazing fixedly at him.

10

In the autumn the Petersburg streets chill one to the marrow, the streets caress one with fingers of ice; when one leaves the street and enters an establishment, the street continues to throb in one's veins like the ague.

The stranger experienced all this when he entered the sweaty steaming vestibule, tightly crowded with blue, gray, and tan greatcoats, lop-eared caps, and all manner of overshoes; the odor of steam hovered here. And from the dining room came all sorts of sounds:

"Aaa! . . . A-ha-ha-ha! Ha-ha-ha! . . ."

The restaurant consisted of a single dirty little room; the floor was spotted with lute; there was a fresco on the walls depicting Peter the Great surveying from a hill a squadron of his fleet.

"Will you have vodka with pickles?"

"No, without."

As he sat there, he asked himself: why had the man inside the carriage looked so frightened? First his eyes had popped; then they looked petrified; and, finally, they had closed. His head had jerked back and dropped; the hand on his chest had quivered convulsively . . .

The hors d'oeuvres on the counter were growing stale; a heap of overdone cutlets on faded lettuce leaves were turning sour.

At a distant table a huge fellow sat sweating: he had a droshkydriver's beard and wore a blue jacket and greased topboots. He was gulping down one glass of vodka after another. He called to the waiter:

"Got anything?"

"A melon?"

"I know your melons! Soap and sugar!"

"A banana?"

"That's an indecent fruit . . ."

Three times already the stranger had swallowed the tart poison. And his consciousness, separated now from his body like the handle of a machine lever, began to revolve round his organism.

For an instant the stranger's consciousness cleared: where was the *bundle*? There it was—beside him.

The meeting with Ableukhov had suppressed his memory.

"What do you say to a slice of watermelon?"

"Your watermelons are a joke. Only good to make your teeth crunch. . . . I want something tasty . . ."

"You'd better have another drop of vodka!"

"What about having one?" The sweating big-beard asked, winking at the stranger.

"I've already had a couple."

"I want you to have one on me—for company's sake!"

A thought struck the stranger. He glanced at the bearded fellow suspiciously and grabbed at the *bundle*; he covered it with a newspaper. Then he asked:

"Are you from Tula by any chance?"

"Not at all!"

There was a pause. The stranger thought hard or, rather, his thoughts, separating themselves, thought independently for him. They revealed to him the dismal nature of the whole scene, with its smell of tarpaulin, hawsers, and herring . . .

"In commercial business?"

(Oh, Lord!)

"No!"

"You aren't? Well, I'm a cabby."

"My brother-in-law is a driver and works for Konstantin Konstantinovich."

"Well, what about it?"

"What about it? Nothing!"

Suddenly—

11

Apollon Apollonovich applied his mind to the business of the day. The reports of the previous day lay on his desk, heaped with papers bearing his marginal comments. Marks in blue pencil meant "Go ahead"; those in red said "Make inquiries!"

In the space between the departmental stairs and his study, Apollon Apollonovich exerted his will in order to change the center of his consciousness; the heap of papers he expected to find on his desk served this purpose; it rose to the surface of his consciousness; Apollon Apollonovich applied his mind to the business of the day.

"Herman Hermanovich!" he exclaimed, addressing a passing official, "do try and get things ready—you know the case I mean . . ."

"The affair of Deacon Zhrakov!"

Then he suddenly remembered (after an interlude of forgetfulness) those eyes—the eyes of the derelict. How astonished they had looked, how they had flamed with sudden rage. . . . He remembered the movement made to protect the *bundle.* . . . What a revolting fellow! Then it occurred to him that he had seen the fellow before, somewhere, at some time . . .

Apollon Apollonovich opened the door of his study.

There stood the desk. A log fire crackled in the fireplace. Apollon Apollonovich halted, warming his numbed hands, but his mind continued to play and form its own misty images.

"Nikolai Apollonovich . . ." he murmured to himself, while his mind posed a question.

Apollon Apollonovich walked back to the door and, struck by

a sudden thought, stopped short. He had remembered something; and what he remembered came as a surprise:

He had seen the derelict once before—and just imagine it!—in his own house.

Yes, he remembered him coming downstairs; he remembered his son, Nikolai Apollonovich, bending over the banister, talking to someone: Apollon Apollonovich, important dignitary that he was, did not claim the privilege of informing himself about his son's acquaintances. His sense of tact hindered him from asking the simple question:

"Now tell me, Nikolai, old chap, who was that visiting you?"

Nikolai Apollonovich would have lowered his eyes and replied: "No one in particular. Just a visitor ... ."

That was why Apollon Apollonovich had not at this time shown any interest in the personality of the derelict whom he had glimpsed in the hall; the stranger had the same tiny mustache and the same startling eyes—eyes one could have beheld only at night in the Chapel of Panteleimon the Martyr at the Nikolsky Gate in Moscow, or in a frontispiece portrait to the biography of some great man; and now and then in a neuropathic clinic.

Even then, in the entrance hall, those eyes had dilated, moved, and flashed lightning. Now this singular coincidence troubled him.

Apollon Apollonovich suddenly glanced through the open door: desks and more desks! What a mountain of work! And all those heads bent over their work! What a seething, mighty business this manufacturing of paper was!

The mind's play of this recipient of many distinguished Orders was conspicuous for strange, very strange, virtues: his box skull was the repository of mental images that had their immediate impact upon this phantasmal world.

It would have been far better had Apollon Apollonovich not allowed a single idle fancy to roam beyond the confines of his skull, for his every thought evolved stubbornly into a temporary image in space and continued its uncontrolled actions—outside his Senatorial head.

Apollon Apollonovich resembled Zeus in this: goddesses and genii issued from his head. One of these genii, the stranger with the tiny mustache, sprang into existence, like an image, and ran amok in the yellowish spaces, asserting that he had not emerged from the Senator's own head. He imagined that these idle fancies were really the stranger's, and that they possessed the virtues he had assigned to them.

These fancies either vanished or assumed substance.

His dominant fleeting thought was that the stranger really existed; this idea then retreated to where it had come from—the Senator's brain.

The circle then closed.

Apollon Apollonovich was indeed like Zeus: hardly had his brain given birth to the Stranger, another Pallas Athene, than the goddess of wisdom assumed yet another form.

This new image was the Senator's house.

The lackey was mounting the stairway—and what a handsome stairway it was! Its steps were soft and yielding, like the convolutions of the brain. More than once eminent dignitaries had ascended it; the lackey had already reached the main reception hall . . .

What a handsome spacious room it was! The windows and the walls had a frigid air about them. . . .

From sheer habit, the Senator invested all objects with certain tokens.

Thus—

—at some remote time Apollon Apollonovich had come upon the bosom of nature all abloom, and having come upon the bosom of nature all abloom which, in our eyes, bears distinct tokens—such as violets, buttercups, cloves—it had no heterogeneity for him, but merely a kind of homogeneity. And when we would have said:

"Here's a buttercup!"

Or—

"Here's a forget-me-not!"

Apollon Apollonovich proclaimed very simply and briefly:
"Here's a flower!"

Apollon Apollonovich, for some reason, thought that all
flowers were bluebells.

He would have characterized his
own house with the same laconic brevity. For him it consisted of
walls (forming squares and cubes), of windows fashioned from
squares and cubes, of parquet floors and tables; beyond this, everything was a mere matter of detail . . .

The pictures, piano, mirrors, mother-of-pearl incrustations on
the tiny tables—all these, glimpsed in passing, were merely an
irritation of his brain, if not an indisposition of the cerebellum.

An illusion of a room erected itself in his mind, only to be dissipated, leaving no trace. When a door slammed somewhere in the
small hollow corridor, it was like a throbbing of his temples.

Apparently there was no dining room beyond the slammed door,
only a cerebral expanse: sinuosities, gray and white substances,
knobby glands; the heavy walls of sparkling sputters (conditioned
by the afflux) consisted of a leaden and painful perception resi-
dent in the occipital, frontal, temporal, and sincipital bones.

Apollon Apollonovich sat at his desk, poring over affairs of state
and feeling that his head was six times as large and a dozen times
heavier than it should have been.

12

The streets of Petersburg possess one indubitable quality: they
transform the figures of passers-by into shadows.

The mysterious stranger, having originated like a thought, became associated for some reason with the Senator's house; he had
floated spontaneously to the surface on the Nevsky Prospect in the
wake of the Senator.

From the street crossing, where the stranger had run into the
Senator's carriage, to the little restaurant on the Millionaya, we have
obligingly described the stranger's path.

When the stranger disappeared into the restaurant, two silhouettes were cutting through the fog. One was tall and burly—a hefty

fellow; but it was impossible to distinguish his features (silhouettes, after all, have no faces). But one could distinguish his raised open umbrella, his overshoes, and fur cap with earflaps.

A mangy little figure, quite short in stature—such was the general impression of the second silhouette. His face, to be sure, was visible; but an immense wart, a shameless accident of nature and its chief feature, effectively screened the rest of the face. Such was its function in the world of shadows.

The dark pair paused before the door of the restaurant.

"H'm?"

"This is the place . . ."

"So I thought."

"What measures have you taken?"

"I've placed a man inside the restaurant."

"H'm . . . I'll have to . . . h'm! . . . Well, I wish you luck!"

The undertaking had evidently been put on a clockwork basis.

"H'm?"

"What's the matter?"

"It's this damn head cold of mine."

"My advice is you'd better take your salary . . ."

"No, you won't understand me!"

"Maybe I will. Damn it, I can't get enough handkerchiefs."

"What?"

"It's this running nose!"

"I don't work for a wage. I'm an artist!"

"Of a sort . . ."

"What?"

"I use tallow candle as a cure."

The diminutive figure drew a soiled wet handkerchief from its pocket. It said:

"Don't forget to report: Nikolai Apollonovich has made a promise . . ."

"A tallow candle is a fine cure!"

"Tell them everything!"

"In the evening you dab your nostrils with a bit of tallow—in the morning it's gone."

The handkerchief once more resumed its operations under the wart. The two shadows drifted into the foul mist. Soon the shadow of the burly man re-emerged from the fog; it glanced absent-mindedly at the slender spire of Peter and Paul. Then it entered the restaurant.

13

Suddenly is familiar to you by now.

It stealthily approaches from behind; it often heralds its approach before it actually appears. The anxiety is excruciating. You have an increasing perception of evil behind your back. It is as if a horde of invisible spirits had entered behind you, and you turn to the woman in charge with the plea:

"Madam, would you mind shutting the door? It makes me nervous. I don't like sitting with my back to the door."

Everyone laughs. You also laugh: as if *Suddenly* did not exist!

Suddenly the stranger in the little restaurant turned his head. He felt as if something slimy were being poured down his neck. He could see nothing behind his back; yet he had a definite perception of the *invisible* approaching him from there, through the door.

When the stranger glanced away from the door, there entered through the same door a burly nasty fellow, whose footfalls made the boards creak as he approached the stranger. His sallow shaven face was turned slightly sidewise and floated on the softness of his second chin; the face had a greasy look.

At this point the stranger again turned his head. The newcomer waved his fur cap with earflaps at him. He greeted the stranger:

"Alexander Ivanovich . . ."

"Lippanchenko!"

Lippanchenko wore a gaudy silk red tie; it was very bright and was pierced with a pin crowned with a paste diamond. He wore a striped dark tan suit and a pair of gleaming light tan shoes.

Sitting down at the stranger's table, he shouted:

"A pot of coffee, please! And some cognac, too! I haven't finished the bottle you're keeping for me."

There was a din of conversation all around:

"Have you had a few drinks?"

"Yes."

"Well, you're a proper swine, if I may say so."

"Be careful there!" The stranger shouted as the burly fellow was about to place his elbow on the newspaper covering the bundle.

"What's that?" Lippanchenko asked. Edging away, he removed the newspaper and saw the bundle. His lips trembled:

"Is that the . . . the . . .?"

Lippanchenko's lips continued to tremble; they resembled slices of salmon—not the red variety, but the yellow oily kind.

"How could you be so careless, Alexander Ivanovich?" Lippanchenko stretched his fingers toward the bundle; his fingers were thick and stiff, adorned with imitation stones which seemed to call attention to his puffy fingers and dirty nails. A close scrutiny of these fingernails would have revealed traces of tawny tints corresponding to the coloring of his hair. Lippanchenko resorted to dye.

"Just think, old chap, a single movement—that of my elbow, for example—might have caused a catastrophe."

And, with great caution, Lippanchenko moved the bundle to a chair.

"Yes, to be sure," the stranger replied mordantly, "it would have been the end of both of us."

The surrounding din was as loud as ever.

"Don't you call me names!"

"I'm not calling you names."

"Yes, you are. You're reminding me that you're paying the bill."

"Go on, eat your fill. That'd be better . . ."

"Take charge of it, my dear Alexander Ivanovich. Take this bundle at once to Nikolai Apollonovich." Lippanchenko eyed the bundle with misgiving.

"Why shouldn't I keep it myself?" the other asked. "The bundle should be safe with me."

"That's not so good. You might be arrested. But *there* it would be safe."

And reaching over, the burly fellow whispered something in the other's ear:

"Shoo-shoo-shoo- . . ."

"Ableukhov, you say?"

"Shoo . . ."

"What, Ableukhov? . . ."

"Shoo . . ."

"With Ableukhov? . . ."

"Yes, not the Senator, but his son. And give him this letter too. I have it here . . ."

Lippanchenko's low forehead was uncomfortably close to the stranger's face. His small eyes grew furtive, his lips imperceptibly trembled and sucked in the air. The stranger, straining hard, listened to the whispers of the heavy man. This was not easy, for his whispered words were drowned in the noise of the restaurant. The rustle of those repugnant lips seemed to convey horrible meanings; they might have been whispering of worlds and planetary systems, but in the end the whispering dissipated itself in triviality:

"Hand him the letter . . ."

The surrounding din went on:

"What's the truth?"

"The truth—the truth . . ."

"I know . . ."

"If you know, get busy with your plate and eat your fill . . ."

Lippanchenko's striped suit reminded the stranger of the wallpaper in his flat on Vasilyevsky Island. It was the color that he associated with his insomnia, an insomnia that evoked in his memory the ominous face with narrow Mongolian eyes persistently peering at him from the wallpaper. When he had examined the place by daylight, he found only a damp spot upon which a woodlouse crawled. In order to divert his memories from this agonizing hallucination, he surprised himself by becoming garrulous:

"Just listen to the din!"

"It's a lot of noise, right enough!"

"Speaking of sounds," the stranger said, "it's odd how some of them—sometimes a mere syllable or even a letter—can suggest ideas. Despair, dejection, devil, dentistry, derelict, delirium, oh yes, and death—all these words have the same ominous opening syllable. . . . Do you follow?"

"Of course," Lippanchenko answered, torn from his own thoughts.

"There are also words which convey triviality," the stranger resumed. "But there are others so full of meaning. When you hear the word 'hawk,' you instantaneously have an image of a sharp hooked beak; when you hear 'scavenger,' you at once have the vision of a foul creature that consumes carrion; when you say 'fish,' you think of something cold-blooded. Then there's 'soap,' which suggests something slimy. And can you think of anything more formless than 'clod'? . . ."

The stranger broke off. As he sat before him, Lippanchenko looked indeed like a formless clod, and the smoke from his cigarette slimily soaped the atmosphere. Lippanchenko sat there as in a cloud. The stranger eyed him in disgust and thought: "Tfu, a reptile, a dirty Tartar . . ." Before him sat something that was merely an ugly sound, a beastly syllable . . .

At the neighboring table someone stammered:

"De-de-de-de . . . de-de-de . . ."

"Excuse me, Lippanchenko, are you by any chance a Mongol?"

"What a strange question!"

"Well, as you know, all Russians have a strain of Mongol blood."

14

Nikolai Apollonovich's quarters consisted of a bedroom, a study, and a reception room.

The bedroom was occupied by a huge bed covered with a satin counterpane. Oak bookshelves, filled with leather-bound books, stood against the walls: silk draperies hanging along their exposed side glided on a bar fitted with rings.

The furniture in the study was upholstered green. There was a handsome bust—of Kant, needless to say.

Two and a half years had passed since Nikolai Apollonovich had

risen before noon. Previously he used to wake at nine and don his
tightly buttoned student's uniform. At that time he was not yet in
the habit of pacing his rooms attired in a Bokhara dressing-gown;
a skullcap had not graced his Oriental reception room. Two and a
half years had also passed since Anna Petrovna, the mother of
Nikolai Apollonovich and the wife of Apollon Apollonovich, had
abandoned her home and run off with an Italian singer. Only after
her flight had Nikolai Apollonovich begun to pace the parquet floor
in his Bokhara dressing-gown. His morning chats with his father
over coffee had thus automatically ceased.

The Senator now drank his coffee considerably earlier than his
son. But Nikolai Apollonovich began to breakfast in his dressing-
gown, his Tartar slippers, and his skullcap.

A brilliant student was transformed into an Oriental.

Nikolai Apollonovich had just received a letter in an unfamiliar
handwriting: some paltry rhymes over the impressive signature:
"*Flaming Soul.*" In quest of his spectacles, Nikolai Apollonovich
wandered up and down the room, turning objects upside down.

"A-ah . . .

"The deuce take it . . ."

Like his father, Nikolai Apollonovich was in the habit of speaking
to himself.

His movements were impulsive, like his father's; and, like him,
he was not an impressive figure. He had restless eyes in a normally
smiling face but, when he lapsed into deep contemplation, his
glance became stony, and the lines of his livid face hardened, rigid
and cold, like the countenance of an ikon; the forehead revealed a
certain nobility—it was chiseled with tiny swollen veins which
throbbed visibly, a sign of incipient sclerosis.

The blue veins blended with the circles around his enormous eyes
of a dark cornflower color; when disturbed, his pupils dilated and
made his eyes look black.

Nikolai Apollonovich wore a Tartar skullcap. Under it, his luminous flaxen white hair somewhat softened his sober features. Such
flaxen hair was unusual in an adult, although infants, especially in
White Russia, often had such hair.

Here, in his room, Nikolai Apollonovich had achieved his growth
within a self-defined center of predetermined thoughts, confining

a whole series of logical premises; and the table in this room seemed the only center of both the visible and the invisible universe.

This center he himself had inferred.

Yet scarcely had Nikolai Apollonovich succeeded in dismissing from his mind all those mundane trivialities and incoherences which bore the name of World and Life when the same external absurdity impinged upon his serene mood.

Nikolai Apollonovich tore himself away from his book:

"Well, what is it?"

A timid and respectful voice sounded from behind the door:

"Someone to see you, sir."

Behind his locked door he had been deliberating step by step upon the conditions that might lead to a unified system, and he had become conscious that his body was merging with the "all," with the universe; his head had seemed to usurp the shape of the electric bulb projecting from the lamp socket.

And in this happy state, Nikolai Apollonovich truly became a creative substance.

He loved to isolate himself; and the slightest rustling sound or step disturbed his consciousness.

"What is it?" he called again.

From the remote space behind the door came the reply:

"You have a visitor."

At this, Nikolai Apollonovich's face assumed a satisfied expression.

"Ah, it must be the costumer," he thought. "He must have brought my costume."

Gathering up the folds of his dressing-gown, he strode in the direction of the hall; he leaned over the balustrade and shouted:

"Is that you? The costumer?"

Soon Nikolai Apollonovich reappeared in his room with a carton under his arm. He relocked the door and hurriedly cut the cord around the carton. Removing the cover, he drew from the box a small mask with a black lace beard and a sumptuous, flaming red domino with rustling folds.

Presently he stood before a mirror, garbed in red velvet, holding the mask over his face. The black lace of the beard fell to his shoulders, forming fantastic wings right and left.

After this masquerade Nikolai Apollonovich, looking extremely satisfied, replaced the red domino and the small black mask in the box.

15

Tufts of clouds drifted in a greenish swarm, moving without pause over the boundless expanse of the Neva's broad embankment. From the Petersburg side, the slender spire of Peter and Paul vanished into the clouds.

A dark strip of soot, rising from the chimneys, described a funereal arc and dipped its tail in the water.

The Neva seethed; the siren of a small passing steamer sounded clamorously, the steel sides of ships beat against the piers and lapped the granite of the embankment.

As he peered into the muddy contaminated water of the Neva, Nikolai Apollonovich's silhouette was clearly outlined against this somber background of soot which hovered above the damp stones of the embankment balustrade.

He had paused before the big black bridge.

An unpleasant smile hovered on his face. He was torn by the recollections of unrequited love. Nikolai Apollonovich was remembering a certain foggy night. That particular night he had tried to climb over the balustrade. He had swung one leg over and, turning his body, he was about to swing the other leg over. . . . Then he had paused. Nothing happened. Nikolai Apollonovich had timorously withdrawn.

As he recalled this unsuccessful attempt, Nikolai Apollonovich looked pitiful and absurd; swathed in his greatcoat, the cape flouncing in the wind like a long flapping wing, he resembled an armless hunchback.

At the approach to the bridge, where two gray lions mockingly placed one granite paw over the other, he suddenly spied the back of a passing army officer entangled in the folds of a voluminous greatcoat. He hailed him:

"Sergey Sergeyevich!"

For an instant the officer's face and his trembling lips betrayed his hesitation: should he recognize this acquaintance or not? However, the hesitation was fleeting, and a greeting ensued:

"Oh, it's you? . . . How do you do?"

"Which way are you bound?" Nikolai Apollonovich asked, although he was fairly certain that Sergey Sergeyevich intended to walk along the Moika, and equally certain that he himself wanted an excuse to go that way.

"I'm going home," the officer replied.

"We're going the same way then."

Before Nikolai Apollonovich's eyes rose the vision of a large yellow house, between whose windows a row of lions' heads was festooned above a coat of arms encircled in a stone garland.

Gingerly, they tried not to touch upon the past. Interrupting each other, they casually discussed the popular unrest of the past few weeks and its effect on Nikolai Apollonovich's philosophical studies.

Thus they reached the Moika. And there was the bright, three-story, five-columned edifice. Above its first story was the familiar series of modeled ornaments: ring after ring, and inside each ring the same coat of arms—a Roman helmet between two crossed swords. They passed this building; and then they came to *the* house, and its windows . . .

"Well, goodbye," the officer said. "You're going farther, I think."

Nikolai Apollonovich's heart began to beat rapidly; he had been preparing to ask a question, but no—he desisted. Alone, he stood in front of the door that had just been slammed; recollections of his unrequited love—or, more accurately, of his unsuccessful infatuation—gripped him again.

This bright five-columned house, with its strip of sculptured reliefs and its series of circles with the coat of arms repeated in each—a Roman helmet between two crossed swords—was firmly imprinted on his memory.

Then Nikolai Apollonovich emerged on the Nevsky Prospect.

In the evening the Prospect presented a rectilinear stream of light. Down its middle the apples of electric light were evenly strung out. Along the sides played the constantly changing gleam of shop signs; here, rubies of flame suddenly flashed and vanished; there, emeralds as suddenly sparkled and disappeared.

Nikolai Apollonovich did not see the Nevsky; his eyes still held the vision of that house, of its windows and the shadows behind the windows; and he heard gay voices: the voice of the Cuirassier, Baron Ommau-Ommergau, and—*her* voice . . .

16

Apollon Apollonovich remembered that some of his officials, his underlings, occasionally joked good-naturedly at his expense.

One day, as the door swung open, Apollon Apollonovich entered and caught them in the middle of such a jest. He said nothing, however; he was impervious to this sort of thing.

He merely walked to the window and looked out. Two pairs of eyes glanced at him from a window across the street and beheld, like a blur upon the pane, the unfamiliar face of an old man.

Here, in the sanctum of an important department, Apollon Apollonovich had evolved into a kind of king-pin of governmental departments and green-topped writing desks. Here he seemed to be a point of energy-radiating power, an impulse of energy-stimulating power. He was a force in the Newtonian sense, and such a force is an occult force.

His consciousness was detached from his personality, fabulously sharpening and concentrating in a single point between his eyes and his forehead, and generating a tiny flame which scattered shafts of lightning; his thoughts—lightnings, as it were—uncoiled swiftly, like serpents, from his bald head; a clear-sighted person, without doubt, would have recognized in his head the head of the Gorgon—Medusa.

The Senator's consciousness was separate from his personality: the latter, indeed, seemed to him to be merely a skull case, quite empty of content.

In his official armchair, he used his consciousness to intersect his existence; the circulars, which he issued from this place, cut across the line of everyday life, of vegetative existence.

It was only here that he achieved an elevation, that he soared madly over Russia, provoking his enemies to compare him ominously to a bat.

On this particular day Apollon Apollonovich was unusually alert; he refused to glance at the report placed before him. For some reason, on this particular day, Apollon Apollonovich had come to the conclusion that his son, Nikolai Apollonovich, was a scoundrel.

From his window he was able to see the caryatid at the entrance: the bearded fellow hewn from stone.

The bearded fellow had first risen above the din of the streets in the year 1812. Crowds had fought below him in 1825; crowds had gathered here again in this year of 1905. Five years had passed since Apollon Apollonovich had first watched from this same window that same stone smile; the tooth of time was nibbling away at it. In these five years, many things had happened: Anna Petrovna had fled to Spain; Vyacheslav Konstantinovich was gone; yellow heels had audaciously trodden the ridges of Port Arthur's heights; China was restless, and Port Arthur had fallen.

The door opened. His secretary, a young man with an Order dangling on his chest, came flying into the room, the edge of his overstarched cuff clicking respectfully. To his timid question, Apollon Apollonovich replied loudly:

"No, no! Do exactly as I tell you. And do you know . . ." Here Apollon Apollonovich's voice faltered, and he said something quite incoherent.

In the office, legends circulated concerning his incoherence when distraught.

17

Apollon Apollonovich Ableukhov, in his gray overcoat and tall black cylinder hat, his stony face reminiscent of a paperweight, speedily stepped from his carriage and, removing a glove, ran up the steps of his house.

He entered the hall. He handed the cylinder to the lackey.

"Be so good as to tell me, does the young man come here often?"

"Young people come here sometimes, Your Excellency."

"I mean a young man, with a—small mustache?"

"With a small mustache?"

"Yes, yes, with a small mustache—in an overcoat rather the worse for wear."

A gleam suddenly appeared in the doorman's eyes.

"Yes, Your Excellency . . . such a young man did come to see the young master once."

"With a small mustache?"

"Exactly, sir."

Apollon Apollonovich paused and reflected; then, impulsively, he ascended the stairs.

A gray velvet rug covered the stairs; a similar gray rug covered the wall. Polished antique weapons graced the wall of the stairway; a Lithuanian helmet gleamed under a rusty green shield; the hilt of a knightly sword flashed brightly; there were rusty swords here, halberds hung on a slant. . . . On the landing, a lusterless monolith supported a stilled Niobe, her alabaster eyes raised in affliction.

Apollon Apollonovich firmly opened the door, his bony hand pressing on the cut-crystal handle.

18

A mysterious phosphorescent stain drifted across a dead clouded sky. It permeated the misty heights and lighted roofs and chimneys. Here the waters of the Moika ran past; on one side of the canal the familiar three-story house loomed, revealing its upper projections.

His head buried in his fur collar, Nikolai Apollonovich sauntered along the river bank. Intangible feelings divided his soul; they were both painful and sweet. . . . He was thinking: can this be love? Then, suddenly remembering, he trembled.

A shaft of light flashed by. An elegant black carriage sped past. The lamps near its hollow windows glowed blood-red. Playfully their lights shimmered over the waters of the Moika. The phantasmal contours of the lackey's cocked hat and of the wings of his cape flashed by, moving with the light, from one patch of fog into another.

Nikolai Apollonovich remained standing in front of the house for a considerable time; then, unexpectedly, he vanished through the gate.

It swung open before him, striking his back with a thud as he passed. The darkness embraced him, and everything fell away from him—it was as if something had died in him. At this moment Nikolai Apollonovich was not thinking of death; he was absorbed in his personal gestures, and his actions assumed a fantastic character in the darkness. He sat down on the cold step inside the gate, buried his face in his fur collar, and listened to the beating of his heart.

Nikolai Apollonovich continued to sit in the darkness.

The granite curve of the Winter Canal unfurled in a wide ribbon of sleet; the Neva seethed and foamed under the pressure of the moist wind; the soundlessly stirring surfaces shimmered; and the moon lighted the walls of the four-story palace.

A mood of desolation invested the scene. No one, nothing, was stirring. Only the small canal showed signs of life; the water flowed. A woman's shadow sped from the yellow house on the Gagarinsky embankment, where it lingered every evening, peering into a window.

A vista of open spaces widened before her, revealing everywhere greenish bronze statues, those of Hercules and Poseidon among them. Vast shapes loomed beyond the Neva—contours of islands and houses; amber eyes peered into the fog; it seemed as if someone were crying.

High up, arms shaped from clouds sorrowfully formed misty bodies; swarms of clouds ascended above the tumultuous waters of the Neva, racing toward the zenith; and, when they touched the zenith, the phosphorescent stain fell upon them.

The shadow of the woman, whose head was buried in a muff, sped along the Moika toward the same house entrance to which she fled every evening and where now, on a cold step, behind the gate, sat Nikolai Apollonovich. She closed the gate behind her; it slammed; the dark embraced her; it was as if she had left everything behind; the little dark lady thought only of simple earthy things. Already she had stretched a hand toward the bell when she noticed the outline of what appeared to be a mask raised toward her from the step.

When the inner door opened and a shaft of light dispelled for an instant the darkness of the entrance, the exclamation of the frightened maid confirmed what she had seen. In that instant, in that single flash of light, she had glimpsed something incredibly strange: the little lady flung herself through the open door.

Behind her, out of the darkness, rose a rustling buffoon with a shaking bearded mask.

In the dark she discerned a fur-collared cape falling from human shoulders, and two red arms reaching out toward the inner door. Then the door closed, cutting off the stream of light and plunging the outer entrance into darkness again.

In an instant, Nikolai Apollonovich had leaped into the street. A piece of red silk dangled from the folds of his cape; thrusting his nose into his collar, he wandered off in the direction of the bridge.

When he reached the iron bridge, he turned his head, but saw nothing. In the gusts of the Neva wind, over the damp railings, over the green waters seething with bacilli, he saw only a bowler, a stick, a greatcoat, ears, nose, and a mustache.

19

We have glimpsed Senator Ableukhov and the Senator's idle thoughts in the shape of his house, in the shape of his son, who also carried idle thoughts in his head; and finally, we have glimpsed another idle shadow—the shadow of the stranger.

This shadow was traced on the Senator's consciousness only by chance, and there it acquired its ephemeral existence; but Apollon Apollonovich's consciousness was a shadowy one, because he also was ephemeral: his was an unnecessary existence. It was mere idle cerebral play.

Cerebral play is only a mask. Under this mask, however, an invasion has been launched into the mind by powers unknown to us. Although Apollon Apollonovich is but a creature of fancy, yet he will succeed in frightening others with his staggering existence, with events that intrude upon the night. Apollon Apollonovich has all the attributes of this existence: the play of his mind is likewise endowed with those attributes.

Once his brain had begun to play with the idea of the mysterious stranger, then the stranger began to exist; that stranger would not vanish from the Petersburg prospects, at least not as long as the Senator persisted in thinking as he did; for, after all, thoughts too have their own particular existence.

Our stranger will therefore be a stranger of flesh and blood! And the two shadows of my two strangers will also be real shadows!

Those dark shadows will doubtless follow on the Senator's heels, just as the stranger himself will doubtless follow on the Senator's heels. The senile shadow of the Senator will follow on your heels also; he will come riding after you in his black carriage and you will never, never forget him!

CHAPTER TWO

Though in books and by word of mouth
Men will try to make mock of me,
I am a citizen, as you must know,
And in that sense a democrat.

—PUSHKIN

1

Our citizens do not read the newspaper feature *Diary of Events*. In October of 1905 our worthy citizens most likely read the editorials in *Comrade*, if they were not subscribers to the very latest newspapers.

All the other truly Russian Philistines willynilly pounced upon the *Diary of Events*. I, too, pounced upon it. Reading the *Diary* kept me well-informed. Who bothered to read of burglaries, witches, and ghosts? Everyone read only the editorials. But no one will remember the facts recorded herein.

Here are some newspaper excerpts of the time, which include stories of burglaries, rapes, thefts of diamonds, the disappearance from a tiny provincial town of an author with jewels amounting to a considerable sum. There was also much pure fantasy, enough to make the head of a reader of Conan Doyle spin.

The Diary of Events:

"*October 1*. Relying on information communicated by a lady medical assistant, N. N., we note an enigmatic occurrence. Last evening she happened to pass by the Chernishev Bridge. There she observed a singular spectacle: a red domino dancing on the bridge. The figure wore a black mask."

"*October 2*. According to a female teacher, M. M., we are in a position to inform the esteemed public of a singular event. The lady was instructing her morning class. The windows of the classroom face the street. Suddenly, a cloud of dust spiraled up near a window. The teacher and the pupils rushed to the windows in order to learn the cause of the strange spectacle. Imagine the confusion of the class and its teacher when, out of the cloud of dust, they saw emerge a red domino, which promptly pressed a black face-mask against a pane. The O. O. School promptly suspended all classes . . ."

"*October 3.* At a spiritualist seance held in the apartment of the Baroness R. R., the audience had just formed a circle. Suddenly, in this circle, a red domino appeared and brushed against the tip of the nose of Councilor S., a physician attached to the G. Hospital, leaving a mysterious burn. According to rumor, a lilac stain will now permanently mar the tip of Dr. S.'s nose."

Finally: "*October 4.* The citizens of the suburb of S. fled at the appearance of a red domino. A series of protests are being pre-pared. A hundred Cossacks have been called to the scene."

A newspaper contributor is an active worker in the press. As a collaborator in the Press (the sixth continent of the world), he receives a penny a line for his service, or maybe twopence, or threepence, or six, or a shilling, as the case may be.

Such are the esteemed virtues of newspaper correspondents of the Right, the Middle, the Moderately Liberal, and the Revolutionary newspapers; and here is the key to the truth of the year 1905—the truth of the *Diary of Events* and its subtitle "The Red Domino." The contributor to the newspaper in question had utilized what he had heard from the hostess of a certain house; the responsibility for the story of the red domino should be placed not on the shoulders of the esteemed contributor, but on those of the lady from whom he had heard it . . .

This woman happened to mention that she had just passed a red domino in a dark vestibule; her story happened to fall under the heading, *Diary of Events*; and, having fallen there, quickly developed into a series of fabricated events.

2

Sofya Petrovna Likhutina was distinguished for her extraordinary vegetative qualities. She had an extremely supple body and aston-ishing black hair, which would have covered her waist and reached to her calves, had she allowed it to fall loose. She frankly did not know what to do with her hair which, despite its black magnificence, failed to conceal the down on her upper lip that ominously threatened to develop into a tiny mustache in the years to follow. She had a startling complexion: pure pearl, of a pale rose tint that suggested tender apple blossoms. When Sofya Petrovna was embarrassed, she turned visibly crimson.

Sofya Petrovna's eyes were large and dark blue. Perhaps they should be called orbs rather than eyes—orbs that either sparkled or grew dim. At moments they seemed dull, faded, lost in their deep sockets, and appeared surprisingly malignant and squinting. Her lips were very red and overly large, but her teeth—ah, her teeth—were true pearls! How lovely they looked when she laughed—the laugh of a child. This laughter conferred a certain beauty to her parted lips. Then there was her waist, her very supple waist: all the movements of her waist and mobile back were either impulsive or languid.

She dressed in a black frock buttoned at the back and this complimented her magnificent form. Sofya Petrovna was only twenty-three, but she had prematurely achieved the figure of a woman of thirty.

Ah, Sofya Petrovna!

She lived in a small flat on the Moika. Cascades of the brightest, most lavish colors fell from the walls, which alternated between flame and sky-blue. Japanese fans, laces, draperies, and bowknots decorated the walls, while the satin lampshades projected paper wings, like tropical butterflies.

Army officers of her acquaintance always called her Angel Peri, erroneously confusing the meanings of these two words.

Sofya Petrovna Likhutina had hung several Japanese landscapes of Fujiyama on the walls. These landscapes had no perspective; the rooms themselves, tightly packed with divans, armchairs, sofas, fans, and freshly cut Japanese chrysanthemums, revealed no perspective either: the only perspective was offered by the satin-lined alcove from which Sofya Petrovna would come fluttering, and by the door which swung open whenever Sofya Petrovna entered. Fujiyama made a fitting background for her fabulous hair; in the morning, when Sofya Petrovna Likhutina, in her rose kimono, swept from the door toward the alcove, she looked authentically Japanese. There was no perspective.

The rooms were small: each was occupied by one very large object. The enormous bed was the principal piece in the little bedroom; a table and sideboard filled the dining room; and the object that filled her husband's room was of course the husband.

How could there be any perspective here?

All six tiny rooms were centrally heated; the flat was hot and stuffy. The window panes perspired; the visitors perspired; the maid, and the husband perspired; Sofya Petrovna Likhutina herself was covered with perspiration like a chrysanthemum with warm dew. How could there be a perspective here?

Indeed, there was none.

3

The man who looked after her chrysanthemums was a regular visitor to Angel Peri's small conservatory. During his visits he praised her Japanese landscapes and offered his views on art. Angel Peri would volunteer the information: "This landscape is by the brush of Hadusai . . ." when, of course, she meant Hokusai; the captivating angel always confused proper names, and not only names. Her mistakes always offended the visiting art critic, who finally refrained from expressing any views on art. This did not prevent the Angel from buying more landscapes, on which she did not hesitate to spend her last penny.

Sofya Petrovna made no effort to entertain her visitors. If the guest happened to be a man of fashion and a gallant, she giggled throughout the visit whether he spoke jestingly or seriously. She would giggle and giggle, turning crimson; perspiration would settle on her little nose. The gentleman, in his turn, would also turn red and perspire uncomfortably. He would be astonished at her child-like laughter, which was not at all sophisticated. He might think her a demi-mondaine; but she would haul out a tiny box with a slot, inscribed "Charity Fund." And then Sofya Petrovna Likhu-

tina or Angel Peri, would exclaim: "You told a fib just then! You
must pay!" (Sofya Petrovna had established a Charity Fund on
the basis of such fibs: the visitor had to pay for every bit of nonsense he uttered.) Baron Ommau-Ommergau, of Her Majesty's
Cuirassiers; Count Aven, also a Cuirassier; Shporishev, of the
Life Guards; and Verhefden, special duty officer attached to Ableukhov—all young men of the world—uttered fib after fib, and
put coin after coin into the tin box.

If Sofya Petrovna's visitor turned out to be a musician, a music
critic, or simply a music lover, then she would produce her idols
—Duncan and Nikisch. With rapturous expressions, gesticulations
rather than utterances, she would explain that she was prepared
to learn meloplastics in order to perform in Bayreuth the dance
of Valkyries' flight. And the musician or music critic or music
lover, shaken by Sofya Petrovna's incredible pronunciation of
names, would conclude that Sofya Petrovna Likhutina was an
empty-headed little woman, and would then counter her with gay
chatter. Sofya Petrovna never missed a fashionable opera; nevertheless musicians who played before smart audiences rarely visited
her flat. Count Aven, Baron Ommau-Ommergau, Shporishev and
Verhefden, however, came often. At one time, Nikolai Ableukhov,
as a student, frequented her home: then, suddenly, he stopped
coming.

Sofya Petrovna's visitors fell naturally into two categories: social
visitors, and simply visitors—well—those who were not quite
comme il faut. These latter were, so to speak, the desirable visitors
—desirable for the easing of the soul. They had not angled for
their invitations; Angel Peri brought them into her drawing room
by force. In their presence Angel Peri sat with compressed lips;
she neither giggled nor sulked nor teased, but remained timid and
mute. As for the guests, they wrangled continuously, and the words
most often heard were "revolution" and "evolution." They represented neither the golden nor even the silver youth, but rather the
copper youth, who had received their educations through hard work
and were lavish only in their use of the phrase, "social revolution,"
and again, "social evolution." Angel Peri found it difficult to distinguish between these terms.

4

Among the young people who visited the Likhutins frequently was a certain radiant personality: a girl student, Varvara Evgrafovna.

Under the influence of this radiant creature—just imagine it!—Angel Peri had honored a radical meeting with her presence. Under the same influence, she had passed around the tin receptacle with the ambiguous inscription, "Charity Fund." Those for whom the meeting had been organized were not, of course, expected to contribute, but sums were duly extorted from Count Aven, Baron Ommau-Ommergau, Shporishev, and Verhefden. Under the influence of Varvara Evgrafovna, Angel Peri had learned by heart the *Manifesto* of Karl Marx. It was during this period that Nikolai Ableukhov had daily visited the Angel, and it had been possible then, without risk, to introduce him to Varvara Evgrafovna (who had fallen in love with him) and to Baron Ommau-Ommergau, Her Majesty's Cuirassier.

After Nikolai Ableukhov had stopped coming, Angel Peri contacted the spirit world, but kept this a secret even from her regular visitors, even from Baron Ommau-Ommergau; her secrecy attained incredible dimensions.

Sofya Petrovna Likhutina had still another regular visitor: Sergey Sergeyevich Likhutin, an army officer. Strictly speaking, he was her husband; he was a regimental quartermaster; he left the house early in the morning and rarely returned before midnight; he would greet the visitors simply, utter a mild fib for form's sake and drop a small coin into the tin box if Aven and Ommau-Ommergau happened to be there, or he would nod his head modestly at the words, "revolution" and "evolution," drink a cup of tea, and then retire to his tiny room. The society visitors referred to him as "the soldier," but the radical young men had a less pleasant name for him.

When possible, Sergey Sergeyevich Likhutin refrained from fibs and from the words, "revolution" and "evolution"; he would not have minded going to the Baroness's spiritualist seances, but he never expressed his desire; nor did he insist on his rights as husband. He was no despot in his relationship with Sofya Petrovna·

he had married her two and a half years earlier in opposition to the wishes of his parents, rich landowners, who had cursed and disinherited him.

There was still another visitor: Lippanchenko, a Ukrainian, a common sensual fellow, who called Sofya Petrovna not angel, but darling: he confined himself, however, within the bounds of decency and therefore had entrée to the Likhutin home.

Sergey Sergeyevich Likhutin, a very good-natured husband and lieutenant in a famous regiment, tolerated the revolutionary acquaintances of his wife; he maintained a complacent attitude toward her social acquaintances. As for Lippanchenko, he merely endured him. This Lippanchenko was a sly fellow, who seemed to be a blend of Mongol and Semite; he wore a red necktie, fixed with a paste diamond pin, and unashamedly dyed his hair brown. Lippanchenko admitted to exporting Russian pigs.

Likhutin had no love for Lippanchenko; indeed, he had heard some dark rumors about him. Likhutin loved almost everyone and, at one time, had particularly loved Nikolai Apollonovich Ableukhov. They had known each other since boyhood; Nikolai Apollonovich had been best man at Likhutin's wedding and a daily visitor at their Moika flat. Then he had disappeared without a trace.

Sergey Sergeyevich had not been to blame for this.

5

On the very day when, in church, Nikolai Apollonovich had held the solemn crown over Sergey Sergeyevich's head, Sofya Petrovna Likhutina had been deeply impressed by this handsome, shapely best man, by the color of his eyes, the pallor of his face, and the fairness of his hair. His eyes did not yet peer through pince-nez, as they were to do later, and his face was framed by a gold collar of a kind she had never seen before, and . . . Nikolai Apollonovich had become a frequent visitor: at first he came every fortnight, then once a week and, finally, every day. Soon Sofya Petrovna observed that Nikolai Apollonovich's face had become a mask. She saw him rubbing his perspired hands in a distraught way; she saw the frog-like expression of his smile; and these things unhappily screened his face from her. As soon as Sofya Petrovna noticed these things, she understood that she had been in love with the other face; from under his frog-like smile she tried to evoke the face she had first known and restore her lost infatuation. She tormented Ableukhov; she jealously followed his movements, studied his tastes and aspirations—all in an effort to recover her loss. She grew desperate; in her desperation, she resorted to her dancing. Then one of her cuirassiers appeared on the scene; and so did Varvara Evgrafovna with the tin box for collecting fines for "fibs."

Since then, Sergey Sergeyevich Likhutin himself had become a "visitor" to his own little flat on the Moika. He became a quartermaster and, leaving the house early in the morning, never returned until midnight.

Sofya Petrovna found her freedom difficult to endure; she had a small forehead and, besides, she was torn by her feelings; she was a woman. Women cannot bear chaos, and chaos was being awakened in Sofya Petrovna's soul. In every woman a sinner is concealed; but once her crime is committed, she feels like a saint.

Duality characterized Nikolai Apollonovich; there were two of him. Such duality is usually a woman's prerogative; duality is a feminine rather than a masculine trait; in truth, integrity is the symbol of the male. As soon as a trinity manifests itself, the domestic hearth becomes untenable.

If either Sergey Sergeyevich Likhutin or Nikolai Apollonovich had been real unities rather than dualities, a trinity would have been established. Sofya Petrovna would have found harmony in union with a man; and the gramophone, her dancing, Lippanchenko, and all the rest of it, would have gone by the board.

But there was no unity in Ableukhov. Everything that happened was the result of that.

6

During the final months of her acquaintance with Nikolai Apollonovich, Sofya Petrovna had behaved very provokingly. She practiced gymnastics to the tune of "Siegfried's Death" on the gramophone; while exercising, she raised her long rustling skirt to her knees; her leg came in contact with Ableukhov more than once. It was hardly astonishing that, on one occasion, he had tried to embrace her; but she had slipped from his arms, coldly rejecting his advances. Then she resumed her tactics again. One day Nikolai Apollonovich could endure it no longer; in a passion, he threw her onto the sofa. She bit his lips and, when Nikolai Apollonovich recoiled with pain, a slap across his face resounded through the Japanese room.

"Oh, you . . . you monster! You frog! You red clown!"

Nikolai Apollonovich answered dispassionately:

"You're a Japanese doll!"

He stood erect and dignified; his face assumed the remote expression she had noted at their first meeting, and, remembering this, her love flamed again. When he left her, she flung herself on the floor, scratching and biting the rug. Then she jumped to her feet, stretched her arms toward the door and cried:

"Come back!"

The only answer was the slamming of the street door. Nikolai Apollonovich fled toward the Petersburg Bridge. On the bridge, he reached a fateful decision: he decided to commit suicide. The expression "red clown" had stung him deeply.

Sofya Petrovna Likhutina never saw him again. At the same time, quite reluctantly, she drifted away from her radical circle and its slogans "revolution"—"evolution." Varvara Evgrafovna appeared at the flat less frequently; on the other hand, Count Aven, Ommau-Ommergau, Shporishev, and Verhefden came more often, and Lippanchenko most of all. With all these visitors, and even with Lippanchenko, Sofya Petrovna giggled to her heart's content; and sometimes she would ask provokingly:

"I'm a doll—am I not?"

They answered with "fibs." As for Lippanchenko, he said:

"You're a darling, a pet, a honey." And he presented her with a yellow-faced doll.

When she told her husband about Ableukhov, he made no reply and went to his room as if retiring to bed. He sat down to write a letter to Nikolai Apollonovich, in which he stated that he, Sergey Sergeyevich, lieutenant in such-and-such regiment, insisted—the word *insisted* was underlined—that he, Nikolai Apollonovich, should stop coming to his house. His own behavior, however, did not change at all. As before, he left the house early and returned at midnight, and kept uttering his polite "fibs." Whenever he met Baron Ommau-Ommergau, he frowned slightly; but when he saw Lippanchenko, he nodded his head mildly at the words "revolution"—"evolution," finished his cup of tea and quietly retreated to his room.

He was tall, had a fair beard and owned a nose, mouth, hair, ears, and eyes; it was a pity he wore dark blue spectacles which concealed the color of his eyes and their wonderful expression.

7

During those frosty days of early October, Sofya Petrovna was in a state of extraordinary perturbation. When left to herself she would wrinkle her low forehead and flare easily into anger. Or she would walk to the window and wipe the perspiring panes with an exquisitely transparent batiste handkerchief. The glass would squeak under the rubbing. The view opened on the canal, and one day she caught sight of a gentleman in a cylinder hat. Deceived in her presentiment, Peri bit the damp handkerchief, and ran to put on her fur coat and hat; pressing her little nose into her muff, she sauntered from the Moika to the Embankment. She even ventured into the Chinizeli Circus and stared at a natural monster: the bearded woman. More often, however, during this period she would drop into the kitchen and exchange whispers with Mavrushka, the young housemaid, who was suitably clothed in apron and cap. In these moments of agitation her eyes squinted.

One evening, in Lippanchenko's presence, she laughingly pulled the pin out of her hat and stuck it into her little finger.

"Look, I feel no pain. You can see . . . I'm a doll."

Lippanchenko understood nothing. He said:

"You're no doll. You're a darling!"

The Angel flew into a rage and drove him from the flat. Lippanchenko seized his cap with the earflaps and fled.

One day she ran to the window in the little conservatory and wiped the pane. The canal came into view and also a carriage speeding along it. Nothing more.

What more could there be?

Some days earlier Sofya Petrovna Likhutina had returned from the Baroness R. R.; at the Baroness's there had been table rapping, and the table had jumped: nothing more. Yet Sofya Petrovna's nerves were on edge and, after the seance, she wandered through the streets. The vestibule of her house had not been lighted; inside the dark entrance she clearly saw a black spot, a mask, fixing her in a kind of stare. Below the mask, she could discern something red. She pulled at the bell. When the door was flung open and a stream of light fell upon the steps, Mavrushka cried out and waved her hands; Sofya Petrovna dashed into her apartment. Mavrushka had time to see a red domino with a black mask and a fan-like beard of black lace behind her mistress's back. Luckily Sofya Petrovna did not turn around, for the red domino held out toward Mavrushka a blood-red sleeve, from which a visiting card projected. Later, Sofya Petrovna studied the card upon which, instead of a noble coronet, a skull and crossbones were imprinted, and beneath them the words were written: "I shall expect you at the masquerade—on such-and-such a date."

Sofya Petrovna was terribly disturbed for the rest of the evening. Who was the red domino? It must be Nikolai Apollonovich, she thought. Hadn't she called him a "red clown"? Well, here he was, the red clown. If it were he, how categorize such conduct toward a defenseless woman?

Caddishness, caddishness, caddishness.

She wished her husband were at home; he would teach that shameless fellow a lesson. She flushed, squinted, bit her handkerchief and—perspired. She hoped a visitor would call!

But no one came.

Suppose it was not Nikolai Apollonovich at all? She could not conceal her distress: it was hard to part with her conviction that he indeed was the fool. A sweet familiar feeling dominated her: she obviously wanted him to prove himself—a perfect cad.

No—it couldn't be Nikolai. He could not be a cad, a mere vulgarian! But who, then, was the red fool? She could not answer the question with any satisfaction. All the same . . .

She ordered Mavrushka to hold her tongue, and went secretly to the masquerade.

Sergey Sergeyevich Likhutin had sternly forbidden her to attend masquerades.

He was a gentle fellow in all things except when his honor as an officer was in question. He would say: "I give you my word of honor as an officer—this can be done, but that can't." And he refused to be moved: such was his inflexibility, his heartlessness. More than once, Angel Peri had come running out of his room frightened and with tears in her eyes.

Among Sofya Petrovna's visitors who discussed "revolution"—"evolution" was an esteemed newspaper correspondent named Neintelpfein. Sofya Petrovna held him in great respect. She had confided in him. He escorted her to the masquerade, where clowns and buffoons, Spanish coquettes, and Oriental women flashed their eyes from velvet masks. With her hand on Neintelpfein's arm, Sofya Petrovna roamed through the rooms. At the same time, a distraught red domino walked about in search of someone, peering through the slits of his black mask fringed with a large fan-like beard of lace.

Sofya Petrovna told the esteemed Neintelpfein of her experiences, concealing of course all the threads. Was he not a respected newspaper correspondent? From that day notes began to appear daily in the *Diary of Events*.

The red domino became the chief topic of conversation: people talked and argued about him. Some saw revolutionary terrorism in the occurrence; others merely shrugged their shoulders in silence.

He also became a subject of conversation in the Likhutins' conservatory. Count Aven, Ommau-Ommergau, and Shporishev, the hussar, displayed a lively interest in the matter, and in this connection contributed not a few fines to the tin box, while the sly Lippanchenko laughed immoderately. Neintelpfein had proved to be a vulgar beast, and failed to appear again in Sofya Petrovna's circle; he was too busy stretching out the number of lines of his *Diary* to cover adequately the occurrence of the red domino. And the excitement continued.

8

Nikolai Apollonovich Ableukhov in his multicolored dressing-gown stood on the landing: leaning over the balustrade, he shouted something in the direction of the entrance hall. At first, silence was the only answer to his outcry; then a protesting voice replied:

"Nikolai Apollonovich, you've mistaken me for someone else!"

Nikolai Apollonovich bared his teeth in an unpleasant grin:

"Is that you, Alexander Ivanovich?"

And then he added hypocritically:

"I didn't recognize you without my glasses."

Mastering his feelings about the stranger's presence there, he glanced down over the balustrade and said loudly:

"You see, I've just got out of bed. I'm still in my dressing-gown." Actually, in the past few nights, Nikolai Apollonovich had seldom been home.

Against the opulent background of the house, the stranger with the tiny black mustache presented a pitiful spectacle; at this moment he stood facing the wall hung with antique weapons. Nonetheless he made an effort to calm Ableukhov, speaking now half mockingly, now like a simpleton:

"It doesn't matter in the least that you're. . . . A mere trifle. You're not a young lady, and neither am I."

There was nothing to be done. Controlling his revulsion, Nikolai Apollonovich was about to descend, but he fortunately lost a slipper: his bare foot caught in the hem of his dressing-gown and made him stumble. The stranger, assuming that he was putting Nikolai Apollonovich to some inconvenience and wishing to save him the trouble of descending, moved impulsively toward the stairs, leaving wet traces from his shoes. At the foot of the stairwell, he paused uncertainly and smiled in a distraught way.

Then, with desperate independence, he shook off his thin overcoat and stood revealed in a gray checked suit, the worse for moths. But when a pompous lackey held out a hand to relieve him of the wet bundle, the stranger flared up:

"No, no! I'll take it with me."

The stranger cast rapid, astonished glances at the perspective offered by the vista of rooms as Nikolai Apollonovich, gathering up the skirts of his dressing-gown, descended to meet him. The shining perspectives seemed agonizingly dismal to both of them. With relief, Nikolai Apollonovich turned his back on them; the smile suddenly slipped from his distended lips; he trembled; a thought revolved in his mind:

"Some sort of charitable fund—for downtrodden workmen, for weapons . . ." gnawed at his soul. "No, no . . ."

At the door of his room, Nikolai Apollonovich turned sharply; again the momentary smile vanished; they looked at each other expectantly.

"Please . . ."

"Don't stand on ceremony . . ."

Nikolai Apollonovich's reception room was the antithesis of his study. It was as lavish in color as his dressing-gown, and this quality was evident in all the objects in the room: in the low divan reminiscent of an Oriental couch, in the dark brown tabouret incrusted with strips of ivory and mother-of-pearl, in the African shield of thick ox-hide hanging on the wall, in the rusty Sudanese arrows with massive helves, in the mottled leopard skin with wide open maw. A dark blue hookah-set and a three-legged censer with a crescent moon graced the tabouret. The most astonishing object of all was a brightly painted cage, in which green parrots rocked on swings.

Nikolai Apollonovich drew the tabouret nearer to the stranger, who seated himself on the edge and pulled out a cigarette case.

"Will you permit me?" he asked.

"By all means."

"You don't smoke?"

"No, I don't.

"But I don't mind others smoking," Nikolai added.

"You could open a ventilator, if you . . ."

"Never mind me. I like the smell of tobacco smoke."

"Oh, you needn't defend the weed, Nikolai Apollonovich. I speak from experience. . . . Tobacco smoke penetrates the gray substance. . . . It chokes up the passages of the brain."

With an air of concern the stranger began to pull at his mustache.

"Just look closely at my face!"

Nikolai Apollonovich projected his blinking eyelids toward the stranger's face.

"Do you see?"

"Yes . . ."

"It's what I call a smoked-out face," the stranger explained. "The face of a hard smoker!"

Nikolai Apollonovich was aware of a choked feeling in the passages of his brain, of a certain turgidity in his organism. But he was no longer thinking of the pros and cons of smoking, but of how to emerge with dignity from a ticklish situation if the stranger should . . .

The leaden pressure he felt had no relation to cheap cigarettes, but was due to the depressed state of his spirit. Nikolai Apollonovich waited with impatience for the stranger to interrupt his babble, the only aim of which was to torment his host with anticipation. Oh yes, he would suddenly come to the point and remind Nikolai Apollonovich that he had once given a promise . . .

In a word, Nikolai Apollonovich had given a pledge that he was bound to fulfill, and not only for the sake of his honor. He had given his promise in a mood of desperation; he had been stirred to do it by his personal failure, but had somehow straightened that out. At first, it had seemed that he would be automatically released from his promise. But this was not to be; the promise held, if only because he had taken no steps to withdraw it. Nikolai Apollonovich had forgotten all about it, but the promise had continued to exist even though he had regarded it as a joke.

The stranger's appearance now filled Nikolai Apollonovich with real fear. He remembered the sad circumstances, all the details of the state of mind which had induced him to make the promise; and he found them deadly.

Why then . . . but no: it was not so much the promise itself as the fact that he had given it to a certain unreliable person!

Nikolai Apollonovich had been studying social phenomena.

But now he looked quite pale, even green: the green tint came from the atmosphere of the room.

"You see, Nikolai Apollonovich,"—Nikolai Apollonovich trembled at these words—"you must know, of course, that I haven't come to smoke cigarettes . . . all that's incidental." The stranger paused. "To be sure, I enjoyed the smoke. But, of course, that wasn't why I came. I've come about a certain matter . . ." And once more he paused agonizingly. "No, not so much about a certain matter, really . . . but about a favor you can do . . ."

There was a bluish tinge to Nikolai Apollonovich's face. He had torn a button from the divan upholstery, and he was now pulling out the horsehairs.

"I feel awkward about it, but how shall I put it?" The other continued. "But remembering that you . . ."

Hearing the last phrase uttered in sharp falsetto, Nikolai Apollonovich almost shouted:

"You've come about my offer? . . ."

He soon recovered himself and added:

"I'm at your service."

But even as he said these words, he realized that his politeness had destroyed him . . .

There was a pause. Then:

"Oh, it's my fault. Here's an ashtray . . ."

9

Those were strange foggy days. Noxious October was striding through the city with icy gait; farther south, it had hung out its foul mists; through the forests, it blew its golden murmur which, descending to earth, turned to a wild autumnal rustle that swept round people's feet in the swirl of red-and-yellow spotted leaves. The sweet whispering of September bathed no more in the leafy wave. Now the orphaned titmouse forlornly hopped from branch to branch; swinging in the wind, these branches whistled their autumnal moan, spreading beyond the parks, the gardens, and the forests.

The icy blasts were already moving upon us in silvery clouds; yet everyone believed in the Spring; a popular cabinet minister had said that he was looking forward to the Spring.

The ploughmen had already ceased scraping the soil. They had flung aside their harrows and their wooden ploughs. In little groups they gathered in their hovels; they talked and wrangled; and then suddenly they surged in a swarm toward the landowner's colonnaded house; the long country nights flared with incendiary fires.

That was the situation in the villages.

It was the same in the towns. In the workshops, in the printing shops, in the hairdressing establishments, in the dairies, in the taverns, everywhere there was the same ubiquitous garrulous person; fresh from the blood-soaked fields of Manchuria, a shaggy cap pulled over his eyes, a Browning in his pocket, he thrust badly composed leaflets into people's hands.

Everyone seemed to be afraid of something, everyone seemed to hope for something; people poured into the streets and formed crowds, and then scattered again. They behaved in the same way in Archangel, in Nizhny-Kolomsk, in Saratov, in Petersburg, and in Moscow. They all seemed to fear something, to hope for something; people poured into the streets and formed crowds, and then scattered again.

A ring of many-chimneyed factories girded Petersburg.

In the morning the great human swarm crept toward them; the streets of the suburbs crawled with this moving horde. In those days, there was no lack of agitation in the factories; the workers had become garrulous; Brownings circulated among them, and— something else.

This agitation, which ringed Petersburg, had penetrated into the very heart of the city. It had first gripped the Islands, then rushed headlong across the Liteiny and Nikolayevsky bridges; on the Nevsky Prospect, it assumed a human polypedal form, and this polypedal swarm changed constantly as it circulated along the Prospect; an observer might have noted the black shaggy cap from the blood-soaked fields of Manchuria: the number of passing cylinder hats was diminishing correspondingly; and the air carried the turbulent shouts of the anti-Government urchins who were distributing revolutionary leaflets between the railway station and the Admiralty.

Those were strange foggy days. Noxious October was marching with icy gait. Violent gusts sent the dust flying through the streets, and a wild autumnal rustle curled submissively round people's feet in the swirl of yellow-and-red spotted words.

Such were the days. Those who ventured at nighttime into the open suburban spaces heard a persistent moan with stress on the note "oo." Oo-oo-oo-oo . . . sounded in the open spaces. It was a sound from some other world, and it attained a rare strength and clarity. Oo-oo-oo-oo . . . such was the sound that came, not too audibly, from the fields on the outskirts of Moscow, Petersburg, and Saratov. But the factory sirens were silent. There was no wind, and no sound even of a dog barking.

Did you happen to hear this October song of the year 1905?

10

Holding on to the marble banister, Apollon Apollonovich caught his toe in the hem of his greatcoat and stumbled. Reluctantly, he slowed down; quite naturally his eyes rested on the large portrait of a cabinet minister who had been his friend.

A chill crept along his spine: the house was cold.

He feared space.

The country landscape really frightened him. He remembered a snowstorm which had once caught him in a region of snow and ice; there, by an unlucky chance, he had been nearly frozen to death.

That had been fifty years ago.

In that freezing hour someone's cold fingers, thrust into his bosom, had roughly stroked his heart: and, ever since, that icy hand had guided him—as he ascended the steps of his career, and he saw the same incredible expanses before his eyes; that icy hand had lured him on; before him lay infinitude: the Russian Empire.

For many years Apollon Apollonovich Ableukhov had remained incarcerated within city walls, loathing the orphaned provincial expanses, loathing the smoke which curled above the huts of remote villages, loathing the ubiquitous jackdaw. Only once, when traveling on an express train, on a responsible mission from Petersburg to Tokyo, had he ventured to intersect these expanses.

Of his visit to Japan, Apollon Apollonovich had never spoken to anyone.

"Russia is a vast icy plateau, full of prowling wolves!" was all he said to the cabinet minister.

The minister had looked at him, stroking his gray mustache with a white hand; but he made no reply and only sighed; he was on the eve of retiring from the service.

But then he died.

Bereft of his friend, Apollon Apollonovich felt desperately alone. Behind him the centuries receded into the immeasurable; before him—the leaden hand pointed to the immeasurable.

The immeasurable sped to meet him.

The Senator seemed to hear his friend's voice calling him from the grave; and the hungry wolves gathered in packs.

The Senator had developed a phobia for space, a phobia sharpened by his friend's tragic death. The image of his friend haunted him night after night: the now stilled image of that soft glance and that white hand stroking a mustache:

> "He was no more—having departed
> From that Russia he had evoked . . ."

This fragment from Pushkin came into his mind as he crossed the immense reception room. Then another fragment succeeded the first:

> "Methinks my turn has come . . .
> Dear Delvig calls me,
> He, the comrade of my zestful youth,
> The comrade of cheerless days,
> The comrade who joined me in song,
> In feasts and lofty aspirations—
> There, into the shadowed throng,
> That fine mind is forever departed . . ."

As he recalled these fragments extremely clearly, he set out to meet some petitioners.

11

Nikolai Apollonovich's conversation with the stranger continued.

"I have been charged," the stranger announced as he accepted the ashtray from his host, "to hand over this little bundle to you for safekeeping."

"Is that all?" Nikolai Apollonovich shouted, hardly daring to believe what he had heard, while his face suddenly revealed his inner conflict. He rose impulsively and made for the bundle. The stranger rose too. When Nikolai Apollonovich attempted to snatch the bundle, the stranger's hand unceremoniously seized his fingers:

"I must earnestly ask you to be more careful, Nikolai Apollonovich . . ."

"Ah . . . yes . . . yes . . ." But Nikolai Apollonovich seemed not to have heard; he picked up the bundle by a corner of the towel.

"Nikolai Apollonovich, I repeat: be more careful!"

Nikolai Apollonovich looked astonished . . .

"Pamphlets? . . ."

"No, no . . ."

Then a precise metallic sound made itself heard: something clicked. At the same moment a mouse squeaked; the soft tabouret was overturned and the stranger was stamping his feet in the corner where he had taken refuge.

"Nikolai Apollonovich, Nikolai Apollonovich!" his voice resounded. "A mouse, a mouse! Do tell your servant to remove it at once! This I can't stand . . . I can't . . ."

"You're afraid of mice?"

Nikolai Apollonovich looked absurd as he gazed with great interest at the tiny gray captive in the mousetrap he now held.

"It's a mouse," he said to the lackey who appeared in response to his call.

"To be sure, it's a mouse," the lackey repeated after him.

Only after the lackey's departure did the stranger reappear.

"It was only a little mouse," explained Nikolai Apollonovich, who had a tender feeling for mice.

Nikolai Apollonovich finally carried the bundle into his room; its weight rather surprised him. As he entered the study he stumbled on a brightly colored rug. Something in the bundle tinkled. The stranger sprang forward; the arm behind Nikolai Apollonovich made the same zigzag gesture that had so greatly alarmed the Senator.

Nothing happened: the stranger then grew talkative.

"My solitude is killing me," he said. "I've completely forgotten how to talk. My words get entangled."

"That happens to many people, you know," Nikolai Apollonovich murmured.

Nikolai Apollonovich placed the bundle behind a cabinet-sized photograph of a pretty brunette. As he did so, he lapsed into thought, and his mouth assumed a frog-like appearance. Behind his back he heard the words:

"I simply get entangled in every sentence. I want to say something and, instead, I say quite another thing. Or else I suddenly have a lapse of memory. I forget the name of an ordinary object. I know that a lamp is called a lamp, but in a little while I begin to doubt the existence of such a word. And there's no one I can turn to."

Had Nikolai Apollonovich heeded the stranger's first words, he would have undoubtedly been more careful with the bundle, and understood that the innocent-looking package was not so innocent; but he was more concerned with the photograph.

"It's hard to live in a Torricelian vacuum . . ." the stranger went on.

"Torricelian?" asked Nikolai Apollonovich, who had not heard the entire sentence.

"Precisely. Yes, in the name of social justice. And what sort of society do I see? A society of wood-lice. Bbbrrr . . . my room's just full of them!"

The stranger had stumbled by chance on his favorite theme and, having fallen on his favorite theme, had quite forgotten the purpose of his visit—the bundle—and the number of cigarettes he had consumed. Like all naturally garrulous persons who are subjected to enforced silence, he sometimes experienced the need to confide in someone, no matter whom, friend or enemy, a house porter, a policeman, a child, or even a dressmaker's dummy in a shop window. He spent his nights talking to himself. The opulent furnishings of the reception room had suddenly revived the need to talk.

"Some would have it that I'm not 'I,' but some sort of a 'we.' On the other hand, my memory has gone to pot: my solitude is slaying me. Often I find myself becoming angry."

At this point the stranger paused. Nikolai had slightly pushed the table and, as he suddenly turned, he noticed that the stranger was pacing up and down his study, carelessly strewing cigarette ash; he had also caught sight of the satin domino which was now in view; and, seeing it all, he flushed deeply; but this merely served to change the subject of conversation:

"What a handsome domino, Nikolai Nikolayevich!"

Nikolai Apollonovich rushed to put the domino away.

He almost snatched it out of the stanger's hand and, like a thief caught red-handed, he hurried to conceal it. Once he had hidden it, he grew more calm. The stranger, however, quickly forgot the domino and returned to his favorite theme.

"Ha, ha!" he exclaimed and, still pacing, lighted another cigarette. "No doubt you wonder how I am able to act. I act according to my judgment. My judgment brings the Party's activities into line. Strictly speaking, I am not in the Party, the Party is in me. . . . Does that astonish you?"

"I must confess it does." Nikolai replied. "I must also confess that I would not dream of collaborating with you."

"All the same, you accepted my little bundle. *Ergo*, we are collaborating."

"You don't call that collaboration?"

"Of course I do. Of course . . ." Then, he suddenly grew silent. He continued to stare at his host and then said quite frankly:

"I've wanted to have a heart to heart talk with you for a long time. I see so few people. You of course are familiar with the methods of social phenomena and you know Karl Marx. But I've read little. Don't imagine for a moment that I'm a voracious reader. I'm not concerned with books or figures."

"What then interests you? . . . A drop of cognac, perhaps. I have some in the sideboard."

"Don't mind if I do .."

Nikolai Apollonovich thrust a hand into the sideboard and brought out a cut-crystal decanter and two small cut-crystal glasses.

Nikolai Apollonovich was very fond of cognac.

As he poured the cognac, he thought this might be his opportunity to suggest that he had changed his mind about doing anything for the Party, but cowardice prevented him from revealing his cowardice. Besides, why bother to do it by word of mouth when he could do it just as well in a letter?

"The fact is," the stranger resumed, "I'm now reading Conan

Doyle. To be sure, my range of reading must seem barbarous to you. Among other things, I am reading a history of gnosticism —Gregory of Nyssa, the Apocalypse. . . . That, I must tell you, is my rightful privilege. Somehow, I am the colonel of the movement, promoted, as it were, for my long service to the staff. As for you, Nikolai Apollonovich—you, with your method and mind, are merely a corporal. Still, you're a theoretician, and generals are rather weak on theory. They are the bishops. In bishops' eyes a young academician, who has studied Harnack inside out, is nothing but a superfluous ecclesiastical appendage. And that's exactly what you are in the eyes of the Party—a mere appendage!"

The stranger fell into thought, poured himself a glass of cognac, drained it, and poured himself another.

"You were exiled, weren't you?" asked Nikolai Apollonovich.

"Yes. I was sent to the Yakutsk region."

A silence followed. The stranger drained his glass.

"I made good my escape from Yakutsk. I was hidden under cabbages in a barrel. Now I am an underground worker. Don't get the idea for a moment that I acted in the name of a Utopia or in your railway manner of thought. After all, I was a Nietzschean. We're all Nietzscheans. You, too, are a Nietzschean. You may not acknowledge this. All the same, for us Nietzscheans, the masses, when moved by social instincts—as we might say— become transformed into an executive apparatus in which all people—even people like you—are a keyboard upon which the nimble fingers of the pianist—please note my phrase—play, as they overcome all difficulties. Such are we all!"

"Sportsmen of revolution, you mean?"

An awkward silence fell upon them again. Nikolai Apollonovich was pulling a horsehair out of the couch. He disliked theoretical discussion. He was accustomed to arguing properly.

"Everything is based on contrasts," the stranger resumed. "A desire to be useful to society drove me to Siberia, but the farther I penetrated into the void, the more I shed my Party preconceptions or categories, as you would call them."

In the greenish fog outside the window, a platoon was marching; soldiers in greatcoats marched by, their upturned bayonets glinting black in the fog.

Nikolai Apollonovich experienced a strange chill.

"What is that?" he asked, raising his head.

"Nothing in particular. Your father's just arrived in his carriage."

Apollon Apollonovich disliked the appearance of his rooms when the furniture was protected by dust-covers; the parquet floors sounded hollow and precise.

The main reception room looked like a vast corridor. From the center of a circle of stuccoed fruit on the garlanded ceiling a chandelier of multiple glass fragments was suspended in a muslin cover; the crystal pendants trembled.

The parquet floor shone like a mirror.

Long-legged chairs with gold grooves, upholstered in plush, were ranged along the white walls. Columns of white alabaster rose everywhere: on one of these stood an alabaster Archimedes. Some solicitous hand had hung frames on the walls; the pale paintings in them were imitations of Pompeiian frescoes.

The solicitous hand had been Anna Petrovna's. Apollon Apollonovich pursed his lips at the thought. Holding something large and round, he entered his study and locked the door. The vast expanses outside evoked in him an intangible nostalgia; there outside, a wholly fantastic being seemed to menace him.

12

The stranger grew nervous: the alcohol had begun to take effect. Conversation always made him aware of the sinfulness of his spirit, and made him hate his own words. It was obvious that these innocent conversations deeply weakened him. The more he talked, the greater became his desire to speak, until he had an astringent feeling in his throat. He was unable to stop until he had exhausted himself. As he spoke he unloosed the paroxysms of the persecution which he remembered from his dreams. He had three nightmares each night: Tartars, Japanese, or other Orientals blinked their eyes at him. Above all, he was not a little astonished to find that, during these nightmares, he heard an absurd and wholly senseless word—heaven alone knew where it came from—the word *enfranshish*; with the aid of this word, he wrestled with some unknown power. A sinister face would also appear on a fragment of his yellow wallpaper. These sinister manifestations were always preceded by a surge of anguish, evoked when he sat too long in any one place. This drove Alexander Ivanovich out-of-doors and into the taverns. His consumption of liquor was followed by a feeling of shame and suggested the image of the stockinged leg of a naïve girl student; and all this always ended with the nightmare in which the word *enfranshish* appeared.

"You're listening to my babble, Nikolai Apollonovich. Actually, I'm not arguing with you, but only with myself. A *vis-à-vis* is nothing to me. I talk to walls and streetposts. I never listen to what other people say. I hear only what concerns me personally. I wrestle with my feelings. Then comes solitude. For weeks on end, I sit and smoke. . . . Do you know the mood?"

"I don't quite. But it must come from the heart."

"My soul is like an endless expanse. Out of it I seem to gaze on all things."

And without waiting for a response, he added:

"My room on Vasilyevsky Island is, to me, a vast incalculable space. I have four yellow-papered walls. No one ever visits me, except Morzhov, and a certain *personality*." .

"How did you come to be there?"

"That *personality* . . ."

"Again?"

"It's always he . . . the guard of a damp threshold!"

"Now I understand why you cast a shadow—the shadow of the Elusive One."

"It all comes from within those four yellow walls."

"How much do you pay for your lodging?"

"Twenty rubles. To be exact, twenty and a half."

"And there you devote yourself to all that?"

"Yes, there. There I arrived at the conviction that all windows are cut out into infinity."

"That must refer to the idea that, at the peak of a movement, one also can see the normally inaccessible depths. What do you see at the peak?"

"Just emptiness."

"Why then all the rest?"

"That's the nature of the disease . . ."

"What do you mean?"

"I mean the disease that is destroying me. I cannot yet name it, but I know the symptoms well. They are intense longing, hallucinations, vodka, smoking; I frequently have a dull pain in my head, a curious sensation in the brain and down the spine, but that is only in the morning. Do you think I alone suffer from this? You, Nikolai Apollonovich, are also ill. Nearly everyone is sick. . . . Please don't contradict me: I know what you will say. All the Party members are afflicted with this disease. But in me these characteristics are more acute. In the old days, years ago, when I met the comrades, I loved to learn things. Our little gatherings lasted for hours. We talked of our affairs, of our noble aspirations, of transcendental things. Afterwards, a comrade would invite me to a restaurant."

"Well, what then?"

"We drank vodka, and the rest of it. Many tiny glasses of vodka. After that, I would look at my companion. If he smiled in a certain way—I can scarcely give you an idea of the kind of smile it was— why, then, Nikolai Apollonovich, I knew at once that I could not depend on him. It meant that my *vis-à-vis* was diseased and that nothing could prevent the softening of his brain. Such a person could not be depended upon to keep a promise"; (at these words Nikolai Apollonovich trembled) "he was capable of theft, betrayal, rape. His presence in the Party was sure to mean provocation. From then on, I could read the meaning of the tiny furrows around his lips. And now I meet this brain disorder, this elusive provocation, everywhere. But I really can give you no idea of the full meaning of that smile. Yet I can detect it unerringly!"

"And you never smile like that?"

"I do!"

"It follows that you are a provocateur?"

"I? Yes, a provocateur—but only in the name of a great idea, or, rather, of a new trend of thought."

"What sort?"

"Shall I define my meaning in words? I might call it a common desire for death. I revel in it."

"Have you been drinking long?"

"Yes, yes. Besides, I feel lecherous. I am fascinated not by women, but—how shall I put it?—by individual parts of a woman's body, and by her clothes: stockings, for example."

"Yes, you know . . ."

But Nikolai Apollonovich did not finish his sentence and, for a while, there was silence. Then the stranger resumed:

"Do you know, my favorite position when suffering from insomnia was to stand against a wall with arms outspread. Once, while standing in this position, flattened against the wall—I must add, Nikolai Apollonovich, that I used to maintain this position for hours—I came to an extraordinary conclusion, which was strangely associated with a phenomenon that can only be understood if the development of my malady is taken into consideration."

On the nature of the phenomenon Alexander Ivanovich seemed to think it best to remain silent.

This phenomenon consisted of a hallucination. He would see a face on the wallpaper, a face with a film of saffron overtones. The face, that of a Semite or a Mongol, stared at Alexander Ivanovich with hatred. Alexander Ivanovich would light a cigarette; the face, Semite or Mongol, would stir its yellow lips through the smoke, while Alexander Ivanovich's ear would catch the word:

"Helsingfors."

After his escape from Siberian exile, Alexander Ivanovich had indeed fled to Helsingfors. There, for the first time, he had met *a certain personality.*

But why Helsingfors?

Alexander Ivanovich's distress communicated itself to Ableukhov; and the twelve cigarette stubs in the ashtray irritated him. He remarked:

"I have a splitting headache. What do you say to continuing our conversation in the open air? Just wait a moment. I'll put on some clothes."

"An excellent idea."

A sharp knock interrupted the conversation. Nikolai Apollonovich was about to investigate it, but Alexander Ivanovich forestalled him; wholly distraught, he flung open the door. A skull with large ears was thrust through the opening, and almost bumped against

the stranger's head; in perplexity, Alexander Ivanovich sprang
back.

In the doorway stood Apollon Apollonovich with a watermelon
under his arm . . .

"I'm afraid I'm intruding. . . . You see, Kolya, my boy, I picked
up a watermelon on the way."

In the autumn, on his way home, it was Apollon Apollonovich's
custom to buy an Astrakhan melon, of which he was inordinately
fond.

For an instant, all three men were silent: each of them experienced an ill-concealed feeling of terror.

"Papa, I want you to meet a university friend . . . Alexandei
Ivanovich Doodkin . . ."

"Pleased to meet you."

Apollon Apollonovich saw before him only a very humble person,
crushed by need.

Alexander Ivanovich saw before him only a pitiful old man.

Nikolai Apollonovich—but he, too, was reassured and calmed.

Apollon Apollonovich attempted to start a conversation. Alexander Ivanovich's replies were incoherent. He blushed and made
no reply to the point. He merely snatched at last words, which
sounded like abrupt exclamations.

"Why, even at high school, Kolya knew all the birds. . . . He had
read Kaigorodov . . ."

Thus, abruptly, did the sixty-eight-year-old man address Alexander Ivanovich. Something like sympathy stirred in the old man.

"What did you say that you and Alexander . . . er . . ."

"Ivanovich . . ."

"And Alexander Ivanovich . . ."

Apollon Apollonovich thought: "Maybe it's for the best, but
his eyes seem to have lost that look . . ." He also thought: "Poverty
is no crime. Only why had they been drinking cognac?"

"Where are you going?" Apollon Apollonovich asked.

"On business . . ."

"What do you say to joining me in a little dinner . . . you and
Alexander Ivanovich?"

Alexander Ivanovich looked at his watch.

"However, I don't want to intrude . . ." the old man said.

"Goodbye, Papa . . ."
"Goodbye, Kolya . . ."

As their steps echoed down the corridor, tiny Apollon Apollonovich remained standing in the semi-darkness, gazing after them.
He stood there, his head thrust forward, and looked after them
with curiosity:
"Alexander Ivanovich Doodkin . . . university student!"

Nikolai Apollonovich stopped before a lackey in the entrance hall
and tried to catch a fugitive thought.
"Oh, yes . . . the little mouse! . . ." Nikolai Apollonovich continued to rub his forehead, trying to remember what he should
express with the help of the verbal symbol "mouse." He often
experienced such moments of oblivion after reading serious trea-
tises.
"Listen! What did you do with the mouse?"
"I set it free on the Embankment."
Reassured about the fate of the mouse, Nikolai Apollonovich, and
Alexander Ivanovich, went their way.
But they went their way because they could feel someone staring
at them over the balustrade: searchingly and sadly.

13

Shaggy Manchurian caps spilled into the street and melted into
the crowd, which grew rapidly; the men in Manchurian caps strode
in the direction of a purple-roofed edifice; the crowd near the
gloomy edifice consisted entirely of men in Manchurian caps. And
how they pressed and shoved into the main entrance! And how
could it be otherwise? The workers had no time for ceremony:
they were in an ugly mood.
At the corner a detachment of police were stamping their feet
near the sidewalk. The sergeant in charge seemed at a loss. Grayish,
in a gray greatcoat, he barked occasional commands, holding his

sheathed sword respectfully and lowering his eyes. Behind him he heard rude comments, gibes, mocking laughter, and even obscenities. . . . He continued to shout:

"Pass on, gentlemen, pass on!"

Behind the fence shaggy-ankled horses snorted persistently. Above the timber-toothed fence shaggy human heads rose; if one looked down on them, one might have noticed *nagaikas*—Cossack whips— in the clenched fists of these men from the Steppes, and rifles slung across their backs. They were fiercely impatient and from time to time leaped into their saddles and pranced about on their shaggy little horses.

This was a detachment of Orenburg Cossacks.

A saffron mist, illuminated with candles, hovered inside the building. Here nothing was visible except bodies, bodies, and bodies: hunched, half-hunched, slightly hunched, and not hunched. Sitting and standing, the bodies covered everything. They occupied the seats of the amphitheater, and the platform was invisible.

"Oo-oo-oo-oo . . ." came a droning sound through space; and above this drone could now and then be heard the words:

"Revolution. . . . Evolution. . . . Proletariat. . . . Strike . . ." And again: "Strike . . ." And again: "Strike . . ."

The droning continued.

The speeches stressed one and the same thing: that here, and there, and there also, the strike had begun; and here, and there, and there also, a strike was preparing; therefore, it was also necessary to strike here, and at once!

14

Alexander Ivanovich was returning by the prospect that ran along the Neva. A light flashed by, revealing the Neva under the arch over the canal. On the curved little bridge he noticed the familiar shadow again.

Alexander Ivanovich was returning to his poor quarters, that he might sit in solitude there and study the life of wood-lice. By observation Alexander Ivanovich had deduced that peace at night depended upon the way in which the day had been spent. He brought home with him what he had experienced in the streets, in the little restaurants, and the tea rooms.

Alexander Ivanovich's experiences of the day trailed behind him like an invisible tail. Alexander Ivanovich lived his experiences in reverse order, for they retreated behind his back. His back seemed to open like a door and, out of that door, a giant body was poised to pounce: this giant embodied the sum total of his experiences within the past twenty-four hours.

Alexander Ivanovich judged it best to return to his room, for there he could shut out these experiences.

He left the illuminated bridge behind him.

Beyond the bridge, in St. Isaac's Square, a cliff rose out of the mist; fronting it, the enigmatic Bronze Horseman loomed, holding out his green bronze arm; above the shaggy buzby of an Imperial Grenadier, a rearing horse shot out of its front hoofs . . .

A shadow concealed the Horseman's huge face; but the palm of his outstretched hand was bathed in moonlight.

Since that pregnant time when the Bronze Horseman had galloped here and had rooted his horse in Finnish granite, Russia had become divided, as had the destiny of the Fatherland; weeping in anguish until the ultimate hour, Russia had been severed in half.

Russia, that bronze steed is your symbol! Your fore hoofs are plunging in darkness, in emptiness; but your hind hoofs have taken deep root in the granite soil.

Will you break loose from the riveting granite, just as some of your witless sons have broken loose from the soil? Or, perhaps, breaking through the fog, you will leap through the air and then, with your sons, vanish in the clouds? For many years, O Russia, you have lost yourself in reflection upon the stern destinies which have flung you hither—in the midst of this gloomy North, where even the sun's setting is delayed for many hours, where time interchangeably flings itself into frosty night or into diurnal radiance. Or, frightened perhaps of leaping, you will again set down your hoofs and, snorting, bear the great Horseman away from these illusory lands into the perspective of spacious plateaus?

But this will not be!

Having reared and measured the air with his eyes, the Bronze Horseman will never set down his hoofs. He will leap over history;

and great will be the tumult when he does so. He will cleave the earth: the very hills will crumble from the fear assailing them, and this fear will make the native plains arch themselves into hills. Upon their crests you shall see rise Nizhny[1] and Vladimir[2] and Uglich.[3]

And Petersburg shall sink.

In those days all the peoples of the earth will scatter in panic. Voices shall be raised in horror, curses fill the air, unheard-of curses. A yellow horde of Asiatics, stirring from their age-long retreats, will redden the fields of Europe with an ocean of blood. There will be—yes, yes—Tsushima![4] And there will also be a new Kolka![5]

On that day the ultimate Sun shall rise and dazzle my native earth. But if you should fail to rise, O Sun, then the shores of Europe will fall under the heavy Mongolian heel, and the foaming, raging sea will surge over these shores; the creatures of the earth will once more descend to the bottom of the ocean—into the primordial, long-forgotten chaos . . .

So rise, O Sun!

A gap in the clouds revealed a patch of turquoise which drifted across the heavens; a phosphorescent spot ran to meet it, and was unexpectedly transformed into a brilliant moon. Everything caught light from it: the waters of the Neva, the chimneys, the granite, the two goddesses above the arch, the roof of a four-story building; the dome of St. Isaac's looked radiant, and a bronze laurel wreath flared brightly. The lights on the islands went out; an ambiguous ship in the middle of the Neva became a fishing schooner . . .

Here, at this point, Alexander Ivanovich had a clear and precise

[1] City on the Volga River, from which Minin and Pojarsky led a revolt in 1611 against the Poles, then ruling in Moscow.

[2] City famous for its cathedrals, Church architecture, and fresco painting, 12th to 15th centuries.

[3] Town where Prince Dmitri died in 1591. Boris Godunov was accused of having him assassinated.

[4] Sea-battle in which the Russian Baltic fleet was destroyed by the Japanese during the Russo-Japanese War, 1905.

[5] River at which the Russians suffered their first defeat by the Mongols, 1223.

vision of human destiny. He could foresee what would come to pass, and what would never be: everything was so clear. But he feared to peer into his own fate; he stood there shaken.

Then the moon cut into a cloud . . .

Once more tufted arms, misty wisps, rushed madly through the sky; ambiguously, a phosphorescent patch began to twinkle . . .

A deafening, inhuman roar! Flashing its headlights and panting from speed, an automobile careened from under the arch toward the river; and yellow Mongolian mugs cut across the square.

15

A road winds from Kolpino: nothing could be gloomier. On the way to Petersburg, if you waken and glance from a train window, you will see nothing but a dead landscape—not a village anywhere, not a human soul; the very earth looks like a corpse.

Kolpino! A place of many chimneys and much grime.

The road from Kolpino follows a winding line of telegraph poles. Along this road trudged Stepka, a worker. He had just been discharged from a gunpowder factory where he had been working. Now he was tramping to Petersburg. Heavy immovable boulders dotted the roadside, striped mile-signs succeeded one another interminably; and the telegraph wires quivered audibly.

Many-storied piles squatted behind factories; factories squatted behind chimneys—there, there, everywhere. No vestige of cloud streaked the sky, and the horizon gasped with soot.

Poisonous fumes filled the air, hovering around and above numerous tall chimneys which in the distance looked like hairs standing on end . . .

But Stepka thought nothing of all this. He had been familiar with the scene long enough: now he was off to other parts.

Toward evening the door of a porter's lodge opened to admit him; the door squeaked. Morzhov, the house porter, raised his head; his plump wife, who suffered from earache, was searching for bugs through a pile of puffed-out pillows.

Stepka hesitated on the threshold. Morzhov was a countryman of his: it was natural that Stepka should seek him out.

A bottle and pickled cucumbers soon appeared on the table; and then Bezsmertny, the cobbler, joined them with his guitar.

"A countryman of mine, yes, a countryman of mine!" Morzhov exclaimed, introducing Stepka with a smirk.

"It's all due to their lack of understanding," Bezsmertny asserted, shrugging his shoulders. He touched a guitar string, and it went *bam-bam* . . .

"And what about your Dad?"

"He's always drunk."

"That's how it is. . . . . He's a fellow-countryman, for all that," Morzhov said in a friendly way, as he picked up a cucumber and bit into it.

"It's all due to their lack of understanding," Bezsmertny, the cobbler, repeated, with another shrug. Again he touched a guitar string, and it went *bam-bam*. As for Stepka, he continued his tale: how some strange folk had appeared in the village, how these strange folk had announced the birth of an infant and the salvation of the world; this latter would soon come to pass.

"It's all due to their lack of understanding! They have no understanding. No, not anyone," the cobbler insisted.

Stepka did not utter another sound. He kept silent about his discharge from the Kolpino factory; not another word did he add about what or how it had all happened. Presently, he broke into song:

> "Dear Annette,
> A kiss I do implore,
> Sweet soubrette,
> Make it three or four!"

Bezsmertny, the cobbler, merely shrugged; then with five fingers he strummed on the guitar. And he sang:

> "I shall never see you again,
> Never again shall I see you . . .
> A vial of ammonium chloride
> Deep in my jacket I hide,

A vial of ammonium chloride
Down my parched throat I pour.
Then shaken, I fall to the pavement,
I shall see my darling no more!"

Not to be outdone, Stepka astonished everyone with this:

"Above temptation and above woe,
The Angel stood with a golden trumpet—
Light, O Light,
O deathless Light!
Shelter us in Thy deathless Light—
We are all children in Thy presence:
Thou art alone eternal
In the Heavens!"

A *barin*, who rented an attic room, overheard all this. He questioned Stepka about the strange folk he had mentioned, about the glad tidings they had proclaimed, and about when all this was to be. The *barin* was a gentleman who had seen better days. Now he had a meager look, and his adam's apple danced when he swallowed his dram of vodka. Stepka gave him sound advice.

"*Barin*, you're a sick man," he said. "Vodka and tobacco will soon make you *kaput*. I once drank like a fish, but then I signed the pledge. It's all because of tobacco and vodka that the Japs were on our neck!"

"How do you know?"

"About vodka? I read Leo Tolstoy—have you read his booklet about it? That's what he says."

"Where do the Japs come in?"

"About the Japs, it's like this—who doesn't know about the Japs? . . . Let me remind you: we had a tornado over Moscow. People said this and that about it—that it was the souls of the slain being swept through Moscow, that they'd come from the other world, and that they'd died unrepentant; and that means there'll be a revolt."

"And what'll happen to Petersburg?"

"I hear the Chinese are building a heathen temple there!"

The *barin* conducted Stepka to his own room and made him sit in front of him. Then, from a small trunk, he pulled out some writing and read it aloud: "Your political convictions are clear enough to me: it's all the devil's work, and you're all possessed."

He read on:

"A portentous time is approaching; only a decade remains before the beginning of the end. Copy this and pass it down to your offspring. Of all future years, 1954 will be the most significant. This concerns Russia; the Church of Philadelphia had its cradle in Russia; now I understand why Solovyov spoke so much about Sofia."

Stepka made noises through his nose. "So, so," he asked, "and what kind of a *barin* wrote that?"

"He's now living in political exile abroad."

"So, so!"

"What will happen?"

"At first there'll be killings, and general discontent; then, all sorts of diseases, pestilence and hunger; clever folk are telling us about agitations: Chinamen will rise against themselves, the Moslems will stir too; nothing will come of it, though."

"And then what?"

"All the rest of it is due to happen about the time 1912 is ending and 1913 is coming in. . . . That's about it! One prophecy says an infant will be born. And there's something, too, about the Prussian Emperor. . . . That's prophecy for you, *barin*: we must build a new Noah's Ark!"

"What do you mean, build?"

"Don't worry on that score, *barin*, there's time! We'll exchange a few whispers on the subject."

"Whispers about what?"

"About one and the same thing: about the Second Coming."

"That's rubbish!"

"Come, O Lord!"

CHAPTER THREE

Though an ordinary mortal,
A second-rate Don Juan is he,
Neither Demon—nor even a gypsy,
Merely a citizen of a capital city is he.

—Pushkin

1

A grand levee was being held in a certain important place. Those who attended wore their most resplendent uniforms.

It was a day of extraordinary events. It was also a clear day. Everything sparkled: the roofs of Petersburg and the spires.

At that important place, where the ceremony was being held, the windows sparkled, and the columns inside, and the parquet floor sparkled too: all was lacquer, gloss, and glitter!

On this extraordinary morning, a minute human figure in dazzling white night clothes suddenly threw aside the dazzling white sheets and leaped from the bed: the figure somehow reminded one of a circus rider. As was his habit, he began the day with gymnastic exercises, squatting down and rising a dozen or more times. Then he sprinkled his naked skull and hands with eau-de-cologne.

After he had completed his ablutions of skull, hands, chin, and ears, Apollon Apollonovich Ableukhov, like other old men, wrapped himself in starched linen, thrusting his ears and his bald head through the aperture of a shirt that was like a coat of mail. Then entering the dressing room, Apollon Apollonovich drew from a wardrobe (as other old dignitaries must have done that same morning) some small lacquered caskets in which, under the lids, on soft velvet linings lay all the rare Orders conferred on him, Orders which would grace the gorgeous uniform with its glittering, golden, shining chest, its white pantaloons and white gloves, and silver scabbard surmounted by an ornate sword hilt. Under the pressure of a yellow fingernail, all ten casket lids sprang open; Apollon Apollonovich pulled out the decorations one by one: the White

Eagle and the corresponding Star, and—the Blue Ribbon; all these
he pinned on his chest. He now stood in white and gold before the
mirror, sparkling and glittering, his left hand pressing the exquisite
sword against his thigh, his right holding the plumed three-cornered
hat and the gloves.

Nikolai Apollonovich had not slept at all that night; late in the
night a cab had driven up to the house, and Nikolai Apollonovich
had sprung in a flurry from the droshky and had begun to ring
the bell with all his might. When the door was opened, he ran
upstairs without stopping to remove his voluminous greatcoat and,
floundering in its folds, dashed through a whole series of rooms.
Mysterious shadows paced outside the yellow house, but Nikolai
Apollonovich walked about his room; at two in the morning, his
footfalls could still be heard; and also at half-past two, at three,
and at four.

Unwashed and drowsy, Nikolai Apollonovich was sitting by the
fireplace when his father appeared. Apollon Apollonovich paused
involuntarily; he stood there reflected in the parquet floors and
in the mirrors between the windows, their gilt frames surrounded
by groups of plump cupids, their flamboyant ribbons forming
golden wreaths; he stood there and tapped his fingers on the small
incrusted table. Nikolai Apollonovich started, sprang to his feet and
blinked his eyes: he saw before him a minute golden-white old man!

Nikolai Apollonovich cursed his own mortal self, and, insofar
as he was the image and the likeness of his father, he also cursed
his father; his spiritual self hated his father. Nikolai Apollonovich
intuitively knew his father, his least sinuosities and his most inarticulate tremors. In his physical perceptions, he was absolutely
like his father. He was unsure where he himself ended or where
the Senator, that bearer of many sparkling Orders, began in him.
He actually experienced rather than saw himself in that splendid
uniform; and something impelled him to stand up and greet the
little old man in white and gold.

"Good morning, Papa!"

Not without a certain very exaggerated naïveté, the Senator replied cheerfully and familiarly:

"My respects, Son!"

Whenever father and son came in contact with each other, they resembled two ventilators that had been turned on facing each other; and the result was a most unpleasant draft.

Their proximity bore little semblance to love; Nikolai Apollonovich regarded love as a humiliating physical act; and, at this instant, direct kinship meant no more to him than a mere organic relationship.

"You're on parade today?" the son asked.

The Senator dovetailed his fingers, then tore them apart. Apparently Apollon Apollonovich wanted to say something and explain his appearance in uniform; but he only coughed. Just then a lackey announced:

"The carriage is ready, sir!"

Apollon Apollonovich, happy to be interrupted, hurried off.

Suddenly Nikolai Apollonovich remembered his father's most recent official circular and decided that his father, Apollon Apollonovich, was a scoundrel.

Meanwhile, the little old man was already ascending the red-carpeted stairs; his legs, as he climbed, formed angles, and this comforted his spirit: he loved symmetry.

Other little old men greeted him: sideburns, full beards, shaven heads and goatees, chests decorated with Orders, as befitted men who were at the wheel of State; at the balustrade stood a small solemn group of gilt-chested men, who discussed the fated course of the revolving wheel until the Master of Ceremonies, wielding a baton, invited them to form a line.

Afterwards, the same little old men gathered again near the balustrade; soon there was a sparkling swarm of them, from which rose the base velvety note of one shorter than the rest who, when the little old men surrounded him, became invisible.

Apollon Apollonovich was busily discoursing when Count Witte, a man of heroic stature, with the bluest of ribbons across his chest, a jaunty air, and squinting eyes, came to join the group, running his hand through his gray hair. Apollon Apollonovich abruptly stopped and with vague heartiness extended his hand toward the hand that had just signed the latest treaty. Count Witte bent low over the Senator's shoulder and uttered a witty remark. The *bon mot* did not, however, evoke a smile either from the Senator or from his aged colleagues. The small group dispersed: Apollon

Apollonovich descended the stairs with Witte; the little old men
followed behind; they were preceded by a hook-nosed, red-lipped,
elderly Oriental ambassador. Against the fiery background of the
red-carpeted stairway, the Senator in gold and white marched very
erectly down the stairs.

It was the hour of the parade: outside, a square of the Imperial
Guard was lined up.

Behind the steel tips of the Grenadiers' bayonets one could see
the white horses of the Cavalry; the unbroken radiant spectacle,
like a golden, compact, reflecting mirror, moved forward slowly to
the assembly point; the motley standards of the squadrons swung
in the breeze; the silver bands played exhilarating martial music;
there were whole squadrons of Cuirassiers and Cavalier Guards;
one could pick out in the ranks some of the huge fair-haired horsemen in breastplates and in white, tightly stretched pantaloons. In
breastplates and helmets, some crowned with silver doves, others
with double-headed eagles, the ranks of the squadron trotted forward. Crowned with a silver dove, the pale-mustached Baron Om-
mergau pranced by; also crowned with a dove, Count Aven passed,
followed by the Cuirassiers and the Cavalier Guards. Through the
dust, like a blood-red cloud, with their plumes lowered, the Hussars
galloped past on their gray chargers. Their pelisses glowed scarlet,
their mantles white; they thundered over the ground, and a gleam
of silver sabers streaked through the air. The red cloud of Hussars
flashed by, clearing the square. Then, out of space, loomed azure
horsemen with silver shimmering breastplates; the squadron of
Guard Gendarmerie, heralded by a trumpet, was suddenly hidden
from sight by a new cloud of dust; the drums rattled. The infantry
marched past.

2

After the slush melted, the Petersburg roofs were bathed in sunlight.

Angel Peri was at home, alone; her husband, the quartermaster,
was out. Uncombed, the Angel fluttered about in her kimono between vases of chrysanthemums and Fujiyama. The satin wings of

the kimono flapped; its wearer, still hypnotized by the same idea, kept biting now the corner of a handkerchief, now the tip of a braid. She still thought Nikolai Apollonovich a scoundrel; but that newspaper man—he was a beast, too!

In order to recover some measure of tranquillity, the distressed Angel curled up on a quilted couch and opened a book: *The Man and His Body*. The Angel had opened this book frequently, but it had always slipped from her hands. Angel Peri's eyelids drooped while her husband whistled and snored.

Baroness R. R. had already asked her: "What do you think of the book, *ma chère*?" But *ma chère* had nothing to say, and Baroness R. R. wagged a finger at her; had she not inscribed this book with the words: "*To my mystical friend*," and signed it, "*Baroness R. R., a transitory shell with a Buddhist spark.*"

Henri Besançon, no doubt, would explain these enigmatic words; and Sofya Petrovna had now and then dipped into the book. Sticking her little nose into Henri Besançon's book, she had detected the Baroness's favorite perfume—opopanax. But then the bell rang and Varvara Evgrafovna flew in.

"What's that?" Varvara Evgrafovna asked, bending over the book. "Yes, what is it?" she repeated. "Who gave it to you?"

"The Baroness . . ."

"Of course. . . . But what is it?"

"Besançon . . ."

"You mean Annie Besant . . . rubbish, isn't it? . . . Have you read the *Manifesto*?"

Sofya Petrovna's crimson lips merely pouted.

"The bourgeoisie, having a presentiment of its end, has taken to mysticism!" Varvara Evgrafovna announced triumphantly, throwing an irrefutable glance at the Angel through her pince-nez. Fortunately, she did not resume the topic; crossing her legs, she began to wipe her pince-nez. "You'll come, of course, to the ball at the Tzukatovs!"

"To be sure, I will."

"Our common acquaintance, Ableukhov, will be there."

The Angel flushed.

"Then, please be good enough to give him this letter." The visitor thrust a letter into the Angel's hand.

"You will give it to him—without fail?" the visitor persisted.

"I'll . . . I'll give it to him," the Angel consented, not without faltering.

"Thanks. Now I must be off . . . to a meeting . . ."

"Varvara Evgrafovna, darling, take me along with you," the Angel pleaded.

"We may get beaten up."

"I don't care. Take me with you!"

"All right, then. Come along. Only don't waste a lot of time dressing, powdering and all that. Hurry, please!"

"At once. It won't take a minute! . . .

"Oh, Lord, hurry, do hurry! . . . My corset, Mavrushka! . . . The black woolen dress, you know the one I mean. And the shoes! No, not these, but the ones with the high heels."

The kimono flew over the table and landed on the bed. Mavrushka, becoming confused, upset a chair.

"No, not like that . . . tighter, tighter, please. . . . You've only got thumbs. . . . Now the garters, quick! How often must I tell you?" The corset began to crackle.

At last, with an ivory hairpin between her teeth, Sofya Petrovna Likhutina casually glanced at the letter addressed to Ableukhov. A recalcitrant wisp of hair fell over her forehead.

That letter, that familiar name! But strangely enough the handwriting was Lippanchenko's!

And now, in her black woolen dress buttoned at the back, she fluttered from her bedroom:

"Well, let's go. . . . Oh, by the way, who's that letter from?"

"?"

"Well, never mind, never mind!"

At the entrance of the house, they stumbled on Lippanchenko.

"Well, well! And where are you going?" he inquired.

"To the meeting, the meeting."

The cunning Ukrainian was not to be put off.

"That's fine. I'll go with you," he said.

Varvara Evgrafovna flushed, stopped short, fixing her gaze on Lippanchenko. She remarked:

"I think I know you. You have a room, I think, at Mantonshi's."

The brazen provincial lost his poise. In confusion, he raised his hat and dropped behind.

"Who is he?" Varvara Evgrafovna asked.

"Lippanchenko."

"No, that's not true. He's a Greek from Odessa, by the name of Mavrokordato. I should advise you not to receive him."

Sofya Petrovna did not listen. Mavrokordato or Lippanchenko —it was all the same to her.

3

They walked along the Moika.

The last leaves, golden and red, rustled in a neighboring garden.

"Oo-oo-oo-oo . . ." sounded in the open places.

"Do you hear it?"

"What is it?"

"Oo-oo-oo-oo . . ."

"I hear nothing . . ."

This wail resounded faintly in the forests and the fields, in the expanses near Moscow, Petersburg, and Saratov. Have you heard this October song of the year 1905?

"It must be a factory siren. There's a strike somewhere."

It was not a factory siren; it was not the wind; it was not even the howling of a dog.

Below, to one side of them, the Moika Canal appeared blue; on the other side stood the familiar three-story colonnaded building with the same familiar series of modeled ornaments: ring after ring, and inside each ring a coat of arms—a Roman helmet between two crossed swords.

Before them, where the canal took a turn to the left of a stone projection, loomed the dazzling dome of St. Isaac's Cathedral against a background of exquisite turquoise.

They had reached the Embankment: the deep waters of the Neva looked green-blue. Far, far away, appearing ever so remote, the islands looked incredibly flat and low; and their buildings seemed so flat too that the deep green-blue waters threatened suddenly to wash over and submerge them. A pitiless sunset hovered

above this green-blue surface, scattering its gleams here and there:
the Troitsky Bridge and the Winter Palace glowed purple.

Suddenly, a clearly defined silhouette appeared above these
green-blue waters and against the background of the red sky; the
flaps of a coat cape beat in the breeze like a pair of wings; carelessly, a waxen face with protruding lips came into view; the eyes
seemed to search for something in the blue expanse of the Neva
and, unable to find what they sought, took refuge under the visor
of a modest cap; the eyes saw neither Sofya Petrovna nor Varvara
Evgrafovna: they saw only the green-blue depths; they rose and
fell—beyond the Neva, where the buildings glowed purple on the
sunken banks of the island. A bulldog, carrying in his mouth a whip
with a silver handle, ran snorting ahead of the silhouette.

As he passed them, the young man barely blinked his eyes,
touched the band of his cap with his fingers, and walked on without
a word. The buildings glowed purple.

Sofya Petrovna, squinting at him, hurriedly hid her face in her
muff and nodded to the bulldog. Varvara Evgrafovna however stared
straight into his face.

"Ableukhov?" she asked Sofya.

"Yes, I think so."

Receiving this answer (she was extremely nearsighted), she
whispered a rhyme to herself:

> "Graceful, noble, pale,
> Hair as white as flax,
> A mind both bold and hale,
> N. A. A.—who is he?
>
> He is for revolution,
> Though a pure aristocrat,
> He is not for evolution,
> Though his father is a rat."

There he was, the transformer of a rotten order; and here she
was ready to marry him when he had fulfilled his appointed task,
which would cause a world-wide explosion. At that instant, she
choked (Varvara Evgrafovna had the habit of swallowing her
saliva).

Sofya Petrovna paid no attention to her. She turned her head. There, on the stone projection, in the brightly glowing assault of the last rays, stood Nikolai Apollonovich, facing in her direction, his back arched, his face buried in his collar, and his cap tilted back. He seemed to smile unpleasantly; and in any case he looked absurd. Wrapped in his greatcoat, he appeared stooped and armless, and the ends of his long cape flapped in the breeze like two awkward wings.

For a long time he stood there in his stooped position, smiling unpleasantly, the awkward wings flapping in the breeze against the red glow; he did not glance in her direction; in any case, he was nearsighted. He was staring at the islands, where the sunken buildings grew dimmer in the purple smoke.

Sofya Petrovna wished that her husband, Sergey Sergeyevich, would walk up to this scoundrel and hit him in the face with his clenched fist and say what he had to say.

The pitiless sunset sent assault after assault from the horizon, animating the water with rosy ripples. Higher up, the small white clouds, like fragments of crushed mother-of-pearl, sank in the turquoise sky. Soon the dark blue, the bluish-green depth, would pour down on the houses, the granite, and the water.

The sunset would be over.

4

Apollon Apollonovich appeared in the doorway. The lackey had already removed the lid from the steaming soup tureen.

Through the open doorway on the left, Nikolai Apollonovich, in a student's uniform, burst into the room; he wore an unusually high collar.

Apollon Apollonovich's eyes drifted from object to object. Nikolai Apollonovich felt awkward: his arms hung helplessly from his shoulders. In an outburst of nervousness, he rushed toward his father and began to knead his fingers.

Apollon Apollonovich impulsively rose before his son—jumped up, one might say.

Nikolai Apollonovich tripped on a chair leg.

Apollon Apollonovich offered his lips; and Nikolai Apollonovich pressed his lips to his father's.

Apollon Apollonovich resumed his seat. He seized the pepper-box. He overpeppered his soup.

"From the university?" he asked.

A frog-like expression appeared on the smirking mouth of the respectful son. Of the "Greek mask" not a trace remained; amiable smiles and furrows poured in a cascade before the unsteady gaze of the distraught father. His hand with the upraised spoon trembled.

"And you, Papa, have you just come from the Department?" the son asked.

"No, from the Minister's."

The Senator, in his office, had come to the conclusion that his son was a scoundrel. Thus, the sixty-eight-year-old father had executed an intellectually comprehensible terroristic act over his own son.

His conclusion, however, had been arrived at in his office, and was by no means intended for the dining room.

"Kolenka, would you like some pepper?"

"No, the salt, please . . ."

Letting his eyes dart from object to object, Apollon Apollonovich, acting according to the tradition of this hour, diligently forced his thoughts to avoid his office.

"As for me, I prefer pepper. It's spicier . . ."

"So!"

"So!"

"Well . . ."

Thus the father engaged his young son or, to be more accurate, himself in conversation.

A leaden silence ensued.

The silence weighed less on the Senator than on Nikolai Apollonovich who, in search of a topic, suffered real agony.

Quite unexpectedly, he said:

"Here . . . I . . ."

"What were you about to say?"

"Nothing in particular . . ."

Again, quite unexpectedly, the words came from Nikolai Apollonovich:

"Here . . . I . . ."

What was he trying to say? He had thought of no words to follow his initial utterance.

Apollon Apollonovich, distressed by his son's verbal confusion, cast a capricious glance at him and said approvingly:

"Well, do say what's on your mind!"

Absurd associations whirled about in the son's head. He managed to squeeze out of himself:

"Here . . . I . . . have read Cohen's *Theorie der Erfahrung!* . . ."

And suddenly he stopped short again.

"What sort of book is that, Sonny?"

In speaking to his son Apollon Apollonovich, following old traditions, alternated in calling him "Kolenka," "Sonny," and "Little Pigeon."

"Cohen, Papa, is the modern exponent of serious Kantism."

"Did you say Comtism?"

"No, Kantism, Papa."

"Didn't Comte refute Kant?"

"But Comte is not scientific . . ."

"I don't know, my dear boy. In my time it wasn't so considered . . ."

Apollon Apollonovich slowly rubbed his eyes and repeated absentmindedly:

"Comte . . ."

Apollon Apollonovich was thinking; his brain was suffering again from an afflux, conditioned by a hemorrhoidal ailment during the entire past week. Fixing his dark blue eyes on his son, he asked:

"What sort of book is it, Kolenka?"

With instinctive cunning Nikolai Apollonovich dilated upon philosophy. The conversation about Cohen was very neutral in character; it served to shelve other topics; some due explanation was postponed (from month to month). Besides, Apollon Apollonovich encouraged such conversations in his son; sometimes, when he came back from the gymnasium, Nikolai Apollonovich would plunge into details about the Roman cohorts; and Apollon Apollonovich encouraged his interest in cohorts. Recently, Apollon Apollonovich had placed his hand on Kolenka's shoulder and exhorted him:

"If I were you, Kolenka, I would read Mill's *Logic*. A useful book. . . . In two volumes. . . . I read it in my time—from cover to cover."

One day Nikolai Apollonovich appeared with a volume of Mill, and Apollon Apollonovich, pretending he did not know, asked him:

"What are you reading?"

"Mill, Papa."

"So, so. . . . That's splendid!"

And now, divided to the end, they unconsciously revived old memories.

Apollon Apollonovich had been at one time a professor of legal philosophy and was prodigiously well-read in the subject; but no trace of that remained. When confronted by the refined pirouettes of collateral logic, he was conscious of an intangible weight and was unable to refute the arguments.

"Yes, one might do justice to Kolenka," he thought. "His intellectual apparatus, one might say, functions."

Nikolai Apollonovich derived some pleasure from the attention with which his father listened to him.

By the time dessert was served, a semblance of friendship had developed; and sometimes it seemed a pity to interrupt the conversation, as though each were afraid of his own isolation.

Finally, they both rose and began to pace the rooms; and the rooms began to grow dark; and distantly, in the drawing room, a fire had flared red and crackled.

Thus, many years ago, they had paced the empty rooms—he, still a boy, and his father; and patting his fair-haired son on the shoulder, the father had pointed to the stars:

"The stars, Kolenka, are far, far away. From the nearest star, it takes the light at least two and a half years to reach the earth. . . . That's how it is, my dear boy!" The tender-hearted father had also written some verses for his son:

> "Little fool, little sap,
>   Kolenka is dancing;
>   On his head a fool's cap—
>   On a horse he's prancing."

Sharply the contours of the tables began to take shape; the glass emitted a ray of light, the inlaid tops began to glisten. Had the father really concluded that his own seed was worthless? Had his son really sneered at him? Perhaps it had all been real; and perhaps it had never been.

Father and son sat in the satin drawing room, aimlessly stretching out the meeting. From time to time, they looked into each other's eyes. The fire in the grate breathed warmth; in its light, Apollon Apollonovich, shaven and old, was silhouetted with large ears and bare skull. With precisely such a face he had been portrayed on the cover of a cheap magazine.

"My dear boy, you often have . . . h'm . . . a visitor . . ."

"Who?"

"Oh, what's his name? . . . A young man . . ."

"A young man?"

"With a tiny mustache."

"You mean Alexander Ivanovich Doodkin! . . . No . . ."

Nikolai Apollonovich reflected a moment, then added:

"Yes, he does call now and then."

"If . . . if it isn't indiscreet to ask . . ."

"What?"

"That he comes here on university matters?"

"If my question sounds inappropriate, then . . ."

"Is he a student?"

"Yes, a student."

"In the technological school?"

"No . . ."

Apollon Apollonovich realized that his son was lying. He glanced at his watch and rose indecisively. Nikolai Apollonovich became acutely conscious of his hands, and his eyes began to blink.

"Yes, there are many branches of knowledge in this world," his father remarked. "Each one of them has its own depth—you're right in that. Do you know, Kolya, I feel tired."

He stood, staring, asking no questions, his head lowered. Nikolai Apollonovich suddenly felt ashamed.

The old hand moved. . . . Two fingers were held out.

"Good night, Papa!"

"My respects!"

A mouse rustled, scuttled and squeaked.

The door of the Senator's study opened: with a candle in his hand, Apollon Apollonovich ran into the indescribable room and there devoted himself to perusing the newspapers.

Nikolai Apollonovich stood at the window.

In a misty frenzy, a phosphorescent patch moved across the sky; a fog crept over the Neva expanses; a greenish hue shimmered over the flying surfaces; and a small red light suddenly flashed, blinked for an instant and vanished into the mist. Beyond the Neva, the huge buildings of the islands loomed, their lights peering silently and agonizingly through the fog . . . it seemed as if someone were weeping there. Overhead, the tufted clouds seemed to stretch forth their vaguely outlined, frenzied arms above the unquiet waters of the Neva.

The Embankment was deserted; the shadow of a policeman passed, black against the fog, and disappeared; the island buildings were fading in the fog; the spire of the Peter and Paul fortress flashed faintly.

Peering through the window, Nikolai Apollonovich noticed a shadowy woman; she hovered nearby and seemed to fix her gaze on the window. He smiled unpleasantly and, putting on his pince-nez, scrutinized the shadow.

No, no, it was not she!

The black shadow soon faded in the fog.

A metal latch clinked in the depth of the corridor; out of its darkness a light flashed. It was Apollon Apollonovich, candle in hand, returning from that indescribable place; his dull-colored dressing-gown and the enormous contours of his moribund ears were clearly outlined in the wavering candlelight; Ableukhov had appeared out of utter darkness, and he disappeared again into utter darkness.

Nikolai Apollonovich suddenly thought: "It's time."

Nikolai Apollonovich knew the meeting would take place that evening, and that she would be there. And again he thought: "It's time."

5

Sofya Petrovna hid her little nose softly in her fur muff; mutely, behind her, the Troitsky Bridge vanished into nothingness; and on the iron bridge, above the damp handrails, over the greenish water seething with bacilli, through the draughts of the Neva wind, vague shadows followed in her steps—a cylindrical hat, a walking stick, a greatcoat, ears, and a nose.

Suddenly her eyes rested, widened, blinked, squinted: under the damp handrails a striped bulldog sat on his haunches, holding a slavered silver-handled whip betwen his teeth. Sofya Petrovna looked farther; under the handrail she saw a waxen face with protruding teeth peeping out of a greatcoat. The man appeared lost in thought. It was a thought which he had pursued in recent days while reciting to himself in anguish some lines of a ballad:

"Thine eyes beheld the purple setting of the sun,
Thou stood on Neva's bank."

There he stood on Neva's bank, his eyes fixed dully on the green water or staring at the low bank opposite and its squatting island buildings where, above the white walls of the fortress, loomed in cold detachment the pitiless, agonizingly sharp Peter and Paul spire, piercing the sky.

Her entire being reached out to him—it was no time for words or reflections! He did not notice her; he stared as glassily as before; and he looked like an armless monstrosity.

She walked away. As she did he slowly turned toward her; he took quick mincing steps, stumbling over the voluminous flaps and becoming entangled in them. At the corner he spied a cab, a speeding cab. Nikolai Apollonovich gave chase. He reached it; but as he grasped the dog's collar and turned to smile at her, the cab sped away.

Suddenly, early snow began to fall; it fell in a shower of minute, animated diamonds, dancing and sparkling. The street lamp cast a bright circle, lighting one side of the palace, the canal, and the stone bridge. The canal ran into the darkness; at the corner a cab was waiting for someone; a greatcoat had been negligently tossed into it.

For a long time Sofya Petrovna stood on the curve of the bridge, gazing reflectively at the steaming water; she had stood on this spot before, sighing about Liza and sadly discussing the tribulations of *La Pique Dame*—the divine, enchanting, fabulous harmonies; and she had hummed in an undertone:

"Tatam-tam-tam! . . . Tatam-tam-tam!"

She caught the sound of running steps. She looked up, but did not scream: a red domino had suddenly emerged from the direction of the palace; it ran about distractedly as if looking for something. Then, spying the woman's shadow on the curve of the bridge, it rushed toward her, stumbling over cobblestones and thrusting its mask forward, a mask with a chilling white beard of lace and malignant slits for eyes. While the mask was running toward the bridge, Sofya Petrovna Likhutina had no time to conclude that this domino was some buffoon, some tasteless practical joker wished to have his little joke. She had no time to realize that there was a human face under the velvet mask and lace beard, and that human eyes looked through the long slits. Under her small forehead Sofya Petrovna seemed to imagine that a gap had opened somewhere in the world and that, out of this gap, had issued this fool who was now running toward her; but she had no idea who this fool might be.

In rustling velvet, the domino rushed stumbling on to the bridge and, like a red flame, fell at the handrail. Suddenly, the bright green garters of his socks showed; the fool at once became a pitiful fool; and then one of his boots slipped from his foot. The fool fell hard on his face. He heard a guffaw:

"Monster! Red fool!"

A hairy form rushed forward; a whistle blew. The fool scrambled into the waiting droshky, and onlookers could observe a red patch struggling to slip on a greatcoat.

A barking bulldog flung itself after the droshky; its short legs flashed quickly by. Two Secret Police agents gave chase in a car.

6

Said one shadow to the other:

"One hears nothing about the red domino."

"So you know about it?"

"I followed him to the very house."

"Well, what are things coming to?"

"The incident hasn't come to a head yet."

"Any evidence?"

"What do you think? You don't suppose I'd deign to search his pockets!"

"Evidence? So you ask for evidence? What about the *Petersburg Diary of Events*? Have you read the *Diary*?"

"To be frank, I haven't."

"But it's our duty to know what Petersburg talks about. If you'd followed the news, you'd have known that it's pretty well established that the domino makes his appearance at the Summer Canal."

"H'm . . ."

"Why don't you ask me who wrote about it in the *Diary*?"

"Well, who?"

"My colleague, Neintelpfein."

"I must admit, I hadn't expected such a trick."

"You think you're smart. But let me tell you, the whole thing is arranged like clockwork. You can remain in blissful ignorance of what's going on, if you like. But I assure you, my man Neintelpfein will cause a sensation."

"I trust you've ordered your agents to leave Nikolai Apollonovich in peace for the time being."

7

She could not reconcile herself to this humilating occurrence. If Nikolai Apollonovich had to humiliate her, he should have done it in some other way: he would have done better to strike her. Had he flung himself in his domino from the bridge, she would have remembered it for the rest of her life with agonizing tremors. She would have remembered it to the day of her death. The spot where Sofya Petrovna's humiliation had occurred was not at all a prosaic one; it was not the sort of place where he should have permitted himself to act in that way. It was not strange that this spot had evoked in her memory the harmonies of *Pique Dame*; there was some affinity between her situation and Liza's (but she could not tell exactly what it was). She had dreamed of meeting Nikolai Apollonovich here in the role of Herman. Herman? . . . But with disgusting timidity Nikolai Apollonovich had sidled up to her and thrust his mask toward her; then, again, he had hurriedly flourished his domino before her, stumbling awkwardly as he did so and, falling, had prosaically revealed his sock garters—that was enough to enrage anyone. Finally, to climax his absurdities, so unbecoming to a Herman, he had fled from the police. He had not torn the mask from his face with a heroic, tragic gesture; nor had he proclaimed in a husky melancholy voice: "I love you." He had not even shot himself. No, the shameful conduct of this fancied Herman had extinguished the light of these days! It had transformed the domino into a harlequin! His embarrassing conduct was quite beyond her. For how could she be a Liza without a Herman? Her heart cried for vengeance.

She rushed to her flat in a rage. In the vestibule she saw an over-coat and a cap: her husband was home. Without taking off her coat, she rushed to her husband. Flinging open his door, she confronted him, her fur around her neck, her fur muff still in her hands, her face flushed and swollen with ugly rage.

Sergey Sergeyevich was preparing to go to bed; his smoking jacket was already on a hanger, and he wore a dazzling white night-shirt, tied around the waist with a tasseled cord. Looking dejected, he knelt before an ikon that sparkled in the light of a lamp. In the dim light of the tiny lamp, the contours of his face, of his pointed beard, and of his hand, stood out in relief; and his face, goatee, hand, and white chest looked as if they had been carved from a hard wood. Sergey Sergeyevich's lips moved faintly against the pale blue flame; his bluish fingers, poised to make the sign of the cross, rested almost motionlessly on his forehead.

Lieutenant Likhutin touched his chest and both shoulders with his fingers, then bowed; only after accomplishing this, did he, rather reluctantly, turn his head. Then rising from his knees, he wiped a fleck of dust from them and asked:

"What's the matter, Sonya dear?"

Her husband's composure, so like the blue flame of the image lamp, irritated and humiliated her. She sank into a chair and, bury-ing her face in her muff, burst into loud sobs.

Sergey Sergeyevich's face relaxed, became softer; a furrow crossed his forehead; a look of compassion crept into his eyes. Sergey Sergeyevich was at a loss how to act. Should he let her cry her fill and look on at the risk of being reproached for indifference, or should he fall at her feet and gently raise her head from the muff, embrace her and cover her with kisses? But he feared to see a grimace of boredom and contempt on her face. So he chose the middle way: he simply patted her trembling shoulder and said:

"Well, well, Sonya . . . well, enough, my infant!"

"Oh, leave me alone, leave me alone!"

"Tell me what's wrong. We can decide then what to do!"

"Leave me alone, leave me alone! You're so coldblooded . . ."

Sergey Sergeyevich walked away from his wife; for a few moments he stood undecided, then sank into a nearby chair.

"Ah. . . . Who's ever heard of a man always leaving his wife alone? Who goes off the way you do to look after army provisions? Always away, and never caring what happens to one!"

"Sonya dear, you're mistaken if you think I don't realize it. You see what comes of not listening to me!"

"Ah, leave me alone, please!"

"You see, my dear, since I was obliged to move into this room. . . . After all, my dear, I have my pride. And I haven't the least desire to embarrass you. . . . I understand you; I know that it isn't easy for you. . . . I'd been entertaining the hope that some day again. . . . Never fear, I won't insist! I shan't, I tell you. But, please, try to understand me. What you take for indifference, coldbloodedness, and all that, does not arise at all from any coldness on my part. . . . Never fear, I shan't insist!

"Maybe, my dear, it's because you wanted to see something of Nikolai Apollonovich Ableukhov? I think something must have happened between you two. . . . Do tell me everything, please do! Maybe, between us, we can settle the matter."

"Don't you dare mention him to me! He's a scoundrel, a scoundrel, I tell you! Another in his place would have put a bullet through his head long ago. . . . Ah, you! You'd better leave me in peace!"

Then incoherently, in great agitation, she told him everything, everything.

Sergey Sergeyevich Likhutin was a simple man. Simple persons are much more disturbed by inexplicably absurd behavior than by sheer badness or even by murder. It is not hard to understand ordinary human betrayal; once you understand it, you almost find justification for the act. But how explain to the average honest person an act bordering on the fantastic, such as falling to one's haunches, for example, and waving one's frock coat? There was no justification for such mad acts. No, it was preferable that a normal man should embezzle government money and go unpunished than to squat down on his haunches and perform silly antics.

In his mind, Sergey Sergeyevich had evidently pictured the red

domino squatting in the unlighted entrance hall, and he blushed
until he looked like a carrot; the blood rushed to his head. As a
child, he had played with Nikolai Apollonovich; later, his friend's
capacity for philosophy had astonished him; nobly, he had allowed
Nikolai Apollonovich to come between himself and his wife, and
now. . . . Sergey Sergeyevich Likhutin worked himself into a rage
as he permitted himself to imagine clearly the clownish grimaces
in the unlighted entrance. Greatly perturbed, he paced the small
room, raising his clenched fist each time he made a sharp turn; it
was his habitual gesture in moments of deep disturbance. Sofya
Petrovna knew this gesture well; and she now became alarmed at
the silence which provoked this movement.

"What are you thinking?" she asked.

"Oh, nothing in particular."

And Sergey Sergeyevich, his fingers clenched, continued to pace
the little room.

What an outrage! Nikolai Apollonovich had actually dared to
stand behind the entrance door!

The lieutenant was completely dumfounded by Nikolai Apollonovich's conduct; he experienced a nasty feeling mingled with horror;
it was the sort of feeling that seizes one when watching an idiot
perform certain functions or the actions of horrible furry-legged
insects. His perplexity, humiliation, and horror were transformed
into a terrible fury. Not only had his letter been ignored, but this
stupid act had heaped insult on the honor of an officer. Sergey Sergeyevich vowed to crush this terrible spider. Having made this
decision, he continued to pace the room, his face lobster-red and
his fingers clenched, swinging his muscular arm at each sharp turn.
He frightened Sofya Petrovna; she sat with half-open puffed lips,
with tear-stained cheeks that she made no attempt to wipe, attentively observing his pacing figure from her chair.

"What are you thinking?" she repeated her question.

Sergey Sergeyevich replied in a gruff voice: there was menace
in the voice, sternness and repressed fury.

"Nothing in particular."

At this moment Sergey Sergeyevich experienced something like
repulsion for his beloved wife; it was as if he thought she had some
share in the ignominy of the red domino.

"You had better go to your room and have a good sleep, and leave this matter to me."

Sofya Petrovna, drying her tears, rose from her chair and obediently left the room.

Sergey Sergeyevich continued to pace the room; now and then he coughed rather unpleasantly and with a kind of deliberation: khe-khe-khe-khe. . . . Sometimes his wooden fist, hewn out of a strong aromatic tree, was lifted above a little table; and the small table threatened to fly into splinters.

Then he unclenched his fist.

Sergey Sergeyevich undressed, lay down on his bed and covered himself. Then, abruptly, he threw the blanket from him; he fixed his eyes blankly on a single point and, unexpectedly even to himself, whispered loudly:

"I'll shoot him, like a dog . . ."

From the other side of the wall, Sofya Petrovna's offended voice asked:

"What are you thinking?"

"Nothing in particular . . ."

Sergey Sergeyevich dove under the blanket and pulled it over his head: there he continued to sigh, implore, and threaten . . .

Sofya Petrovna impetuously pulled off her dress; all in white, she threw herself on the bed. She buried her little face, crowned with a mass of black hair, in her hands. A cascade of objects littered the floor; Mavrushka's duty was to pick them up for her mistress, for, when Sofya Petrovna called for a certain object and it was not immediately brought, she sent things flying round the room: blouses, handkerchiefs, dresses, hairpins, hatpins.

Sofya Petrovna listened to her husband's tireless pacing; at the same time on a resounding piano overhead someone was playing a familiar melody: a polka-mazurka which, while still a child, she had danced with someone in laughing abandon. Under the spell of these innocent sounds, her anger turned to weariness; she felt apathetic toward her husband in whom, as she now realized, she had awakened jealousy toward *the other*. Sergey Sergeyevich's awkwardness had provoked a definite repulsion in her; he could not have done worse if he had broken into the small, sacred casket that she kept locked in a drawer and that contained her letters. The shameless behavior of Nikolai Apollonovich was not without solace: she only regretted that he had fallen at her feet in such a clumsy, pitiful manner; nevertheless, she still wanted to claw him to pieces—a thing she had never wished to do indeed to her husband; she never felt like kissing or tormenting him. It was now clear that her husband had nothing to do with the whole affair; but she had told him everything. She could not bear her husband's contact either with herself or with Nikolai Apollonovich. The lieutenant of course would draw the wrong conclusions from the episode; he would make neither head nor tail of it. Sofya Petrovna listened to the sounds of the polka-mazurka and to the footfalls behind the wall; her pale little face peered out from the abundant locks of blue-black hair and rather dimly glanced at her trembling knees.

Her glance then fell on the dressing-table mirror and, under the mirror, she suddenly spied the letter that she had promised to deliver at the ball. She had entirely forgotten about it. Her first impulse was to return it. How dared they inflict this letter on her? She would have sent it back if her husband (would he never get to bed!) had not interfered in it all. At the moment, under the influence of her inner protest against "this interference," she viewed the matter in a very simple light: why not open the envelope and learn its secrets? She had the right to do it—how dared he have secrets? In an instant, Sofya Petrovna had reached the dressing table and seized the letter. Again, hearing a whisper on the other side of the wall, she called out:

"What are you thinking?"

"Nothing in particular."

The bed creaked mournfully; all was silent. With trembling fingers Sofya Petrovna unsealed the letter. . . . As she read, her puffy eyes grew large and round; a dazzling light conquered their dimness and her face gradually changed color: at first a rosy rose, it turned scarlet when she had finished reading.

Nikolai Apollonovich was now wholly in her hands; if she wished, she now had the power to avenge her suffering by inflicting on him a crushing blow. Her own little hands could inflict this blow; he had tried to frighten her with his clownish masking, but he hadn't the cunning to carry this out properly; let him now be effaced; let him assume the role of Herman! Yes, yes, yes; by passing on the letter, she would inflict this blow on him. For an instant her head grew dizzy at the thought of what she was proposing to do. It was too late to restrain herself, to avoid taking the path she was determined to follow. Let it all come to pass! Let the red domino become a bloody domino!

The door suddenly creaked. Sofya Petrovna had barely time to crush the letter in her hand. On the threshold stood her husband, all in white—in underwear. The entry of this alien man in such improper garments provoked her to fury:

"You might have come in properly dressed."

Sergey Sergeyevich beat a confused retreat, and then reappeared in a dressing-gown. She had meanwhile managed to hide the letter. With unpleasant and unusual firmness, he turned to her simply:

"Sofya . . . promise that you won't go to the ball tomorrow night . . ."

Receiving no reply, he went on:

"I hope you'll give me this promise. It's a matter of prudence."

There was no reply.

"I should wish after all that's happened . . ."

Faltering, he resumed:

"I've given my officer's word for you that you will not appear at the ball."

Meeting with continued silence, he said:

"If, on the other hand, you refuse, I shall be forced to forbid you to go."

"I shall go, all the same," she answered at last.

"No, you shall not!"

There was menace in the way Sergey Sergeyevich spoke.

"I will go."

In the ensuing silence, only Sergey Sergeyevich's breathing was audible. It made him clutch at his throat. Twice he shook his head as if making an effort to repel the inevitable. Having succeeded with an incredible effort in suppressing an outburst, he quietly sat down.

"Don't you see," he began again, "I did not demand any details from you. You, yourself, of your own will, came and confided in me."

Thought of what he had just heard forced him to descend into an abyss of depravity, down whose surfaces his own wife was slipping. What could be more vicious than the very absurdity of the incident? He felt there was something more here than the usual man-woman affair. It was not merely a betrayal or a fall. No, no: there was evidence here of some kind of excess that, like prussic acid, had now poisoned his life forever; the odor of bitter almonds assailed him, and he was conscious of the infusion of something stifling. He felt acutely aware of one thing: if Sofya Petrovna, his wife, went to the ball at the Tzukatovs, she would meet the domino —and then his world would crumble.

"Can't you see," he faltered, "after what has happened. . . . Don't you understand that all this is sheer nastiness, nothing but nastiness. That's why I swore that you wouldn't appear there. Have some pity for yourself, and for me, yes, even for . . . him, because otherwise . . . I . . ."

Sofya Petrovna's indignation at her husband's interference grew with every instant. How dared he enter her bedroom and give these absurd orders? As she lifted the hem of her robe from the floor, she realized that she was not fully dressed; hastily pulling the robe about her, she moved away into a corner and, from that dark corner, shook her head:

"Perhaps I might not have gone, but now I will certainly go. I'll go, I will!"

Something like a shot sounded in the room: there was an inhuman wail, a falsetto cry—the man of wood had jumped from his seat. The chair fell with a crash; the blow of a fist had split a small table in two; the door slammed. Then all was silent.

The sounds of the polka-mazurka overhead suddenly came to a stop; there was a stamping of feet in the apartment. Voices were raised: the indignant tenant overhead began to pound his floor with a broom.

Sofya Petrovna shrank from all this and, in her shame, broke into sobs. She experienced such fury for the first time in her life; only a few moments ago he had been standing in front of her. . . . No, he was not a human being . . . not even a wild beast . . . but just a mad dog.

8

Apollon Apollonovich's bedroom consisted of four walls and a single cut-out window hung with a lace curtain; the sheets, the towels, and the pillow-slips were immaculately white; the valet had sprayed the sheets with cologne.

Apollon Apollonovich did not call the valet to help him undress.

Quickly he took off his dressing-gown, meticulously folded it, and put it on the chair with his jacket and other clothes. Then, in his underwear, he did some exercises before going to sleep.

He flung out his arms and legs, twisted his body, squatted down twelve or more times, and then, lying on his back, worked his legs up and down.

He was particularly assiduous in his exercises when troubled by hemorrhoids.

Then he pulled the blanket over him before embarking on the journey—that is what he called sleep.

Burying his whole head except the tip of his nose under the blanket, he hung in a timeless void.

What sort of a void? What about the walls and the floor? And all the rest of it? . . .

Apollon Apollonovich was always aware of two dimensions: one, a material dimension of walls and carriages; the other, not exactly a spiritual, but a material one, too. . . . Above Ableukhov's head Ableukhov's eyes discerned lights and beams and iridescent colors —the dancing spots of revolving centers; they darkened the boundaries of space, and space played with space . . .

Sometimes he would close his eyes, and then open them; the misty spots and the stars, like the scum of the seething depths, would quite unexpectedly assume precise forms: crosses, polyhedrals, swans, light-permeated pyramids. Then these shapes would fly apart.

Apollon Apollonovich had his own secret: a world of contours, tremors and perception—a universe of singular phenomena. All this he saw before dropping off to sleep. On his way to sleep he recalled all the former inarticulations, rustlings, crystallographic figures, stars flitting in the murky darkness (one such star had drenched the Senator with a boiling golden liquid as crawling sensations ran up and down his skull): he remembered everything he had seen on the eve, so that he might not have to remember it again.

Before the final moment of diurnal consciousness, Apollon Apollonovich had noticed, as he dropped off to sleep, that a gurgling whirlpool was suddenly assuming the shape of a corridor that vanished in infinity; but what astonished him most was that the corridor began with his head and was the endless continuation of his head, whose crown had suddenly opened into infinity. Thus, the old Senator had the impression that he was seeing not with his eyes, but with the center of his head; that is, he, Apollon Apollonovich, was not Apollon Apollonovich, but *something* which had taken root in his brain and was gazing out of this brain. If the parietal bones should be opened, anything might run the length of the corridor and be precipitated into the *abyss*.

This was the Senator's second dimension.

Wrapped in the blanket, head and all, he was already suspended above the bed; the lacquered floor had already fallen away from the legs of the bed into the unknown—and, at the same moment, he heard a distant clicking noise, like the clatter of hoofs.

This clicking noise came nearer.

It was a strange, a very strange, an extraordinarily strange circumstance: his ear was cocked to the moon; and—there was no doubt about it—he could hear a knocking.

He thrust his head out.

A star moved toward the parietal bones and disappeared instantly; instantly, too, the lacquered squares of the floor moved near the legs of the bed. Apollon Apollonovich, all in white, looking like a plucked fowl, suddenly pressed his yellow heels against the rug.

Then he fled into the corridor.

The moon lighted the rooms.

In his nightshirt, a lighted candle in his hand, he traveled through the rooms. The bulldog with a clipped tail followed his disturbed master, clinking his collar and slobbering.

The Senator's hairy chest, like a shallow lid, was lifted by his heavy, stertorous breathing; his pale green ear pricked up. The Senator looked strange in the pier-glass: his arms and chest were sheathed in blue satin, which flashed metallically. Apollon Apollonovich was now wearing armor. He looked like a tiny knight; and in his hand he seemed to hold a flaming brand rather than a candle.

Apollon Apollonovich gathered courage and rushed into the salon; the clicking noise came from there.

"Tra-ta. . . . Tra-ta-ta . . ."

"On the basis of what statute in the *Code of Laws?*"

As he asked this, he observed the good-natured bulldog panting amiably at his side; but someone in the hall impudently replied:

"On the basis of the extraordinary law!"

Angered by this answer, he rushed into the hall.

The flaming brand melted in his hand: it filtered through his fingers like air. A tiny ray, it came to rest at his feet. The clicking noise was made by the tongue of some villainous Mongol; he had seen the face before when staying in Tokyo; yet it turned out to be Nikolai Apollonovich: he had seen him also in Tokyo. Apollon Apollonovich did not attempt to understand this: he rubbed his eyes with his hands (somehow these two points—the dimension of his hands and the dimension of his face—had come into contact). And the Mongol (Nikolai Apollonovich) was bearing down on him with a covetous purpose.

"On the basis of what law?" the Senator asked again.

"And what paragraph in the Code?" he added.

"There are no paragraphs, and no laws!" The answer came from space.

Weightless, bereft of sensation, suddenly deprived of gravity, of every physical sense, he fixed the space of his eyes (he could not say positively that his eyes fixed it, because all bodily sensation had left him); he realized too that he no longer had any parietal bones, that in their place there was a gap; Apollon Apollonovich saw in himself this round gap which formed a blue circle. At the fatal moment when according to his calculation the Mongol, who was imprinted in his consciousness but was now no longer visible, was about to reach him, something resembling a roaring wind in a chimney rapidly began to pull his consciousness through the blue parietal breach—into infinity.

A scandal had occurred (his consciousness noted this occurrence, but he could not remember when)—the wind blew Apollon Apollonovich out of Apollon Apollonovich.

Apollon Apollonovich flew through the round breach into the darkness above his head which was somehow like the planet earth, and there he was scattered asunder into sparks.

There was primordial darkness; and the consciousness struggled within it—no universal consciousness, but a quite simple one.

The consciousness now turned back, releasing two perceptions: they descended like two arms. What they perceived was a sort of shape (very like the bottom of a bath) filled with stinking filth; the perceptions splashed about in this bath of filth; soon they had become stuck to the sides of the bath. The consciousness now fought to get out, but something heavy weighed down the perceptions.

Then the consciousness saw its habitation: a little yellow old man, whose bare heels were pressing against a rug.

The consciousness, it seemed, was the little old man himself; as he sat on his bed, the little old man listened to the distant clatter.

And then Apollon Apollonovich suddenly understood: his journey through the corridor, through the salon, through his head—had been only a dream.

And no sooner did this thought occur to him than he awoke: it had been a double dream.

He was not sitting, but lying down with his head wrapped in a blanket: the clatter was that of a slamming door.

Nikolai Apollonovich had returned home.

"So . . ." murmured the old man.

"So . . ." he repeated.

"Very well . . ."

But he felt something wrong with his back; he was afraid to touch his spinal column . . .

"*Tabes dorsalis*?" he wondered.

CHAPTER FOUR

God grant I may preserve my wits . . .

—Pushkin

1

Only occasionally did the gloomy pedestrian quicken his pace. It took him some time to cross the vast expanse of the Field of Mars.

The Summer Garden was overcast.

The statues were boarded up; they stood on end like coffins. These coffins lined the paths; they sheltered nymphs and satyrs from the tooth of frost and time: time sharpens its teeth for all things—for the body, the soul, and the stones.

This garden had grown more desolate and gray than before. The grotto had fallen into ruin; the fountains had ceased playing; the summer portico had tumbled down; the waterfall had vanished; the garden had shrunk and taken refuge behind railings.

Peter the Great himself had planted this garden, watered these plants with his own watering-pot; he had imported cedars from Solikamsk, barberries from Danzig, apple-trees from Switzerland. He had erected fountains.

The Summer Garden had spread far, encroaching on the Field of Mars, and its paths were lined with attractive plants; enormous shells from the Indian Ocean lifted their horns; with an ear to the opening it had been possible to hear a chaotic din; near the grotto people used to drink wine.

In later days, under the posed figure of an antique statue that extended its fingers into the twilight, whispers and sighs could be heard, and the jewels of strolling young ladies had sparkled. This was in the springtime, on Whit Monday; the evening atmosphere had thickened, shattered by a single mighty organ-like voice, which

111

emanated from the gently dreaming elms; from there a green light suddenly flashed, casting a wide aura; there, amid green lights, musicians in bright red hunting habits, holding up their horns, made the neighborhood resound melodiously to their languid lament.

It had once been like this, but no more; now the paths were desolate; a flock of frenzied birds circled and swooped above Peter the Great's little house.

Nikolai Apollonovich, clean-shaven, was striding along a frosty path; his eyes were strangely bright. This very day, when he had decided to concentrate diligently on his studies, he had suddenly received a little note: a request to keep an appointment in the Summer Garden. The note was signed "S." This "S" must stand for Sofya, but of course she had disguised her handwriting.

Nikolai Apollonovich looked perturbed; for a whole week he had allowed dust to accumulate on an open page of a Kantian commentary. And now he experienced a sweet emotion . . . intangible and remote as yet; nonetheless, he felt those nameless tremors. Was this a sign of love? He had denied its existence.

He was already glancing nervously around, seeking the familiar figure in a black fur coat and black fur muff; there was no one like that about. Not far away he saw a shapeless, bundled female figure rise from a bench; the figure advanced to meet him.

"You didn't recognize me?"

"Oh!"

"It seems you don't know me even now? Yes, I'm Solovyova."

"Varvara Evgrafovna!"

"Do let's sit down here . . ."

Painfully, Nikolai Apollonovich sat down. His tryst had been made for this very spot; here was certainly a piece of bad luck! Nikolai Apollonovich wondered how he might end this chance meeting as quickly as possible; he looked right and left; but the person he had come to meet was nowhere in sight.

"Did you receive my note?"

"What note?"

"With the signature 'S'?"

"Why, is that you?"

"To be sure . . ."

"Where does the 'S' come in ?"

"What else could it be? As you know, my family name is Solov-yova."

His dreams collapsed.

"I . . . wanted . . . I thought. . . . Did you get my little poem signed '*Flaming Soul*'?"

"No, I haven't received it."

"What do you mean, you haven't received it? Can the police be intercepting my letters? Oh! I just wanted to ask you something about the meaning of life . . ."

"Excuse me, Varvara Evgrafovna, I have no time."

"I don't understand."

"Goodbye! You'll have to excuse me, please. We'll have a chat at a more convenient time."

Varvara Evgrafovna gripped the lapels of his greatcoat; he rose decisively; and with decision he held out his hand. She could think of nothing to stop him; and he fled from her, greatly annoyed, his face buried in his fur collar. The leaves stirred on the ground; they spiraled in dry circles around the hem of his greatcoat. The whirling leaves swept impetuously along the pathways; a lone red leaf came flying and clung momentarily. A darkish net of inter-secting branches lost itself in the steel horizon; he reached this spot and went on beyond; a flock of frenzied crows rose at his approach and circled around Peter's tiny house; the net of branches began to swing and to hum; and he heard sounds of weary dejection, merging with an organ-like voice from the past. The twilight deep-ened; there seemed to be no present; it looked as if those gloomy trees might tremulously put on a familiar green radiance, and hunters clad in scarlet might raise their hunting horns and extract waves of organ music from the zephyrs.

2

It was already late when Angel Peri, from her pillows, reluctantly opened her innocent little eyes, but she found it hard to keep them open; so she permitted herself to remain in a half-dreamy state; under her crown of hair stirred all sorts of incoherences, disturb-ances, suggestions of hints. Her first thought was of the ball that

night: she would be there! But when she tried to develop this
thought, her little eyes closed and those perturbations and suggestions of hints returned; one thing stood out clearly: Pompadour,
Pompadour, Pompadour! And what was Pompadour? To her the
word Pompadour suggested: Valenciennes lace, silver slippers,
pompoms! For days she had been arguing with her seamstress.
Madame Farnua had not wanted to concede to her on the question
of blond lace. "Why blond lace?" But how could she do without
blond lace? In the beginning Madame Farnua had said to her: "It's
not a question of your taste or mine: you've got to respect the
Pompadour style!" But Sofya Petrovna had shown no willingness to
yield and, as a result, Madame Farnua had offered to send back
the materials: "Take them to Maison Tricotons: they'll not think
of contradicting you there." What, go to Tricotons? That was
simply unthinkable. So she had abandoned the idea of blond lace
and of a *chapeau bergère*; but she could not do without a *pannier*
for the skirt.

On this they had compromised.

As she plunged into her reflections about Madame Farnua, Angel
Peri had an agonizing premonition of something else; and that
something had happened. In her daydream she had no inclination
to clutch at the fleeting impressions of yesterday's events. In the
end however she suddenly remembered: the *domino* and the *letter*;
and, at this thought, she sprang from her bed. Then again she
remembered: there had been another, a third word, before she had
fallen asleep. That third word was: husband!

Scarcely had she stumbled on this familiar word when she rushed
toward her husband's closed room, fully expecting to find her
husband, Lieutenant Likhutin, gone about his official duties as was
his custom. To her astonishment the room was locked against her:
Lieutenant Likhutin was inside.

Then she remembered the unpleasant scene of the previous
evening; so she slammed her bedroom door in turn. He had locked
himself in! She could do the same! But having turned the key,
she noticed the splintered table.

"Madame," Mavrushka's voice asked, "do you want coffee in
your room?"

"I don't want any . . ."

"Madame, someone's come!"
"From Madame Farnua?"
"No, from the laundress!"

Silence.
Near noon a Cuirassier called with a two-pound box of bonbons from Kraft's. His bonbons were accepted; he was refused.
About two o'clock a Lancer of the Life Guards called with a box of bonbons from Balle's: he was also refused.
A Hussar of the Life Guards was also refused.
At about ten in the evening a young girl from Madame Farnua's arrived with a carton; the maid promptly admitted her; presently a tittering was heard; the door of the bedroom clicked, and a curiously tear-stained little face was thrust out; a voice cried impatiently:
"Come, don't dawdle with that package!"
Just then a head peeped out from the study: it glanced around and withdrew again.

3

An enormous red sun hovered above the Neva; the buildings of Petersburg seemed to have dwindled away, transformed into ethereal, mist-permeated amethyst lace; the windows reflected the golden glow; the tall spires flashed rubies; and fiery flares invaded the recesses and the projections and set fire to the caryatids and the cornices of the brick balconies.
The palace flamed blood-red; Rastrelli had built it: in those days the old palace had stood like an azure wall amid a series of white columns; the Empress Elizaveta Petrovna had gazed upon the stretches of the Neva. In Alexander I's day the palace had been repainted yellow; during Alexander II's reign, it was repainted again, this time a ruddy red.
Slowly the rows of walls darkened against a waning lilac sky; sparkling torches burst into flame; and slight flames flared up here and there.

The past was glowing in all this.

A medium-sized plump woman, all in black, was wandering beneath the windows of the yellow house; her trembling hand held a small handbag of obviously foreign make; she suffered from shortness of breath; her fingers now and again touched her chin, which showed gray hairs; with trembling fingers she tried to open her handbag, which refused to yield; finally, she managed to open it and take out a handkerchief: she turned back toward the Neva and burst into tears.

At last regaining control of herself, she hurried to the entrance and rang the bell.

The door was thrown open. The old man in gold braid, having opened the door, thrust his bald head forward and half closed his running eyes in the unbearable glare from beyond the Neva.

The woman was agitated; she seemed overcome with emotion or else with timidity.

"You don't recognize me?"

The lackey's bald head quivered and bent over the lady's handbag, hanging from her arm:

"Oh, little mother, *barinya*! . . . Anna Petrovna!"

"Yes, here I am, Semenich . . ."

"By what good fortune? Where from?"

"From Spain. . . . Well, I've come to see how you manage here without me."

"Come in, my lady. . . . Please!"

The same velvety carpet covered the stairs; the same ornamented ancient weapons shone on the walls; the same Lithuanian cap and the same two-edged sword; under the watchful eye of the mistress, they had been hung here and there; everything sparkled as before: the Lithuanian cap and the cross-hilted sword.

"Only there's no one at home: neither the young *barin* nor . . ."

Above the balustrade, as before, stood the white alabaster pedestal.

"How do you get on without me?"

"So, so, my lady. . . . No change, just as before. . . . Apollon Apollonovich—you've heard about him?"

"Yes, I've heard."

"Yes . . . all the honors. . . . The Tsar has been gracious! . . ."

"And Kolenka?"

"As to Kolenka—Nikolai Apollonovich—he is, how shall I put it, such a knowing young fellow! And handsome, too!"

The walls were lined with high-legged chairs; everywhere between the chairs cold pedestals stuck out, topped by cold masculine alabaster figures; elsewhere were pale-toned paintings—copies of Pompeian frescoes; everywhere there was lacquer and luster; the heart ached as before with the old hostility; oh, yes: in that lacquered house the spirit of misfortune hovered silently and fatally.

"Are you staying with us, my lady?"

"I? . . . No, I'm stopping at a hotel."

In this gray misty light, staring points appeared in the windows: lights, great, small, minute; gathering strength, they grew into large red patches; from above fell night, blue, purple, and black.

4

Bells sounded.

Creatures in blue, white, and rose gowns fanned themselves with chiffons, fans and silks, permeating the air with the aroma of violets, lily-of-the-valley, tuberoses. Their delicate shoulders, generously powdered, would soon perspire; before the dancing began, the little faces, the shoulders and the bare arms, seemed paler and thinner than on ordinary days; white fans were unfolded; and dainty slippers moved restlessly.

Bell after bell sounded.

Strong-chested persons in constricted evening coats, in uniforms, in hussars' jackets—lawyers, hussars, and others of no particular distinction and without beards—continued to arrive; they exuded anticipatory joy and held themselves in restraint; they glanced around at the gauze-enveloped groups; already here and there, a fan, like a female wing, beat at the breast of some personage; a deep-chested hussar dropped flirtatious hints. And against the scarlet of a hussar's uniform the delicate contours of a flushing profile could be seen faintly outlined.

Strictly speaking, the Tzukatovs were not giving a ball: it was ostensibly a children's evening, in which the elders wanted to take part. A rumor circulated that masks would appear; their appearance, indeed, astonished many of the guests. The host, the possessor of a pair of silvery side-whiskers, was familiarly called Koko. In this dancing house he was known as Nikolai Petrovich, the head of the house and the father of two girls: one eighteen, and the other fifteen years old.

Flourishing fluffy fans, these sweet creatures wore net dresses and silver slippers.

The bell rang once more; the door of the brilliantly lighted salon flew open; a pianist entered, compactly attired in a dress suit; he reminded one of a crane. The pianist spread out his sheets of music, gently blew the dust from the keyboard and aimlessly pressed the pedal; at this moment he rather resembled an efficient locomotive machinist testing the boilers. Convinced of the good condition of the instrument, the pianist raised the tails of his evening coat, sat down on a stool, squared his shoulders, and let his fingers slip over the keyboard; for an instant all was still; then a thunderous chord rocked the walls.

Nikolai Petrovich Tzukatov, his bald head shining, his fingers teasing the silver lace of his whiskers, his chin clean-shaven, strutted about pairing off couples, now uttering an innocent joke to some young girl, now thrusting his fingers into the sturdy chest of some mustached man.

The air palpitated with sparks and tremors. The piano thundered. Tzukatov shouted instructions to the couples paired off for dancing.

He had danced all through his life; now he was about to stop dancing. No cloud had ever darkened his soul, always as radiant as his shiny bald head, or as his shaven chin which, between his whiskers, peeped out like the moon from the clouds.

He had spent his life dancing. He had danced as a boy, and danced better than anyone. On finishing high school, he had danced himself into acquaintance; on finishing college, he had danced himself out of this circle of acquaintances and patrons. Nikolai Petrovich had then danced away his existence in the civil service; he had danced away his estate; and danced at balls; with remarkable ease he had brought into his house the traveling companion of his life, Liubov Alexeyevna; she had brought a fine dowry with her; and now Nikolai Petrovich danced at home; his two daughters had also danced themselves out of childhood into young womanhood.

And now he was dancing himself to a finish.

5

During the gay waltz the reception room was a necessary adjunct to the salon: it provided a refuge for the mothers. Liubov Alexeyevna, taking advantage of her husband's good nature and of the fact that their house was profoundly impersonal and neutral, charged her husband with supervising the dances while she herself saw to it that various persons met each other and became acquainted: the provincial official with the city official; the journalists with the director of a department; the demagogue with the Judeophobe.

Apollon Apollonovich sometimes visited this house and even lunched here.

While Nikolai Petrovich was weaving in and out of a contredanse, more than one interesting meeting was taking place in the impersonally affable reception room.

Here people were dancing too—in their own fashion.

A number of visitors had gathered here. There was one man of truly antedeluvian appearance, with a distraught face and an oddly cut evening dress; he was a professor of statistics; from his chin hung a tufted beard and a voluminous mane fell to his shoulders like a piece of felt.

In view of the current political events, something in the nature of a *rapprochement* was being prepared between a group that supported moderate humane reform and the patriots; the *rapprochement* was conditional, the result of a host of meetings. The partisans of gradual humane reforms, greatly shaken and frightened by the effects of their reforms, began to cling to the partisans of existing norms, but they had so far made no effort to meet the latter; the liberal professor had taken the initiative and was the first to step across this threshold. He had appended his signature to the latest protest; and, at the last banquet, he had raised his goblet to the promise of Spring.

The professor had entered the salon where he felt lost: his lip had fallen; confused, he reached for his handkerchief in order to wipe the moisture from his lips; he blinked at the flying pairs of figures dancing a quadrille.

As he entered the reception room in the tremulous light of the pale blue candelabra, a voice made him pause on the threshold:

"My dear lady, don't you see the connection between the Japanese War, the Jews, and the Mongolian invasion? The tricks of the Russian Jews and the emergence of the Boxers in China are closely connected . . ."

"Of course, I understand!"

The professor stood there uncertainly: he was a liberal, an advocate of very humane reforms; this was the first time that he had visited this house in the expectation of meeting Senator Ableukhov, who was nowhere to be seen; instead, there was an editor of a conservative newspaper. The professor of statistics began to breathe heavily, to blink angrily, and to tug at his tufted beard.

At this moment the hostess's double chin had already turned toward the professor and then toward the editor of the conservative newspaper; utilizing her lorgnette, she introduced one to the other. They glared at each other in perplexity and exchanged a handshake.

The professor, distraught, sat down in an armchair; but the editor behaved as if nothing unusual had occurred. . . . Only Ableukhov could rescue him; the professor's eyes sought him in vain.

Again he heard the voice:

"So you understand, my dear lady, the activities of the Jews and the Masons?"

The professor found this too much for him; turning to the hostess, he remarked:

"Allow me, lady, to interpose the modest word of science: such words can have only one source: they come from people who want pogroms!"

In the salon, the pianist with an elegant gesture struck a thunderous bass note. With a facile movement of one hand he turned a page of music; with the other lifted high in the air and his spread fingers poised between the notes and the keyboard, he motioned to the host, at the same time revealing the enamel of his dazzlingly white teeth.

In response to the pianist's gesture, Tzukatov thrust his chin from between his side-whiskers and gave him a sign; then with lowered head he ran forward and placed himself at the head of the dancing pairs, twisting one of his side-whiskers with two fingers. He was followed by an angelic creature who aimlessly flourished a heliotrope scarf. Tzukatov shouted directions in French, and the pairs turned to the corridor, a scene of animation. Here servants were flying back and forth; little tables, benches, and chairs appeared from nowhere and were carried somewhere; a large platter of sandwiches and a stack of fragile plates followed.

Pair after pair filed into the corridor and sat on the chairs.

Little spirals of cigarette smoke rose in the corridor, in the smoking room, and even in the vestibule. From the corridor it was possible to see a corner of the dining room; here the sandwiches, the bottled wines, and the effervescent drinks were being deposited.

The pianist was the last to leave the salon; having wiped his perspiring fingers, and having passed a cloth over the keyboard, he hesitantly turned into the lacquered corridor, assuming once more the shape of a crane; he thought of tea and sandwiches with anticipation.

A woman with a double chin appeared in the doorway. She peered through a lorgnette.

Some distance away the professor of statistics had stumbled upon the provincial official who like himself seemed at a loss; the professor greeted him amiably, and with his two fingers caught a button of his frock coat as if it were a safe haven. Presently were heard the words:

"According to statistical evidence . . . the annual consumption of salt by the normal Dutchman is . . ."

6

The masks were expected. But no masks had yet arrived. Apparently it had been only a rumor.

The doorbell rang tremulously. Some unbidden guest must have suddenly invited himself to this house; here he might take refuge from the fog, from the sleety street. No one answered the bell; he rang again.

A ten-year-old girl ran into the vacant glitter of the salon. There she heard the sound of an opening door; she saw the cut-glass handle turn; through the gap of the doorway a black mask thrust itself forward.

A black beard of wavy lace was followed by a red velvet domino; the little girl smiled with joy, clapped her hands, and cried out: "The masks have come!"—then ran back to the assembled guests where, amid drooping tufts of bluish tobacco smoke, the misty heavy-limbed professor was faintly outlined.

The domino, crossing the threshold, dragged his red velvet flaps across the parquet floor; spots of red, like pools of blood, were reflected from square to square; heavy feet stamped to meet the newcomer.

The provincial official paused, distraught, plucking at the tuft of beard. Apparently trying to be witty, he quacked:

"Mm . . . yes—yes . . ."

The domino advanced upon him, his bright red arm thrust forward:

"Excuse me, sir."

"There's a real prank for you!" the provincial official muttered. He shrugged and abruptly decided to return to the spot where, in the bluish electric light, the professor of statistics was still standing immobile amid the spirals of tobacco smoke; he almost knocked down a swarm of scurrying young women who waved their ribbons and cotillion favors.

These young women had come running to see the newly arrived "mask"; the red domino had paused in the doorway; the cheerful outcries had become a confused murmur which eventually died down; a silence succeeded.

Someone asked:

"Tell us, domino: was it you who were roaming about the streets?"

Someone else asked:

"Gentlemen, have you read today's *Petersburg Diary*?"

"Well, what about it?"

"It mentioned the domino again."

"That's all rubbish!"

"No—by no means!"

Then one of the young women, after peering sharply at the un-expected visitor, whispered something to her friend. The other replied:

"That's sheer nonsense!"

"No—not at all!"

"Here's something for you!"

The last exclamation came from a young cadet who sent a rus-tling stream of confetti flying to the domino above the heads of the young women. A colored paper streamer came hurtling at the same moment and, cutting a curve, fell to the floor. The domino did not respond; he merely stretched out his arms.

"Let's go, girls!" someone said.

They all turned to leave.

Only one young woman, who had been standing closer to the domino than the others, lingered for an instant; she scrutinized him from head to foot, unaccountably sighed, and then walked away; but she turned to look at him again.

7

In a fog, Nikolai Apollonovich noticed the provincial official; in a labyrinth of mirrors the figures of laughing young women floated before him; and when he was assaulted from this labyrinth by re-mote questions, accompanied by a handful of confetti, he wondered as in a dream . . . about the relation of appearance to reality; he himself tended to regard all things as mere reflection; and they, for their part, accepted him as an apparition from another sphere: now he had banished them.

Then the remote echoes of events reached him again; he turned his head: dimly, phantasmally—somewhere there, somewhere there —he perceived a small figure cross the salon: a meager little man, without hair, mustache, or eyebrows. Nikolai Apollonovich felt a strain from having to squint through the slits of his mask, and besides he was nearsighted. Somewhere in front, he had seen the contours of a pair of greenish ears. Something familiar, singularly intimate, had crossed his line of vision and, in order to see it better, he strained toward the tiny figure. As it fixed its gaze on him, the tiny figure recoiled as soon as their glance met, and it even seemed to clutch at its heart: Nikolai Apollonovich saw before him a face of his own blood, a veritable network of wrinkles from forehead to chin; he was staring directly at his father. Apollon Apollonovich, fingering the links of a fine watch chain, fixed his alarmed gaze on the approaching domino; and he seemed to have guessed something. Nikolai Apollonovich experienced unpleasant sensations: he found it painful, even through the slits of the mask, to look into those staring eyes which even normally forced him to lower his own. He also found it painful to observe fear and helplessness in those eyes; Nikolai Apollonovich fancied that he had been recognized. But this was not so: Apollon Apollonovich had merely concluded that some tactless joker was attempting to terrorize him with the red symbol.

He began to count his pulse. More than once Nikolai Apollonovich had observed this gesture of his father's, which was usually furtive—evidently the Senator's heart slowed down at times. Seeing this gesture now, the son felt something like compassion. But Apollon Apollonovich hurried away despite his heart condition.

Suddenly the doorbell rang: the room was soon filled with masks; black Capuchin monks, holding hands, formed a circle around the red domino and began a wild dance; the hems of their cassocks swept the floor, the pointed ends of their cowls bobbed up and down; their Capuchin robes bore the emblem of a skull and crossbones.

The red domino tried to fight his way out of the ring; the Capuchins pursued him; they ran down the corridor and into the dining room. The company at the table welcomed them by tapping their plates.

"Capuchins! Masks! A buffoon!"

The young women jumped from their places, as did the hussars and the lawyers. Tzukatov, with a goblet of Rhine wine in his hands, was shouting a toast when someone remarked:

"Gentlemen, this is too much . . ."

The speaker was dragged off to dance.

The pianist in the salon straightened his spine and made his long hair shake in response to the trills which his fingers executed on the keyboard; his opening treble slowly deepened into bass.

Gazing at her black Capuchin, a girl in violet fixed her eyes on her partner's eye-slits, lifted her train, revealing a tiny silver slipper, and glided into the dance.

They were soon followed by women in Spanish costume, the Capuchins, and a band of devils; fans, bare backs, and scarves filled the room.

8

Everything was running away and becoming blurred: the walls and floor seemed to recede; out of a fountain of objects, out of the froth of muslin and lace—there—there—a beauty with fluffy hair and a beauty spot on one cheek came forward: a real Madame Pompadour!

The hair in ringlets was gray; her slender little fingers clutched a powder puff poised above a powder box; with a black mask in one hand and her pale blue waist tightly laced, the figure leaned forward; the décolleté revealed her heaving breasts; the narrow cuffs of her sleeves were lost in waves of Valenciennes lace; waves of lace surrounded her deep neckline and fell below it; her *pannier* skirt, wafted, as it were, by zephyrs' breath, was garlanded with a kind of silvery grass; silvery pompoms decorated her slippers. In this costume, she lost, oddly enough, some of her prettiness; her rather sensual lips looked coarse; her eyes squinted; she now had a witch-like air about her.

Mavrushka had handed her a radiant wand with a gold handle and fluttering ribbons. As Pompadour was about to grasp it, she discovered a note in her hand: "If you leave the house tonight, you will never enter my house again. *Likhutin*."

Madame Pompadour merely smiled, staring into the greenish depths of the mirror: there in the depths she saw a waxen face emerge; she turned around.

Behind her stood an officer: her husband. She burst out laughing

and, slightly raising her skirt by the bows, glided smoothly away
from him with a series of curtseys; her crinoline swung and rustled;
and when she reached the doorway, she smilingly thumbed her nose
at her officer husband with the hand from which dangled the velvet
mask; then with a peal of laughter she called out:

"Mavrushka, my fur coat, please!"

Then Lieutenant Likhutin, her husband, outwardly calm and smiling into her mask, clinked his spurs; and with dignity held her fur
coat for her, and with even greater dignity wrapped her coat over
her shoulders; then he opened the door wide and with a polite gesture ushered her into the darkness; when she passed, rustling, into
the darkness, her humble servitor again clinked his spurs together.
The darkness absorbed her and the front door slammed.

Sergey Sergeyevich Likhutin, with the same brusque gestures,
walked through all the rooms of his apartment extinguishing the
electric lights.

9

The pianist, with an elegant thundering gesture, struck the bass
of the keyboard; with the other hand he nimbly turned a page of
music. Nikolai Petrovich Tzukatov unexpectedly thrust his clean-
shaven chin from between his whiskers and commanded: "*Pas de
quatre, s'il vous plaît!*"

Nikolai Apollonovich, failing to recognize Madame Pompadour,
gave her his hand. Glancing at her red cavalier from under her
mask, Madame Pompadour gave him a limp hand; with the other,
which held her waving fan, she lifted her azure train and revealed a
slipper.

And they glided, glided into the dance.

"Don't you recognize me?"

"No."

"I have a letter."

The first pair—the domino and the marquise—was followed by
other pairs: harlequins, women in Spanish costumes, creatures in
muslin: fans, silvery backs, and scarves.

One arm of the red domino encircled the azure waist; the other
hand, seizing his partner's, groped for the letter. The dark green,

the black, and the clothed arms of all the pairs, as well as the red arms of the hussars, seized the slender waists of their heliotrope, pearly, rustling dancing partners.

Apollon Apollonovich was concealing the symptoms of an imminent heart attack. This evening's attack had been provoked by the sight of the red domino: red was indeed the emblem of the chaos threatening Russia.

Apollon Apollonovich was ashamed to show fear.

As he recovered from his attack, he glanced continually toward the ballroom. The images that flashed by there nauseated him. He saw a monster capped as a double-headed eagle; the dry figure of a little knight with a bright sword in the semblance of a ray of light was cutting across: the figure ran on, vague and dull, bald, without mustache, with prominently outlined ears and a diamond order on his chest. Out of the crowd of masks and Capuchins a single-horned creature rushed upon the little knight and broke his ray of light: in the distance something tinkled and fell like a beam. This picture made Apollon Apollonovich conscious of a previous event, and he immediately grew aware of his spine, thinking he had *tabes dorsalis*; he turned away from the ballroom towards the drawing room.

At his entry everyone rose; the professor of statistics pounced on him:

"What good fortune to meet you! I'm indeed glad to see you. I have something to discuss with you, Apollon Apollonovich."

To which Apollon Apollonovich replied drily:

"But you must know that my reception hours in the Department are from one to two."

This answer barred all approach to the Government. . . . All possibility of mediation was destroyed; the professor had no alternative but to abandon this house and resume his toasts at banquets without further restraint.

The editor of the conservative newspaper orated:

"You think that the ruin of Russia is being planned when social equality is advocated. Think what you like! They intend to make of us a sacrifice to Satan."

"How, please?" the hostess asked.

"If you're astonished, it's only because you haven't kept track of things."

"Allow me to say," the professor put in, "that you're relying too much on the fabrications of Taxil . . ."

"Taxil?" the hostess interrupted, reaching for a notebook in which she promptly jotted down the name:

"Taxil?"

"They're preparing to sacrifice us," the editor insisted. "The higher degrees of Freemasons profess palladism. This cult . . ."

"Palladism?" the hostess again interrupted, and once more began to take notes.

"Pa-lla. . . . How did you say it?"

At this moment decanters of cool cranberry juice were brought in on a tray: they were placed in a room joining the drawing room and the ballroom. Disengaging herself from a partner, a girl with flushed cheeks would now and then come running and, impatiently stamping her little feet, hurriedly pour herself a glass of the rather sour liquid from a decanter and gulp it down. Or her cavalier would snatch the glass from her hand and finish the remainder. Each happy pair would then hurry back to the seething salon where the white-gloved cavalier would return his arm to his partner's waist and they would glide into the dance again.

"Taxil fabricated a humiliating expose against the Masons—and it was believed. Later Taxil admitted its falsity: his declaration to the Pope was sheer mockery directed against the obscurantism of the Vatican; and for this he was excommunicated."

A fussy little man with a huge wart near his nose entered; rubbing his hands, he smiled at the Senator, and took him aside:

"You see . . . Apollon Apollonovich . . . the Director of the N. N. Department is proposing to confront you with a ticklish question."

The little man's whispers in the Senator's pale ear, and Apollon Apollonovich's rather apprehensive questions, were generally audible:

"Speak plainly . . ."

"Precisely. The question must be obvious to you."

"So it's my son?"

"It's a pity the jest has assumed an unpleasant character, that the press . . ."

"But, as you know, the Petersburg police were instructed to . . ."

"To be sure, but only for his benefit."

"You say it's the domino?" the Senator asked.

"The very same."

The fussy little man suddenly indicated the neighboring room, where the stooping domino in impetuous strides was dragging his satin cape over the parquet floor.

10

Passing through the ballroom, the domino reached a corner of the room; he tore open the envelope; a note rustled in his nervous hands. To see better, the domino pushed his mask over his forehead: the lace of the beard in two fluttering flaps winged his face. His hands trembled and the note in his hand trembled; sweat showed on his forehead.

The domino no longer saw Madame Pompadour, who was observing him from another corner; all his attention was concentrated on the note. The velvet flaps of his domino had parted, revealing the customary costume beneath—a dark green frock coat; Nikolai Apollonovich drew a pair of gold-rimmed pince-nez from his pocket and, putting them on his nose, bent over the note.

Suddenly he recoiled; his terrified gaze was directed at Sofya Petrovna, though he actually did not see her; Sofya Petrovna, unable to endure this gaze, wanted to flee. At this moment several persons entered the room, and the domino nervously hid the note between his fingers; but he had forgotten to lower his mask and stood there with half-open mouth, staring blankly.

A girl ran into the room and paused before the pier-glass. Placing a small foot on a chair, she began to lace her slipper.

Suddenly she noticed the domino and exclaimed:

"So it's you? How do you do, Nikolai Apollonovich? Who could have known it was you?"

Nikolai Apollonovich quickly ran away—into the ballroom.

Two rows of female dancers stood there, shimmering with rose, pearl, heliotrope, blue, and white silks; shawls, scarves, veils' adorned the shoulders.

Two rows of male dancers also stood there, in black and green suits, the hussars in red with gold collars and shoulder straps.

Impetuously, Nikolai Apollonovich rushed past them, trailing the blood-red velvet after him across the lacquered squares.

The flight of the red domino with raised mask and uncovered face created an immediate scandal. People left their places; there was hysteria; the other masks also removed their disguises in fear. Recognizing the fleeing Ableukhov, Shporishev caught him by the sleeve:

"Nikolai Apollonovich, for heaven's sake, what is the matter?"

But Nikolai Apollonovich merely grinned, trying to force a smile which came to nothing; very soon the doors shut behind him.

The young women began to exchange impressions; all at once, the knights, the harlequins, the Spanish women, having furtively removed their masks, lost all significance; the two-headed monster ran up to Shporishev and said to him:

"What's the meaning of it all?"

Shporishev recognized the voice: it was Verhefden's!

The consternation that prevailed in the ballroom was soon communicated to the drawing room: in the pale blue tremulous light the guests looked distraught, their contours mistily outlined in the tufts of bluish tobacco smoke; in their midst the Senator's meager little figure was vaguely outlined with compressed lips, sideburns, and sharply defined ears: he had been portrayed in this way in that sensational periodical he loathed so deeply.

In the ballroom guesses were made about the singular behavior of the Senator's son; it was conjectured by some that it had been conditioned by mysterious and dramatic circumstances, and the rumor spread that Nikolai Apollonovich was *the domino* that had caused such a sensation in the press.

11

Sofya Petrovna Likhutina paused, like a lost soul, in the middle of the ballroom.

She had a sudden vision of the consequences of her terrible vengeance. The letter was now in his hands; she hardly comprehended what she had done, for she had failed to grasp the full import of the note. But now for the first time its meaning became clear: the note had invited Nikolai Apollonovich to throw a bomb which, it seems, was already in his desk; it had been suggested that he throw this bomb at . . .

Sofya Petrovna stood among the masks, wondering what it all meant. It must be some cruel, scurvy jest, of course; apparently they intended to frighten him; for he was . . . a coward. But suppose . . . the letter meant what it said? Suppose. . . . Did Nikolai Apollonovich actually have a bomb in his desk? And suppose someone had heard of it? Would he be arrested? . . .

Then she impulsively turned about; the Valenciennes lace fluttered and her skirt flashed its festooned garland. A group of gray-haired matrons was ready to leave the gay ball; here was one stretching her neck and calling her daughter; there, another adjusting a miniature lorgnette to her eyes, was distractedly looking for someone; the perturbing atmosphere of a scandal hung in the air. Whispers were audible.

"Did you see? Do you understand it?"

"Don't speak of it! It's terrible."

"I always said, *ma chère*, that he'd brought up a scoundrel. Tante Lise said the same thing. Nicolas, too."

"Poor Anna Petrovna! I'm beginning to understand her now."

"There he is, himself!"

"What terrible ears!"

"He's destined for the Ministry."

"He'll ruin the country."

"He should be told."

"The Tzukatovs are playing up to him—it's simply sickening to watch!"

"They'll never dare to say why we're leaving . . . Madame Tzukatova descends from a line of priests."

But suppose . . . Nikolai Apollonovich did actually have a bomb in his desk? What if he accidentally dropped it—he was so *distrait*. Perhaps in the evening he sat reading at the desk? Sofya Petrovna clearly pictured that sclerotic, blue-veined forehead bent over the desk—and in the desk was the bomb too! A bomb was something one must not touch. And Sofya Petrovna shuddered.

Suddenly, a portly man in the costume of a Grenada Spaniard approached her; she tried to escape him, but he followed her wherever she went:

"You're no *barinya*—you're just a darling!" he said.

"Lippanchenko!" She gestured with her fan. "Lippanchenko! Please explain to me . . ."

"Don't play the ingenue!" Lippanchenko interrupted her.

"Lippanchenko!"

"I want you to know that I saw you handing that letter to Nikolai Apollonovich," he said, laughing smugly.

"Come, let us go out into this marvelous night . . ." he urged. She tore herself away from him.

Clicking his castanets, he went in pursuit of her.

But suppose . . . it was no jest; suppose. . . . But no, no! Such horrors cannot be perpetrated on this earth—no such wild beasts could force a witless son to. . . . It *must* be a practical joke. It was so stupid—she did not enjoy such jokes even when played by friends. As for him—such jokes frightened him too; he was a coward, to be sure—she remembered him running away at the Little Canal . . .

No, he hadn't conducted himself like Herman: he had slipped and fallen, showing his underwear. And now a naïve joke by his revolutionary friends had frightened him out of his wits. Nikolai Apollonovich had apparently not recognized her when she had passed him the letter; he had run the length of the ballroom, the object of derision. Let Sergey Sergeyevich Likhutin now teach the fool a lesson! Her husband must challenge him to a duel.

Sergey Sergeyevich Likhutin! . . . Since the previous evening his conduct had been indecorous; he had snorted and clenched his fist; he had attempted to see her in her bedroom in his underwear; he had dared to pace heavily next door until dawn.

The events of that evening were now confused in her mind: his witless outcries, his bloodshot eyes, his clenched fist! Had he really gone out of his mind? He had been acting suspiciously for some time; there was his silence which had lasted three entire months; there was his suspicious daily flight to his work; she now felt herself wretched and abandoned: she longed for her husband to embrace her, lift her up in his arms, like an infant, and carry her away . . .

Instead, here was this nasty Spaniard bothering her again:

"Well, well? Won't you come with me?"

Where was Sergey Sergeyevich? She was now afraid to return to the Moika flat where her husband would be lying in wait for her like a wild beast.

She stamped her feet.

"I'll show him!"

And again: "I'll teach him!"

Sofya Petrovna shuddered when she recalled the grimace with which he had handed her cape to her. What an attitude he had taken! How she had laughed when, lightly lifting her *pannier* skirt by its festoons, she glided away from him with many curtseys! Why hadn't she thought of a curtsey when she was transmitting the letter to Nikolai Apollonovich? Curtseys became her. But she was afraid to return home.

But here it was even more terrible; nearly everyone had left, that is, all the young people and the masks; the host was still telling anecdotes; but without the harlequins the ballroom looked empty. Sofya Petrovna passed from room to room. Suddenly she spied a white domino which appeared from nowhere—

—someone tall and sad, someone she seemed to have met a multitude of times, all wrapped in white satin, who had come to meet her in the emptying salon; the brightness of his eyes flashed from the slits of his mask, radiated from his whole body, from his stiffening fingers.

Trustfully, Sofya Petrovna greeted the charming domino:

"Sergey Sergeyevich!"

There could be no doubt: he had repented of his behavior; he had come to escort her home.

"Surely it is you?"

The tall sad man slowly shook his head and commanded her to be silent.

Trustfully, she took the white domino's hand: how cool the satin!

Her hand rustled in contact with the white arm; already she hung on it helplessly; his arm seemed stiff; a tuft of beard, like a small bundle of wheat ears, showed under the white lace.

"Have you forgiven me?" she asked.

She was answered by a sigh from the mask.

"Why are you silent?"

The tall sad man made no reply.

They were already in the vestibule: inexpressible feelings surrounded them; inexpressible feelings were all about them. She took off her black mask and plunged her face into her muff; the tall sad man donned his greatcoat, but did not remove his mask. Then Sofya Petrovna stared in consternation at her tall escort: she was astonished that he had not been handed an officer's greatcoat, but merely a thin, worn overcoat from the sleeves of which his hands, like lilies, so strangely protruded. She drew nearer to him to escape the scrutiny of the servants who were watching the scene. Inexpressible feelings were all about them.

But, as they stood on the lighted threshold, the tall sad man slowly shook his head and bade her be silent.

The sky hung low and the air was thick with damp mist through which glimmered the reddish patches of street lamps; above one of these patches, over the entrance to an official building, hung a caryatid; it seemed about to fall. A section of a small neighboring house in the shape of a bay window and some wooden sculptures jutted forward; the presence of her mysterious companion loomed above Sofya Petrovna.

"Cab!" he called, waving his arm in the fog.

Then she understood everything: the melancholy figure had a caressing voice—

⸱ —a voice she had heard a multitude of times (not so long ago, indeed that very day): in a dream, and she had forgotten about it! . . .

The voice was beautiful and caressing, and there could no longer be any doubt: it was not the voice of Sergey Sergeyevich. Yet she ardently desired that this excellent stranger might be her husband. Her husband had failed to come and take her home.

But who could this be?

The mysterious presence raised his voice: it grew stronger and stronger; and beneath the mask there seemed to be Someone Immeasurably Vast. Silence beat against the voice; a dog barked. The street flowed away.

"Who are you?"

"You all reject me: I watch over you all. You deny me and then you summon me . . ."

For an instant Sofya Petrovna understood who was confronting her: sobs contracted her throat; she wanted to fall at the slender feet of the unknown, to wind her arms round his slender knees, but just then a droshky came rolling up, and the driver leaned forward in the light of the street lamp; the presence helped her into the droshky; when she imploringly held out her quivering arms, the presence bade her be silent.

The droshky had already moved off: if only it would stop and turn back to the radiant spot where He had stood an instant before and where He no longer was.

12

Sofya Petrovna Likhutina had forgotten the past; the future was drowned in the black night; the irremediable crept over her; the irretrievable embraced her; her home, her flat, and her husband had all left her; and she no longer knew where she was going; behind her, a fragment of the recent past had just broken off: the masquerade, the harlequins, and even the tall sad presence; she did not know where she had come from.

The entire day was breaking off behind her; her wranglings with Madame Farnua over the Maison Tricotons moved farther away in search of support for the consciousness; the impressions of yesterday—but the whole day had fallen apart like the stones of a broken pavement; thundering, the day had fallen into a dark abyss. There was the sound of a blow, shattering stone.

The love of that fatal, unhappy summer flashed through her mind, and fell away from her memory; there was the sound of another blow, shattering stone; flashing, the stones fell: the conversations she had in the spring with Nikolai Ableukhov, the years of her married life, her wedding: some void was tearing them from her, swallowing them piece by piece. And the metallic stone-shattering blows continued. Her whole life flashed past and fell apart; she might never have lived, never been born. The void began immediately behind her, everything there had fallen apart; and this void stretched into the ages; there she heard nothing but thud on thud: the fragments of many lives all falling away; the ringing hoof beats of a metal steed pounded on stone: behind her, it was trampling on the fragments; there, behind her, the metal Horseman was pursuing her.

She turned and beheld a spectacle: the Mighty Horseman. . . . There!—two flaming nostrils had lighted the gloom with their streaks of fire.

Sofya Petrovna recovered: overtaking her droshky, an officer sped by with a torch held aloft in the fog. A heavy brass helmet gleamed and, in the officer's wake, a fire-engine roared past, thundering and flaring.

"What's going on? A fire?" she asked, turning to the cabby.

"They say the islands are on fire," the driver reported out of the fog. Then the droshky stopped at the Moika.

Everything now seemed terrifyingly banal to her, as if there had never been masks dancing or the Horseman. The masks were mere wags in retrospect, and the tall sad presence just an obliging man. Sofya Petrovna bit her lip in vexation: how could she have so muddled her relations with her husband and whispered admissions of false guilt in strange ears? And now the gossips would spread their versions . . .

Indignantly she pushed open the front door; indignantly the door banged behind her. Darkness enveloped her and, for an instant, the inexpressible too; but she was thinking of how she would order Mavrushka to set a samovar and how, while it was heating, she would lecture her husband; then, when Mavrushka had brought in the samovar, she would attempt reconciliation.

Sofya Petrovna rang the doorbell; the bell resounded through the nocturnal apartment; she would soon hear Mavrushka's hurried step. But no step was heard. Sofya Petrovna felt slighted, and rang again..

Her husband, who was waiting impatiently, she thought, would conclude that the maid had fallen asleep, and would then himself open the door. But nothing happened. What did it mean?

Sofya Petrovna continued to ring the bell; she could hear its clamor inside. . . . No one! She put an ear to the keyhole; she thought she could detect someone breathing stertorously behind the door. Lord Jesus Christ! Who could be breathing like that?

Mavrushka? No, not Mavrushka. . . . Her husband? Yes, it was he. But why didn't he answer or open the door then?

With a presentiment of evil Sofya Petrovna began pounding desperately: "Open the door!"

But the stertorous breathing continued—it was terrifying.

"Sergey Sergeyevich! Enough of this, please!"

There was silence.

"What's the matter with you? Please!"

Something moved behind the door.

"What's that, please? Oh, Lord, I'm afraid, I'm afraid . . ."

There was a loud wailing cry as someone ran from the door: feet shuffled, chairs were moved. The lamp clicked and a table was pushed noisily. Then silence.

Presently, there was a terrifying crash; it sounded as if the ceiling had collapsed and the plaster were falling; one sound, above all, impressed Sofya Petrovna: that of a heavy human body falling from a height.

13

Apollon Apollonovich Ableukhov, in a manner of speaking, could not stomach any needless excursions from the house; there was his obviously calculated visit to a Cabinet Minister with a report which the Director of the Ministry of Justice had brought to his attention.

Apollon Apollonovich could not stomach needless face-to-face conversations. There were telephone connections from his desk to all departments. Apollon Apollonovich listened to the hum of telephone wires with pleasure.

Once, when answering a question from some department, the speaker at the other end had hit the mouthpiece of the receiver with the palm of his hand: Apollon Apollonovich felt as if he had received a blow on the cheek.

Every verbal exchange had a clear and direct goal, straight as a line. He saw everything in the light of tea parties and cigarette smoking: he had a notion that Russians were essentially drunkards and nicotine fiends—on the score of the latter, he had proposed an increase in the tax on tobacco; Russians, he thought, always flaunted a red nose; but he, Apollon Apollonovich, like a bull, resented everything red.

He himself had a tiny gray nose and a slender waist, the waist of a sixteen-year-old girl; he was rather proud of this.

Apollon Apollonovich had gone to the Tzukatov ball with but one aim in view: that of striking a blow against the department which was flirting with the moderate party, which was suspected of wishing to institute some slight reforms rather than to undermine public order. Apollon Apollonovich loathed compromise.

Apollon Apollonovich did not consider it a pleasure to be obliged to sit at the Tzukatovs and to watch the convulsions of dancing feet and the blood-red folds of absurd costumes; he had seen the same red rags elsewhere: in the public square, before the Kazan Cathedral; there the red rags had been called flags.

The red rags at the Tzukatov soirée had struck him as an unfitting jest in the presence of the head of a department; as for the convulsions of dancing feet, they merely made him think of dancing as a melancholy measure that helped the prevention of crime.

Apollon Apollonovich thought irritably: allow these apparently innocent dances to continue and they eventually will spread to the streets.

He himself had danced in his youth: the polka-mazurka and the lancers.

One circumstance had induced this melancholy mood in him: the absurd domino had provoked an attack of angina. Was it an attack of angina? He still had some doubts. That grimacing domino had crossed his path in the salon.

Apollon Apollonovich tried to recall where he had seen those grimaces before, but he could not remember.

Apollon Apollonovich sat through it all, erect as a yardstick; a porcelain cup was held in one hand, while his legs with their thin calves descended in a perpendicular line to the rug; the lower part of his legs described, in relation to the upper part, a ninety-degree rectangle; he might have been an Egyptian figure such as was depicted on that rug.

Apollon Apollonovich was expounding the system of prohibitions to the professor of statistical data, leader of the moderate party, and the editor of the conservative newspaper who came from a family of liberal priests.

He found it difficult to do anything with either of them: they both had portly stomachs, and both of course had red noses, a sure sign of heavy drinking. One was a priest's son; and Apollon Apollonovich had an understandable weakness: he simply could not bear the sight of a priest's son. Whenever, in the course of duty, he was obliged to discuss any matter with a priest, he was always keenly aware of how badly his feet smelled.

Suddenly Apollon Apollonovich felt uncomfortable, sandwiched between the frock coat of the priest's son and that of the moderate traitor; his agitation was increased by the shock to his eardrums: the pianist had let his fingers drop on the keyboard, and the musical chords had fallen on his ears like a scraping of glass.

Apollon Apollonovich now became convinced that the convulsive feet were a criminal trait: that of the young dancers; and then his attention again focused on the domino. He labored to recall where he had seen him before; he could not remember. But when a scurvy little man obsequiously ran up to him, Apollon Apollonovich suddenly became extremely animated.

The contemptible little man was a key figure in that transitional period of which Apollon Apollonovich disapproved in principle; but . . . what could he do? If such a figure did exist, he had to come to terms with it. The nice thing about the distasteful man was that, knowing his own value, he did not, like the professor, indulge in phrase-making; nor, like the editor, did he pound the table outrageously with his fist; he served the department without superfluous words. Apollon Apollonovich valued this vile person, because for one thing he did not claim equality with his masters; in short, he was an unabashed lackey. Apollon Apollonovich was always on terms of excellent courtesy with lackeys.

Apollon Apollonovich plunged into conversation with the unpleasant little man.

But what he was now called upon to hear dumfounded him: the

blood-red domino, of whom he had just been thinking, was none
other than. . . . No (here Apollon Apollonovich grimaced as if he
had just seen someone cut a lemon)! It was simply incredible: the
domino was his own son!

His own son? Perhaps he was Anna Petrovna's son more than
his by virtue of a chance predominance of the maternal blood; and
in that maternal blood, according to the records, there was a priestly
taint—Apollon Apollonovich had made these genealogical investiga-
tions after his wife's flight. Priest-blood had contaminated the
Ableukhov stock by contributing this nasty son; never had there
been anything like this mongrel in all the generations of the Ableukhov family.

What dumfounded the Senator above all was that the Jewish
press was already making the most of his son's disgusting behavior;
Apollon Apollonovich even regretted that he had not followed the
events recorded in the *Diary of Events.*

Apollon Apollonovich rose and would have fled to the next room,
but a young high school boy came running to him; Apollon Apollonovich was on the point of extending his hand to him, when on
closer inspection the boy turned out to be someone he did not know.
. . . Apollon Apollonovich, having mistaken the direction of the
room, almost ran into a mirror in his confusion.

With excessive nervousness Apollon Apollonovich went to the
card tables; he managed to retain an outward semblance of calm
and courtesy and a polite curiosity about a number of things: the
statistician told him something about the Ploshegorsk Government;
and the provincial official informed him of the need for pepper in
Newfoundland.

A fresh outburst of whispers and giggles suddenly reached him;
the convulsion of dancing feet suddenly ceased: for an instant his
spirit was calm. Presently, however, his mind saw things with terrifying clarity; the fatal presentiment was confirmed: his son was a
scoundrel: he had worn a domino and a mask, and had given the
Jewish press material for their vile articles!

He, Apollon Apollonovich, would now lose his post: how could he
preserve his position without washing away the ignominious, vicious
stain of his worthless son?

Apollon Apollonovich proffered his finger to everyone and hurriedly fled from the drawing room, escorted by his hosts; as he sped through the ballroom, he noticed a group of gray-haired matrons standing and whispering, and a word reached his ear:

"A chick!"

Apollon Apollonovich could not bear the sight of headless chicks exposed for sale in poultry shops.

14

Nikolai Apollonovich had left the Tzukatov house a quarter of an hour before the Senator; but he was in a state of exhaustion and remained standing in front of the entrance. As if in a somber trance, he stood in the icy street, automatically counting the number of waiting carriages and following with his eyes the movements of a tall sad-looking man who looked after the order of things.

Suddenly the tall sad-looking man walked past him: he was the police inspector, and he wagged his flaxen beard angrily at the student in the greatcoat.

In a trance, Nikolai Apollonovich saw the reddish stain of the street lamp in the mist and a projecting fragment of the tiny neighboring house; the house was black, one-storied, and adorned with wooden sculptures.

Scarcely had Nikolai Apollonovich stirred from the spot when he noticed the spatter from a puddle; there below him were something resembling feet, but he was not conscious of them (he felt he had no feet); that was why he seated himself on the lowest projection of the tiny black house.

He could not have done anything else; he opened his greatcoat, revealing the red domino; he thrust his hand into one pocket, then another, and finally drew out a small rumpled envelope; he read the note again, trying to discover in it some trace of jest or mockery:

"*Remembering the summer proposal, we make haste, comrade, to inform you that you are being intrusted to carry out the task . . .*"

—Nikolai Apollonovich skipped a line because his father's name was mentioned. Then he read on: "*The material necessary for the act has already been delivered to you in the form of a bundle; it is desirable that the task be carried out in the very near future . . .*"

Farther—there was a slogan: this and the handwriting were both familiar to him: the note had been written by the Unknown.

He could not doubt its meaning.

Nikolai Apollonovich's arms and legs felt paralyzed; he had lost his will power.

He tried to think idle thoughts: of the number of books he had on a certain shelf, of the embroidery patterns on the flounces of a skirt of a woman he had once loved—that this was Sofya Petrovna did not occur to him.

Then he tried not to think at all: how could one understand such a thing? It actually had happened; it crushed him, it was incredible; if he were to begin thinking about it, he would have only one alternative: to cut his throat . . .

In his soul something wailed piteously, like a bullock under the knife. He tried to snatch at surface things; he stared at the caryatid. . . . But no! He had never seen anything like it: it hung over a flame. And there was the tiny black house.

No!

There was nothing normal about that little house; there was nothing normal about anything: everything within him was in a turmoil, was rent apart; he was torn from himself.

There were his feet. . . . No, no! They were not feet, but soft fleshy parts dangling aimlessly.

The entrance of the house where he had recently acted so stupidly was now intermittently pouring out guests; carriages rolled away, their lights flashing in the fog. With an effort Nikolai Apollonovich stirred from the projection on which he was sitting and wandered into a neighboring lane.

The lane was desolate, like his soul. For a minute he tried to convince himself that the events of the transitory world had no effect upon the mind, and that the thinking brain was merely a phenomenon of consciousness; the authentic contemplative spirit was capable of lighting the way for him: even in the face of this. . . . Yet all around him was this fated *this*: it erected fences around him; at his feet he noticed a chink in a gate and a puddle.

But no light came from anywhere.

His consciousness strove vainly to light his way, but no light came forth: the darkness was terrifying! Glancing around him, he crept up to the patch thrown by the street lamp: under the patch he could hear the water running into the gutter; the water carried an orange rind.

Again Nikolai Apollonovich glanced at the note:

"*Remembering the summer proposal . . .*" A proposal had been made to him; he had forgotten it: he had remembered it only once; then there had been the surging episode of the domino; he cast his glance over the recent past: there had been a woman too: yes, a woman.

Now his consciousness had no center: he could only see the gap under the gate; and there was the same empty gap in the soul; as he stood there staring at the gap under the gate, Nikolai Apollonovich lapsed into thought. Where and when had he stood like this before? Then he remembered: thus he had stood in the gusty Neva wind when he had leaned over the parapet of the bridge and stared at the bacilli-infected water. Everything had happened before! A multitude of times!

"*We make haste to inform you that . . .*" Nikolai Apollonovich read; then he turned his head: he heard footsteps approaching behind him; an incomprehensible shadow loomed in the gusty lane. Glancing over his shoulder, he made out: a bowler hat, a cane, a greatcoat, a wart, and a nose.

Passers-by paid no attention to him: he heard only their steps and the pounding of his heart. Nikolai Apollonovich turned his head and peered through the dirty fog: he could still hear the violent thud of steps; he stood a long time, his head bowed (everything had happened before!), and his mouth open; he presented an absurd enough appearance: an armless figure (he still wore his cape) with the flaps of his greatcoat dancing in the wind like a pair of wings . . .

"*The material necessary for the act has already been delivered to you in the form of a bundle containing a bomb . . .*" Nikolai Apollonovich snatched at this phrase: no such bundle had been conveyed to him! All this was a jest. . . . Did he have a bomb?

In the form of a bundle?

Then he suddenly remembered: the bundle, the suspicious visitor,

the day in September, and all the rest of it; he had accepted a
bundle, and the bundle had been wet.

An unutterable terror seized him: he felt cramps in his stomach:
the darkness enveloped him. His "I" was merely a dark receptacle,
at best a crowded storeroom; and here in the dark where his heart
was, there was nothing but a shell that went on swelling and assuming the form of a red sphere; the sphere continued to expand until
it burst: everything burst. . . . The scurvy little man with the wart
near his nose paused two paces from him to perform a natural
function in front of the old fence. He turned his face toward
Ableukhov:

"From the ball, I take it?"

"Yes, from the ball. . . . To be sure: to go to a ball is no crime."

"I know that . . ."

"Well?"

"I can see a piece of a domino under your greatcoat."

"What of that?"

"It was seen yesterday, too."

"How?"

"At the Summer Canal . . ."

"Well, sir?"

"In short, you are *the* domino."

"What domino?"

"Yes—the very same."

"I don't understand you, sir—walking up to a stranger and . . ."

"You're by no means a stranger. You are Nikolai Apollonovich.
And you are the *Red Domino*, about whom they're writing in the
papers."

The dreadful little man showed no signs of abating:

"I know your father: I've just had a chat with him."

"You surely don't believe in all those nasty rumors?" Nikolai
Apollonovich asked in great agitation.

Having attended to his need, the little man buttoned his coat
and winked familiarly:

"Which way are you going?"

"To the Vasilyevsky Island," Nikolai Apollonovich growled un-
truthfully.

"I too am going that way."

"I mean—to the Embankment . . ."

"It seems you don't know where you're going. In that case, we'd better stop at a restaurant."

15

Apollon Apollonovich Ableukhov, in his gray greatcoat and tall black cylinder hat, fled in fear to the main door.

Someone shouted his name; the black shape of a carriage moved forward into the range of the street light, exposing the coat of arms: a unicorn goring a knight. Apollon Apollonovich was about to jump into his carriage and speed through the fog when the main door was once more flung open and the scurvy little man, the purveyor of truth, appeared and fled down the street to the left.

Apollon Apollonovich changed his mind; touching the edge of his cylinder hat with his glove, he ordered the driver to return home without him. The history of his life in the past fifteen years held no record of such an act: pressing his hand to his heart, he ran after the little man, waving his other hand.

The wind swept his black cylinder from his head; Apollon Apollonovich squatted on his haunches to rescue it from a puddle; he shouted at the retreating back:

"H'm . . . listen! . . ."

The retreating back paid no attention.

"Stop, please!"

The person called then turned his head. Recognizing the Senator, he ran back to meet him; amazed at the spectacle, he promptly helped him to retrieve the cylinder from the puddle.

"Your Excellency! Apollon Apollonovich! By what ill fortune? . . . Permit me!" With these words the scurvy little man handed the cylinder to the eminent dignitary, who first wiped it with a coat sleeve.

"Where is your carriage?"

Apollon Apollonovich interrupted him:

"The night air is good for me."

Both started in the same direction.

Apollon Apollonovich raised his eyes at his companion. He blinked and said, not without awkwardness:

"By the way . . . I'd like to have your address, Pavel Pavlovich."

"Pavel Yakovlevich!"

"Pavel Yakovlevich. I have a poor memory for names."

Apollon Apollonovich, unbuttoning his greatcoat, drew out a notebook bound in leather; they paused under a street lamp.

"My address is subject to change. More often I'm on the Vasilyevsky Island, Eighteenth Line, Number 17. At the cobbler's, Bezsmertny's. Address me as the district clerk, Voronkov."

Apollon Apollonovich arched his brows; his features expressed astonishment:

"But how . . ." he began, "how . . ."

"You mean, how come my family name is Voronkov when I call myself Morkovin? . . . My real address is on the Nevsky . . ."

Apollon Apollonovich thought: "What can we do about it? Such figures are necessary in this transitional period, within the bounds of the law—it's a sad necessity, but a necessity for all that."

"Your Excellency, I'm engaged at present, as you know, in the work of detection."

"Yes, you are right . . ."

"A crime of official importance is being plotted. . . . Be careful, there's a puddle. . . . A crime is . . ."

"So that's it?"

"Before long we expect to uncover it. . . . Here's a dry place. Allow me to take your arm."

Apollon Apollonovich was crossing a square: his fear of space was reawakened and made him cling to the little man.

He tried to summon his courage as an icy hand grasped his own and guided him past the puddles; the way seemed endless as he followed the icy hand; expanses ran to meet him. Apollon Apollonovich cast a respectful glance at this custodian of the established order:

"Is it a terroristic act?" he inquired.

"Yes, it's a plot to slay a high dignitary."

Apollon Apollonovich had received a threatening letter informing him that, if he accepted the newly offered post, he would receive a bomb for his pains. Apollon Apollonovich despised anonymous letters; he had torn up the letter and accepted the post.

"Do you mind my asking who the intended victim is to be?"

Something strange occurred just then; all the objects around him seemed to shrink and draw nearer; and Mr. Morkovin looked like an old acquaintance; a smile passed over his lips:

"What do you mean, who? *You*, of course, Your Excellency, *you*!"

Apollon Apollonovich could not quite realize that this hand from which the glove had been removed, these feet, this so weary heart, under the expansion of the gases of some bomb, could . . .

"But why?"

"Why ask? It's all very simple . . ."

Simple? Apollon Apollonovich was incredulous: challengingly, he stroked his side-whiskers (they would go too!) and pursed his lips (there would be no lips either!); then he suddenly felt himself shrinking; he lowered his head and looked at the rivulet running down the pavement at his feet. All around him were whispers and murmurs: the senile whisper of autumnal days.

Mr. Morkovin began to feel pity for the old man and added:

"Your Excellency need have no fear; the strongest measures have been taken; we shall not allow it: you're in no danger either today or tomorrow. . . . It will all pass . . ."

Morkovin thought involuntarily: "How the man has aged: he is a mere ruin . . ." Apollon Apollonovich turned the beardless aspect of his face toward Morkovin and smiled sadly.

Presently, however, Apollon Apollonovich looked happier and younger; erect as a yardstick, he walked on through the dirty fog, his profile reminiscent of a mummified Pharaoh.

Spotted with reddish patches of lamplight the night grew darker: they passed gates, walls, fences, courtyards; whispers and murmurs came from them.

How damp, how unwholesome it all was!

16

After following his disobedient wife, Sergey Sergeyevich, white as death and smiling ironically, clinked his spurs and paused before the door; after Sofya Petrovna had provokingly rustled past him, angry Sergey Sergeyevich had walked from room to room, making vigorous gestures and extinguishing the electric lights.

Why did he exhibit his emotions in precisely this way? What connection could there be between this spirit of mischief and the lights? There was no connection except in the mirrors: the angular reflection, as it faced the mirror, seized itself by the slender neck —ai, ai! There was no real connection.

The switches clicked, plunging the man and his gestures into darkness. Perhaps this was no longer Lieutenant Likhutin.

Imagine his terrible state: to be thus reflected in the mirrors—a man who allowed some domino to bring dishonor to his honest house, who was now honor-bound not to allow his wife to cross his threshold. By all means, imagine his terrible state; nevertheless, this was Lieutenant Likhutin—no other.

The switches clicked one after another. Mavrushka was disturbed; she came out of the kitchen.

"What's happening?" she growled.

"Get out!" came the coughing reply in the darkness.

"What do you mean, *barin*?"

"Get out of here!"

"But I must make the beds!"

"Get out, get out!"

The voice followed her to the kitchen:

"Leave the house altogether!"

"How can I, *barin*?"

"Get out at once, I tell you!"

"I've no place to go!"

"Don't argue! Get out!"

"*Barin!*"

"Get out!"

Mavrushka took her fur coat and, lingering at the door, wept. She was frightened. The *barin* was not at all himself: she ought to go to the house porter, to the police station, and report the matter, then find a place to stay.

At the slightest domestic upset ordinary people lose their wits. . . . Since the previous evening Lieutenant Likhutin had suffered an unbearable pain in his head; he felt as if he had banged his head against an iron wall. . . . Likhutin bellowed and swayed his head, conscious of the sharpest pain in his brain, while across the walls moved the lights cast by a small steamer passing on the Moika, throwing strips of radiant light on the waters.

Likhutin continued to bellow and to sway his head: all his thoughts had become entangled, everything had become entangled. He began by analyzing his wife's behavior; he ended with a conclusion unflattering to himself: he had lived like a visitor in his own house. Far better to cover the mirrors: there was no consolation in observing the conduct of a married officer with his wife; he had no wish to watch the reflection of a wretch such as he had confessed himself to be; he could detect nothing in himself that deserved better.

What was he to do now? It had all begun yesterday: but why *begun*? Except for the masquerade, he had nothing against Ableukhov. In any case, his brain refused to serve him in this delicate question; the blood rushed to his head; he resorted to a cold towel on his temples, but this did not help much: something beat in his head, something played a game there, tugging at his veins!

He struck a match; his face in the mirror resembled the face of a madman. He glanced at his watch: two hours or a hundred and twenty minutes had elapsed: should he count the seconds too?

"Twice sixty makes one hundred and twenty!"

He clutched his head in his hands.

"Carry one . . ." His mind seemed to have splintered against the mirror. "Twelve—carry one . . ." His thoughts became entangled; Likhutin paced the room in the dark. "Twice six makes twelve; plus one; then two zeros: that makes seven thousand two hundred seconds."

Exulting over this complex labor accomplished by his brain, Sergey Sergeyevich inopportunely revealed his joy. Suddenly he remembered and his face recovered its gloom.

"Seven thousand two hundred seconds since she left home: two hundred thousand seconds—no, everything's at an end!"

At the expiration of two hundred seconds, the two hundred and first second marked the fulfillment of an officer's word of honor: he had endured seven thousand two hundred seconds—they had been like seven thousand years. Sergey Sergeyevich felt that he had been confined in this darkness with his unbearable headache from the very day of creation. Likhutin busied himself in a corner; he crossed himself; then from a box he pulled out a rope and made a noose: it refused to draw tight: in despair he ran into his tiny study, dragging the rope after him.

What was he doing but keeping his word! . . . He took a piece of soap and squatted on the floor; he soaped the rope over a basin; his actions assumed a fantastic character.

He climbed on the table after removing the cover; he placed a chair on the table and, climbing on the chair, cautiously removed the hanging lamp; then he attached the soaped slippery rope to the hook that had held the lamp; he crossed himself and paused; slowly he lifted the noose.

At this moment a brilliant thought flashed in Sergey Sergeyevich's head: he must shave first . . .

With this thought in mind, Likhutin returned to his study; in the light of a candle he began to shave his bearded neck—but his skin was tender, and soon his neck was covered with scratches. He shaved both neck and chin, but after his razor had unexpectedly nicked off the end of his mustache, he had to shave the rest of it; he could not be caught with half a mustache.

When Sergey Sergeyevich had finished shaving, he looked like an idiot.

There was no point in delaying. . . . But, at this instant, the doorbell rang. Vexed, he flung aside his razor; his fingers were thick with mixed lather and hairs. What was he to do now? For a minute he thought of postponing his undertaking; there was no time to lose, he must hurry; the doorbell rang again. He sprang onto the table and removed the noose from the hook; the rope refused to obey his soapy fingers; he climbed down again; stealthily, he crept into the vestibule; he noticed that the black-blue darkness had paled in the rooms; it had grown gray; in the gray darkness the objects were clearly delineated: he was able to see the chair on the table, the lamp lying on its side, and the wet noose.

In the vestibule he pressed against the door, remaining completely motionless; his agitation had reached that point of oblivion when to act was unthinkable. He had also begun to notice his stertorous breathing; he heard a woman's outcries behind the door; he suddenly shouted at the top of his voice and, as he did so, he realized that everything was lost. He rushed to finish what he had begun; he jumped on the table again, stretched out his neck; he quickly pulled the noose around his neck, covered with scratches, keeping two fingers between the rope and his neck.

Then for some reason he gave a shout, and pushed away the table with a foot; the table on brass casters rolled back. That was the noise Sofya Petrovna had heard.

17

An instant . . .

Sergey Sergeyevich's feet jerked; he saw distinctly the reflections of the street lights on the ventilators of the heating-stove; he heard distinctly the pounding and battering on the door; he noted that the two fingers he had placed between the noose and his neck were now being pressed painfully against the skin—he tried to release them, but could not do so. He thought he was suffocating; he heard a crackle, and imagined that his veins had burst; then the ceiling plaster crashed; Sergey Sergeyevich went down (to his death, he imagined). But Sergey Sergeyevich rose from the dead, having received, as it were, a mighty kick; he came to himself and understood that he was not risen from the dead, but had merely landed on the floor. Conscious of a sharp pain in his backbone, and of his fingers pressed between the noose and his throat, Likhutin strove to pull his fingers out; the noose widened.

Then he understood: he had narrowly missed hanging himself. He sighed with relief.

The inky blackness had turned gray: Likhutin realized that he was sitting senselessly there; in the gray light he discerned the Japanese landscapes on the walls barely blending with the night; the ceiling had lost the lace-like design of the light of the lamp he had removed.

Sergey Sergeyevich's sigh broke involuntarily. He had seriously planned to settle all his difficulties on earth. He might have realized this intention, but there it was: a rotten ceiling—blame the builder for that! His sigh of relief had no reference to his personality, only to his physical easing; he sat there on his haunches, aware of everything; Sergey Sergeyevich's spirit was composed.

His thoughts grew clearer; a dilemma presented itself: what now?

His revolvers had been put away; it would be hard to find them.
. . . As for using the razor—he did not like the notion at all! . . .
There was no time to be wasted. Sofya Petrovna, no doubt, would
promptly rush to the house porter; they would telephone the police;
a crowd would gather; they would break down the door; they would
rush in and find him, Lieutenant Likhutin, sitting on his haunches,
with a rope round his neck, amid fragments of fallen plaster.

No, no! He must not allow this: the honor of his uniform was
even dearer to him than his word of honor. Only one thing remained: to make peace promptly with his wife and to explain away
the plaster.

He flung the rope under the sofa and, in a most humiliating way,
ran to the door.

Still panting, he opened the door and paused indecisively on the
threshold, ashamed of his failure to hang himself. But having torn
himself from the lamp hook, he now seemed to have freed himself
from rage within him. He was no longer angry at his wife, no longer
angry at the behavior of Nikolai Apollonovich. For had not he
himself behaved in an outrageous manner, by deciding to hang
himself and succeeding only in tearing a hook from the ceiling?

No crowd came rushing into the room as he had expected; Sofya
Petrovna alone flew into the room and broke into sobs:

"What's the matter? Why this darkness?"

Sergey Sergeyevich was speechless.

"What is all the noise?"

Sergey Sergeyevich merely pressed her cold fingers in the darkness.

"Why are your hands all soapy . . . Sergey Sergeyevich, what's
all this?"

"You see, Sonya dear . . ."

"Why are you so hoarse?"

"You see . . . I . . . I . . . stood by the little gate in front—very
carelessly, you know—and . . . well, I got hoarse . . ."

He was confused; he stammered.

"Please don't, please don't," he almost shouted, restraining his
wife's hand which was about to switch on the light. "Anyway, not
here, not now—not in this room."

He dragged her toward the study.

There the objects were clearly delineated; dawn was at the window, and Sofya Petrovna beheld an indescribable object: the blue face of a strange idiot.

"What have you done? You've shaved yourself! You look like an utter fool!"

"You see, Sonya dear," he whispered hoarsely, "there was a circumstance here . . ."

But she would not listen: in unaccountable distress, she rushed to inspect all the rooms.

"You'll find the place in disorder. . . . The ceiling cracked and came down . . ."

Oblivious of his words, Sofya Petrovna stood staring at the pile of plaster in which, darker than the other pieces, the hook stood out; the table had been pushed aside and, from under the sofa, a portion of the noose stuck out; Sofya Petrovna bent down to look at it.

Suddenly everything seemed to light up; the glow of pink rippling clouds, like a web of pearl, penetrated the room; a bluish radiance crept in; everything was permeated with shyness, with the question: "What then? What then?" Tremors ran over the windows, over the spires; the spires glowed a delicate red. Voices spoke within her soul, a light flashed there; a pale rose ray fell upon the rug and upon the doorjamb.

Sofya Petrovna reached out a hand toward the rope: kissing the rope, she wept quietly: transcendently, the image of her remote and newly returned childhood rose before her, and stood behind her back; she turned her face, and saw her husband standing there —tall, lanky, sad, and shaven:

"Forgive me, Sonya darling!"

She flung herself at his feet, weeping:

"My poor Sergey, my darling!"

What they whispered, one to the other, must remain between them—something intimately their own.

The tufted rosy cloud, ascending from the funnel of a tiny passing steamer, hovered above the Moika; from the stern a green strip shone, beating against the bank and turning amber; surging from the bank, ripples broke against the strip which met them with resistance; and the ripples began to shine like a swarm of annulated

serpents, broken again by the appearance of a rowboat among
them; the serpents were cut into strings of diamonds, spinning
out into silvery threads, shimmering on the watery surface like
twinkling stars; then the agitation of the water ceased, and all the
stars were extinguished. On the Moika's bank loomed a green,
white-columned building: a fragment of the Renaissance.

18

Out of the darkness loomed the tall wall of a house; two Egyptians
supported the balcony with their hands. Apollon Apollonovich
walked past many such weighty edifices until he finally reached the
poor district inhabited by the common people.

A door swung open; white vapors assailed his nostrils, wrangling
obscenities struck his ears, as did the tinkling sounds of a balalaika
and a voice singing; he listened to the voice:

> "With our spirit we draw to Thee, Father,
> Heavenward in our thoughts we soar.
> And for our food from our hearts
> We thank Thee, O Lord."

The door banged shut. In the man of the people Apollon Apollonovich had suspected something petty, fleeting beyond the window panes of his carriage; now all the perspectives had shifted . . .
here was the man of the people, and here his voice.

An interest in the man of the people awoke in Apollon Apollonovich, and for a moment he wished to knock at the door and discover
him; then he remembered that "the man of the people" was plotting
to . . . his cylinder hat tipped over his forehead, his tired shoulders
sagged—

—Yes, yes: they had blown into fragments: no, not him, but
someone else sent by destiny; Apollon Apollonovich recalled
the gray mustache, the greenish hollows of fixed eyes, they
both had bent over a map of the Empire one day (it
had been the day before he was—). . . . They had blown
to fragments a *primus inter pares*. . . . They say it lasts but

a second; afterward—it is as if there had been nothing. . . .
What does it all mean? Every man in the government is a
hero, but—br-r—br-r-r . . .

Apollon Apollonovich Ableuk-
hov straightened his cylinder as he penetrated into the rank life of
"the man of the people"; into the network of walls, gateways, fences
covered with mud, into the very rank, rotten, empty, and public
lavatory; it now seemed to him that this very rotting fence hated
him; *they hated him.* Who were they? An insignificant bunch? Here
the action of his brain moved up misty plateaus: all the plateaus were
rent apart: the giant map of Russia rose before him, so small a man.
Were *they* really enemies? That gigantic complex of tribes inhabit-
ing these spaces? *One hundred million?* No—more? . . .

"From the chill crags of Finland to Colchis' fiery skies . . ."

What? *They* hated? . . . Yet there was the whole expanse of
Russia. Hated him? . . . They were plotting . . . plotting. . . . No . . .
br-r . . . br-r. . . . It was only the play of the brain. A poet's words
came to him:

"It's time, friend, time! Peace is the heart's desire.
Day follows day, And each day bears away
A part of being. But you and I propose
To share our life. But what's beyond? To die."

With whom, then, did he intend to live? His son? His son was
a scoundrel. With "the man of the people"? "The man of the people" was plotting to. . . . At one time he had intended to live out
his life with Anna Petrovna, and on his retirement from government
service move to a cottage in Finland; but, instead, Anna Petrovna
had left him, and he could do nothing about it.

Apollon Apollonovich clearly realized that he had no companion,
no fellow-traveler in life—until this moment he had not given much
thought to the matter; nevertheless, to die at his post would
embellish his life. Now he felt childishly sad and quiet—he experienced a feeling of comfort. And the murmur of the rivulet running
down the pavement was like the murmur of a prayer . . .

The nocturnal darkness began to wane; it had turned gray, and
was then shot through with light; the reddish street lights grew

faint, mere dim dots, peering through the gray fog; the gray file of lines and walls casting the faintest shadows and revealing the glow from windows looked like an aerial lace-work of very delicate and exquisite design.

A poorly dressed young girl of about fifteen ran toward him; behind her, apparently in pressing pursuit, came the dark form of a man. Apollon Apollonovich, imagining himself a knight, removed his cylinder:

"My dear young lady, may I offer you my arm? It is rather dangerous for young women to walk alone in the streets."

The young girl stared at the dark little figure holding the cylinder hat in a gesture of respect.

They walked together in silence; everything seemed wet and old, ebbing into the past; Apollon Apollonovich had noted all this before, though remotely. And now here it all was—the gateways, the tiny houses, the walls, the young girl pressing timidly against him, a young girl for whom he was no Senator, but just a kind old man.

They reached a green little house with a rotted gate; the Senator courteously raised his cylinder; his gesture seemed pathetically aged; his dead lips murmured something . . .

Somewhere to one side, flames flashed; suddenly, everything became radiant; the rosy ripples of the clouds, shot through with mother-of-pearl, mingled with the flames. The walls and shapes now became more clearly delineated: entrances, caryatids, brick cornices, balconies.

The Petersburg morning was transformed into lace: five-story houses were the color of sand; the bright red palace glowed like fire.

CHAPTER FIVE

There will be a new dawn tomorrow,
The day will blaze with light,
But I, perhaps, shall sorrow
Among the shades of eternal night.

—PUSHKIN

1

Nikolai Apollonovich turned and fixed his gaze on the small man.
"Whom have I the honor of addressing?"

"Pavel Yakovlevich Morkovin."

The face told him nothing: there was only a bowler, a cane, a
greatcoat, a wart, and a nose.

"You seem very nonchalant."

An apple of bright light suddenly flashed, then a second, and a
third—this line of electric fruit indicated that they had reached
the Nevsky Prospect, where all night long restaurants displayed
their bright red signs, beneath which feathery women glided among
cylindrical hats and bowlers.

Nikolai Apollonovich realized that the circumstances of his meeting with the enigmatic Pavel Yakovlevich would not permit him to
end the meeting without injury to his dignity; he must learn from
the stranger what had happened between him and his father. He
was reluctant to leave without knowing this.

The Neva came into view: the stone projection of the Summer
Canal; here the wind tore into them; and, beyond the Neva, loomed
the shapes of islands and houses; their amber eyes, peering through
the fog, gave the impression of weeping.

Here was the square: a massive rock rose, revealing the upraised
hoofs of a rearing horse; a shadow concealed the rider. There
was a fishing schooner on the Neva.

Now they were crossing the bridge.

Ahead of them strode an odd pair: a middle-aged sailor wearing
a cap with earflaps and a red beard streaked with gray; and his
bulky companion, with black hair, tiny mustache, a tiny nose, and
a dark green hat of lambs' wool.

"Odd, isn't it, Nikolai Apollonovich, that we should have walked precisely to this spot!"

"Allow me to . . . ."

"You're not bored by any chance?"

"No, I'm just sleepy . . . ."

Nikolai Apollonovich shrugged. With a fastidious gesture, he opened a restaurant door.

A thick white vapor from pancakes struck his nostrils; a hatcheck fell into the palm of his hand, leaving a burning sensation.

"They all know me here . . . Alexander Ivanovich, Butischenko, Shishiganov, Pepp . . ."

Nikolai Apollonovich's curiosity was awakened by three things: first, the stranger had stressed acquaintance with his father; then, he had mentioned Alexander Ivanovich; finally, he had spoken of Butischenko and Pepp, names that rang familiarly.

"She looks interesting," Pavel Yakovlevich commented, nudging him to look in the direction of a prostitute with a Turkish cigarette in her mouth. "You take an interest in women?"

"What?"

Everyone in the room was talking loudly.

"Who?"

"Ivan!"

"Ivan Ivanovich!"

"Ivan Ivanovich Ivanov . . . ."

"It's all a lie!"

"Ivan Ivanovich Ivanov is a swine!"

The player piano suddenly bellowed forth its cacophany. Ivan Ivanovich Ivanov, who had been sitting near the piano, stood up, flourishing a bottle.

How came he to be in such a sordid place, and at this time?

The terrible barbaric raucous machine belched forth wild sounds like a volcano about to erupt, as its cracking voice sounded through the restaurant:

> "R-r-rest, oh, m-my s-soul's pas-s-sion . . .
> Sle-e-ep, oh, m-my hope-l-less heart . . . ."

"Ha-ha-ha-ha-ha-ha! . . ."

2

"Well, admit it. . . . Hey there, two glasses of vodka! . . . Admit it . . ." shouted Pavel Yakovlevich. He looked fat and smug, his yellowed face spread out, baggy and creased. "I venture to guess that I'm a riddle to you. . . . Well, young man?"

"What is it?"

"What do you think of my behavior in the street?"

"Will you have another?"

"By all means!"

Pavel Yakovlevich was preoccupied with his attempt to thrust a trembling fork into a slippery mushroom:

"You must admit it was rather strange out there!"

"What was strange?"

"There—by the fence. . . . No, waiter, I don't want any sardines!"

At the neighboring tables sat members of a mongrel race, neither human beings nor shadows, merely denizens of the islands, a strange race, neither one thing nor another.

"How about a third?"

"Well, let's have a third . . ."

"And what do you think of our conversation near the gate?"

"About the domino?"

"To be sure!"

"I can only repeat what I've said . . ."

Nikolai Apollonovich was revolted; he wanted to turn away from those evil-smelling lips, but he controlled himself. His own lips stretched into a smile. Taut, they danced and trembled at the corners like the legs of a tormented frog when in contact with a live wire.

"Well, then, don't attach any importance to my remarks about the domino. I mentioned the domino only for the sake of meeting you."

"Excuse me for mentioning it," Nikolai Apollonovich interrupted, "but there's olive oil running down your chin."

"You must agree, though, that your being the domino was a good, if wild, guess on my part. . . . I said to myself: 'Pavlusha, here's your chance! Stop at that fence and urinate. Use it as an excuse for striking up an acquaintance!'"

They left the counter and walked toward a table.

"Waiter, a clean tablecloth, please! . . . And some vodka!"

They sat down, resting their elbows on the table. Nikolai Apollonovich was conscious of being drunk as much from fatigue as from the vodka. All the colors and sounds pounded at his brain.

"Yes, yes, there's a curious point in that. . . . Fine, I'll have some kidneys and madeira. Will you have kidneys?"

"What's the point?"

"Two portions of kidneys, please. . . . What's the point? Well, then—I have a confession to make. There are ties uniting us . . ."

"What?"

"Ties of birth."

"What do you mean?"

"Ties of blood . . ."

The waiter placed the kidneys before them.

"Don't think for a moment that these ties. . . . Waiter, salt and pepper, please! . . . have to do with the shedding of blood. Why do you tremble? One would think you were a young girl! Here's the pepper."

Like his father, Nikolai Apollonovich peppered his food too much.

"What did you say?"

"Here's the pepper . . ."

"About blood . . ."

"About ties? By ties of blood I mean ties of kinship, of course."

Pavel Yakovlevich fussed with the napkin which he thrust into his collar.

"Excuse me, I'm afraid I don't understand. What exactly do you mean by ties of blood and kinship?"

"You see, Nikolai Apollonovich, I am, as it were, your own brother . . ."

Nikolai Apollonovich almost rose from his chair. His nostrils quivered nervously, and his hair seemed to have a will of its own.

"To be sure, I'm illegitimate. I'm the result of your father's love for a seamstress . . ."

The Ableukhovs greatly valued the purity of their blood; Nikolai Apollonovich cherished the purity of the Ableukhov blood.

"Your Papa," the little man resumed, "had an interesting little romance in his youth . . ."

Nikolai Apollonovich thought Morkovin would continue with: "which came to an end with my appearance . . ."

"Which terminated in my appearance in this world."

That had happened at some time—long ago.

"Let's drink to it!"

The player piano continued its wild anguish and, with it, the terrible old days seemed to return in overwhelming force and fill the room with weeping.

"My father . . ."

"Our common father."

"Our common father, if you like."

"You shrugged then," Pavel Yakovlevich interrupted. "What's the meaning of that shrug, may I ask?"

"The meaning?"

"Yes. Let me tell you: you shrugged, Nikolai Apollonovich, because you consider our relationship a humiliating one. . . . Will you have gravy? . . . You'll excuse me if I apply the psychological method to you. I have to feel my way, old chap."

Nikolai Apollonovich screwed up his eyes; his fingers drummed on the table.

"Let me reassure you, then, about our kinship. I was just feeling my way. . . . I must acquit you, and offend you, too. . . . There remains only to say: we are—brothers . . . but by different parents."

"What?"

"The fact is, it was all a joke about Apollon Apollonovich. I permitted myself to lie about that little romance—ha-ha-ha—there wasn't any such thing! . . . Your father is a singularly moral character!"

"How, then, are we brothers?"

"By conviction . . ."

"How is it possible for you to know my convictions?"

"You're a convinced terrorist, Nikolai Apollonovich."

"A terrorist?"

"Precisely. Allow me to say that I did not mention those names without reason: Butischenko, Shishiganov, Pepp. . . . That was by way of a delicate reminder. . . . And Alexander Ivanovich Doodkin, the Elusive! . . . Ah? Ah? Now you get me? You do, don't you? But don't worry: our theoretician is a rogue . . . ooh . . ."

Nikolai Apollonovich, throwing his head back, roared with laughter. Pavel Yakovlevich echoed him.

The huge fellow at the next table turned his head angrily and stared.

"I'll tell you," Nikolai Apollonovich announced quite seriously, "you're mistaken: my relation to terrorism is a negative one."

"How can you say that, Nikolai Apollonovich? After all, I happen to know everything: about the little bundle, about Alexander Ivanovich, about Sofya Petrovna . . . I know it—in the course of duty . . ."

"You're in the service?"

"Yes, in the Secret Police . . ."

3

For an instant they had reached a standstill; over the edge of the table Pavel Yakovlevich had caught a button of Nikolai Apollonovich's coat. With a guilty smile Nikolai Apollonovich drew out a leather-bound notebook.

"If you please, I'd like to inspect that little book!"

Nikolai Apollonovich did not resist: his ordeal of mental torture had passed all bounds.

Pavel Yakovlevich, bending over the little notebook, projected his head in such a way that it gave the impression of being attached not to his neck, but to his hands; for a moment, he looked like a monster: blinking his small eyes set under an unkempt, woolly, smelling head, his face distorted by a laughing grimace, he let his ten fingers fly above the tabletop as he turned the leaves of the notebook. His fingers suggested a ten-legged spider.

It was clear that Pavel Yakovlevich wished to frighten his companion by giving the impression of a police search—just a joke on his part; grimacing with laughter, he flung the notebook back to Nikolai Apollonovich.

"Tell me, why do you submit to this? . . . I'm sure I don't look as if I were going to question you. . . . Don't be frightened: I've been attached to the Secret Police by the Party. . . . You're agitated without cause."

"You're not pulling my leg?"

"By no means. . . . If I were a police officer, I'd have you arrested, because the gesture you made was sufficiently suspicious. Why, the way you put your hand to the pocket where the notebook was gave the impression that you were hiding a document of importance . . . that gesture gave you away! . . . You agree?"

"Please . . ."

"Allow me to remark: you committed a blunder. You took out your quite innocent little notebook when no one had even asked for it. You took it out, no doubt, simply to distract attention from something else. You did not achieve your aim. On the contrary, you called attention to the fact that you were hiding another document in your pocket. You're too careless. . . . Just glance at that page! It contains a little secret. Read it, and enjoy it!"

"Why are you putting me on the rack? If you're really the person you pretend to be, then your conduct and your insinuations are unworthy of you!"

Nikolai Apollonovich stood up amid the fumes, his mouth open but not laughing, his fair hair framed about his face; he bared his teeth like a beast at bay, then, turning contemptuously, flung a fifty-kopeck piece on the table.

The neighboring tables were already empty; suddenly the electric lights were extinguished; the reddish light of a candle flared into being; the shadows of the walls softened; the edge of a painted wall came into sight, revealing the Flying Dutchman—Nikolai Apollonovich was giddy from seven persuasive glasses of vodka; but the middle-aged sailor rose from his place and vanished into darkness.

Morkovin, straightening his frock coat, glanced at Nikolai Apollonovich with reflective tenderness. For a minute or so neither spoke a word.

Finally Pavel Yakovlevich said, "I must tell you: it's just as hard for me as for you . . ."

"Why not be frank, comrade?"

"Well then, let's go back to the day of your promise. . . . Nikolai Apollonovich, you must be an odd fellow, indeed, to imagine even for a moment that I dragged after you through the streets just for the fun of it!" Then he added solemnly, "The Party, Nikolai Apollonovich, awaits an answer from you."

Nikolai Apollonovich was descending the steps; one end of them had receded into the darkness; at the bottom, near the door, *they* were standing. Who *they* were, he could scarcely say; there were the dark contours and a turgid green mist shot through with a dimly flaring phosphorescence; and *they* were waiting for him.

When he passed by, he felt eyes fixed on him from either side: one of the observers, a giant bathed in the light of the street lamp, towered near the door in bronze majesty. His metallic face, burning with a phosphorescent light, stared at him; his green ponderous hand threatened him:

"Who is it?"

"He who is destroying us—irretrievably."

The restaurant door slammed behind them. Again the bowler moved along the wall at his side.

"And if I refuse?"

"I shall arrest you . . ."

"Arrest—me?"

"Don't forget, I'm a . . ."

"A conspirator?"

"An official of the Secret Police!"

"What will the Party say to that?"

"The Party will justify me. Taking advantage of my position in the Secret Police, I'll exercise vengeance against you on behalf of the Party . . ."

There was a pause. Then Pavel Yakovlevich resumed: "Nikolai Apollonovich, all jokes aside: I'm in dead earnest. I must remark that your doubts, your indecisiveness, distress me. You should have thought of all that earlier . . . you could have refused then; but two months have passed. You were negligent. You have three alternatives—choose among them: arrest, suicide, or murder. Do you understand me now?"

Nikolai Apollonovich turned his head: he saw nothing, no one, behind him. Above the damp parapet, above the greenish, stagnant waters, only the wind greeted him, weeping; here, on this very spot only two and a half months ago, Nikolai Apollonovich had given his dreadful promise!

The square was desolate; the buildings of the Senate and the Synod loomed silently. With curiosity Nikolai Apollonovich raised his eyes to the immense shape of the Horseman. The Horseman had seemed to vanish, a short while ago, swallowed in shadows; now, however, the metal of the face had creased in a smile.

The clouds were torn, and a green vapor was wafted from the seemingly melting bronze to drift in the moonlight, which suddenly flowed through the clouds. For an instant everything burst into light: the water, the roofs, the granite. The Horseman's face and his crown of bronze laurels were ablaze, and so was that ponderous arm stretched out in an attitude of command. The arm seemed to shake, the rearing metallic hoofs seemed about to crash down on the rock, and the Horseman's voice seemed to resound through Petersburg:

"Yes, yes, yes . . . it is I. . . . I destroy—irretrievably! . . ."

For an instant, the whole truth was clear to Nikolai Apollonovich. He understood. He was under an obligation.

Screaming with laughter, he fled from the Bronze Horseman:

"I know . . . I am lost—irretrievably lost . . ."

In the distance a sheaf of flame sped by. It was a black carriage belonging to the Court; its lights were bright red; the spectral contours of the lackey's cocked hat and of the wings of his uniform cape sped with the flame—from mist into mist.

4

There was not a moment to lose! Something must be done. He himself had disseminated the theory that there was no sense in compassion. Before a silent group, he has expressed his ideas— his disgust for the wrinkled ears . . . skin . . . of the *barins* . . .

He hailed a cab.

The Admiralty thrust forward its eight-columned side: for an

instant it glowed rose, then vanished from sight; on the opposite
bank of the Neva, the walls of an old building were tinted a carrot
color; to the left, in front of a black and white sentry box, a grenadier paced; he shifted his gleaming bayonet from one shoulder to
the other.

It was a clear morning. The flashing dawn had transformed the
Neva into pure gold over which sped the funnel of a tiny steamer.
Suddenly Nikolai Apollonovich noticed a thin little human figure
hurrying along the sidewalk. He immediately recognized it as his
father's! Nikolai Apollonovich wanted to slow the cab in order to
increase the distance between him and his father . . . but it was
too late. His father turned toward the cab. To avoid recognition,
Nikolai Apollonovich stuck his face into his fur collar; and his collar
and cap were all that remained visible.

Apollon Apollonovich heard the sound of a cab behind him; when
it drew level with him, he had time to observe the hunched figure
of a young man closely wrapped in a greatcoat. When the youth
peered from behind his collar, the Senator had already turned the
other way. On seeing him, the eyes of the pompous young man
widened perceptibly; they were full of terror as they followed
the old man . . .

Nikolai Apollonovich sprang from the cab. Full of inward anger
and presenting an absurd figure entangled in the folds of his greatcoat, he awkwardly dashed toward the main entrance of his home.

He tugged violently at the bell: why did Semenich not hurry to
open the door? He knew that the dry little figure of his father, who
should have been in his carriage, would soon emerge from the mist.
On either side of the flight of steps he saw the gaping mouth of a
griffin, rose-tinted by the rising sun, and claws holding the rings
for flag staffs; and under the griffins, cut in stone, was the Ableukhov coat of arms: a unicorn goring a knight. The thought
flashed through his mind, like a fish skimming the surface of the
water, that Apollon Apollonovich, who lived beyond the threshold
of that door, was himself the gored knight. And at the same time
without rising to the surface, the thought mistily glided that this
old family coat of arms applied to all the Ableukhovs, and that he,
Nikolai Apollonovich, was also being gored—but by whom?

This mental play of nonsense lasted less than a second: and

yonder he could already discern the little figure hurrying home through the fog at a rapid pace. Apollon Apollonovich, in his cylinder, reminded him of death; unable to account for such strange thoughts, Nikolai Apollonovich pictured his father in the act of sexual intercourse; and with new force the thought of his conception filled him with the familiar nausea.

The tiny figure approached. Nikolai Apollonovich became aware, to his shame, of the familiar confusion which had taken possession of him.

He suddenly ran down the steps and rushed to meet his father. With a furtive look, he exclaimed:

"Good morning, Papa!"

As he looked at this young man, so diffident in appearance, Apollon Apollonovich thought of him as a scoundrel; but embarrassed by his presence, he murmured:

"Yes, that's so. A fine morning. . . . And so we meet . . ."

The stone griffins stared at them. . . . At this moment the main door opened, and the familiar odor of the house greeted the Ableukhovs. Mutually embarrassed, they managed to squeeze through the doorway simultaneously.

5

Both were aware that they must hold a conversation, that the time had come for a talk. After handing his cylinder to the butler, Apollon Apollonovich became involved with his galoshes. Nikolai Apollonovich could not guess if his father was familiar with the history of the red domino; he threw his splendid silvery beaver coat over the butler's arm. Then in his domino he confronted his father, in whose mind a verse stirred:

> "Tints of fiery color
> I'll spread on my palm,
> That, from an abyss of light,
> He may rise, as red as fire."

With his veined hand Apollon Apollonovich pulled at his sideburns.

He stood there, ironically chewing his lip; the skin of his face was a mask of wrinkles, while the skin of his skull grew taut. He realized the necessity for an explanation; the fruit was ripe and . . . suddenly—

—Apollon Apollonovich dropped a pencil on the stairs; Nikolai Apollonovich, following from habit his father's movements, jumped forward to retrieve the pencil. Apollon Apollonovich tried to stop him; he stumbled and fell, catching the stair with his hand. Unexpectedly his head came into contact with his son's fingers; Nikolai Apollonovich caught sight of the violent pulsation of an artery on his father's neck; it frightened him. He pulled back his hand, but too late; under the contact of the cold hand, the Senator's head jerked violently, and his ears twitched. Like a nervous Japanese, teaching jiu-jitsu, he jumped aside, then straightened himself, his knees cracking.

All this lasted but an instant. Nikolai Apollonovich handed the pencil to his father.

"Here it is!"

A meaningless incident had pushed them together, and set off an explosion of feelings and thoughts. Apollon Apollonovich felt extremely embarrassed. To exhibit fear in response to an act of respect was ignominious—after all, the young man in red was his own son, and to fear him was unnatural. He rested on his knees looking up into his son's face; Apollon Apollonovich was vexed; suddenly he recovered his dignity and said through tightly pressed lips:

"Thank you. I hope you sleep well . . ."

Nikolai Apollonovich felt the blood rush to his face; although he thought he had merely flushed, his face had grown purple. Apollon Apollonovich, seeing his son's face, felt his own reddening and, to conceal his flush, he dashed up the stairs with a sort of coy grace.

Nikolai Apollonovich found himself alone deep in reflection; but the butler's voice broke into his mood:

"How could I forget! . . . Dear *barin*, something's happened!"

"What has happened?"

"How shall I put it? . . . I hardly dare . . ."

Nikolai Apollonovich paused on a step of the gently lighted velvet-covered stairs; from a window a network of crimson patches fell upon the spot where his father had stumbled; they looked like bloodstains on an ancient sword.

"Yes, sir . . . what an event! Your mother, sir . . . our lady, sir. . . . She's come back!"

Nikolai Apollonovich's mouth worked from sudden nausea; he gaped at the dawn and stood there, red as a flame.

"She's arrived!" the servant repeated.

"Who's arrived?"

"Why, Anna Petrovna . . ."

"Who is she? . . ."

"Your own mother, sir. . . . What's the matter, *barin*, you act like a stranger. It's your mother, sir, who's come . . ."

"What?"

"Yes sir, from Spain, back in Petersburg. First, a messenger came with a letter. She's stopping at a hotel. . . . Well, as you know . . ."

"Know what?"

"It happened when His Excellency, Apollon Apollonovich, had just left the house . . . the messenger came with the letter. . . . I put the letter on the table, and gave the messenger twenty kopecks . . .

"Then, what do you think? An hour had not passed when—oh, Lord!—the lady herself turned up! She must have known no one was home . . ."

The six-pointed mace glittered; between the wall and the window, a column of purple light cast by the early glow floated; particles of dust danced in the air. Nikolai Apollonovich thought that this must be the way blood danced in his veins.

"I opened the door. . . . There was an unfamiliar lady, simply dressed in black. . . . So I say to her, 'What can I do for you, lady?' And she says to me, 'Mitry Semenich, don't you know me?' Then I kissed her hand. 'Well, who'd have thought it. If it isn't Anna Petrovna herself . . .' Yes, it was Anna Petrovna herself. . . . God give her health! She stared at me, stared and then tears filled her eyes. 'I want to see,' she says, 'how you're getting on without me . . .' And she takes a little handkerchief from her foreign hand-bag. . . . I had orders not to let her in. . . . But how could I help not letting in the *barinya* . . . and she . . ."

Instead of showing astonishment, compassion, or joy, Nikolai Apollonovich dashed upstairs, dragging behind him the blood-red satin like a tail.

Having interrupted Semenich, Nikolai Apollonovich fled because he had clearly pictured a scoundrel—in whose hand was a pair of scissors with which he had flung himself on a little old man in order to cut a pulsating artery; the scissors were dripping with blood, and the little old man, beardless, wrinkled, and bald, had broken into sobs; sitting on his haunches, he had put his hand to his neck in a desperate attempt to stem the flow of blood . . .

This was the image that rose in his mind while he had been standing on the stairs with his father looking up at him. The image had recurred, and he had not yet recovered from the shock. It had made him fly up the stairs and stamp loudly through the rooms.

6

The rooms were already radiant with sunlight; the tiny incrusted tables reflected its beams; all the mirrors were filled with a clown, because the salon mirror, which faced the reception room, reflected a clown. The clown moved about distractedly, and each mirror reflected another. All the mirrors reflected the clown who ran into the reception room and then paused as in a trance, because he saw himself, now in one mirror, now in another, and because he saw, too, a skeleton in a tightly buttoned frock coat and with a bare ear and a wispy sideburn on each side.

Apollon Apollonovich, seeing a marionette instead of his son in the mirror, waited for him. He closed the door to the salon, cutting off all retreat; this affair must be concluded. Like a surgeon proceeding quickly to an operating table, upon which lay scalpels, saws, and drills, Apollon Apollonovich rubbed his hands and approached Nikolai Apollonovich; he paused before him, took out his eyeglass case, turned it between his fingers, put it away again, and coughed:

"Still in your domino, I see."

"To be sure. I was at a masked ball. So I had to wear a costume, too . . ."

At the same time he thought: the skin and the bones, and the blood . . . everything to the last muscle, this entire structure, was in danger of being torn to bits; if he was to escape this fate today, he would face a fresh prospect tomorrow . . .

Casually intercepting this glance in the sparkling mirror, Apollon Apollonovich turned about, catching the end of a phrase:

". . . then we played *petits jeux.*"

Apollon Apollonovich made no reply. *That* glance was now directed at the parquet floor. Then Apollon Apollonovich remembered: this "clown" had once been a tiny body, which he had carried in his arms with paternal tenderness. The fair-haired youngster, donning a fool's cap, had once climbed on his shoulders, and Apollon Apollonovich had hoarsely chanted:

> "Little fool, little sap,
> Kolenka is dancing;
> On his head a fool's cap—
> On a horse he's prancing."

He had carried the child to this very mirror; it had reflected both the old man and the boy; he would point out the reflection to the boy:

"Look, son, do you see those strangers?"

Kolenka used to cry and scream at night. And now Apollon Apollonovich saw before him a large, strange body. . . . And Apollon Apollonovich began to walk about in slow circles:

"You see, Kolenka . . .

"I must, Kolenka, have a . . ." he continued, sinking into a deep armchair. "That is—I hope—you and I may have a talk. Have you time now? The question, a distressing one, consists in that . . ." he stumbled on the word and ran again to the mirror. At this moment chimes sounded; death-in-a-frock-coat stared from the mirror toward the reception room. Suddenly the mirror cracked; like lightning, a twisted gash cut across it and remained fixed there, in a zigzag line. To the superstitious, this would have seemed an ill omen.

Nikolai Apollonovich was evidently trying to postpone the explanation; it seemed superfluous; time would settle the matter. He regretted that he had not escaped from the reception room in time.

"Papa, I must admit I was expecting this," he said.

"Are you free?"

"Yes, I'm free."

He could not tear himself away from his father, and remained standing in front of him.

"Kolenka, you had better go to your room and gather your wits. If you find something in yourself that will not hinder us from a discussion, come and see me in my study."

"Very well, Papa."

"And, by the way, remove your circus rig . . . I don't like it."

"What?"

"No, I do not like it! I dislike it completely!"

Two bony yellow fingers beat rhythmically on the card table.

7

Nikolai Apollonovich remained standing by the card table: his eyes scanned the little boxes, the shelves protruding from the walls. Here he had often played games; here he had often sat—in this very armchair, whose light blue satin seat was decorated with a design of festoons; here hung David's *Distribution des aigles par Napoléon premier*, showing the Emperor in crown and porphyry.

What should he tell his father? Should he lie again, even if lies were futile? Lie—in his position? Nikolai Apollonovich recalled that he had often lied as a child.

The grand piano, of fashionable design and yellow color, rested on casters on the parquet floor. His mother used to sit there, and the familiar sounds of Beethoven used to shake the walls.

The sun flowed in: the thousand-armed old Titan lighted up the spires, the roofs. . . . But the sun today looked like an immense thousand-pawed tarantula, which had thrown itself in mad passion upon the earth . . .

A sudden radiance flooded the room, making him squint; the lampshade showered amethysts; sparks glistened on the wing of the

golden cupid; and the surface of the mirrors burst into flame . . .
and one of them was cracked.

"But how . . . what . . . shall we . . .?"

Nikolai Apollonovich raised his face.

"What shall we do about the *barinya?*" a voice asked.

He saw Semenich.

"I really don't know . . ."

Semenich chewed his lips.

"Shall I report to the master?"

"Doesn't Papa know?"

"I haven't dared to . . ."

"Well, go and tell him . . ."

"Very well . . . I'll go and tell him." And Semenich walked into
the corridor.

All, all, all: the sun's radiance, these walls, this body, this soul—
all will fall away; already everything was crumbling; and, in its
place, nothing but delirium, an abyss, a bomb.

A bomb—just a rapid expansion of gases. . . . The roundness of
the expansion evoked a forgotten fantasy.

As a child he had deliriums; sometimes at night a ball would
loom up bouncing—a ball either of rubber or made from the matter
of very strange worlds; and it produced a dull lacquered sound on
the floor: *pépp-péppep*, and again, *pépp-péppep*, and again; expanding terribly, it had often assumed the appearance of a rotund
gentleman; the gentleman, becoming a sphere, would continue to
expand and grow, threatening to fall on him:

"Pépp. . . . Péppovich. . . . Pépp . . ."

Then he would explode into fragments.

And Nikolai would shout the most absurd things—that he too
was growing round, that he was Zero. Everything in him was becoming Zero . . .

His governess, Karolina Karlovna, in a white blouse, her hair in
curlers, would stare angrily at him through the yellow nimbus of
candlelight, but the circle would continue to widen. Karolina Karlovna would repeat:

"Little Kolenka, be quiet now. You're growing . . ."

She did not look at him, but went on karolling, karolling, karolling . . .

Pépp Péppovich Pépp . . .

"Am I delirious now?"

Nikolai Apollonovich put his fingers to his forehead: delirium, an abyss, a bomb.

Through the window, far beyond where the river banks lay low, and the island buildings squatted, the torturously sharp spire of Peter and Paul, gleaming unmercifully, pierced the high sky.

Semenich's step sounded in the corridor. There was no point in delaying: Apollon Apollonovich was waiting.

8

The Senator's study, in addition to the writing desk, contained many bookshelves lining the walls; the shelves sagged under the weight of the books; a textbook on "planimetry" lay in the middle of the table.

Before going to sleep, Apollon Apollonovich would often open this book to solace his restless mind with his favorite forms: parallelepipeds, parallelograms, cones, and cubes.

On this exhausting morning the leather back of the upholstered armchair tempted him to lean back, but he refused the temptation. Apollon Apollonovich was very fastidious; he sat perfectly erect at his table and waited for his useless son. He pulled out a drawer and, under the letter "R," extracted a small diary labeled "Observations"; in it he began to jot down his impressions. He was interrupted by an apprehensive sigh. Turning round, he broke his pen.

"*Barin*, Your Excellency . . . I venture to report to you. . . . You see, the *barinya*, our lady . . . I venture to report to you . . ."

Apollon Apollonovich turned an immense ear toward Semenich.

"What is it . . . ah? Speak louder, I can't hear you."

Semenich, trembling, bent over the pale green ear which waited expectantly.

"The *barinya* . . . Anna Petrovna. . . . She's come back . . ."

"What!"

"From Spain—to Petersburg . . ."

"What do you mean?"

"She went to a hotel. . . . You'd barely left the house, sir, when a messenger arrived with a letter. I put the letter on the table, and I gave the messenger a twenty-kopeck piece. . . . Then, hardly another hour passed, when suddenly I heard the doorbell ring."

Apollon Apollonovich sat rooted in his chair in calm detachment, with arms crossed, immobile, without a thought; his gaze rested on the titles of some books: *The Russian Code of Law. Volume One. Volume Two.* On the table, in front of some packets of papers, gleamed a gold inkwell, penholders and pens, and a heavy paperweight upon which stood a silver mouzhik holding up an infant.

"I open the door, Your Excellency. . . . There's a lady there . . .

"Says I, 'What can I do for you? . . .' She looks at me and says, 'Mitry Semenich . . .' I kiss her hand at once. 'If it isn't Anna Petrovna . . .' Says she, 'I want to take a look and see how you're getting on without me . . .'"

Apollon Apollonovich opened a drawer and drew out a dozen cheap pencils. He took two of them between his fingers and the wood cracked under his fingers. To express his anguish, Apollon Apollonovich always broke packets of pencils, which were kept specially for this purpose in a drawer under the letter "B."

While he broke the pencils, he managed to maintain his dispassionate expression; and no one glancing at him would have known that this stern *barin* nourished a secret desire to girdle the earth with an endless prospect as with a chain.

Semenich left the room. Flinging away the broken pencils, Apollon Apollonovich looked younger; quickly rearranging his tie, he jumped up and paced back and forth in extreme nervousness. At this moment he resembled his son, as he had looked in a photograph taken the previous year.

Then, blow after blow from distant rooms made themselves heard. Apollon Apollonovich paused and was about to lock the door of his study, but on reflection decided that he had heard only the slamming of a door in the drawing room. There was also the excruciating noise of someone coughing and the shuffling of slippered feet.

The door opened: Nikolai Apollonovich stood on the threshold in the uniform and sword which he had worn under the domino. He also wore a Tartar cap and house slippers.

"Well, Papa, here I am."

Apollon Apollonovich made no reference to the domino, but spoke instead of something else.

"You see, Kolenka . . . your mother, Anna Petrovna, has come back."

"So that's it," Nikolai Apollonovich thought, pretending to be agitated.

"Of course. I know . . ."

Only then did he actually realize that his mother had returned. He promptly resumed his habit of watching the old man's neck and ears. . . . The embarrassment, the virginal shyness with which the old man . . .

"Anna Petrovna, my dear, has committed an act which—I find it difficult to express myself—it is hard for me, Kolenka, to condone . . .

"In a word, her action is well known. You must have noticed that I have refrained from discussing it in your presence, bearing in mind your natural feelings . . ."

They were unnatural . . .

"Yes, Papa, I understand you."

"Of course!" Apollon Apollonovich thrust two fingers into his waistcoat pocket and began to pace the room diagonally from corner to corner. "Of course, her return to Petersburg is something I did not expect."

Apollon Apollonovich fixed his gaze on his son and raised himself on his toes.

"It's a complete surprise to us all. Who could have expected it?" Nikolai Apollonovich put in.

"That's what I say: who could have imagined it?" Apollon Apollonovich shrugged helplessly. "That she would return?" Again he started pacing about the room. "Her unexpected return can end, as you may suppose, in a complete change," he raised his finger and thundered, "in our domestic position or, again, everything may remain as it is."

"Yes, I see that."

Apollon Apollonovich raised his infinitely sad eyes.

"Kolenka, really I don't know, but I think. . . . It's hard to explain to you, taking into consideration your natural feelings . . ."

Nikolai Apollonovich suddenly felt a surge of love for the old despot, who was destined to be blown to bits.

He rushed toward his father and was about to fling himself to his knees, to repent and implore forgiveness. But the old man pursed his lips and waved his hands in repugnance.

"Oh no! Don't, please! I know what you want! You've heard me. Please leave me in peace."

He rapped with two fingers, and pointed to the door.

"You, young man, are trying to lead me by the nose. You, dear sir, are no son of mine. You're a terrible scoundrel!" Apollon Apollonovich shouted.

Nikolai Apollonovich escaped into the corridor. Those two protruding ears would be turned to slush.

8

Nikolai Apollonovich violently opened the door to his room and, rushing through it, upset a chair. He ran quickly to the table.

"Oh . . . where is it! . . . Ah! . . . It must be here . . . good!"

He often talked aloud to himself. He was impatient but the drawer refused to budge. When it finally opened he began throwing out packets of letters carefully tied together, a large cabinet-size portrait of a pretty woman and then, under the portrait, he found the small bundle. He balanced it in the palm of his hand; it was quite heavy. He put it down.

Nervously untying the knots of the towel, he resembled the Senator when a young man. His trembling fingers could not untie the knot; and there was no point in trying to, since everything was clear. Nevertheless, he finally managed to undo the knot. His astonishment was extreme.

"A bonbon box . . . ah? . . . and here's a ribbon! . . ."

When he tore off the ribbon his hopes were crushed; instead of candies from Balle, the bonbon box contained a sardine tin.

He casually noted the clock mechanism attached to the side: at the side, a metal key had to be turned in order to wind the black hand to the desired hour. Nikolai Apollonovich felt that he would never be able to turn this key: there was obviously no means to interrupt the course of the mechanism. To cut off further retreat Nikolai Apollonovich gripped the little key between his fingers. Either because his fingers trembled or because he felt dizzy, he fell headlong into that abyss which he had wanted to avoid: the little key turned to one o'clock, to two, and Nikolai Apollonovich suddenly recoiled from it, gazing distractedly at the table. He saw the sardine tin, which had once contained plump sardines; he himself had avoided sardines since the day he had gorged himself on them. It was an ordinary sardine tin, rounded at the corners.

"No!"

This sardine tin had terrible contents!

But the life which the conscious mind could not grasp was already active; the hour and the minute hands crawled around; and the seconds ticked in a circle; they would continue to do so until the instant when—

—the terrible contents of the sardine tin would suddenly rush to expand immeasurably; then, the sardine tin would explode . . .—

—the gases would scatter in circles, tearing apart the table with a roar; in the explosion the body would be torn to pieces and mingle with the splinters; there would be a spatter of gases and flesh . . .—

—in a hundredth of a second, the walls would crash and, expanding, their contents would whistle heavenward: a mass of splinters, stones and blood. Trails of smoke would fly over the Neva.

Having turned the key, he would put the little box somewhere in the white bedroom or, else, he would crush it under his heel.

His ears tingled; he felt sick as though he had swallowed the bomb like a pill. He would never crush it!

Only one way remained: to throw it into the Neva, and there was still time for that. If he turned the key twenty times, there would be a respite; but he delayed. He sank lethargically into an armchair; drowsiness overcame him. His weakened thought, breaking away from his body, drew some senseless, idle arabesques . . .

Nikolai Apollonovich had devoted his best years to the study of philosophy. Magic was alien to him; it dimmed and obscured the perception of the source of perfection. To the philosopher, Reason was perfection, his god. Nikolai Apollonovich respected the founders of great religions.

Nikolai Apollonovich respected Buddha in particular, assuming that Buddha had surpassed all religions in two respects: psychologically, by teaching men to love even animals; theoretically, by applying a system of logic which had been developed by Tibetan lamas. He remembered having read the logic of Darmarkirti with commentaries by Darmotapri.

Then, from time to time, he had experienced a strange sensation before passing through a doorway: it had seemed to him that there was nothing behind the door; that the door, if opened, would give on to an infinite cosmos; and that, if he stepped over the threshold, he would plunge below and fly past stars and planets—in an atmosphere of two hundred seventy-three degrees of cold.

10

Senselessly, he sat staring at the sardine tin: he saw and did not see it; he heard and did not hear it. His head fell to the table, on the box, while he stared into a bottomless abyss through the open door leading to the corridor.

Someone was staring at him through that door, from the infinite cosmos: the head of some god peered in and vanished; his Kirghiz-Kaisatsk ancestors had been in communication with Tibetan lamas; and they stirred in the blood of the Ab-Lai-Ukhovs. This heritage attracted him to Buddhism; in these sclerotic veins heredity beat in a million cells.

His dream was interrupted. A dumb torturous tread approached. An ancient world, like the horns of automobiles assaulting him, was fortified by the ancient sound of chanting: "Passion's surge —grow quiet . . . drowse . . . without . . ."

A roar came from the doorway. An ancient head appeared.

Nikolai Apollonovich sprang to his feet.

Whose head was it—Confucius's or Buddha's? An iridescent dressing-gown rustled in the doorway. He suddenly remembered his own Bokhara dressing-gown with its pattern of iridescent feathers . . . the dressing-gown upon whose smoky sapphire background crawled minute sharp-beaked golden-winged dragons. The cap with five tiers resembled a mitre; a many-rayed nimbus shone above the head. In the center a wrinkled face held its mouth open. Thus, the exalted Mongol entered the room. Ancient breezes blew.

Nikolai Apollonovich thought Kronos was visiting him in the guise of a Mongolian ancestor. In the hands of the Unknown he sought the blade of the traditional scythe; there was no scythe; the aromatic hand, like the first lily, held an Oriental plate with a heap of rosy apples: the apples of Paradise.

He rejected Paradise: Paradise or the Garden was inconsistent with his conception of the higher Kantian good. He believed in Nirvana.

And by Nirvana he understood—Nothingness.

Nikolai Apollonovich remembered now: he was an old Turanian. He had been reincarnated in the ranks of the high Russian nobility in order to fulfill the ancient commandment: to shatter all foundations. The Ancient Dragon must nourish himself on corrupt blood and consume everything in flame; the ancient Orient had poured a rain of bombs on the age. Nikolai Apollonovich, an ancient Turanian bomb, was about to explode now that he saw his native land; a Mongolian expression crept over his face. He looked like a mandarin of the Middle Empire dressed in a frock coat to visit the West on a secret mission.

The ancient Turanian, temporarily clothed in an Aryan domino, hurried to the stack of notebooks in which were outlined the propositions of a reasoned metaphysics; the stack of notebooks added up to an immense undertaking covering the whole of life: the Mongolian aspect of it was transparent in the well-defined points and all the paragraphs—a mission intrusted to him before birth.

The visitor, a dignified Turanian, stood there. His arms rose rhythmically, and his attire flapped like beating wings; the smoky background cleared, deepened, and suddenly became the sky, streaked through gaps of air into the small study. A dark sapphire crevice was visible in the room crowded with bookshelves—the dressing-gown had become an immense crevice through which it was possible to see the sparkling stars. . . . The indigo air, distilled with stars, blew through the room.

Nikolai Apollonovich rushed to meet his visitor—as one Turanian greeting another—with a notebook in his hand:

"Kant. (Kant too was a Turanian.)

"Value, as a metaphysical nothing!

"Social relations, based on values.

"The destruction of the Aryan world by a system of values.

"Conclusion: a Mongolian affair."

The Turanian replied: "The problem has not been grasped: Paragraph One—is the Prospect.

"Instead of values—numeration: by houses, stories, rooms—to the end of time.

"Instead of a new order—the regulated circulation by the citizens of the Prospect.

"Not the destruction of Europe—but her immutability . . .

"A Mongolian affair . . ."

He had been condemned. The wrinkled face drew closer: he glanced at the ear, and realized that the old Turanian, his mentor in the ways of wisdom, was no other than Apollon Apollonovich; and it was against him that he had raised his hand.

And this was the Day of Judgment.

"What is it? Who is it?"

"Your father . . ."

"Who?"

"Saturn . . ."

The Last Judgment was upon him.

There was neither Earth, nor Venus, nor Mars: only revolving rings; then a fourth planet was shattered, and an immense Sun was being concentrated into a new world. Mists drifted past; Nikolai Apollonovich had been thrown into infinity; distances flowed by.

Then he was on earth again; the sword of Saturn hung in the

air, and the continent of Atlantis had been destroyed. Nikolai Apollonovich was now a depraved monster. Afterwards, he was in China; and Apollon Apollonovich, the mighty ruler, had commanded him to slaughter thousands, and this he had done. At that time, hordes of Tamerlane's horsemen had been pouring in, and Nikolai Apollonovich had galloped into Russia on a horse from the steppes; then he had been reincarnated as a Russian nobleman and had resumed his old habits: he had slaughtered more thousands, and now he wanted to throw a bomb at his father. But his father was Saturn. Time had completed its revolution: Saturn's reign had returned.

Time had stopped moving; everything was perishing.

"Father!"

"You wanted to blow me to bits—that's why everything is perishing."

"Not you, but . . ."

"Everything is crashing down, falling on Saturn . . ."

The air beyond the window was darkening; everything had melted, expanding infinitely; everything was spinning at a terrible speed.

"*Célà . . . tourne . . .*" roared Nikolai Apollonovich, who had lost his body without noticing it . . .

"No, *ça . . . tourne. . . .*"

Although his body was missing, he still preserved a sense of his body; the invisible center, formerly his consciousness, seemed to preserve the semblance of his previous state: logic had become bone; syllogisms were wound with sinews; and the content of logic was covered with flesh. Thus, "I" again revealed its image as substance, though it was not body; and in the explosion an alien "I" was revealed. It had come from Saturn, and to Saturn it returned.

He sat bodiless as before, but within a body. Outside there was a sound: *tourne-tourne.*

The revolution of years ran backward.

"What is our chronology?"

But Saturn—Apollon Apollonovich—answered with a chortle:

"We haven't any, Kolenka. Our chronology, my dear, is simply zero . . ."

"Ai! What, then, is the meaning of 'I am'?"

"Zero . . ."

"And zero?"

"A bomb . . ."

Then Nikolai Apollonovich realized that he was a bomb; and, bursting, he would be detonated.

He awoke from his dream: his head was resting on the sardine tin.

A terrible dream. . . . He could not remember it. Nightmares of his childhood returned: Pépp Péppovich Pépp, swelling from a tiny ball, in a sardine tin—

—Pépp Péppovich Pépp was a Party bomb: it ticked inaudibly; Pépp Péppovich Pépp would swell and swell. And Pépp Péppovich Pépp would explode!

"What?

. . . Am I delirious?"

Again he felt a surge of dizziness. What was he to do? Only a quarter of an hour left: should he turn it back?

He turned the key twenty times, and it clicked twenty times. His deliriums departed to make the morning another morning, day another day, evening another evening; but, at the end of the night, the movement of the key would halt. The walls would crash.

CHAPTER SIX

Pursued where'er he went
By the Bronze Horseman
Wildly galloping . . .

—PUSHKIN

1

Alexander Ivanovich opened his weary eyes: the night had been an event of gigantic proportions.

The transitional state between dream and waking felt like a jump from a fifth-story window. His senses had opened a breach, and into this breach he had plunged.

Waking had quickly precipitated him from there: his entire body ached. He was conscious of shivering violently. He had tossed all night long; something, certainly, must have happened . . .

The delirious flight continued along misty prospects, up and down the rungs of a strange ladder. Actually, he was suffering from a fever, which was raging through his body. Memory struggled to be heard, but eluded him; he tried vainly to connect things. Frightened—he had always feared sickness in solitude—he was determined to see it through.

"I must have quinine. . . . Yes, and strong tea . . . with raspberry preserves . . ."

He sighed involuntarily.

"I should abstain. . . . Perhaps I should not read *The Apocalypse* . . . maybe I should not look in on the house porter . . . nor chat with Stepka . . ."

Thinking of tea, Stepka, and *The Apocalypse* comforted him.

After washing his face in cold water from the faucet, he again felt the surge of the irrational. He glanced around his twenty-ruble garret room, a squalid place. His bed was made of cracked boards placed across wooden trestles, showing the stains of dried bedbugs. The boards were covered with a very hard mattress; the red and

189

blue stripes were faded from the woven bedcover; traces of them had been removed not by dirt but by many years of hard use.

A small ikon depicting the prayer of Seraphim Sarovsky hung in a corner: under his shirt Alexander Ivanovich wore a cross.

In addition to the bed, the room contained a small planed table, such as is commonly used for holding wash basins and is usually sold in country markets. It served both as a writing table and a night table; there was no wash basin. Alexander Ivanovich used a spigot and a sardine tin for his piece of Kazan soap. There was also a clothes rack, under which showed the tip of a worn slipper. In a dream he had once seen a slipper behaving as if it were alive, like a dog or a cat; it had shuffled along autonomously, crawling about in the corners with a rustling noise; when he had offered to feed it some soft musty bread, the shuffling creature had bitten his finger; he had awakened. A bulging tan suitcase, which had lost its original form, was also in the room.

All the decorations of the room were overshadowed by the color of the very ugly and somber wallpaper: dark yellow, darkish brown with damp stains. At night wood-lice crawled over it.

Alexander Ivanovich Doodkin surveyed his habitation; he longed to be outdoors, in the unclean fog, rubbing shoulders, mingling with other backs and greenish faces, on a Petersburg prospect.

Layers of October fog clung to the windowpane; he felt a desire to be overwhelmed by the fog, to drown in it the nonsense which irritated his brain, to extinguish the surges of delirium by exercising his legs. He wanted to stride from prospect to prospect, from street to street, until his brain was numbed, and then collapse at a tavern table and burn out his organs with vodka.

He put on his thin overcoat and thought, "I really ought to take some quinine! But what's the good of quinine?

"I'd better have some strong tea with raspberry preserves! . . ."

2

The stairway . . .

It was forbidding, shadowy, damp; it pitilessly echoed the sound of steps. Everything had occurred that night; he had passed here; it had been no dream.

The fatal silence deepened, intensifying an occasional rustling sound; in the suspenseful atmosphere he heard sounds like the swallowing of saliva, sounds of the moans of time. From above, through the windows, the murky twilight fell in tufted shapes, and dim turquoise shadows spread soundlessly under foot.

The moon shone through. But shaggy, smoky cloud formations rushed toward the moon: the turquoise air became imbued with gloom.

Alexander Ivanovich suddenly remembered that he had run up this stairway the day before, dissipating his strength without the faintest hope of overcoming—overcoming what? Some shape was pursuing him.

And it was irreparably destroying him.

The stairway . . .

On a gray day it was prosaic enough: dull thuds could be heard, the sound of cabbage being chopped, of a rug from apartment four, half-torn and smelling from cat, being beaten on the banister, and of sneezing caused by dust.

The edges of the doors were covered with oilcloth. One door after another. . . . The oilcloth of one door had been torn away, horsehair stuck out of the rips; on another door a card was pinned, reading "Zakatalkin." Nothing more—neither his full name nor his profession. Behind this door someone was diligently sawing away at a familiar tune on a fiddle; someone was singing:

"To my dear native land . . ."

Perhaps Zakatalkin was a fiddler in a restaurant orchestra.

3

Away, out into the street! . . .

He had to stride forcefully until his brain was numbed, until he dreamed no longer, stride through Petersburg and lose himself in the damp rushes, in the vapors from the seashore, cut loose, reject everything, and find himself in the dim lights of the suburbs.

Apprehensively, he started down the stairs; he stopped abruptly, noticing a figure in an Italian cloak and a fantastically bent hat hurrying along, desperately swinging a heavy cane.

The strange figure rushed right into him, almost colliding with his chest. Alexander Ivanovich Doodkin's head swung up and he saw before him a perspiring forehead with a quivering vein; by this vein he recognized Ableukhov.

Nikolai Apollonovich cut him off with a menacing whisper: "You understand, of course. I *cannot*, and I *do not want to*. In a word, I *shall not do it!*"

"!"

"I refuse, irrevocably. You can tell them so. And I want you to leave me in peace."

Nikolai Apollonovich turned; twirling his heavy cane, he ran back down the steps.

Alexander Ivanovich thudded down the stairs shouting after him: "Nikolai Apollonovich, stop!"

He caught Ableukhov by the sleeve, but the latter tore away across the courtyard. Alexander Ivanovich, in desperation, threw open the door and overtook him in two leaps. He grabbed the flying hem of Ableukhov's Italian cloak. They struggled for a moment in the pile of wood. Choking with anger, Nikolai Apollonovich shouted loud insults at him.

"So you call this action Party work? To have me surrounded by spies? To follow me like shadows . . . I see through it all, let me tell you! Oh, Lord, and you . . . you . . . you . . ."

Tearing himself free again, Nikolai Apollonovich dashed off.

4

They were both running along the street.

"Nikolai Apollonovich!" Doodkin kept shouting excitedly. "You must agree—we can't separate without some explanation . . ."

"There's nothing more to talk about!" Nikolai Apollonovich yelled over his shoulder.

"Explain it more clearly," Alexander Ivanovich insisted. His face and voice expressed injury and astonishment. Nikolai Apollonovich could not help noticing it.

He turned more calmly, but with lachrymose bitterness:

"What is there to explain? . . . I have the right to demand. . . .
It is I who suffer, not you or your comrades . . ."

"What do you mean?"

"To have given me that bundle . . ."

"Well?"

"Without an explanation, without warning . . ."

Alexander Ivanovich flushed.

"And then to vanish . . . and to threaten me with the police
through someone else . . ."

Alexander Ivanovich smirked nervously:

"Stop. What police? What do these insinuations mean, anyhow?"

Nikolai Apollonovich shouted hoarsely:

"I'll . . . I'll . . ." He moved nearer Doodkin. "Why, I'll . . .
deal with you right now . . ."

One summer evening Alexander Ivanovich had noticed an old
woman sitting and biting at her lip at the window of a small shining
house nearby. He knew that the bomb had been brought to his
garret from that little house. He shuddered involuntarily.

From the ravings of the Senator's son about the police and
about his irrevocable refusal, he could only grasp one thing:

"Listen, the package is the main issue . . ."

"Yes. You gave it to me for safekeeping."

The conversation was being continued near the little house where
the bomb had originated: the bomb, having now become a mental
bomb in conversation, had described a complete circle.

"Nikolai Apollonovich, you've hurt me. What is there reprehen-
sible in my behavior?"

"What do you mean?"

"The Party," he pronounced the words in a whisper, "only asked
you to keep the package safe for a while. You agreed, didn't you?
That is all. . . . If you don't want to keep it, then I'll stop by and
collect it."

"Please don't assume this innocent mask! It's not just a question
of keeping a bundle."

"Sh-h! Not so loud, please! People might hear us . . ."

"Yes. . . . I could have understood that. . . . Don't pretend that
you don't know."

"What is the matter, then?"

"It's a question of coercion."

"There's been no coercion."

"And the spies."

"I repeat, there's been no coercion. You agreed freely."

"Yes—last summer I . . ."

"Go on!"

"Yes, I agreed in principle or, rather, I offered . . . and, perhaps, I even promised, assuming that there would be no compulsion, just as there is no compulsion in the Party. But if you exercise compulsion, then you are simply a gang of intriguers. . . . Well, what then? . . . I promised, but I certainly thought the promise could be retracted . . ."

"Just a minute . . ."

"And could I know that my offer would be twisted like that . . ."

"Just a minute. I must interrupt. . . . What promise are you talking about?"

"*That* promise!"

Alexander Ivanovich immediately recalled that Nikolai Stepanovich Lippanchenko had said something in the tavern to the effect that Nikolai Apollonovich was to . . . but he did not want to remember it! He said quickly:

"I'm not talking about *that*. *That* is not it."

"What do you mean? The whole issue lies in that promise: in the promise which has been interpreted in the cruelest way, and irrevocably."

"Not so loud, Nikolai Apollonovich. What's cruel about it?"

"What do you mean!"

"Why, the Party asked you to keep it safe for a time. That's all."

"Is that all?"

"All . . ."

"If the matter concerned only the bundle, I'd understand you; but, you see . . ." He waved his hand. "Don't you see, we're getting nowhere."

"You keep raving about coercion. Come to think of it, rumors have reached me, too . . ."

"Yes?"

"About the act of violence which you proposed to us. The intention came from you!"

Alexander Ivanovich remembered what Lippanchenko had told him in the tavern. Nikolai Apollonovich had proposed, through an intermediary, to do away with his father. He remembered Lippanchenko adding that the Party had only one alternative: to reject the proposal. The unnatural choice of the victim, the cynicism bordering on infamy involved in the choice, had revolted his sensitivity. Although Alexander Ivanovich had been drunk during his entire conversation with Lippanchenko, which had seemed like a play of intoxication rather than sober reality, yet he remembered it all.

"I must admit . . ." he said.

"To demand from me," Ableukhov interrupted, "that I . . . with my own hand . . ."

"So that's it . . ."

"It's unbelievable!"

"Yes, it is horrible. I don't believe it, Nikolai Apollonovich. . . . Indeed, I thought you'd have fallen in the estimation of the Party . . ."

"You think it vile?"

"Excuse me . . ."

"There, you see! You call it horrible, yet you had something to do with it!"

Doodkin suddenly became agitated.

"Just a moment!"

Seizing a button of the Italian cloak, he kept his eyes fixed on one point.

"Don't say another word! We're reproaching each other, yet we both agree on the nature of the act. . . . It is vile, isn't it!"

Nikolai Apollonovich shuddered. "Of course it is!"

A silence followed. Nikolai Apollonovich, pulling a handkerchief from his pocket, stopped and wiped his face.

"So am I . . ."

They looked at each other with perplexity. Alexander Ivanovich again touched the edge of the cloak.

"In order to clear this up, answer me one thing: that promise was not your idea then?"

"No! Certainly not!"

"You were not implicated in this murder then—even in thought?

I ask you this because the mind sometimes unwittingly expresses itself in gesture, intonation, glance, even in the trembling of lips..."

"No, no. . . . That is . . ." Nikolai Apollonovich paused, for he caught himself in a suspicious current of thought. He blushed.

"I did not love my father . . . and more than once I expressed my. . . . But that I should think of . . . never!"

"I believe you."

Unfortunately, Nikolai Apollonovich blushed deeply; and having done so, needed to explain himself. But Alexander Ivanovich shook his head, having no desire to touch upon the nuance of the incommunicable thought which had flashed upon both of them.

"Don't bother . . . I believe you. . . . I have something else on my mind. Tell me honestly, do you think I'm implicated in this?"

Nikolai Apollonovich looked in astonishment at his naïve companion. He stared at him, blushed, and, in order to hide a thought, heatedly shouted:

"As I see it, yes! You helped him."

"Whom?"

"The Unknown . . ."

"The what?"

"The *Unknown* demanded that . . ."

"What!"

"The execution of this cruel act."

"Where?"

"In a nasty note."

"I don't know any such person."

"The *Unknown*," Nikolai Apollonovich insisted, "is a Party comrade. . . . Why are you astonished?"

"I assure you, there is no such person as the *Unknown* in the Party!"

"What? No *Unknown* in the Party?"

"Not so loud, please! . . . No . . ."

"For three months now I've been receiving notes . . ."

"From whom?"

"From him . . ."

They stared into each other's eyes: the eyes of one dropped, terrified; a spark of faint hope flashed in the eyes of the other.

"Nikolai Apollonovich," began Alexander Ivanovich, and a strong confusion, conquering fear, suffused his cheeks with red spots. "Nikolai Apollonovich!"

"Well?"

But Alexander Ivanovich could not regain his breath.

"Go on—don't torture me!"

Alexander Ivanovich shook his head and did not reply. Something inexpressible held him silent, but his struggle was visible in his face. He said with some effort:

"I assure you—I give you my word of honor. I had no part in this . . ."

Nikolai Apollonovich did not believe him.

"Well then, what does it mean?" He stared blindly down the street. It had visibly altered. "I feel no easier. I had no sleep last night!"

A gust swept in from the sea. The last leaves fell in a quiet shower; and Alexander Ivanovich knew it all by heart, knew that days of blood and terror would come, that everything would crash after the last leaves had done their dance.

5

"So *he* was at the ball?"

"Yes, *he* was . . ."

"And talked to your father?"

"Precisely. He mentioned you."

"Then he met you in the lane?"

"Yes, he took me to a little restaurant."

"What did he say his name was?"

"Morkovin . . ."

Nikolai Apollonovich babbled on, bending his grinning profile; his tragic mask contradicted his lizard-like shiftiness. He continued to pour out all he knew about the ball, his masquerade, the flight across the salon, his stop by the projection of the little house, the gate, the note and finally, the tavern.

Abracadabra! It all seemed an imaginative mental exercise, and irreparably destructive.

A great swarm of bowlers and cylinder hats rolled along the street toward them. An ostrich feather foamed by.

Noses were thrust forward everywhere: eagle noses and cock noses; duck noses and hen noses; a green nose and a red nose. They all rolled forward to meet them, hurriedly and abundantly.

"So you think it's a mistake?"

Having made a shy advance, Nikolai Apollonovich shivered. Alexander Ivanovich tore himself away from the contemplation of noses.

"It's no mistake, but dirty interference. There's a method in this design—an attempt to smother Party initiative."

"You must help me . . ."

"Inadmissible mockery," Doodkin interrupted, "made up of nonsense and rank lies!"

Alexander Ivanovich held out his hand to Nikolai Apollonovich and noticed casually that his companion was shorter than he.

"Well, you must keep your nerve . . ."

"It's easy for you to speak of nerve. But I had no sleep last night . . ."

Alexander Ivanovich soothed Ableukhov.

"I am sure I can solve this messy riddle. I'll start inquiries, and . . ."

He faltered. Lippanchenko had information. But was he in Petersburg?

"And? . . ."

"I'll give you an answer tomorrow."

One fact in particular had amazed Alexander Ivanovich.

6

The crowd of shoulders formed a cohesive and slowly moving mass. Alexander Ivanovich's shoulder glued itself to the mass and, obeying the impulse of the mass, moved upon the Nevsky Prospect. The bodies of those who were thrown upon the pavement were transformed into one general body, like grains of caviar. The pavements of the Nevsky formed a sandwich field where individual thought became part of the general thought of the polypedal creature which crawled along it.

Mutely, the multiple feet crawled and shuffled; the throng was a pastiche of individual members.

There were no individual persons on the Nevsky, but only a crawling, growling polypod, sprinkling forth a variety of voices, broken down into a variety of words; intermingling, the words wove themselves into phrases, meaningless phrases which hovered like black smoke over the Nevsky. And swelling against it, the Neva pressed against its massive cage of granite.

The crawling mass was terrifying. For centuries it had run along the Nevsky. Higher, above the Nevsky, time ran. Here, above, the order was flexible, but below there, it was immutable. Time had certain limits. But the vast human polypod had no limits; all its links were interchangeable. It was always the same: its head was curled beyond the railway station; its tail was thrust into the Morskaya. The links shuffled along the Prospect.

7

"You understand me, I hope," Nikolai Apollonovich repeated. "You do understand me, Alexander Ivanovich?"

"Yes, I understand you."

"There's life in that sardine tin," Nikolai Apollonovich affirmed. "The clock mechanism ticked so strangely . . ."

Alexander Ivanovich suddenly asked, "What sardine tin is that?" Listening more attentively, he realized that his companion was referring to the bomb.

"I started it. It was dead, so to speak, when I received it . . . I turned the key. It began to gasp like a man waking up. That set it off . . ."

"So you started it going?"

"Yes. It will go on for twenty-four hours . . ."

"What have you done! Throw it into the river at once!" Alexander Ivanovich exclaimed, gesturing with his hands.

"It's made me see double . . ."

"The sardine tin?"

"Generally speaking, I've had some odd, constantly varying experiences in connection with it. . . . Only the devil knows what. . . . I felt revulsion. . . . All sorts of nonsense, disgust . . . a strange revulsion against the tin itself and the sardines it had contained—I can't bear sardines! The revulsion grew . . . as though directed against an insect buzzing in my ear. It prodded me to action . . ."

"H'm . . ."

"It was like food for which I had an aversion. . . . I felt sick . . . as though I had swallowed it . . ."

"Swallowed it? How awful!"

"I myself had become the bomb. It was ticking in my stomach."

"Not so loud. People might hear you!"

"They won't understand anything, though."

"Do you know," Alexander Ivanovich commented with interest, "this ticking is an odd thing: when you listen to it, now it's one thing, now another. I once frightened a neurasthenic. I began to tap with my finger in rhythm to the conversation. He began to stare at me, grew pale, stopped talking, and finally barked out: 'What is it?' I answered, 'Nothing . . .' and went on tapping. Just think of it! The fellow had a fit. His feelings were hurt and, afterwards, he wouldn't even greet me . . ."

"No, no, it's impossible to understand it easily. . . . I had a sort of delirium . . . memories that troubled me . . ."

"Something out of childhood?"

"It was as though a bandage had been torn from all my sensations. . . . Something stirred above my head—do you know the feeling? My hair stood on end. I understand it now, I grasped it last night; my whole body, as it were, stood on end; it bristled, legs and arms and chest. Everything quivered, pulsated, ran onward—faster and faster, and was transformed into a tremendous feeling, as though of being torn apart and pulled in different directions: first, the heart came out; then, like a switch out of wattling, the vertebrae came out of the spine."

"And you, Nikolai Apollonovich, felt like a Dionysus in agony. Jokes aside though, will you speak on another level . . . not according to Kant."

"But I've already told you: all the bandages were torn from

my sensations. It wasn't according to Kant, that's certain. Far from it!"

"That's a case either of logic carried into the blood or of stagnation; you had received a shock—your blood rushed to the brain. In your very words, I can hear the blood pulsing . . ."

"I felt myself swelling, swollen. I had been swollen for hundreds of years perhaps; and there I was walking about, a swollen monster. . . . It was terrible."

"That was mere sensation."

"I'm not . . . ?"

"On the contrary: you've grown thinner."

"I stood staring at that sardine tin. . . . No, it was not *I* who stood there, but a giant with an idiot head. There was a prickling sensation in my body. I could hear it clearly—about six inches 'from the body! . . . Just think of it! I had been turned inside out."

"You were simply beside yourself."

"It's all very well for you to say 'beside yourself'—the expression is allegorical, not based on sensation. This was different. The sensations had overflowed the organs, had suddenly expanded in space, like a bomb . . ."

"Tss!"

". . .In fragments! . . ."

"When I came to your house with the bundle, I asked myself why *I* was I. But you didn't understand me."

"But now I understand *everything*—it's sheer terror . . ."

"Not terror, but a Dionysian agony. Nothing literary of course . . ."

"The devil knows!"

"Be calm, Nikolai Apollonovich, you're very tired. It's not sensible, you've gone through so much!" Alexander Ivanovich felt a desperate need to escape from this conversation and to consider these events.

8

He wanted to stride, to walk out and, finally, to collapse exhausted in a tavern where he might think and drink.

He himself had been instructed by a certain *person* to deliver a letter to Ableukhov. Although he had the letter when he gave the bundle to Ableukhov, he had forgotten to hand the letter over. Instead, he had asked Varvara Evgrafovna to transmit it to Ableukhov. That might have been the fatal letter. But it was impossible. According to Ableukhov, the letter had been handed to him by some masked person at the ball.

Alexander Ivanovich was reassured. It could not have been the letter intrusted to him by Lippanchenko. He had just arrived at this conclusion and was about to intersect a stream of droshkies, when someone called to him.

"Alexander Ivanovich!"

Trembling, perspiring, Nikolai Apollonovich was pushing through the crowd.

"Just a minute!" he panted.

"Oh Lord!" Alexander Ivanovich sighed.

"Alexander Ivanovich, it's hard for me to leave you now. . . . I have to tell you something else . . ." He led him to the nearest shop window.

"There's another thing . . ."

"Nikolai Apollonovich, I'm in a hurry. On your business . . ."

"Just a second . . ."

Nikolai Apollonovich looked inspired.

"I must tell you: I grew to be infinite, and all the objects grew in proportion: the room and the spire of Peter and Paul. No space was left for further growth . . . and finally, in the end, there seemed to be another principle—a wild, fantastic one. Perhaps I lack the means of conceiving it. The sense organs were replaced by *zero*. . . . I conceived something that was not quite *zero*, but *zero minus* something, *minus* five, for example . . . "

"Listen, tell me," Alexander Ivanovich interrupted, "did you get the letter through Varvara Evgrafovna?"

"Letter? . . ."

"Not *that*, not the note—but the letter sent you through Varvara Evgrafovna . . ."

"Oh, you mean those verses signed '*Flaming Soul*'?"

"I don't know what was in it."

"Yes, yes, I received it. . . . No—what was I saying? Oh yes —zero *minus* something . . ."

"Lord, are you still harping on that! You should read *The Apocalypse . . .*"

"I've heard you say that before. . . . I'll read it without fail. When you reassure me . . . about all *this*, I'll feel a renewed interest. I'll stay at home, drink bromide, and read *The Apocalypse.* The effect of last night hasn't worn off yet; everything seems now one thing, now another. Just look! Here's a shop window . . . full of reflections; a gentleman has just passed by, and look. . . . Here are *we*, do you see? It all seems so strange . . ."

"Yes, strange," Alexander Ivanovich consented with a nod. In the matter of "it seems so strange," he was a specialist.

"Or consider mere objects. . . . The devil alone knows what they are: now they are one thing, now another. . . . Take *that* tin, for example: it's just a tin, and yet something more . . ."

"Tsss!"

"A tin of terrible content!"

"Pitch that sardine tin into the Neva, the sooner the better; and then everything will fall into its natural place again . . ."

"No, it will not . . ."

It must be admitted that Alexander Ivanovich was at a loss how to stop this babbling; he did not know whether to try to calm him or to break off the conversation.

"Nikolai Apollonovich, you have been brooding too long over Kant in your corked-up, unventilated room. A storm has hit you; you've listened to it, and heard yourself in it. . . . But your state has already been described; it has been the subject of observation . . ."

"Where, where?"

"In *belles-lettres*, in poetry, in books on psychology, in occult research."

Alexander Ivanovich smiled at the ignorance of his learned companion and continued: "The psychiatrist . . ."

"Well?"

"Would call it . . ."

"Yes—yes—yes . . ."

"Well, something like—you might call it pseudo-hallucination . . ."

"What?"

"That is the cause of symbolic sensations which do not correspond to the irritation of a sensation."

"Well, what then? To say *that* is to say nothing!"

"Yes, you're right . . ."

"No, that does not satisfy me . . ."

"Of course, a modernist would call it the sensation of the abyss, and search for an image corresponding to the symbolic sensation."

"So it's an allegory?"

"Don't confuse allegory and symbol. Allegory is a symbol which has become current literature. For example, there is the accepted concept of your 'beside oneself.' A symbol is the naming of the experience you have had with that sardine tin; a better term for it would be the elemental pulsation body. That is what you really experienced; the shock made your elemental body tremble within you. For an instant, it separated itself from your physical body, and you therefore underwent that experience. According to the beliefs of other schools, the experiences of the elemental body can transform literary meanings and allegories into real meanings, into symbols; the works of mystics abound in symbols; and after what you have gone through, I'd advise you to read these mystics . . ."

"I told you I would, and I mean to . . ."

"As for your recent experiences, they might be classified as experiences beyond the grave: Plato speaks of them when he cites the evidence of the Bacchantes. . . . There are experimental schools that consciously evoke perceptions and then laboriously transform a nightmare into a form of harmony, in the process studying the rhythms, movements, pulsations, and introducing into the sensation of expansion the sober clarity of consciousness. For example . . . but why stand here chattering? You should go home and throw that tin into the river. . . . Then sit tight. Don't stir or go anywhere; I've no doubt you're being followed. Drink your bromide—you've taken a lot . . . although it's better to leave the bromide alone. Too much of it will leave you incapable of anything. . . . Well, I really must be off—on your business."

Alexander Ivanovich slipped into the stream of bowlers, turned and called: "Throw that tin into the river!"

His shoulders joined other shoulders: the headless polypod carried him away.

Nikolai Apollonovich shuddered. He must return home, stick *it* into his pocket, and throw it into the Neva!

Nikolai Apollonovich felt that he was expanding again; at the same time, he became aware of a slight drizzle.

9

The street crossing opposite looked black; a caryatid stood there.

The Institution of which Apollon Apollonovich was the head loomed above it.

The bearded caryatid of the entrance had rashly pushed a hoof into the wall, and it looked as if it would break away from the wall and crash down.

What the caryatid saw was mutable, inexplicable, inarticulate: the drifting clouds. Below, it beheld the pavement where a rustling of passing feet made a muffled sound and where all the faces looked green; by staring at them it was impossible to tell that there was a rumbling of important events somewhere.

The procession of bowlers provided no clue to the thunder of great events: in the town of Ak-Tiuk, in the Kutaisk Theater; in Tiflis, the police had discovered a factory making illegal bombs; in Odessa the library had been closed; meetings were being held in all the universities of Russia; at the iron foundry in Revel, red flags had been unfurled . . .

From the procession of bowlers no one could have deduced that there was a strike on the Moscow-Kazan railroad; that windows had been smashed and storehouses raided; that work had stopped on the Kursk, Vindavsk, Nizhegorod, and Muromsk railroads; that traffic everywhere was at a standstill. No one could have suspected that events were occurring in Petersburg as well; the typesetters of all the Petersburg printing houses had elected delegates and had held a meeting; factories were on strike; and so were the shipyards and the Alexandrovsk plant.

But the public still circulated in the streets: bowlers still flowed in a sluggish stream.

On this gray day the massive doors were thrown open, and a gray shaven doorman in gold galloon signaled to a coachman; the horses lunged forward to the entrance, while the doorman suddenly grew dumb and rigid. Apollon Apollonovich Ableukhov—shrunken, bent, unshaven, his face puffy and his lower lip protruding—raised his black-gloved hand to the black brim of his cylinder hat.

He glanced indifferently at the doorman, the carriage, and the coachman, at the large black bridge and the expanse of the Neva, where the many misty chimneys showed so faintly and where the island rose, ashen pale and indistinct.

The carriage door with its heraldic unicorn was slammed shut, and the carriage sped into the fog—past the tonelessly black cathedral, past the Nicholas monument, to the Nevsky Prospect, where a red fustian standard flapped in the light breeze. The silhouettes of the carriage, the coachman's cocked hat, and the wings of his mantle cut into the shaggy throng. The Manchurian caps, cap bands, peaked caps—in unison all burst into song.

The carriage stopped.

10

"Mais j'espère que oui"—a foreigner's voice sang out.

Alexander Ivanovich disliked eavesdropping.

The sky was growing dark and blue.

Alexander Ivanovich had crossed the threshold before his footsteps were heard.

The air was heavy with the fragrance of mingled perfume and medicine.

Zoya Zakharovna was solicitously trying to attend to some foreigner. "I hope you will carry away a fine impression of Russia. Things are happening . . ."

"Mais j'espère . . ."

Zoya Fleish swiveled her somewhat distraught glance from the Frenchman to Alexander Ivanovich; her eyes bulged; she was a large-headed brunette of about forty, heavily powdered.

"You must see *him*?" she inquired at random. Her casual
question was charged with latent hostility, perhaps even hatred,
but her smile concealed it in the same way that sticky sweet candy
sold in certain shops hides dirt.

"I think I'll wait for *him*."

Alexander Ivanovich reached out for a pear: Zoya Zakharovna
moved the fruit bowl away. Pears were all right, but there was no
force in them.

A voice was chanting somewhere in the rear, a broken voice
with an impossible accent; it was just incredible to sing like that.
It sounded like a man with dark hair, sunken chest, and the eyes
of a roach; a consumptive probably, someone from Odessa or a
Bulgarian from Varna; a propagandist full of hate.

In the meantime, Zoya Fleish rambled on: "Yes, yes, yes, we're
living through historically significant experiences . . . audacity
and youth . . . historians will say . . ."

"*Pardon, Madame, monsieur viendra-t-il bientôt?*"

Alexander Ivanovich almost fell over the St. Bernard which
was gnawing a bone.

The cottage windows faced the sea. The atmosphere was a
deepening blue.

The beacon eye winked "one-two-three," and was extinguished;
the somber cloak of a pedestrian was visible; crested waves
curled; lights sprang up along the shore and a siren wailed.

"Here's an ashtray."

But Alexander Ivanovich was very touchy: he threw his cigarette
butt into a flower vase.

"Who is singing?"

"What, don't you know? Then let me tell you—it's Shishnarfiev."

"He's remarkably artistic," Alexander Ivanovich commented,
and then asked: "A Bulgarian?"

"No, no . . ."

"A Persian?"

"From Shemakha. He escaped the massacre. From Ispahan."

"Oh."

Zoya Zakharovna turned to the Frenchman.

Alexander Ivanovich was thinking about Zoya: her features
might have been assembled from several different beautiful women:

the nose from one; the mouth from another; the ears from a third. However, the combined effect was irritating.

The Frenchman was besieging her: "*Excusez, dans certains cas je préfère parler personellement . . .*"

They could see the foaming waves. A boat rocked in the blue twilight; its sharp-winged sails cut the darkness; the bluish night thickened around them.

A cab drove up to the garden. A stout bulky man, suffering from shortness of breath, rolled leisurely out of the vehicle, his arms filled with packages; one hand struggled with a leather purse. A bag fell from under his arm into a puddle and burst open, sending some apples rolling in the mud. An ill-omened head, in a cap with earflaps, drooped low over the chest; in a tired manner the small deep-set eyes fixed on the window.

In that face Alexander Ivanovich suddenly intercepted an expression of joy, of purely animal joy: the joy of anticipating supper after a day of hard labor. Like a beast returning to its lair, the man looked gentle, outwardly amiable, ready to rub his muzzle against his female and to lick his pups.

It was the *person*.

"Lippanchenko!"

"How do you do?"

The dog leaped up and fell with his paws upon the *person*'s chest.

"Go away, Tom!"

The *person* tried desperately to protect his purchases; his square face was a mixture of amusement and helpless irritation.

"He's slobbered all over me again!"

The dog's tongue licked the tip of his nose; the *person* shouted helplessly, "Now, Tommy!"

He stopped laughing, and shot rather brusquely, "I'll be with you presently. Here I'm . . ."

His hanging lip quivered; it suggested: "Even here I have no rest."

The *person* fidgeted in the corner: his galoshes refused to come off; standing in the corner he dug into the pocket of his greatcoat; his hand crept out with a toy—a sort of Humpty-Dumpty figure.

"This is for the cook's daughter, Manka . . ."

Zoya Zakharovna turned to the Frenchman: "This way, please!"
And she flung at Doodkin: "You'll have to wait a while."

11

"Zoya Zakharovna . . ."

"Yes?"

"Shishnarfiev is an active representative of Young Persia—an
artistic nature. But where does the Frenchman come in?"

"If you know too much, you will be old before your time," she
snapped at Alexander Ivanovich, her extremely large bosom sinking under her bodice.

Once more he grew aware of the mingled odor of perfume
and medicine—the kind of medicine that reminds one of a dentist's
office; it was not very pleasant.

"You persist in remaining an anchorite."

"Whether I do so or not, it's all the same. Someone has to be
an anchorite." He added mischievously: "I ought to tell you:
you look disturbed, and that doesn't become you."

"Is that why you scattered cigarette ash over the tablecloth?"

But Alexander Ivanovich, reaching for a pear, retorted: "How
stingy you are!"

She had already removed the pears from the table, and pears
were his favorite fruit.

"Here's an ashtray."

"I was reaching for a pear."

But Zoya Zakharovna made no move to offer him a pear.

He gazed through the half-open door: he saw human shapes.
The small Frenchman was gesticulating; the *person* was fidgeting
with papers, snatching first at one, then at another; and he was
also scratching the back of his neck—a gesture of self-defense.

Tom slowly put his muzzle on the *person*'s knee; he stroked the
dog absently. Alexander Ivanovich's scrutiny was cut short.

"You have not been to see us lately."

"No. . . . Didn't you just call me an anchorite?"

Her aim was made clear by her remark: "You are not offended
with him, by any chance?"

"What an idea!" But he did not sound convincing.

This *Lippanchenko* had offended many people. He spoiled. . . . Yes, this *Lippanchenko* was an assumed role. . . . Without *Lippanchenko*, he would have been caught long ago. *Lippanchenko* protected them all . . .

Alexander Ivanovich, becoming aware of an unpleasant odor, moved away.

"Tell me," Zoya said, seizing a pulverizer, "where will you find another such worker? Who would ever agree—please tell me—to lay aside all personal sentiment and become simply *Lippanchenko?*"

Alexander Ivanovich was thinking there was too much of *Lippanchenko* about the *person*.

"I assure you . . ." he began.

"Aren't you ashamed to abandon him like this, to hide from him," she interrupted. "It's not nice to break off close relations with Kolechka . . ."

And now Alexander Ivanovich remembered that the *person* was really Kolechka.

"Well, what if he does drink sometimes, and have his fun. . . . After all, better men have had their dissipations."

Alexander Ivanovich smiled. She resumed: "Do you remember Helsingfors, and the fun we had in the rowboats?" There was a tone of sadness in Zoya Zakharovna's voice. "And afterward there were all those scandalous rumors."

"What sort?" He shuddered.

"Just think of it—scandalous rumors about Kolechka! You think he doesn't suffer, doesn't have nightmares!" The phrase "nightmares" caught Alexander Ivanovich's attention. "How they talk about him. They don't seem to be aware of all he's sacrificed. . . . He's silent, he's pining away, he's gloomy . . . he doesn't look at all well"—Zoya's voice was tearful—"with his unfortunate appearance. Please believe me: he's just a big child!"

"A child?"

"Yes, child! Look at the toy he just brought!" She pointed to the doll, and her bracelet sparkled. "When you will leave, you will spread more rumors about him, while he . . . he . . ."

"He what?"

"He'll take the cook's little daughter on his knees and play dolls with her. . . . He is being accused of all sorts of cunning. Oh, Lord! and all he does is play with tin soldiers!"

"So that's how it is!"

"It's a fact. He keeps ordering tin soldiers: boxes of them keep arriving from Nuremberg. That's the sort of man he is!"

Alexander Ivanovich came to the conclusion that the *person* had been compromised. This he had not known, but he took into consideration what he now perceived when he glanced into the room where the others were sitting.

The low-browed head hung down; the searching gimlet eyes strayed from object to object; the hanging lip faintly trembled and made sucking noises; the entire face composed itself into a *strange whole* that excited repulsion. It compelled Alexander Ivanovich to carry the memory of it back to his attic, where he paced to and fro, tormented by inexpressible thoughts that existed nowhere else.

Attentively, he studied these oppressive, heavy-set features.

That curious bony structure of the forehead . . .

Outwardly it gave the impression of determination: to understand, whatever the cost, whatever the outcome; to understand or else to break into fragments. This forehead expressed neither passion nor perfidy; it strained to understand, unillumined by thought. . . . But it could never understand: it was a very low forehead, full of intersecting furrows that made him appear to be crying.

Those searching, piercing eyes . . .

When he raised his eyebrows, the eyes became minute.

They were sad eyes.

The lip which sucked in air suggested the lip of a suckling eighteen-month-old baby; it would not have been astonishing to see a nipple between his lips. In the absence of the nipple, the movement of the lip imparted an ugly quality to the face.

As for his playing with tin soldiers—well!

This analysis of the monstrous head revealed one thing: the head was that of a man prematurely born, whose feeble brain had been prematurely overgrown with enormous excrescences of bone that made the head resemble a gorilla's. Under the bones there may have been already in progress that unpleasant process commonly known as the softening of the brain.

The combination of feebleness and rhinoceros-like stubbornness had created a chimera: this chimera sprouted in the night—on dark yellow wallpaper—and had produced a real Mongol.

12

It was a strange affair.

In his relations with Alexander Ivanovich, the conduct of a *certain person* had, until now, borne the character of unexceptional obligations; for months he would disseminate flattery. . . . And Alexander Ivanovich had believed in this flattery.

Yet he had also felt physical revulsion; lately, he had avoided the *person*, for he had been experiencing an agonizing crisis of complete disillusionment. But the *person* had overtaken him everywhere; he had mockingly challenged it, and the challenges had been accepted with cynical laughter.

He knew that the *person* was laughing at the business they had in common.

To the *person* he affirmed that the program of their Party was insolvent, and *he* had agreed; the *person* knew it, for he had helped to plan the program.

He had tried to shock *him* with his credo and the affirmation that the Revolution was a sacred affair; the *person* had no objection to mysticism; *he* had listened attentively, and tried to understand.

But *he* could not understand.

The *person* had accepted all his protests and all his extreme conclusions in humble silence. Then *he* had clapped him on the back and dragged him off to some little bistro for a cognac. The *person* would say, "I'm only a tiny rowboat, and you're a battleship."

Nevertheless, *he* had driven him to an attic and hidden him there; the "battleship" had remained moored at the wharf—without a crew—and all its movements had been limited to progress from one tavern to another.

He had retained only one impression: that if he should suddenly need serious help, the *person* would come immediately to his assistance.

And this was the opportunity.

He firmly believed that the *person* would be able to untangle everything.

Yet lately the *person*'s tone had been changing, becoming unpleasant, humiliating, taut, not unlike that of an official receiving petitioners.

It sounded like "There, you must take your medicine!"

After the Frenchman had left, the *person* did not emerge immediately from his study. He continued to sit at his writing table as if Alexander Ivanovich did not exist, as if he did not know him or want to know him.

Dusk was falling.

In the darkening twilight of the study the *person*'s jacket stood out in yellow relief; his square head was again lowered, presenting his broad back and unwashed neck; his back seemed arched, somehow indecent, derisive, as if full of mockery there in the dusk. Alexander Ivanovich felt so repelled that he spat on the floor.

There, on splayed feet, rested this awkward monstrosity.

Alexander Ivanovich turned his back on *that* back, and began to stroke his mustache nonchalantly, but it was only pretense. He wanted to leave and slam the door behind him; but this was out of the question, for Nikolai Apollonovich's peace of mind depended on the prospective conversation.

This back-to-back attitude was impossible to maintain for long; *that* ungainly back exercised a certain magnetism. When he turned, the *person* also turned, staring fixedly, his low-browed head looking like a wild boar's ready to strike with its tusks. The manner of his turning displayed an obvious intention to inflict humiliation; and the stare malignantly said: "So that's you, eh?"

Alexander Ivanovich clenched a fist in his pocket and turned away.

He grunted twice to draw the *person*'s attention to his impatience —he must assert himself without antagonizing the *person*. But his grunting was like a school boy's timid spasm when facing his teacher. What was the matter with him? Why this timidity? He was not afraid of the *person*: he was more afraid of the hallucination on his wallpaper.

He grunted once more: this time the *person* responded.

"Just wait a little . . ."

Why this tone?

At last the *person* raised himself slightly; the palm of his hand traced a gesture of invitation in the air.

Alexander Ivanovich was upset. His anger was revealed in the nervous hesitation of his speech: "You see. . . . I've come to . . ."

But the *person*, leaning back in his armchair and drumming on the table with a chewed finger, muttered dully:

"I must ask you, my dear fellow, to be brief."

And pressing his chin against his adam's apple, the *person* fixed his gaze on the window.

"Well?"

And he screwed up his little eyes.

Alexander Ivanovich Doodkin flushed red. He found it difficult to squeeze out a single phrase. The *person* was silent.

The withered red leaves whirled beyond the window, rustling; and the tree branches formed a misty net which began to swing, whistling as it swung. Confused, helpless, entangled in his words, Alexander Ivanovich explained the Ableukhov episode. As he proceeded, the *person* looked grimmer and grimmer; at that point in his narrative when he mentioned the secret agent Morkovin, the *person* made a significantly deprecatory gesture, giving the impression that, up to this point, he still respected the narrator's conscience, but from that point on he regarded the narrator as devoid of conscience. Then the *person*'s patience snapped.

"And what did you say?"

"I told him everything!" Alexander Ivanovich exclaimed.

The *person* whispered faintly, "That wasn't right. . . . Aren't you ashamed?"

Then Shishnarfiev appeared in the adjacent room; his voice, that of a young Persian, could be heard, although his body was hidden by a palm tree.

Alexander Ivanovich felt terror; the words of his terrible confidant concealed a menace. He squirmed in his chair.

The bones of the *person*'s forehead drew close to his own forehead.

"I must cool you off. The letter to Ableukhov was written by me."

This statement was made with dignity, and was condescending to the point of gentleness.

"What do you mean?"

"Yes, I wrote it, and you conveyed it. Or have you forgotten?"

The word "forgotten" was pronounced to give the impression that Alexander Ivanovich had known all this and was only shamming ignorance now.

"I handed your letter, I assure you, not to Ableukhov, but to Varvara Evgrafovna . . ."

"Enough, Alexander Ivanovich. The letter, as you know, was addressed to him. . . . You're merely quibbling."

"So you are the author of the letter?"

"Does that astonish you?"

"Me?"

"Excuse me, but I should say that your astonishment is only concealed by your simulation . . ."

Alexander Ivanovich, outraged, screamed at his host: "Either I've lost my mind—or you . . ."

The *person* winked at him. "Now, old chap, don't think I haven't caught you napping. . . . Do you think it's right to act like that?"

Pretending to restrain his laughter, the *person* laid a persuasive hand on the other's shoulder and added: "That's not good. In fact, it's bad, very bad . . ."

That same strange, depressing yet familiar feeling of disaster, which he had experienced in front of his dark yellow wallpaper, now gripped him. He felt guilty.

"It's bad, very bad," the *person* said, staring at him.

A silence followed.

"The accusation is a serious one, yes, a serious one, so much so that . . ." the *person* sighed.

"What are the facts?"

"They concern you: a dossier is being collected . . ."

It needed only this!

Rising to his feet, the *person* cut off the end of a Havana cigar, made an ambiguous gesture, and proceeded to the dining room. He shouted toward the kitchen: "I'm dying of hunger!"

Then he returned.

"There are your visits to the house porter. . . . Your friendship with the police, with the house porter . . . with the district notary Voronkov . . ."

Observing the questioning look, full of terror, the *person* continued in whispers: "Do you know who Voronkov is?"

"Who is he? And what do you conclude from this?"

"You allow yourself to meet a detective, to share a bottle with a detective!" Lippanchenko exclaimed, laughing.

"What are you saying!"

"That you have participated in provocation is not yet established. But I warn you, for friendship's sake, old chap, you are playing with fire . . ."

"How!"

"Drop it, I say!"

It was clear the *person* meant that Alexander Ivanovich should not insist on an explanation of the Ableukhov matter, that he commanded weapons of defamation.

Alexander Ivanovich had hardly gathered courage to reply when the same sinister symbol of his hallucination momentarily flashed by him; and the bones of *that* forehead were strained in tense stubbornness—to break his will or to be shattered in fragments.

And the bones of that forehead broke his will.

As in a trance, Alexander Ivanovich bowed his head as the *person* made a new assault: the square head bent over him. The little eyes wished to say: "Eh, eh, eh. . . . So that's how it is?"

Alexander Ivanovich felt the saliva rise in his mouth.

"All Petersburg knows it."

"Knows what?"

"About the failure of T. T. . . . ."

"What!"

"It's a fact."

If the *person* had deliberately wanted to divert Alexander Ivanovich's thoughts from any possible revelation about his conduct, he could not have chosen a better subject. The news of the failure of T. T. struck his victim like a thunderbolt.

"Oh, Lord Jesus Christ!"

"Jesus Christ," repeated his host, mocking him. "You already knew it. Till the experts give their evidence, let's assume. . . . Only please, not a word about Ableukhov."

Alexander Ivanovich wore an idiotic expression; and the *person*, his mouth open in a wide grin, taunted him: "Don't pretend that Ableukhov's role, and our reasons for wanting to punish him with his allotted task, are unknown to you. That amoral scoundrel has managed to play out his role; reliance on sentimentality like yours has worked too."

The *person* softened; by acknowledging that Alexander Ivanovich suffered from sentimentality, he had, as it were, generously eliminated the accusation made a minute before. At the word "sentimentality," a weight fell from Alexander Ivanovich. He tried to convince himself that he had been mistaken.

"His calculation had been correct: the noble son loathed his father, and intended to do away with him. But, at the same time, he poked his nose among us with his essays, collecting scraps of information here and there, which eventually he could hand over to his papa . . ."

"But, Nikolai Stepanovich, the boy wept . . ."

"You're an odd fellow. Tears are the theatrical props of an intelligent detective. You, too, are given to crying . . . but I don't want to say that you too are guilty."

(All this was untrue. His lie had for a moment terrified Lippanchenko; subconsciously the thought flashed upon him: "A bargain is being made; it is being suggested that I believe in the planted calumny or, if not believing it, agree to it. The price for removing this lie against me is . . ." All this had flashed upon him behind the threshold of his consciousness: the truth itself was locked away there. And he was already beginning to think that he believed this calumny.)

"Alexander Ivanovich," Lippanchenko went on, "you are innocent; but, as for Ableukhov, well, I'm keeping a dossier in this

drawer. This dossier I shall hand over to the Party for judgment."
His tone had a genuine note of affliction (the bargain had been
successfully concluded).

"Later," he resumed, "please believe me, I'll be understood;
but at present the situation demands that the disease be removed
promptly by the roots. . . . I am acting on my own decision, and
please believe me: it took all my courage to sign the sentence,
but then . . . dozens of men are perishing . . . all because of the
Senator's son. Peppovich and Pepp have been arrested. Please
remember, you yourself nearly died. Do you remember Yakutsk.
. . . So you have decided to take up the cudgel? Cry then, cry.
Dozens are perishing!"

Darkness had fallen. The closets, the armchairs, the tables—
everything receded into the darkness; here Alexander Ivanovich
sat all alone. Darkness had entered his soul: he was crying. The
person had left the room.

Alexander Ivanovich recalled the various shades of the *person*'s
speeches. In all probability, the *person* had not lied: his suspicions
might be explained by his own unsound state. The nightmare
might easily be connected with the ambiguous symbol; his psy-
chical sickness, rooted in alcoholism, was already present; his
hallucination about the Mongol and "Enfranshish" had done the
rest. What was that Mongol on the wall? Mere delirium!

"*Enfranshish, enfranshish . . .*" What was that?

Naturally, he was not amiably disposed toward the *person*; it
was also true that he was obliged to him. But his repulsion and
terror were unjustified.

He was ill. . . . Darkness surrounded him; it had penetrated
his soul; and in that darkness, he sat and wept.

Then he also remembered that Nikolai Apollonovich had once
read a paper in which the destruction of all values had been
called for; the impression had been unpleasant, and furthermore,
to tell the truth, Nikolai Apollonovich had evinced some curiosity
in Party secrets. Appearing in the guise of an awkward, distraught,
degenerate person, he had poked his nose into everything; his
disturbed appearance might very well have been assumed. A spy
of the higher type could, of course, have acted outwardly as

Ableukhov had done. Alexander Ivanovich was becoming convinced that Nikolai Apollonovich had acted very strangely.

As he convinced himself of the close complicity of Ableukhov in the failure of the T. T. affair, his feeling of depression left him, and something almost carefree entered his soul. He loathed the Senator, but he was sometimes fond of Nikolai Apollonovich. And now the Senator's son had joined the Senator in creating a mood of revulsion and desire to root out the whole of that tarantula breed.

"Disgusting filth! Oh, and dozens are perishing . . ."

The wood-lice and even that yellow wallpaper were preferable; better far even that *person*, who at least had the grandeur of hatred about him; with the *person* he might unite in the wish to destroy.

Then the *person* came back into the room and laid a hand on his shoulder.

"Come, have a bite to eat. You need it. But not a word after supper . . . it's not a cheerful subject. . . . And no need for Zoya Zakharovna to know about it—she's very tired . . . I too. . . . We're all exhausted. . . . Nerves. . . . We're all nervous. . . . Come, let's eat."

They drank with their supper.

<h2 style="text-align:center">13</h2>

Alexander Ivanovich rang the bell, but the house porter failed to appear; only a barking dog behind the gates responded to the ringing; a midnight cock crowed. Then all was still, and the Line of the street ran on—into emptiness.

Alexander Ivanovich experienced something like pleasure: his homecoming was delayed. Within those plaintive walls he heard rustling, crackling, squeaking.

In the darkness, he would have to achieve twelve cold steps and then, turning, another twelve. He would have to do this eight times.

Ninety-six hollow-sounding steps; then he would face the felt-upholstered door and apprehensively insert the half-rusty key. It was risky to light a match. The flame might reveal something unpleasant, maybe a mouse . . .

That was why he delayed before the gates.

But then—

—Someone, whom Alexander Ivanovich had seen more than once, emerged from the vista of the Eighteenth Line; quietly he entered the circle of light cast by the street lamp; and then it seemed as if the light were streaming from his head, and from his stiff fingers . . . .

Alexander Ivanovich recalled: a little old woman in a straw hat had once greeted this gracious stranger and had called him Misha.

Alexander Ivanovich always shivered when the tall sad stranger never failed, in passing, to turn upon him his all-seeing eye, his sunken cheeks.

"Oh, if only! . . . If only he would stop and hear me out!"

But the tall sad stranger passed on without stopping.

Alexander Ivanovich turned and was about to call quietly to the stranger.

But that spot, where he had irrevocably turned, was empty. Only the yellow light of a street lamp blinked there.

He rang again; the wind moaned in the gateway and forcibly struck an iron sign on the opposite side: the reverberating clang of iron sounded in the dark.

14

The gates creaked.

Morzhov, the house porter, let him in. Retreat was cut off.

"You're late."

"Business . . ."

"Still lookin' for a job?"

"Yes, a job . . ."

"That's natural, jobs are scarce these days. . . . Why not try the local police office?"

"They wouldn't take me there . . ."

"Naturally."

Morzhov used to send his wife, who suffered from earaches,

to Alexander Ivanovich with slices of pie and invitations; on holidays, they drank together in the house porter's quarters.

Alexander Ivanovich hated his attic; he was often cooped up there for weeks; it was too risky to go out.

Voronkov the notary, and Bezsmertny the cobbler, would join them at the porter's; and, lately, Stepka also haunted the rooms. From the house porter's place he now heard singing:

> "Some don't love a clerk,
> But I do, do,
> For him I'd go beserk,
> 'Tis too true.

> "I like smart folk
> I really do,
> They have clever talk
> And know a thing or two . . ."

"You have guests again?"

"We're having a bit of fun . . ." Morzhov answered, scratching the back of his neck.

Alexander Ivanovich suddenly remembered that Voronkov, the notary, would turn up there; for some reason, the *person* knew about him.

> "I want a dress fine-spun,
> O mother dear,
> I want to have some fun,
> O never fear . . ."

"Well . . . why not drop in?" Morzhov cut him short.

He would have accepted gladly—it was warm there and there was liquor; in his attic he would feel lonely and cold, but Voronkov would be *there*—the devil alone knew who *he* was!

"It'll do you good," Morzhov insisted.

"No, I'd better not."

Morzhov left him. He opened the door of his quarters, allowing a glimpse of the cheer inside; then banging the door, he shut out the hum, the smells, and the cheer.

The moon lighted the tiny courtyard; Alexander Ivanovich made his way between the stacks of firewood to the entrance.

They were watching Alexander Ivanovich. It had begun one day when on returning home he had noticed a stranger descend the stairs; the stranger had said to him:

"You are *bound* to Him."

Who was *He*? Who had bound him to Himself? Alexander Ivanovich had impulsively run away from the stranger, who made no effort to pursue him.

On another occasion he had met in the street a man with a terrifying face; some unknown woman in great fear had grabbed Alexander Ivanovich's sleeve.

"It's terrible. . . . Did you see him? . . . What does it mean?"

But the man had passed on.

At still another time, hands had gripped him on the landing and had tried to push him over the handrail. When Alexander Ivanovich had freed himself, the stairway was empty . . .

Recently he had heard more than once an inhuman cry . . . from the stairway. . . . A single cry, and no more.

Each time he heard this cry, the other tenants denied hearing anything.

Only once had he heard this cry elsewhere—in the vicinity of the Bronze Horseman; it was in every way the same cry; an automobile drove past at that moment. Stepka, who occasionally strolled with him at night, had also once heard the cry; to Alexander Ivanovich's importunities he had sullenly replied:

"Is it you *they* are after?"

And not another word. After that, Stepka began to avoid Alexander Ivanovich. And Stepka did not say a word to either the house porter or to the cobbler.

Alexander Ivanovich also remained silent.

Whom were *they* seeking? And why?

Alexander Ivanovich glanced toward the attic window. An angular shadow was moving restlessly behind the pane. He felt in his pocket, and was relieved to find his key. But who could be *there* —in his locked room?

Were *they* searching his room? It would be better not to run into a search. He might be incarcerated—thrown into the Peter and Paul fortress.

"You are being sought . . ."

Alexander Ivanovich had been prepared to face anything; he had even enjoyed mentally toying with the various possibilities.

15

So this was it: *they* were waiting for him; *they* were waiting for his last nocturnal homecoming. *They* were waiting for him. Who were *they*? Two shapes: a beam of light fell from a third-story window.

White patches of light rested there in terrifying calm.

The banister cut into these white patches. The two shapes lurked near the banister; they let him pass: one standing to the right, the other to the left; they neither stirred nor trembled. In the dark he was aware of their unblinking eyes.

Should he approach them and whisper words to exorcise them: "*Enfranshish, enfranshish!*"

Or should he, feeling the sharp scrutiny of the observers on either side of him and conscious of their presence behind his back, yet refuse to hurry his pace!

But unable to restrain himself, Alexander Ivanovich rushed upstairs and stopped only on the top landing. How stupid of him!

Bending over the handrail, he apprehensively looked down and lit a match at the same time; by its light he clearly saw the silhouettes: one of them was Makmudka, who occupied a basement apartment. In the failing light of the match, he saw Makmudka whispering to a prosaic little man in a bowler hat, a man with a hook nose and an Oriental face.

The match went out.

It had betrayed Alexander Ivanovich's arrival; above him, he heard a shuffling of feet, and he heard a suave voice in his ear:

"Andrey Andreyich Gorelsky?"

"No, Alexander Ivanovich Doodkin . . ."

"No, no, I mean according to your passport."

Alexander Ivanovich trembled: he had an illegal passport; his real name was Alexey Alexeyevich Pogorelsky, and not Alexander Ivanovich Doodkin.

"What is it you wish?"

"Your room . . . h'm . . . is locked. . . . And yet there is someone in there. . . . I thought I had better wait for you at the door . . ."

"Who is in there?"

"Someone answered me. His voice sounded common."

"Thank heaven," thought Alexander Ivanovich, "it must be Stepka."

"What do you want?"

"We have mutual friends—Nikolai Stepanovich Lippanchenko, who treats me like his own son. . . . I've ventured to call on you. . . . I live in Helsingfors, and I'm on a visit here. I am a native of the south . . ."

Alexander Ivanovich imagined that his visitor was lying: he had heard that story before; but perhaps the whole thing had been a dream.

"It's an unclean business," he thought, "but I must not let him know."

"Whom have I the pleasure of addressing?" he asked.

"Shishnarfne. . . . We met before . . ."

"Shishnarfiev? . . ."

"No, Shishnarfne—the *iev* ending was added to make my name sound Russian . . . I saw you today—yes, yes, at Lippanchenko's. I sat there for two hours waiting for your conversation to end; and I couldn't wait any longer. Zoya Zakharovna gave me your address. I've been wanting to meet you. . . . Indeed, I've looked forward to meeting you for quite a while . . ."

"You say we met before?"

"Yes, don't you remember? In Helsingfors . . ."

Alexander Ivanovich remembered: he had seen him in a Helsingfors café. His visitor watched him with suspicious eyes.

It was in Helsingsfors that Doodkin had experienced the first symptoms of his menacing sickness: the inspired flights of cerebral play.

At that time he had been developing his paradoxical theory on the necessity of destroying culture; the age of humanism, now grown stagnant, was at an end; since history has always provided a purging storm, humanity was now on the eve of a healthy barbarism which was thrusting its way upward from the lower classes —a revolt was brewing against the established forms and all exoticism, against the bourgeoisie (and its feminine modes). Yes, yes, Alexander Ivanovich had indeed propagated the idea of burning libraries, universities, museums, and of calling in the Mongols (of whom he was later frightened).

He had preached this doctrine in the Helsingfors café, and someone had asked him, too, what he thought of Satanism.

Shishnarfne had sat at the same table, a little to the side.

His preaching of barbarism had come to an unexpected end in Helsingfors; in a dream, Alexander Ivanovich had seen himself whisked off into interplanetary space as punishment for some unspeakable act. The dream had been rather amorphous, but it had put an end to this preaching; he did not remember committing the act, but this dream marked the beginning of his malady; and he did not like to remember it.

Then he had taken to reading The Apocalypse.

The mention of Helsingfors produced its effect: he thought involuntarily, "That is why during the past several weeks, my mind has been harping for no reason on *Hel-sing-fors, Hel-sing-fors.* . . . Then, again: *Shishnarfne* . . . it has a familiar ring . . ."

"Will you allow me to enter?" Shishnarfne resumed. "I've become tired waiting, I must admit."

"If you please . . ." Alexander Ivanovich shouted in a fit of involuntary fear.

"Stepka will come to the rescue . . ." he thought.

'But how could Stepka have entered?" he worried. "I have the key." Then feeling in his pocket, he realized the key was missing. The key in his pocket was that of his suitcase.

16

By the light of a low candle, Stepan lay on the trestles of his bed, bending over an old Slavonic text such as is used in the Orthodox Church.

Alexander Ivanovich recalled Stepka's promise to bring him a
Breviary—he was interested in a prayer of Vasily the Great relative to demons.

"Stepan, I'm so glad to see you!"

"I've brought you, *barin* . . ." Stepka began but, noticing the
newcomer, added, "what you asked for."

"Don't go. Sit down. . . . This is Mr. Shishnarfne."

At this point the candle-end burned so low that it set fire to
the paper wrapped round its bottom, and the dance of the wavering
flame was reflected on the walls.

"No, *barin*, I must go," Stepan announced, fidgeting and looking
warily at the visitor.

He picked up the Breviary. Alexander Ivanovich was at a loss
what to do. Stepan would not forgive him. He was undoubtedly
wondering at this moment, "What does he want with a Breviary
when he lets the likes of him come in? . . . Such folk are rarely
allowed anywhere."

Stepan had his suspicions, he thought. But what would he do
without Stepan?

"Stepan, do stay," he pleaded.

"He's come to see you, not me. . . . It's you *they* are after . . ."

The door slammed behind Stepan. Alexander Ivanovich wanted
to shout after him and ask him to leave the Breviary behind, but
shame prevented him. The flame stopped dancing on the walls;
the paper had burned out and everything looked green.

He invited his guest to sit at the table: he himself remained by
the door so as to reach the stairs ahead of his visitor should it
become necessary.

The visitor leaned on the window sill; his silhouette was outlined aganst the green expanse outside where the moon was gliding
by.

"It seems I'm disturbing you . . ."

"Don't give it a thought. I'm very glad," Alexander Ivanovich
reassured him as his hand tried the door handle.

"Well, you see, I've been wanting to see you. All the more
since I have to leave very early in the morning."

"You're leaving?"

"Yes, I'm going to Finland, then Switzerland. . . . To be sure, my home is in Shemakha, but the climate there is bad for me . . ."

"Yes," Alexander Ivanovich replied. "Petersburg is built on a swamp."

"For the Russian Empire Petersburg is a point of importance," the silhouette continued. "Just look at the map. Our capital city, adorned with monuments, is . . ."

"You say, *our* capital city," Alexander Ivanovich interrupted. "But it isn't yours at all. *Your* capital city is, I think, Teheran. . . . To you, as an Easterner . . ."

"But I've lived in Paris and London. . . . Yes, this, *our* capital city," the black silhouette went on, "belongs to the land of spirits —conventional references do not apply here. Baedeker is silent on this point. The uninformed provincial, of course, deals with the visible administration: he has no shadow passport."

"What do you mean?"

"It's very simple: in Papua, you will expect to find Papuans! Baedecker gives us due warning. But you can imagine meeting a horde of Papuans on the way to Kirsanov, though, to be sure, France is arming them with the idea of bringing them to Europe —take my word for it, I am relying on your theory of the destruction of culture; do you remember? . . . I listened to you with great sympathy in that Helsingfors café!"

Alexander Ivanovich was chagrined to hear his theory cited. After his terrible dream, he was quite prepared to admit the connection between his theory and Satanism.

The silhouette at the window was becoming attenuated; he looked like a sheet of black paper pasted on the window frame. His voice, however, sounded clearly in the middle of the cube of four walls and was approaching perceptibly nearer Alexander Ivanovich. His voice formed an autonomous, invisible center!

"The Papuan is an earthy creature," the voice continued. "You can stumble upon a Papuan with the aid of strong liquor, to which you have certainly done honor in these past days and which has certainly made our meeting possible. Moreover, in Papua there are certain institutions approved by the Papuan Parliament . . ."

The visitor had become a mere patch of soot on the moonlit window pane; on the other hand, his voice grew increasingly stronger until it sounded like a stertorous recorded shout.

"The biology of the shadow has not yet been studied. Its demands are difficult to grasp; it enters with bacilli which we swallow with the water from conduits . . ."

"And with vodka!" Alexander Ivanovich interjected.

"No. With vodka you absorb *me* into your system. . . . In any case, the real tragedy is that we belong to the invisible world —the world of shadows."

"Is there one?" Alexander Ivanovich screamed, preparing to run from his cell and forestall his visitor. Here was a man who had entered his room, a three-dimensional creature who pressed against the window, becoming a silhouette (that is, two-dimensional), and then just a smear of soot. Now this black soot had decomposed and become shining lunar ash; then this too vanished, leaving no silhouette. The entire substance of the man had assumed a purely vocal nature . . .

"Mr. Shishnarfne," Alexander Ivanovich began, addressing space—for there was no Shishnarfne.

"Petersburg is a four-dimensional body," the voice crackled in response, "and is only marked on the maps with a dot; this dot is where the surfaces of existence come into contact with the global surfaces and the tremendous astral cosmos—in the twinkling of an eye the dot is capable of projecting an inhabitant of the fourth dimension, from whom there is no protection even within walls. A minute ago I was at the window sill, and now I've appeared in . . ."

"Where?" Alexander Ivanovich wished to cry out, but he could not, because his own throat gave forth the loud answer: "In your throat . . ."

Alexander Ivanovich grew frenzied when his throat said: "A passport is needed. . . . In any case, you are registered there: your passport is written within you. You yourself will fill in the details with an extravagant act. That will come, that will come!"

If, at that moment, Alexander Ivanovich could have detached himself from himself, and then observed himself, he would have been terrified: he would have seen himself with his hands on his stomach, shouting loudly into the void: "When was I registered with you?"

"Then—after the act!"

Suddenly the veil was snatched away: he remembered his dream. In Helsingfors, when he was being whisked through space.

He *had* committed the act.

He *had* joined them; Lippanchenko was merely the image that hinted at this; *their* force had entered into him, rushing from organ to organ, seeking the soul inside his body, and gradually taking possession of everything.

And while *this* was happening, he had imagined that *they* were seeking him; but *they* were already within him.

"Yes, our expanses are not yours; they run in reverse order. . . . Ivanov is, in fact, a Japanese: Vonavi."

Then he understood: "Shishnarfne—Shishnarfne."

From the apparatus in his throat came the reply: "You have called me . . . and here I am . . ."

Enfranshish had come to claim his soul.

Alexander Ivanovich leaped from his room, and turned the key.

"Yes, yes. . . . It is I . . . I destroy—irrevocably . . ."

The moon answered. Faintly at first, two gray, white, pale patches, phosphorescently radiant, shone in the deep darkness.

17

The attic was unlocked. Doodkin rushed in.

By night the attic was strange. The floor was thickly covered with dirt: your feet sank into it; you might stumble over a log and find yourself on all fours; then you would see some seemingly white, intersecting beams of moonlight; you would try and walk through them. Suddenly . . . a wooden beam would crack into your nose.

The motionless white patches turned out to be his underwear, a towel, and a sheet; a faint breeze made the patches— underwear, a towel, and a sheet—waver.

Sighing with relief, Alexander Ivanovich held his breath.

Through the broken windows a song was audible:

> "Buy me a fine-spun dress,
> O mother dear . . ."

Alexander Ivanovich listened; he could hear only normal sounds: the cracking of a beam, broken silence, a woven net of rustling sound, a creak in the corner, the air tense with unheard steps, someone swallowing. In a word—just normal sounds, nothing to be afraid of.

He had no desire to leave the attic. He walked among the underwear, the towel, and sheet; he thrust his head through the broken windows; he breathed peace and universal nostalgia.

Looking through the window, he was able to see with dazzling clarity the square courtyard below, which looked like a miniature; the stacks of timber gleamed silver in the moonlight. The party in the porter's quarters was still going on. Voices were hoarsely singing:

> "O Lord, I see my wickedness:
> Folly shut my eyes to truth,
> Folly blinded me . . ."

Voronkov the notary, and Bezsmertny the cobbler were singing in the basement. Alexander Ivanovich wondered if he should join them.

The sky was clearing; an island roof flashed in a stream of silver.

The Neva was seething.

The siren of a late steamer wailed desperately, and the receding eye of a lantern glowed; the Embankment stretched away; above the yellow, gray, tawny-red box-like houses, above the gray columns, the tawny-red rococo and baroque palaces, loomed the somber walls of an enormous church, with its gold dome thrust sharply into the world of the moon: St. Isaac's.

And the Admiralty pierced the sky like an arrow.

The square was deserted.

The rearing metal hoofs under the Horseman fell clanking upon rock; the horse snorted into the incandescent fog; the Horseman's figure detached itself from the crupper; a clanking spur pricked the horse's flank.

The horse leaped from the rock.

Its powerful resonant clatter echoed across the bridge, toward the islands. The Bronze Horseman flew on: the muscles of his metal arms strained; fierce hoofs pounded the cobblestones; and the horse's neighing rang clearly, like the whistle of a locomotive, and the steam from its nostrils splashed luminous spray into the street. Cab-horses shied and passers-by shut their eyes.

Line after Line of avenues was passed; and soon a large part of the left bank had fallen behind. . . .

Alexander Ivanovich walked away from the window, calm, pacified, chilled; the white patches—the underwear, the towel, and the sheet—wavered.

He decided to return to his room.

18

He sat on the bed, recovering from his nightmare; where the visitors had been, a wood-louse was now crawling: the visitors were gone. The nightmare was succeeded by an interval of lucidity.

His consciousness gleamed, wavering like the moon.

Within these four walls he pictured himself as a captured convict. All the space of the universe was a desert, like his room! . . . Universal space was the ultimate achievement . . . but a beggar's room might appear luxurious in comparison with the impoverished setting of universal space.

Recovering from his nightmare, Alexander Ivanovich mused on his success in surmounting his emotional mirage.

"Vodka! . . . Smoking! . . . Lust!"

His head drooped: from sickness, fear, and persecution, from insomnia, cigarettes, and alcohol.

The attack of insanity was clear again; he knew the truth about insanity: it was the account rendered by his discarded senses to his self-conscious "I." *Shishnarfne* was a symbol and an anagram;

it was not he who followed and pursued, but the organs that pursued the "I." Alcohol and insomnia were gnawing at his body. He was tied to the spaces; he was beginning to disintegrate—the spaces had cracked; bacilli were crawling into the cracks of his sensation; specters rose in the spaces. . . . Who was Shishnarfne? The reverse side of magic: *Enfranshish?* A dream stimulated by vodka? Then *Enfranshish* and Shishnarfne were but stages of his alcoholism.

"I must stop smoking and drinking."

Suddenly he trembled. He had been guilty of a betrayal. He had given up Nikolai Apollonovich for fear of Lippanchenko; he remembered their vulgar bargaining and the betrayal. Without believing, he had believed; his real treachery had consisted in this. Lippanchenko was *the* arch traitor: that he had betrayed them all, this Alexander Ivanovich knew very well, but he hid this knowledge from himself (Lippanchenko had power over his soul) and there lay the root of his sickness—in his discovery that Lippanchenko was a traitor. Alcohol and debauchery were only a consequence of this. His hallucinations were merely a link in the chain forged by Lippanchenko. Because Lippanchenko knew that he knew, he clung to his power and would not let go.

As a result of his wish to dissipate that terrible suspicion, Lippanchenko had subjugated his will. He had merely stimulated that suspicion by communicating with Lippanchenko who, suspecting his, Doodkin's, suspicion, could not allow him to take any steps. Thus, they had bound themselves to each other. He had poured mysticism into Lippanchenko, and Lippanchenko had poured alcohol into him.

Alexander Ivanovich clearly recalled that scene with Lippanchenko. That cynic and villain had outmanoeuvered him. He recalled the hideous fold of Lippanchenko's neck, its insolent grin, and how Lippanchenko had noticed him staring at it and had read the whole truth in that stare.

Lippanchenko had then tried to frighten him, to stun him with his assault, and to mix the cards; he had offered him a way out: belief in Ableukhov's treachery. And he, Doodkin, had actually believed in it: the act had taken place; and the affair had been concluded.

That was what his nightmare had been about.

He remembered his first meeting with Lippanchenko. The first impression had not been a pleasant one; Lippanchenko had displayed curiosity as to all the weaknesses of his associates. The provocateur knew how to make the most of his own clumsy appearance and his dull blinking eyes.

The more closely Alexander Ivanovich had studied Lippanchenko and the better he had observed his physical features, the more he likened him to a tarantula.

A feeling as strong as steel entered his soul.

"I know what I shall do!" he exclaimed.

It would all end in a way not conceived before. His mission became clear.

Suddenly . . .

19

Alexander Ivanovich heard a reverberating sound from below, a sound that was then repeated on the stairs. Thud followed thud; the sound of metal striking stone became distinct and crescendo-like as the steps came nearer. They sounded like peals of thunder on the stairs. He strained his ears: would the door burst open and admit a monster?

He heard the metal *thing* on the landing; it was closer now, thundering and clattering like so many heavy falling weights. It sounded as if the stairs were being shattered. Finally, it crashed upon the landing of his own floor.

The door flew open with a crash, and the murky recesses were filled with smoky greenish clouds. Through the shattered door vast moonlit expanses became visible from the landing, and the dark room now opened upon the inexplicable. On the threshold, surrounded by walls radiating the greenish light of vast spaces, loomed a huge luminous body with a bowed head, garlanded and green, and a ponderous greenish arm outstretched.

The Bronze Horseman confronted him.

The lusterless mantle hung down heavily, and only the shoulders and the scaly armor gleamed. Evgeny's fate was about to be repeated: the moment the walls of the building vanished in greenish space, the past was revealed.

"Now I remember . . . I have waited for this . . ." Alexander Ivanovich exclaimed.

The bronze giant had been galloping through ages of time and, reaching the present moment, had completed a cycle; ages had sped by; Nicholas I had ascended to the throne; and, after him, the Alexanders; and Alexander Ivanovich Doodkin, himself a shadow, had restlessly overcome the ages day after day, year after year, roaming up and down the Petersburg prospects—awake and in dream. The clanging thunder of metal had pursued him and all the others, shattering their life.

Apollon Apollonovich was one such blow of metal on stone; Petersburg another; and so was the caryatid which was always on the verge of falling. Pursuit was inevitable, and so were these blows; there was no escape from them in the attic; no escape from Lippanchenko. The attic was only a snare; these blows would shatter it . . . and they would also fall upon Lippanchenko.

These blows would make fragments of Lippanchenko, pulverize the attic, destroy Petersburg; and Ableukhov's bald head would likewise be broken.

The Bronze Horseman greeted him: "How do you do, son?"

He took three steps that snapped like splitting boards; he lowered his metal body, cast in bronze, into a chair, and let his green gleaming elbow drop with its full weight of bronze clanging onto the table. Slowly the Emperor removed the bronze garland from his brow; the laurel leaves clanged as they fell.

He drew out a glowing clinking pipe and, motioning to it with his eyes, said: *"Petro Primo Catherina Secunda . . ."*

He put the pipe between his lips: the green smoke of molten bronze was lifted toward the moon.

Alexander Ivanovich—the new Evgeny—understood at last: he had wasted a whole century running about between December and October. While being pursued without anger through the villages, the cities, driveways, up and down stairs, he had been forgiven . . .

In the Horseman's hollow head a thought flared; his ponderous hand, which could crush stone, fell, red-hot, on his collarbone and broke it: "Die . . . suffer . . ."

The metal visitor, molten under the moon, sat confronting him. Red-hot and scorching, he turned white-hot over the stooping Alexander Ivanovich and poured himself forth—pouring his metal being into his veins.

20

"What is it?"

Something red was crawling on the pillow . . . brrr. . . . His conciousness recorded it.

"A bedbug . . ."

He raised himself on one elbow.

"Is that you, Stepka?"

He saw a teapot and cup.

"A cup of tea, that's fine."

"You're burning with fever . . ."

He noticed with astonishment that he was not undressed. He was even wearing his overcoat.

"What brought you here?"

"Just looked in. I saw you lying here and groaning, tossing about. . . . You're burning, like a flame."

"I'm well enough, Stepka."

"Well? Hardly! I made some tea for you."

At night he had felt hot water pouring through his veins—this he suddenly remembered.

"Yes, brother, I certainly felt hot last night . . ."

"Cooked in alcohol, that's why!"

"There were devils here . . ."

"Yes, you'll see the Green Serpent if you go on drinking."

"And all of Russia, my friend, as well . . ."

"What?"

"I . . . will see the Green Serpent . . ."

"Christ's Russia . . ."

"You're wandering . . ."

"You'll get the *d.t.*s drinking."

Delirium tremens was stealing over him—no doubt of that.

"Run down to the druggist. . . . Get me some quinine."

"Of course I will."

"And, Stepka, dear chap, you might also get me some raspberry preserves—for the tea."

"Raspberries are an excellent sudorific," he thought. But he had hardly finished washing his face when something flared up within him, confusing reality with delirium.

While he had been talking to Stepka, he had a sense of something waiting for him behind the door, something primitive and familiar. There—behind the door! He sprang up. Opening the door, he saw the landing. The railing hung over an abyss; and Alexander Ivanovich stood there, over this abyss, clicking his dry tongue and shivering with fever. He had a strange taste of bronze in his mouth.

"No—*it* must be waiting in the courtyard," he thought.

But he saw nothing, no one, in the courtyard.

"Where can it be? In a metal place . . ."

It would undoubtedly reappear.

Only a memory of a memory remained—of the matter at hand, but this could not be postponed.

As if on springs, he strode toward the foggy street crossing. He caught sight of a gleam in a shop window. . . . There were objects shining there.

A tiny cheap shop on the corner. The window had a display of knives, forks, scissors. He entered. From an inner office the drowsy face of the proprietor emerged and sulkily approached the counter. He turned his narrow forehead to the customer.

"I'd like . . . I'd like . . .."

Hardly knowing what to buy, Alexander Ivanovich got his sleeve enmeshed in the teeth of a small saw which made a tinkling sound. The proprietor surveyed him suspiciously. Alexander Ivanovich was still wearing the overcoat in which he had slept; it was crumpled and covered with mud; and he wore no cap; his bristling hair was disturbing.

The proprietor, controlling himself, muttered: "Is it a saw you want?"

"No . . . you see, a saw's not quite the thing . . . it would be awkward, with a saw. . . . You haven't a Finnish . . ."

"No, I have no Finnish knives," the man cut him short.

His eyes seemed to say: "If I gave you a knife, heaven alone knows what you'd do . . ."

A resemblance of some sort astonished Alexander Ivanovich; at this moment the proprietor turned his back and then flung a back glance at him that would have sent a bull reeling.

"Well, it's all the same. A pair of scissors then . . ."

He stood shaking over his purchase.

"No, no, never mind the wrapping . . . I live quite near . . ."

He put the scissors in his pocket. They were the kind fops use to trim their nails. He rushed from the shop.

The proprietor's square, low-browed, stubborn-looking head turned an apprehensive glance after the departing figure. There was something about it he could not understand.

That bony forehead could not grasp it at all; the forehead was narrow, with intersecting furrows that made the proprietor look as if he were crying.

CHAPTER SEVEN

*I am weary, friend, weary: my heart implores rest.
Days speed after days . . .*

—PUSHKIN

1

We left Nikolai Apollonovich just when Doodkin had pressed his hand and darted nimbly into the stream of black bowlers, while he himself was experiencing the sensation of expanding.

Up to that instant delirious impressions had been accumulating in him; in the last twenty-four hours he had experienced monstrous events: the Summer Garden, the red satin domino, the ball, the yellow hunched Pierrot, a light blue mass, the note, his flight, the repugnant strange gentleman, and—Pépp Péppovich Pépp, and—that sardine tin . . . which was still ticking.

The sardine tin, which was capable of transforming everything in its vicinity into slush . . .

We left Nikolai Apollonovich by the shop window. It began to drizzle, and umbrellas were unfurled.

Nikolai Apollonovich stood by the shop window deep in thought: the monstrous depression had no name; this monstrous horror had lasted twenty-four hours or eighty thousand seconds—all points in time; each instant attacked and was in turn attacked; instants swiftly scattered in circles, slowly transforming him into a swelling sphere, which finally burst and made him slither away into emptiness. Thus, like a traveler in time, he fell into the unknown . . . until the next instant.

This terrible state had no name.

Thoughts began to pound, issuing from the heart rather than the brain; an original, well-considered plan was formulated, a comparatively safe but devious one. Could Nikolai Apollonovich himself have thought of that plan?

For the past few hours fragments of thoughts had floated before his eyes like shimmering sparks, like the gay stars of a Christmas tree. They showered continuously, from dark to dark, passing through the place lighted by consciousness. The figure of a contorted clown appeared; then a gaudy Petrushka rushed past at a gallop—from dark to dark—passing through the place lighted by consciousness. It glittered, an objectively kinetic image; when the thoughts merged together, his consciousness sketched a shocking, inhuman meaning into them. "I'm a scoundrel . . ." Nikolai Apollonovich spat out in disgust.

But his father had also come to that conclusion.

No, no!

These swarming thoughts were autonomous. He did not think them: they conceived themselves; they thought, sketched, and formed themselves; they thumped in his heart and drilled in his brain; crawling out of the sardine tin, they rose above it. He had hidden the sardine tin . . . apparently . . . in the table drawer, and escaped from the accursed house to roam the streets.

But even in the streets the thoughts persisted, forming, outlining, sketching; insofar as his mind produced thoughts at all, it had itself become a sardine tin which ticked with thoughts.

Thus, the plan had impinged on the field of his consciousness at an unsuitable moment, just when Nikolai Apollonovich—who had reached the hallway of the University—was leaning carelessly against a column and chatting with a lecturer. Then something exploded within him: he shuddered, started, and tore himself away. He had suddenly realized that he himself was the author of the plan.

He rushed toward the Vasilyevsky Island in the direction of the Eighteenth Line. The driver of his cab heard an intermittent whispering behind him.

"Yes, if you please? Ah? What falsity, what pretense. . . . To save his skin . . ."

He jumped out of the droshky and, crossing the asphalt courtyard past the stacks of logs, flew upstairs; without knowing why, from curiosity perhaps, he glanced into the eyes of Doodkin, who had brought the bundle because the "refusal" had been merely a pretext.

Here he had met Doodkin; and we know what followed.

If he had run across the street, he might have felt with his hand the massive building which piled its weight above the street. As soon as it began to drizzle, that façade began to swim in the mist.

The massive stone structure became unmoored; under the rain, it raised a lacework of contours and barely distinguishable lines —a rococo of sorts: this rococo drifted away into nothing.

There was a wet glitter on the shop windows, house windows, and chimneys; a rivulet gushed from the water drain; drops of rain splattered the pavement and turned it brownish-gray; and speeding tires splashed by, snorting.

His heart, touched by all that had happened, began to thaw; feelings stirred, shaking his soul and turning it inside out.

Nikolai Apollonovich stood in the rain, surrounded by the open umbrellas of passers-by; he felt giddy and leaned against the shop window for support. A childhood incident came to his mind.

He saw himself with his governess: his head was pillowed on her lap and she was reading:

> *"Wer reitet so spät durch Nacht und Wind?*
> *Es ist der Vater mit seinem Kind . . ."*

Wild gusts of wind were blowing outside in the rebellious darkness where the chase was on.

Then. . . . Apollon Apollonovich—tiny, gray, old—was teaching him a French contredanse, counting the paces, beating time with his hands. Unaccompanied by music, he sharply, rapidly stressed the feet of Goethe's poem in Russian:

> "Who rides so late through the night wind?
> It is the father with his child . . ."

The chase had caught up!

> "In his arms the child lay dead . . ."

2

Nikolai Apollonovich suddenly yearned desperately to be back in his birthplace, in the nursery. He must shake off everything else; he had to learn everything over again, as one learns in childhood; he heard the sounds of his youth. The high-flying cranes—in the din of the city the cranes are not heard, yet they fly above the city. Somewhere, on the prospect, amid the rumble of droshkies and the clamor of newsboys, amid the hoarsely coughing automobiles—here, on the pavement, a country man, like one entranced, may pause and raise his bearded face to the sky:

"Tsss! . . ."

"What is it?"

"Just listen . . ."

"To what?"

"There. . . . Do you hear the cry of the cranes?"

At first nothing is heard; then the sound is caught: a dear forgotten sound. How strange it seems . . .

The cranes are crying.

You lift your head: the third, the fifth, the tenth. In the blue sky you see them, those familiar cranes, flying north!

A crowd of the curious gathers, a small crowd in fact. A policeman, unable to resist his curiosity, joins them. He raises his head skyward:

"The cranes! . . ."

Thus, the shrill cries of the cranes sound above the roofs. In the same way is heard the voice of childhood.

A sorrowful presence, never before encountered, now entered into Nikolai Apollonovich; penetrating the bright glow of his eyes, he shuddered.

"You are always pursuing me!"

"What? . . ." He attempted to catch the reply.

"I pursue you all . . ." the voice answered.

Nikolai Apollonovich stared into space as though expecting to identify the owner of the voice. He was not there.

But who was *that*? Across the street? By that large building —under those layers of balconies?

Like Nikolai Apollonovich, *he* stood by a shop window, under an umbrella. . . . He was staring, but his features were indistinguishable. Nothing unusual in that! Here was he, Nikolai Apollonovich, on this side. And on the other—*that* man. A chance passer-by, an independent observer? "I've a mustache," he might have been saying. But he was clean-shaven . . .

His overcoat seemed familiar, but in what way? And he wore a cap. Should he approach him . . . pretending to look at the wares displayed in the window? And once there, pretending to be absentminded, study him closely! And then cast himself at his mercy!

"I'm ill . . . deaf. . . . Comfort me!"

And then hear the answer:

"Rise . . . go. . . . Sin not!"

But, of course, there would be no answer.

The sorrowful figure would offer no reply: there could be no answer; there might be one—in hours, in a year, in five years or, perhaps, in a hundred or a thousand; yes, there must be an answer!

In less than a second, everything would change. And all these strangers—those who passed each other in a moment of mortal danger—would meet again!

No one could be deprived of the joy of reunion.

3

"What am I dreaming of—at such a moment?" Nikolai Apollonovich asked himself.

Time was passing and the sardine tin was ticking; he should go home to his desk at once, wrap the tin carefully in paper, put it in his pocket, and throw it into the Neva.

He had already turned his eyes away from that huge pile of a house, where the stranger with open umbrella stood.

He looked again in the stranger's direction.

The man had not stirred. He was waiting for something, perhaps for the rain to end. Nikolai Apollonovich plunged into the human stream.

He thought he saw the stranger move too. His mind on the stranger, he saw him barely avoid running into a droshky as he attempted to cross the street, his umbrella almost torn away by the wind.

At a distance, the stranger looked more sorrowful and less agile.

"He looks like an idiot," Nikolai Apollonovich concluded. "His overcoat is flapping, his umbrella is torn, and his galoshes are only half on!"

Nikolai Apollonovich suddenly felt hostile toward the man; he was about to turn away, when the stranger, almost rubbing noses with him, raised his hand to his cap.

"Ah! Ni-ko-lai A-pol-lo-no-vich!"

Nikolai Apollonovich noticed that the person, apparently a bourgeois, wore a bandage round his throat, probably to cover a boil.

"It seems you don't recognize me?"

"Whom have I the honor of addressing?" Nikolai Apollonovich began to inquire when, looking closely, he reeled back, removed his hat and, with a grimace, exclaimed: "What a surprise!"

It was indeed a surprise to recognize Likhutin in this shabbily dressed person. Likhutin was in civilian clothes; he was shaven, and the scarred emptiness of his face had transformed the familiar physiognomy into an unfamiliar one.

"Either my eyes deceive me, or . . . Sergey Sergeyevich . . ."

"You're quite right. In civilian dress . . ."

"No, it's not that . . . not that at all. . . . You look quite different . . ."

"How?"

"You are so changed, if you'll permit me to say so."

"Nonsense!"

"But you are . . . you're shaven . . ."

"What's that? And why not? Yes, I am shaven. . . . Let's forget all that. I'm leaving the service . . ."

"How? . . . Why?"

"For private reasons."

Likhutin drew closer. Nikolai Apollonovich recoiled before his advance.

"You've affairs to attend to, Sergey Sergeyevich?"

"Affairs, which, sir . . ."

Nikolai Apollonovich caught a clearly menacing note in the

Lieutenant's hoarse voice; it seemed to Ableukhov that the other was trying to hold his arm. He stepped off the curb.

"You need not think that I've pursued you all this time just to have you tell me about my neck . . ."

Nikolai Apollonovich had completely forgotten about the domino in this encounter. Sofya Petrovna Likhutina had undoubtedly babbled about the episode at the Winter Canal.

"It needed only this . . ."

Avoiding Likhutin's glance, Nikolai Apollonovich stared at the shop window. But Sergey Sergeyevich, seizing his arm, sharply spoke out.

"I . . . I . . . I . . . have the honor to inform you that from early morning . . . I . . . I . . . I . . ."

"You what?"

"I've been on your trail. . . . Among other places I've visited your house. I sat waiting for you in your room . . . and finally left a note . . ."

"How annoying!"

"Nonetheless, I must have an urgent talk with you. It cannot be put off."

4

"I have something to talk over with you," Sergey Sergeyevich repeated. "I've been inquiring where to find you. I even visited our mutual acquaintance, Varvara Evgrafovna. . . . She and I had a rather serious talk about you. . . . Doodkin. . . . Well, no matter. . . . To be sure, I went to that address. I saw you in the courtyard. You seemed to be running away, and someone was after you. You had a worried look . . . I didn't feel I ought to break in on your conversation."

"Sergey Sergeyevich . . ."

"Anyhow, I followed you—at a certain distance, in order not to eavesdrop. I don't believe in poking my nose into things . . ."

At this point, Likhutin paused reflectively and glanced into the distance—down the Nevsky.

"Listen . . ."

"What is it?"

"Do you hear that hum in the distance—on a note of 'ooh'?"

Nikolai Apollonovich turned his head, observing something odd: all the droshkies were driving in one direction, and the passers-by walked briskly or ran, sometimes turning their heads.

"All the time, Nikolai Apollonovich, you were staring at me, but you pretended not to see me."

"I didn't recognize you."

"I nodded to you."

What was happening?

The passers-by had paused. The broad prospect was free of vehicles; there was no sound of either tires or hoofs.

"Just look!"

In the distance, a thousand-throated din was fast approaching along the prospect; a droshky came speeding by; a shabby looking baron half stood up in it, holding a pole with a flying standard; when the droshky had passed, all the bowlers, cocked hats, cylinder hats, caps, feathers, shaggy hats, rushed from the sidewalk into the middle of the prospect; and from the ragged clouds the pale sun disk momentarily cast a pale yellow glow.

Jostling with their elbows, they ran in the same direction as the others; taking advantage of the human pressure, Nikolai Apollonovich thought to escape an explanation with his companion. After all, the bomb was really ticking away in his desk! But Lieutenant Likhutin refused to lose him from sight.

"Don't try to get away, Nikolai Apollonovich. In any case, I won't let you."

Once more he felt the pressure of Likhutin's hand on his arm; he pausd, simulating indifference.

"A demonstration!"

"All the same, I have business with you."

From some distance away a series of crackling noises became audible; the red eddies of banners became agitated, and then were quickly scattered.

"Sergey Sergeyevich, let's have our discussion in a café. Yes, why shouldn't we try a café?"

"Why in a café?"

"Where then?"

"I was thinking of that too. . . . Why not take a droshky to my flat?"

"But, Sergey Sergeyevich, I wonder whether, in view of certain circumstances not unknown to you, that would be the proper thing to do . . ."

"Quite."

"As an enlightened, humane person, please understand me. . . . In a word, in connection with Sofya Petrovna . . ."

He became entangled and stopped.

They seated themselves in a droshky. It was none too soon. Where the standards had swarmed and whips had been cracked shortly before, the standards had disappeared; the mob was surging back, flying in the opposite direction along the Nevsky.

Nothing could be done now: they turned from the prospect. . . . The bursting clouds poured down their rain. Nikolai Apollonovich wrapped his mantle around him. He was oblivious to the destination of the droshky, and felt only one thing: he was being taken against his will.

The oppressive confluence or, rather, the pyramid of events, bore down on him.

The pyramid is the delirium of geometry: a delirium for which there is no instrument of measurement . . . a delirium which —possibly—may only be measured by means of figures.

Thirty zeros are a real horror, but remove the digit before them, and all the thirty zeros perish. Zero alone remains.

There is no horror in this unit, it is a mere trifle. But a unit plus thirty zeros is a monstrosity . . . it hangs entirely on this single unit, this tiny, thin stick . . .

Yes—it was as a human unit, that is, as a gaunt little stick, that Nikolai Apollonovich had lived, completing his course in time—

—Nikolai Apollonovich, in Adam's garb, was a mere little stick; ashamed of his meager figure, he had never ventured into a Turkish bath—

—no, never in all eternity!

And now, upon this little stick had fallen all the monstrous weight of a number exceeding a milliard milliard; and from within him an inexpressible feeling was surging, swelling out of eternity—

—in the same way that a belly swells from expanding gas, a complaint from which all the Ableukhovs suffered——through all eternity.

In an instant, all that had passed through his mind since morning flashed before him again; his plan suggested itself to him again.

5

His plan was to place the sardine tin under a pillow or, better still, under a mattress. And—

"Good night, Papa!" he would say.

"Good night, Kolenka!" his father would reply.

Then he would go to his room.

He would undress impatiently; turn the key in the lock; and bury his head under a blanket.

He would quiver in his soft bed—because his heart thumped; he would suffer in anguish, and strain to hear sounds; then something would burst . . . a crash would rend the silence, tearing apart the bed, the table, the wall, and also tearing apart, possibly . . . possibly . . .

But what if, instead, he were to hear the familiar shuffling of slippers toward . . . the place unlike any other.

He would have to rise, take some cotton, stuff his ears with it, and bury his head under a pillow. . . . Then he would thrust his head out again—into an abyss of fear.

To wait and wait.

Half an hour would pass, then would come the first green gleam of dawn, turning to blue, to gray; the candle flame would grow dim; fifteen minutes more would pass; the candle would go out; and then each minute would feel like eternity; he would strike a match, and five more minutes would pass. He would console himself that *it* had been delayed, that it would occur only after ten infinitely slow revolutions in time; he would deceive himself—

—nonetheless, the never to be repeated, the unique, prolonged sound . . .—

—the explosion!

Then—he would thrust his naked legs into his underwear—or even pull his undershirt over his head, and with a pale, wry face —yes, yes, yes!—

—leap from the warm bed, stamp barefoot into the dark hall, rushing like an arrow: toward the inimitable sound, sniffing the peculiar odor on the way: a mixture of gases and . . . something else, more terrible than the smell of fire and gas, and . . .

But there would probably be no odor.

He would arrive at a run, choking and coughing, and gape into the black hole in the wall made by the explosion.

There, through the gap, he would see the shattered bedroom and a grim flame lighting all the ornaments amid the curling, belching smoke.

Then he would peer behind the curtain: the red half of the room: there, something would be flowing: the walls would be all wet and sticky, sticky . . . that would be his first and last impression of the room: fallen plaster, fragments of broken parquet, ragged shreds of scorched, still smoldering rugs . . .

Behind him, he would hear the chaotic din of voices, the confused tramping of feet in the corridor, the wailing of the kitchen maid, and the shrill ringing of the telephone (they would be calling the police) . . .

He would drop a candlestick, squat down and pull up his nightshirt; and then a compassionate servant—upon whose shoulders the blame might be easily thrown—would drag him into the next room and begin to pour cold water into his mouth . . .

Then he would raise his head from the floor . . . and fall back in a faint.

To play this role—to the bitter end.

Twenty-four hours later—the priest would read a litany: he would bow his head and hold a lighted candle.

Two days later—his face buried in a fur collar, he would follow the coffin into the street; with an angelic expression on his face, with his cap clutched in a white-gloved hand, he would descend the stairs behind the dignitaries, the old men in gold braid and white trousers.

Eight bald old men!

And yes, yes!

He would testify at the inquest: his testimony—without deliberate intent, of course—would throw a shadow of suspicion on someone else.

> "Little fool, little sap,
> Kolenka is dancing!
> On his head a fool's cap—
> On a horse he's prancing."

As soon as Nikolai Apollonovich had consecrated himself to execute the punishment—in the name of an idea, at that very instant rather than at any other time of the morning when he was tramping up and down the gray prospect, he proved himself the author of the plan. Action in the name of an idea went hand in hand with dissimulation, and perhaps even insinuation, that might involve innocent persons like the valet, for example.

In this evil design patricide and falsehood joined hands.

> "Graceful, noble, pale,
> Hair as white as flax,
> A mind both bold and hale,
> N. A. A. nothing lacks."

He was—a scoundrel.

All that had happened was in the realm of fact; fact was a monster, a whole swarm of monstrosities! Nikolai Apollonovich slept, read, ate; he had even desired Sofya Petrovna.

But he did not eat as others did, and he did not love as others did: his dreams were dull and his food was tasteless; and these symptoms threw light on all his functions.

As a child he had felt ashamed to be called his father's "off-spring"; his observations had led him to connect this word with animal functions, and this made him, Kolenka, weep. He blamed his father for the humiliation of his birth.

Everything was "offspring," that he understood: there were no people, only "offspring." Apollon Apollonovich, his father, was "offspring," too: the unfortunate essence of blood and flesh; and flesh had a way of sweating and spoiling in the heat.

Soul—there was none.

He loathed his own flesh, but had desired another's. From child-hood he had carried the larvae of monstrosities: on maturing, they had crawled forth: all within twenty-four hours!

This frail decrepit vessel must be smashed to smithereens . . .

6

The Department . . .

The torso of the goat-footed caryatid was still there; a carriage and pair rolled up to the house; the doorman in a cocked hat stepped out to open the carriage door surmounted by a coat of arms: a coronet and a unicorn goring a knight; a hand, in leather glove, touched the brim of a cylinder hat in greeting.

A paragraph can come to life.

A paragraph has an astonishing outline: two lines interlocked at an angle. A paragraph is an insatiable consumer of paper: a true phylloxera. There is something mystical about a paragraph: it is the thirteenth sign of the zodiac.

Paragraphs had multiplied in Russia: Apollon Apollonovich directed the circulation of paragraphs; and they flowed through ante-chambers and over red-carpeted stairs.

Apollon Apollonovich was the most popular civil servant in Russia: with the exception of . . . well . . . Konshin (whose signature was on the banknotes).

There were cabinets in the Department . . .

There were also simple rooms; desks in every large room; clerks;

in front of each clerk a pen and inkwell, and an impressive stack of papers; each clerk scrawled, turned the sheets, rustled like dead leaves over a grave . . .

Ableukhov sat every day in his cabinet, legs crossed, arteries strained, his veined hand clutching his coat lapel; the sixty-eight-year-old Senator breathed the very life of paragraphs; and his breathing, like his paragraphs, reached across the expanses of Russia. Apollon Apollonovich, his legs crossed, his mind absorbed, blew out his cheeks—a habit of his—and cold draughts blew through the unheated chambers. Then the wind would begin to blow and, on the outskirts, a hurricane would develop.

Apollon Apollonovich blew!

He was an urbane well-trained gentleman; he sat in his cabinet, and cast a shadow over the passers-by; whistling, his breath spread over vast expanses—in Samara, in Saratov—through ravines, over sand dunes, among thistles, baring patches of sand, blowing up fires in kilns.

Wags might have called him Aquilon Apollonovich rather than Apollon Apollonovich.

7

For five years Apollon Apollonovich had been at the administrative wheel.

Then an unfortunate affair occurred: genius deserted the corruptible body of the bearer of diamond Orders (he had gone mad): he slipped on the ladder of his official career.

At the Tzukatov soirée he was still a person of official importance; but when his son's actions were made public, the Senator's failings were suddenly revealed: there was no doubt about it.

Apollon Apollonovich Ableukhov's name was removed from the list of candidates for a very important post.

Ableukhov's twilight began.

In old age the tight, heavily weighted spring loses its tautness; the aging human brain becomes slack.

In a single night, the once proud and aloof Apollon Apollono-

vich had become a bowed and stooping figure; in a single night
he had fallen apart and allowed his head to hang.

Against the flaming background of the burning Russian Empire
—instead of a gold-braided personage—one beheld a poor hemorrhoidal old man, unkempt, unshaven, perspiring in a tasseled
dressing-gown!

Have you seen famous people, who for a half-century have beaten
off all attacks, become senile?

We all have.

At meetings, at congresses, they mount the platform in glossy
frock coats, with drooping jaws, toothless—we have seen such
persons. . . . We have seen them at home too. Witlessly whispering
stupid jokes in our ears, they will conduct us to their study where,
slobbering, they will proudly point to a little shelf of their works
bound in morocco!

At precisely ten o'clock Apollon Apollonovich usually sat down
to his coffee. Icy, stern, clean-shaven, smelling of eau-de-cologne,
he entered the dining room briskly. But that morning he came
to his coffee unperfumed and unshaven, shuffling in his slippers
across the floor.

He did not even glance at his correspondence; and he did not
acknowledge the servants' greetings.

> "Dear Delvig calls me,
>   The comrade of my zestful youth,
>   The comrade of cheerless days—"

"I say, take the dog away!" the Senator commanded.

At eleven-thirty, as if remembering something, Apollon Apollonovich suddenly grew as nervous as a gray mouse; with mincing
steps he entered the study, his drawers visible under the open flap
of his dressing-gown.

A servant glanced into the room to remind his master of the
waiting carriage.

In consternation, he watched his master roll the small library ladder over the velvety rugs and, to the danger of his life, mount it. After clambering up, the Senator tried the dust on the books with a finger.

He demanded a dustcloth.

Two servants with lighted wax candles took their stand on either side of the ladder.

"Raise the light, please. . . . Not like that . . . not like that. . . . I say—higher, higher . . ."

From a cloud of dust dangled the flaps of the Senator's mouse-gray dressing-gown, and the tassels swung.

Apollon Apollonovich, Actual Privy Councilor, was lost in a cloud of dust. Forgetting everything in the world, he continued to dust the books.

"What dust, what dust . . ." he exclaimed, coughing. "More and more of it. . . . I'm doing a good job of it with this duster!"

The disturbing peal of the telephone sounded: it was the Department. From the yellow house the answer came:

"Yes, he's having his coffee. . . . I'll tell him. . . . Yes. . . . His carriage is ready . . ."

Later the telephone rang again. The answer was:

"Yes, sir, I've already told him. . . . I'll tell him again . . ."

There was a third call.

"He's busy sorting his books."

The bell continued to ring: the silence spoke of forgotten things. The head on the ladder turned:

"Do you hear? . . . The doorbell's ringing . . ."

It might be Nikolai Apollonovich, that scoundrel, or Herman Hermanovich with some papers, or Kotoshi-Kotoshinsky, Count Nolden, or—perhaps—Anna Petrovna . . .

"Your Excellency, one cannot help hearing it. Never fear, someone will open the door . . ."

When the telephone rang the servant would report:

"Allow me to say, sir, the telephone is ringing!"

Each lackey held a candle high; from a cloud of dust under the ceiling the Senator's head would suddenly emerge.

"Yes, yes, yes . . ."

"The doorbell's ringing again . . ."

The servants sensed something unusual; they trembled, silently urging him to hurry.

"It must be the *barinya* . . ."

"Anna Petrovna!"

Apollon Apollonovich—a mousy figure—blinked and began to crawl down slowly, his hairy chest touching the steps of the ladder; on reaching the floor, he ambled toward the stairway, the dustcloth still in his hand; he was panting hard and felt his pulse.

Up the stairway, conducted by Semenich, came a gentleman with side whiskers, wearing a uniform with a tightly fitted waist, white wrist bands, and a Star on his chest.

Drawing his dressing-gown tightly around himself, Apollon Apollonovich peeped from behind the statue of Niobe.

8

If you have ever been in Petersburg, then you will know that entrance: an oak door with mirrored panels.

Day after day, when you pass this door, you will see a gold galloon, a mace, and a cocked hat: the aged doorman drowsily nodding over the *Stock Exchange Gazette.*

Five years had passed and great events had occurred: Port Arthur had fallen; yellow faces had inundated the land; legends about the horsemen of Genghis Khan had been revived.

But the years had changed nothing here: the shoulder, the cocked hat, the galloon, and the beard remained always the same.

When that white beard will stir or the mace move or the galloon catch the reflection of a passing gleam, then you, like one out of mind, will go roaming the Petersburg prospects.

Listen, cock your ears! Do you hear the thud of hoofs on the Ural steppes!

It is the riders of the steppes.

The caryatid, a colossus, hangs as always above the entrance.

Old heavy-bearded man of stone! For many years, summer, winter, and spring, you have smiled here above the din of the street. . . . Timelessness, you stoop over the line of time; ravens find asylum in your beard; the wet prospect below shimmers with reflections; and the dimly lighted slabs of pavement reflect the greenish faces of the passers-by.

What a day it was!

Drops of rain began to beat, patter, whisper; the clerks arrived out of the fog; the doorman opened the doors for them; the clerks hung their hats and ran up the red-carpeted steps of the white marble vestibule, crossed large unheated chambers and found their own cold desks; there was nothing for them to copy; no papers had been brought from the Director's cabinet: there was no one there.

Apollon Apollonovich had failed to arrive.

The waiting became tedious; the clerks whispered in perplexed voices; it was a somber day; the telephone continued to ring.

"Hasn't he left his house yet? . . . Impossible! . . ."

"Have you reported to him? . . . Is he at breakfast?"

The assistant director, in a resplendent uniform, descended the red-carpeted steps.

Within twenty minutes, as he mounted the stairs of Senator Ableukhov's house, he caught sight of his chief in a dressing-gown, peeping from behind a statue of Niobe.

"Apollon Apollonovich, so you're here! I came to learn what was the matter; we've been ringing you all morning. We've been waiting . . ."

"I . . . I . . ." Ableukhov yawned, "have been sorting my library. . . . Excuse my appearance. I'm engaged in domestic affairs."

He pointed to his torn dressing-gown. He dropped the dustcloth on the parquet floor.

"But there's a general strike on . . ."

"What are you saying? I . . . I . . ." At this point the old man's face crumbled into furrows.

"Dust?"

"Yes, I've been dusting with this rag."

The assistant director respectfully bowed before the human ruin; he tried again . . .

But Apollon Apollonovich again interrupted him:

"Dust, as you know, contains the micro-organisms of diseases . . ."

The gray ruin, seating himself in an Empire armchair, suddenly leaned forward, resting an arm on the chair and burying his face in a document:

"What is this?"

"A report—about the general strike."

"Just a minute, I'll look into it . . ." His face grew bitter as he read.

"Just a minute! . ; . Have they lost their wits? . . ."

"Apollon Apollonovich . . ."

"What can they be thinking of? Administrative authority is one thing; futile violation of the law is another."

"But—Apollon Apollonovich!"

Apollon Apollonovich, his jaw trembling, waved his pencil and tied the tassels of his dressing-gown.

"I am a man of the school of Plehve. . . . I know what I am doing. . . . Me-emme . . . me-emme . . ."

He puffed out his cheeks.

Senator Ableukhov's career, built slowly through the years, was crumbling into dust. When the assistant director left, the Senator walked for some time among the Empire chairs; then he left the room to reappear again, dragging a mass of papers which he piled on top of a small mother-of-pearl table.

His dead head rose above the pile of memoranda, notes, and paragraphs.

"That's how it is. . . . I, gentlemen, am a man of the school of Plehve!"

His sharpened pencil, making hordes of question marks in the margins, flew over the documents. He was transacting his last official business.

The Department was alive with whispers; suddenly a door opened.

"Apollon Apollonovich is leaving the service."

Legonin, the chief clerk, burst into tears; from the office of the assistant director a clear voice was heard; the telephone rang, and the assistant director's jaw trembled; Apollon Apollonovich had ceased to be head of the Department.

9

Nikolai Apollonovich stared at the historical landmarks: he passed them without reacting or noticing that, from time to time, the Lieutenant turned to glance at him. The glance he directed at his kidnaped victim seemed full of curiosity.

At one point the wind ripped off Ableukhov's Italian hat, but he caught it as it landed on Likhutin's knee; for a moment his fingers touched Likhutin's and quivered with reptilian fear. Likhutin felt he had been touched by a snake such as men will immediately crush in disgust . . .

Ableukhov recovered.

"I'd advise you, Sergey Sergeyevich, to raise your collar; you have a bad throat, you know, and this weather isn't too good for it . . ."

"What did you say?"

"You might get a frog in your throat."

"After all, I am here on your business," Likhutin suddenly growled.

"?"

"I am not concerned with my throat. . . . I left the service because of your business or, at least, thanks to you."

"You're insinuating something," Nikolai Apollonovich was about to say, but he caught Likhutin's glance.

There was repulsion in it: a crawling snake does not provoke anger, but the impulse to crush it on the spot . . .

Nikolai Apollonovich, shuddering with fear, clutched at the Lieutenant's sleeve with his cold numbed fingers.

"What is this all about? What are you up to? . . . Sergey Sergeyevich, I confess to you . . . I've conducted myself . . . abominably. . . . I can explain it all. I'm sure you'll understand, when I tell you. . . . And really, I've just spent a sleepless night. I suffer from insomnia. . . . The doctors . . ."—he resorted to a lie—"say it's brain fatigue and pseudo-hallucinations."

Sergey Sergeyevich did not reply; he looked at his companion dispassionately. Reptiles do not provoke anger, but merely the impulse to crush them on the spot . . .

"Yes, pseudo-hallucinations," Ableukhov repeated in a pleading

voice. He looked small, awkward. . . . His frightened eyes sought
those of Sergey Sergeyevich.

"I . . . I . . . I . . ."

"We've arrived."

Lieutenant Likhutin stood waiting by the droshky for the Senator's son to climb out. Nikolai Apollonovich was groping in the
droshky.

"Sergey Sergeyevich, I had a stick with me. . . . Could I have
lost it?"

Nikolai Apollonovich stared into the fog with unblinking metallic
eyes, and did not stir from the spot.

Sergey Sergeyevich began to breathe heavily, impatiently, even
angrily. He caught Ableukhov by the sleeve and began to drag
him from the droshky like a bale of goods.

Losing his balance, Nikolai Apollonovich grabbed Likhutin's
hand. Lieutenant Likhutin, who was now in a rage, gripped Nikolai
Apollonovich by the collar.

"I'm coming, I'm coming, Sergey Sergeyevich . . ."

Soon the front door slammed behind them.

10

"I . . . stood here, yes, right here. . . . I stood and . . ."

"Well, Nikolai Apollonovich?"

"Yes, in a nervous faint, yielding to certain associations . . ."

"Associations?"

"So the doctor said. . . . But please don't drag me along. I can
walk . . ."

"Well, don't grab me then. Stop it, please!"

"The doctor said . . . the doctor said it is a rare nervous disturbance—the domino and all that. . . . A mental disturbance . . ."

From the upper landing a complacent voice called to them:

"How do you do?"

"Who is that?" Nikolai Apollonovich asked with a sense of
relief. Likhutin's grip on his arm relaxed.

"I've been standing here and ringing and ringing . . ." the
voice said.

A lighted match revealed a large bouquet of magnificent chrys-anthemums, and behind it the figure of Verhefden.

"Ah, Sergey Sergeyevich, I did not recognize you at first!" Verhefden said. "You've shaved everything! And in civilian dress! And Nikolai Apollonovich is with you. . . . How is your health? After last night, I must admit I was worried about you. . . . You disappeared so suddenly . . ."

After a pause Verhefden nervously resumed: "Am I in the way? I dropped in only for a minute. . . . The fact is, I'm in a hurry . . . work has piled up. . . . Your father, Apollon Apollonovich, is expecting me. . . . We're on the verge of a general strike."

A young woman in starched dress appeared in the doorway.

"Please come in. . . . The *barinya* is at home."

"No, Mavrushka . . . give this bouquet to your mistress. . . . It's a debt I owe." Verhefden smiled at Sergey Sergeyevich and shrugged the way a man shrugs at another man when a woman is concerned. "In payment of my debt to Sofya Petrovna—for the 'fibs.'" Then he quickly turned. "*Au revoir*, my friends. You ought to look after yourself, Nikolai Apollonovich. You look tired and nervous."

Presently Verhefden's steps were heard descending the stairs, and then came the parting shot: "You're spending too much time with books . . ."

Nikolai Apollonovich experienced great difficulty in restraining himself from shouting: "Herman Hermanovich, I'm coming with you. . . . I think we go the same way!"

It was too late: the street door slammed.

Nikolai Apollonovich felt himself captive in the presence of Mavrushka. His face revealed fear; the Lieutenant's, frank satanic joy; perspiring, Likhutin pulled a handkerchief from his pocket; wiping his face, he pushed Nikolai with the other hand across the threshold.

Nikolai Apollonovich resisted and proved as slippery as an eel.

Although he resisted, he eventually found himself inside. Col-lecting his last shreds of independence, he stuttered:

"I shan't be . . . stopping long."

Observing no courtesy, Sergey Sergeyevich pushed him and his broad-brimmed Italian hat into the room full of· Fujiyamas.

Nikolai Apollonovich crossed the entire length of the room without noticing the traces of plaster on the striped carpet being crunched under his feet. The carpet did not get cleaned until later.

A door opened and Nikolai Apollonovich saw two eyes and a stream of hair. He heard the exclamation:

"Oh!"

He turned his head and, seeing Sofya Petrovna, shouted, "Leave us alone, Sofya Petrovna. This is a matter strictly between men!"

Then he found himself before the door of Sergey Sergeyevich's study. The door swung open, and he disappeared into the unknown.

11

Apollon Apollonovich rose from the chair.

He tore himself away from the files of papers that lay before him; the hand holding the pencil with which he had been jotting in the margins trembled above the tiny mother-of-pearl table.

At last he understood.

The carriage with the coat of arms on the door would no longer roll him up to the caryatid; no one would rush to meet him any more; he would see no more the eighty-year-old shoulder, the cocked hat, and the mace; Port Arthur would never be returned; China would rise in revolt; and then—the horsemen of Genghis Khan!

Apollon Apollonovich listened carefully: he seemed to hear a remote thudding. But it was only Semenich coming and going.

Apollon Apollonovich did not like the view of the Neva from his window. He glanced around anxiously: here were the four walls, the hearth; but his activity was at an end.

What then?

Snow rather than walls! They presented a somewhat cold aspect. . . . What then? There was the domestic life, that is, Nikolai Apollonovich, a most terrible—how to put it?—and—Anna Petrovna, back in Petersburg now, in the evening of life . . .

"Me-emme . . ."

It had all been a mental game!

It had all receded beyond the frontier of consciousness; but he suddenly remembered his son, Nikolai Apollonovich—a young man of small stature, penetrating glance, and a tangle of various intellectual interests (he had to do him that justice!).

And he remembered *that* girl (it had been thirty years ago): her swarm of admirers, and himself as a relatively young man, a Privy Councilor already and a successful suppliant.

And that first night: her repressed expression of repulsion under a submissive smile. That night when he, Apollon Apollonovich, Privy Councilor, had violated the girl; the violation had continued for many years; between those smiles of submission, Nikolai Apollonovich had been conceived; lust and submission. Was it so astonishing that Nikolai Apollonovich had turned out to be a complex of repulsion, fear, and lust? He had been obliged to educate this horror, this offspring of theirs, to humanize this horror . . .

They had finally fled from it: Apollon Apollonovich had found his escape in the Department; his wife, Anna Petrovna, in amorous diversions with Mantalini, the singer; and their son, Nikolai Apollonovich—in philosophy, in meetings, in contact with dubious persons. Their domestic hearth had become a filthy sewer.

To this filth he had now returned; but there was no Anna Petrovna, only the locked door of her apartment. He had the key to it, but he had penetrated into this part of the house only twice, and he had caught a head cold there.

Instead of his son there was a pair of blinking, slippery eyes the color of cornflowers, furtive, frightened, masking horror.

And so on, and so forth.

Now that he had left the government service, he would shut the palatial rooms; the corridor with his private rooms and those of his son would remain open. He would confine his life to this corridor; he would wander back and forth, reading newspapers, attending to his organic functions, visiting the place unlike any other, reading posthumous memoirs, and seeing every day the door to his son's rooms.

He might peer through a chink in the door and then jump back; better still, he might have a small hole bored through the wall: his son's life behind the wall would be revealed to him with the precision of a clock mechanism, and he might find new interest in such observation.

"Papa!"

"Good morning, Kolenka!"

And they would part, each to his own room.

But then, having locked his own door, he would be able to squint through the small hole and observe, not without trembling, the mystery revealed. Nikolai Apollonovich was quite a stranger to him.

Such was the life he envisioned for himself.

An unconquerable desire drew him to his son's room. The door creaked: the reception room lay before him. Small and senile, he paused on the threshold. He noticed the disorder: the cage containing the green parrots, the ivory and copper, the Arabian tabouret. He saw the absurdity of it: the red domino, its folds falling from the tabouret on top of the spotted leopard head. He stood lost in thought, gazing with loathing at the domino that had figured so prominently and so briefly . . .

The room suddenly seemed airless to Apollon Apollonovich. The atmosphere was heavy with lead instead of air. Here the most terrible, intolerable thoughts must have been pondered. . . . An unpleasant room!

Apollon Apollonovich stopped to examine a portrait of his son, painted in the spring of the last year: the wry, martyred mouth, the cornflower-blue eyes, the fair hair bathed in light—his son looked fine in his student uniform with slender waist and white glove in his hand; he was clean-shaven, perfumed perhaps; the ceremonial sword had been obscured and cut short by the frame. Then Apollon Apollonovich shuffled into the next room.

The open writing desk attracted his attention. A drawer had been pulled out. Moved by instinctive curiosity, Apollon Apollonovich ran to the desk and snatched up a forgotten portrait which he studied pensively—his sentimental mood had diverted his attention from the open drawer. The portrait was of a young brunette . . .

Mechanically he lowered his eyes, noticing something that made him put down the portrait immediately; he picked up the heavy object. . . . He promptly became absorbed in this strange object with rounded corners; something was clicking inside. He examined it carefully and listened to the ticking: a clock mechanism! In a sardine tin!

He did not like the look of it . . .

To give it a more detailed examination, he carried the object into the drawing room; as he bent over it, he himself looked like a small mousy bundle. . . . He strode over to the corner of the room where a long-legged bronze statue stood on iron legs; he laid the heavy object on a Chinese tray, above which hung a thinly painted, violet glass lampshade, and bent his large bald head over it.

Age had darkened the glass and dimmed the painting.

12

Having run into Likhutin's small study, Nikolai Apollonovich stumbled and fell to his knees.

He jumped up, limping and panting; frightened, he headed toward the oak armchair. He gave the appearance of a bag-like figure with visibly shaking hands, revealing one instinctive purpose: to reach the chair in time, so that, in the event of a rear assault, he might take refuge behind it and, if necessary, run round it, back and forth, in an effort to escape his relentless adversary.

Or, armed with this same chair, he might, if it came to that, overturn it and rush for the window—far better to jump into the street, even if he had to break a window to do it, than to remain alone with this madman.

He had barely reached the chair when he felt a hot breath on his neck; he caught sight of a five-pronged hand ready to fall on his shoulder and of the face of the avenger, red with fury, veins standing out. Just as the hand was about to descend upon him, he leaped over the chair.

The five-pronged hand fell on the chair.

The chair cracked; the crash was followed by an outburst which sounded hardly human, hardly coherent:

"You know why . . . why I . . . I'm meddling in this . . . do you understand? . . . This whole business . . . this business. . . .

Do you understand? . . . For my part . . . not that I have any. . . . Well, do you understand? . . ."

The Lieutenant towered above the cowering figure which, grimacing, put out a protective hand to ward off the unexpected blow.

"Yes, I understand, I understand . . . Sergey Sergeyevich . . . but more quietly, please, I implore you . . ."

He blinked his eyes and tried not to look at that flushed face nor to hear that shrill almost voiceless voice.

"It's a matter . . . in which any decent man. . . . What did I say? Yes, any decent man . . ."

Sergey Sergeyevich's fist pounded the wall immediately above Nikolai Apollonovich's head.

Nikolai Apollonovich, on all fours, eyed the two straddling legs in front of him and, oblivious of the consequences, quickly darted between them. Springing to his feet, he rushed to the door, but the five-pronged paws gripped the hem of his frock coat, tearing away a piece of the expensive material. Sergey Sergeyevich threw it aside and shouted:

"Stop there. . . . Stop! I . . . I'm not going to kill you!"

He flung his victim aside as easily as he had the piece of cloth. Nikolai Apollonovich landed in a corner; almost weeping from the mad absurdity of it all, he grasped for the first time that the raging man was not Likhutin, not an enemy panting with the fury of vengeance, but a demented creature—a creature unfortunately of massive muscular strength.

The raging man momentarily turned his back and walked to the door, which made a clicking sound; sounds were audible behind the door; a sob, the shuffling of slippers; then all was quiet.

Sofya Petrovna had stolen to the keyhole: peeping in, she saw a pair of legs and . . . sock garters . . . in a corner of the room; it seemed very odd. Loud sounds broke from her, her throat gurgled; then came the metallic sound of the clicking lock.

Weeping, Sofya Petrovna jumped away from the door. She perceived Mavrushka, who was also weeping.

"What is it? Oh, dear *barinya* . . ."

"What can it be? . . . What can they be doing, Mavrushka?"

The demented man went on pacing the room diagonally, while Nikolai Apollonovich, flat against the wall, continued to observe him.

Suddenly he stopped pacing; he sat down, leaning his elbows on his knees, with his face buried in his hands; he sighed deeply and fell into deep meditation.

"Oh, Lord!" he exclaimed.

"Save us and deliver us!" he moaned.

Nikolai Apollonovich cautiously took advantage of this quiet interlude.

The worst of the mad paroxysm was apparently over; Nikolai Apollonovich crept from his corner: a sufficiently ludicrous figure, dressed as he was in his formal student uniform, now ripped, still in his galoshes, and a scarf around his neck.

He paused near a small table and, conscious of his pounding heart, deftly snatched up a paperweight.

A rustle betrayed him; he had upset a little stack of papers. Sergey Sergeyevich's subsided paroxysm surged up again; his head turned and he now saw Ableukhov standing armed with the paperweight. Still holding it in his hand, Nikolai Apollonovich sprang back.

Sergey Sergeyevich resumed on an old note:

"Only, please, do me the favor: don't be afraid. . . . Why are you trembling? . . . It seems I'm frightening you. . . . I've torn your coat. . . . I didn't mean it."

"Believe me," Nikolai Apollonovich replied, "the episode of the domino can be explained by the exhaustion of the nervous system. I did not do it just to violate a promise. I did not stand in the entrance because I wanted to . . ."

"Forgive me for tearing a piece of your coat," the Lieutenant interrupted. "I'll see that it's mended. I'll do it myself. I have needle and thread . . ."

"Don't bother, Sergey Sergeyevich . . . really, it's nothing . . ."

"Yes, yes, a mere trifle . . ."

"I mean it's a trifle in relation to our subject: in relation to my standing in the entrance . . ."

"But we're not talking about that!" The Lieutenant gesticulated in irritation and began to pace the floor again.

"Well then, about Sofya Petrovna. . . . What else could it be?"

"Our subject, you see," the Lieutenant said, turning his in-flamed eyes on Nikolai Apollonovich, "is the cause of your being shut up now . . ."

"You see," Nikolai Apollonovich began, "when the brain be-comes entirely subject to associations . . ."

But Sergey Sergeyevich interrupted him:

"You are not in danger here. . . . And here's your piece of cloth."

"He's mocking me," Nikolai Apollonovich thought.

"It's this way: you must remain here. . . . As for me, I shall leave with a letter I shall dictate and you will sign. . . . I shall go to your house, into your room, where I was this morning and where I did not find what I was looking for. Everything was upside down in your room. Should my search prove futile, I shall warn your father . . . because"—he wiped his forehead—"your father is quite helpless in the matter, and everything depends on you, yes, yes, on you alone. . . . I tell you, it must not happen —no, never!"

A note of anger had crept into his voice.

"What?"

"You know!"

Crazy as a loon!

Nikolai Apollonovich listened to his ravings; something inside him trembled; perhaps, this was no mere raving. There was some-thing in it that sounded like a hint incoherently expressed—but a hint of what?

"Sergey Sergeyevich, what are you talking about?"

"What do you mean? Don't you know? . . . About the bomb, of course!"

The paperweight dropped from Nikolai Apollonovich's hand.

"Sergey Sergeyevich, I am astonished that you could believe I would consent to such an abomination. . . . I'm no scoundrel. . . . I'm not a wretch . . ."

Nikolai Apollonovich could not continue.

With a martyred smile, the stooping figure emerged from the corner, his fair hair like a halo framing a high shining forehead above eyes of cornflower blue. He stood affronted and indignant, his palms lifted and clearly defined against a background of red wallpaper.

The Lieutenant, sensing that he had made an error, promptly yielded.

"Yes, I believe you!" he exclaimed with a distraught gesture. "You see," he went on, unable to hide his confusion, "I did not doubt it. . . . My wife told me about it. . . . Someone passed the note to her. She read it, having opened it by mistake," he lied, turning red and growing even more confused.

"Once the letter was opened," the Senator's son remarked with some malice, shrugging at the same time, "then Sofya Petrovna, of course, was justified in revealing its contents to you, as her husband . . ."

"I'm afraid I acted hastily," Likhutin admitted, as his glance again fell upon the torn bit of cloth which somehow fascinated him. "And don't give this a thought. I'll mend the coat myself."

Nikolai Apollonovich, however, was not prepared to pardon him so easily. With a reproachful gesture, he remarked:

"You didn't know what you were doing."

His dark blue eyes expressed noble sadness.

"You shouldn't believe informers!"

Turning his head away, Nikolai Apollonovich wept without restraint. Having freed himself from rude fear, he was now wholly fearless; he wanted to suffer; his emotions had been lacerated, torn to shreds, just as his "I," his ego, had been likewise torn. He yearned for light. But there was no light—only darkness. In place of the "I," of his ego, there was only darkness. He turned away and wept.

"To be sure," he heard a gentle conciliatory voice behind him, "I've made a mistake. I understood . . ."

"You took advantage of your physical superiority . . . and, in the presence of a woman, treated me abominably . . ."

His hand outstretched, Sergey Sergeyevich crossed the room, but Nikolai Apollonovich, now choking with belated rage, went on:

"You, Sergey Sergeyevich, wanted to make sure . . . that I was no patricide? . . . No, Sergey Sergeyevich, you should have thought of that earlier. Instead, you've treated me as though I were—God knows what. And you have torn my uniform . . ."

"That can be mended!"

And before Ableukhov could recover himself, Sergey Sergeyevich dashed to the door shouting:

"Mavrushka! . . . Some black thread, please! . . . and a needle!"

The opening door almost struck Sofya Petrovna, who had been eavesdropping.

"Ah, it's you, Sofya! Be a dear, and get me a needle and thread. Nikolai Apollonovich has had an accident. He's ripped off a bit of his uniform!"

"Never mind, Sergey Sergeyevich! Never mind, Sofya Petrovna!" Nikolai Apollonovich called out.

And grimacing stupidly, wiping his eyes with his sleeve, Nikolai Apollonovich followed his hosts into the room with the Fujiyamas. He raised his head and, noticing the cracked ceiling, turned questioning eyes on Likhutin.

"An accident, Nikolai Apollonovich. . . . I was repairing the ceiling . . . "

13

Bright as a mirror, the samovar on the stand gleamed in the light, but the boiling samovar on the table had not been cleaned. The new samovar was used only for guests; when there were no visitors, the old monstrosity served. Slices of bread lay on the table, covered with a stained tablecloth; near an unfinished glass of soured tea (there was a slice of lemon in it) was a damp patch; and there was a plate with leavings.

But where was Zoya Zakharovna's sumptuous hair? Her head revealed only a single slender plait.

Zoya Zakharovna wore a wig for the benefit of visitors—very likely she was also shameless in her use of rouge—she had been seen as a lovely brunette with smooth enameled skin. Now she looked like an elderly woman with a perspiring nose. She wore a not too clean blouse.

Lippanchenko sat half turned away from the table, his square hunched back obscuring the dirty samovar. He had spread a pack of cards on a little table and was playing Patience, his customary after-supper recreation. He was disturbed; his eyes kept wandering from the cards. Earlier that evening he had engaged in a conversation—a conversation which, for a time, had made him forget Patience and everything else.

Afterward, he had tried to turn his back on the conversation.

He sat without his jacket, his belt loosened to ease the pressure on his stomach; a tail of his shirt stuck out from between his waistcoat and his trousers.

Pensively he watched a roach crawling, large and black—roaches flourished there.

"Well, I can't understand it at all . . ."

"What?"

"Surely a loyal woman, a woman of forty . . . a woman such as I . . ."

He noticed a hole at the elbow of her blouse, through which the skin showed . . . there was a red spot, probably a flea bite.

"What's on your mind, woman? Speak plainly . . . "

"Haven't I the right to ask?"

Lippanchenko swung about in his chair. Her words had apparently provoked him. His little eyes blinked; he seemed on the point of saying something, but refrained. His mind worked slowly. But his impulse to speak the truth was checked.

"H'm . . . yes, yes . . . the five goes on the six. . . . Where's the Queen? . . . Here she is. . . . But there is no Jack . . ."

He glanced quizzically at Zoya Zakharovna, while his stubby reddish-haired fingers pushed one heap of cards on top of another.

"Well, I've got the game cut."

"Why, then, are you angry?"

She rose and walked across the room, her slippers shuffling, her loosened corset protruding over her stomach, her pendulous chin hanging. As she walked, she flung:

"You'd better ask me *why* I'm so concerned . . . why the others are concerned. . . . They shrug their shoulders. . . . So I thought"—she collapsed into an armchair—"I ought to find out . . ."

Biting his lip, Lippanchenko laid out his cards, row upon row. He remembered that he had many things to attend to the next day, that he must dispose of a growing collection of incriminating documents.

"H'm! ... I've a free place ... I must put the King on it. ... Tell me, what is it they're concerned about ..." He gathered up the cards. "It won't come out, the two is hidden ..."

From the bedroom came a rasping sound as of a window being opened. It must be his St. Bernard, Tom.

"Your questions, I want you to understand," Lippanchenko declared, rising with a sigh, "are a violation of Party discipline." And he gulped down the rest of the soured tea.

He dragged himself toward the open door and into the darkness.

"What has discipline to do with me, Kolechka?" she asked, bending over the empty armchair. "Seriously ..."

She did not finish her thought; she was listening to Lippanchenko shuffling in the bedroom.

"There must be no secrets between us," she said to herself.

She turned her head toward the door where Lippanchenko had reappeared.

"You can't conceal from me the fact that you now have secrets!" she exclaimed in greeting.

"There's no one in the bedroom," he interrupted her. Then he added, grumbling, "Why make a scene?"

"What have I done, Kolechka? Don't I love you? ... Am I not afraid for you?"

She put her arms around his neck.

He saw her nose before him, the pores exuding perspiration: what an unhealthy skin! Her eyes bulged, crept into his; they looked like black buttons; they had no light.

"Let me be! Enough! Let me go, Zoya Zakharovna, you're choking me!"

He grabbed her hands and pulled them from his neck.

"You know," he continued, "how sentimental I am, and how weak my nerves are ... I ..."

They lapsed into silence.

After this consoling little exchange, she washed the glass, the saucer, and the teaspoons in sullen silence. As before, he sat half turned away from the table, presenting his square back to both Zoya Zakharovna and the samovar.

Her perturbed eyes surveyed the tablecloth, then fell upon his heavy chest. When he turned, her eyes attentively scrutinized his blinking little eyes: what time had wrought!

His light brown eyes, once alive with humor and arch gaiety, had in the past twenty-five years grown dim and shallow and had become covered with a menacing film; yes, twenty-five years were no brief span; nevertheless, such paling and shrinking were incredible! There were small bags under those eyes. The face had grown sallow, greasy, faded—as shocking as the gray pallor of a corpse. His forehead seemed too bulging, and his ears too large. After all, there were still handsome elderly men left in the world! And he was far from old.

The fair twenty-year-old student—student Lipensky as he was known in Paris—had been transformed, as a result of distending into this forty-five-year-old paunch—*this* Lippanchenko.

14

A small salt water lake had formed on the sandy shore.

White-capped waves from the bay sped along the shore; lit by the moon, billow after billow foamed, reared, and thundered in the distance, then fell, gliding on the shore in tufted foam, and spread over the low shore, lapping the sands and growing sharper as they advanced until, fine as a blade, they shaved the sand and reached at last the tiny salt lake, filling it with brine.

Then the billows receded.

Knotty bushes stretched at some distance from the sea; they swayed sibilantly. Among them a minuscule blackish figure of a man was running without a hat; a rasping sound, a moan, rose from the spot. Fallen trees stretched out of the mist and dampness . . .

The minuscule figure bent over a tree hollow, into the shroud of black dampness.

"My soul, you have departed from me . . . poor me . . ."

Words broke from the heart:

"Remember me . . . poor me . . ."

A bright point wavered on the horizon; a loaded schooner was approaching Petersburg. The point grew larger, glowing like a stalk of wheat bristling with light.

Now it became a broad strip, outlining the dark basket-like shape of the ship with a forest of spars above it.

Many-limbed wooden hands waved in the moonlight; a head loomed out of the brush, cradled in a web of black branches; the moonlight, becoming entangled in the web, gleamed dazzlingly in its meshes; a phosphorescent gleam filled the gaps between the bushes. A commanding hand, pointing to the future, reached out in the direction of a light in the tiny cottage garden where resilient branches among the bushes beat against the railed fence.

The minuscule figure of a man paused and crept imploringly among the phosphorescent gaps, murmuring:

"Really, I shouldn't do it—on mere suspicion, without an explanation."

His eyes were on the lighted window.

Quickly the minuscule figure crossed an open space, his breast coming in contact with the railing that sheltered the garden; he climbed over the railing and stealthily crept along, his feet becoming entangled in the long dewy grass. He stole up to the terrace and, in two leaps, reached the door of the gray cottage. He peered through the window into the room.

They were sitting there . . .—

—Lippanchenko was leaning with one elbow on the table; the other hand was lying free with palm exposed; the peeker's eyes were astonished by the short stubby fingers which looked as if they had been chopped off—

—The tiny figure fled from the door and found itself in the bushes; an outburst of pity enveloped it: "Really, it's impossible to do it just this way . . ."

15

Shifting his huge torso, Lippanchenko suddenly stretched out his arm—and took down the fiddle hanging on the wall.

"One comes home to rest, and . . . "

He reached for the rosin and, with a kind of fury, set to rubbing the bow.

"One is greeted with tears . . ."

He held the fiddle to his stomach and, bending over it, pressed the broad end into his lap; the narrow end he pressed against his chin; with one hand he tightened the strings, with the other he plucked them:

"*Do!*"

And at this, his head leaned farther forward and turned to the side; with an expression half-quizzical, half-jesting, with a shade of sadness, he glanced at Zoya Zakharovna as if to ask:

"Did you hear that?"

She sat down, her face suddenly amiable; she eyed Lippanchenko's strumming finger.

"That's better!"

They nodded to each other: he with the renewed energy of youth, she with embarrassment.

"Ah, what a man!"

"Tren-tren . . ."

"An incorrigible infant!"

Despite his resemblance to a rhinoceros, with an agile movement of his left hand he transferred his fiddle to its proper place, broad end between shoulder and lowered head, narrow end between the fingers of one hand. He moved the bow rapidly, paused for an instant; then, tenderly, the bow came into contact with the strings, moving rapidly across them in nimble strokes; the head and the torso moved in rhythm . . .

The armchair creaked under Lippanchenko, who was stubbornly intent on producing the softest notes; his somewhat hoarse but pleasant bass unexpectedly filled the room. He sang an old love ballad popular in those days: "*Do not tempt me . . .*"

"Sh-sh!"

"Listen!"

"Is that the window again?"

"I must go and look!"

The moon peered from behind the clouds; all the things that had been obscured now took shape; the skeleton bushes stood out darkly, flinging shaggy shadows on the ground; the scattered patches in the air were consolidated into a phosphorescent body with an arm stretched toward the window; the minuscule figure of a man leaped to the window: it was closed, and made a jarring sound when forced open.

Shadows stirred within; someone with a candle was moving behind the curtain windows. A light suddenly appeared in the opened window; then the curtain was drawn back; a portly figure paused at the window and looked out. Then the curtain was drawn and the bulky figure made its way back past the curtained windows. Soon everything was quiet.

The sound of a fiddle and of voices was heard again from the cottage.

The minuscule figure of a man detached itself from the hollow tree, and crept again toward the window.

Presently the old love ballad was heard again:

"The o-l-l-d b-be-gui-l-lin-n-g days ar-re g-go-n-ne,
N-no l-lon-n-ger d-do-o-o I b-be-li-eve in pro-tes-ta-tion-ns...
N-no l-lon-n-ger d-do-o-o I hav-ve f-faith in-n l-love . . ."

Did Lippanchenko realize what he was singing? The bones of his forehead registered ignorance: his small forehead was ridged with intersecting furrows; it gave him the air of weeping.

Lippanchenko was singing his swan song.

At last, picking up a candle, he retired to his bedroom. On the threshold he paused irresolutely, sighed, and grew pensive; his whole body expressed an incomprehensible sadness.

The candlelight cut into the room's obscurity; objects and shadows of objects appeared; Lippanchenko's own tremendous shadow rose from under his heels and wavered in the circle cast by the light.

16

Lippanchenko stood still, candle in hand; the shadows paused with him; the enormous shadowy double—Lippanchenko's soul—reared his head to the ceiling; but Lippanchenko felt no interest in his own shadow; he was absorbed in no enigma, but only in the rustling sounds he heard.

He was revolted by cockroaches and, in the candlelight, he saw them scampering to their dark lairs, rustling as they ran.

Lippanchenko was angered.

He stamped toward the corner to find the floor-brush.

He placed the candle on the floor; holding the floor-brush in his hand, he clambered heavily on to a chair; with the bristling edge of the brush he pursued the crawling insects: one, two, three!—they cracked under the thrashing brush, on the ceiling, on the wall.

"Eight . . . ten . . . eleven . . ."—the victims fell to floor.

Before going to bed he always slaughtered the cockroaches. After gathering them into a little pile he would go to sleep.

He turned the key in the lock, peered under the bed—a habit of his—and set the candle beside him.

He undressed.

With legs spread out, he sat on the bed, naked and hairy, his shaggy chest rounded like a woman's. Lippanchenko slept naked.

At a certain angle from the candle, between the window wall and the wardrobe which formed a recess, Lippanchenko hung his trousers in a way that never varied; it always created the impression that someone was peering out from there.

When he blew out the candle, the impression became stronger. Lippanchenko put his hand on the window shade and it flew up noisily; a coppery light flooded the room. From the white sheet of minute clouds the moon's disk crashed across the room, and . . .

Against the green background of the wall appeared the minuscule figure of a man in a thin overcoat; he smiled with the white lips of a clown. Suddenly, violently, Lippanchenko plunged forward and beat with his stomach and banged with his chest against the door, forgetting that he had locked it; a stream of boiling liquid gushed from his naked spine, from the shoulder down to the small of the back; falling, he understood: his spine had been cut like the hair-

less skin of a cold suckling pig; no sooner had he realized this
than he felt the heat streaming under his navel.

Something hissed and sputtered there; he seemed aware of
escaping gases—his stomach had been gashed open. Dropping his
head over his writhing stomach, he subsided; and he could feel
the flowing stickiness on his stomach and on the sheet.

This was his last conscious impression of prosaic reality; his
consciousness expanded; the monstrous periphery of consciousness
sucked planets into itself; and sensed them—one by one, through
the gashed organs, while the sun swam in the extension of the
heart; and his spinal column had become incandescent by its
impact and collision with Saturn's mass; in his stomach a volcano
was erupting.

His body sat there senselessly, head sagging on chest, eyes fixed
upon the ripped stomach; suddenly the body pitched forward—
stomach against the sheet; one red-haired arm, lit by the moon,
hung dangling above the blood-stained rug; the head with hanging
jaw had fallen back, facing the door; unblinking, it gazed at the
door; the sheet, white in the moonlight, bore the imprint of five
blood-stained fingers; and a thick heel protruded from it.

When people came in the morning, there was no Lippanchenko,
but only a pool of blood and a corpse. There was also a small, pale,
hysterical man with a tiny curled mustache. In his hand he grasped
a pair of scissors. He straddled the corpse as if it were a horse.
His arm was stretched out, and across his face—over his nose,
over his lips—crawled the shadow of a cockroach.

CHAPTER EIGHT

1

These past twenty-four hours!—how much had happened during them in the ever-widening spiritual expanses in which the author's vision had been increasingly involved.

Cerebral play, plumbing the depths, pursued its course within the closed circle described during those twenty-four hours.

The news of Anna Petrovna's return has been mentioned, but was then forgotten.

Those twenty-four hours!

They can be regarded only as something relative—as an instant —or as a period of time of spiritual occurrences—or as a zero: an experience which grows or shrinks into an instant.

The arrival of Anna Petrovna was a fact, a significant fact. . . . There was Anna Petrovna; she had returned, but she had no suspicion of what was happening. One circumstance agitated her: no one had sent her a message; they had simply ignored her arrival —both Nikolai and Apollon Apollonovich.

The sumptuous hotel had confined her to one of its smallest rooms; here Anna Petrovna sat by the hour, gazing at the wallpaper patterns. When she tired of looking at them, she turned to the window, which opened on a grimy wall, on smoke instead of on the sky; and if she looked out the window at an angle, she saw piles of dirty dishes and a washtub.

She rang; a maid appeared. Anna Petrovna gave an ,order: "*Thé complet.*"

Soon a waiter in black tails and starched shirt appeared, balancing a huge tray on the palm of his hand and his shoulder; his glance surveyed the inexpertly mended dress, the Spanish rags thrown on the double bed, the worn suitcase. He lowered the large tray. After depositing the *thé complet*, he left the room.

No one came, nothing happened. She heard laughter and noises in the next room, two chambermaids chattering in the hall. Again her gaze drifted to the window; and the window gave out on a grimy wall, on smoke instead of on the sky.

Suddenly there was a knock at the door. Anna Petrovna nervously spilled some tea on the napkin; as she glanced at an angle through the window, she saw the pile of dirty dishes and the washtub.

The chambermaid handed her a visiting card. Anna Petrovna rose from the table and, with a rapid movement of her hand, smoothed her hair.

"Where is he?"

"In the corridor."

"Ask him to come in."

She heard the noise in the neighboring room, the chatter of the chambermaids, a piano, and the steps rapidly approaching the door. Apollon Apollonovich Ableukhov, before crossing the threshold, tried to discern something in the twilit room. The first thing he saw was the grimy wall beyond the window, the smoke instead of the sky and, at an angle, the piles of dirty dishes and the washtub.

The first thing that struck him was the scanty setting of the little room: could such a room exist in a first class hotel?

But it was really not so astonishing; such rooms were common in first class hotels—in first class capital cities. Yes—"*Premier ordre—depuis 3 francs.*" God save us!

Here were the bed, the table, the chair; on the bed, in disorder, lay a handbag, belts, a black lace fan, a crystal Venetian vase wrapped in a stocking (of the purest silk), more belts, and shreds of lemon-yellow material: all souvenirs of Granada and Toledo.

She could not have received the three thousand rubles he had recently sent to Granada. To a woman of her position it must have been humiliating to drag about all this rubbish.

A silhouette emerged: his heart constricted; on the chair—no, not on the chair!—he saw Anna Petrovna, her figure subsided, plumper, her hair turning gray. The first thing he grasped was that she had developed a double chin, that her stomach was more rounded, but the light blue of her eyes of her once lovely face shone as before.

Apollon Apollonovich crushed the hat in his hand while his eyes darted about the room where all those objects lay scattered: the belts, the black lace fan, the stocking, and the shreds of the lemon-yellow material.

Two and a half years had changed him; two and a half years ago she had stared at his stone-chiseled face over the mother-of-pearl table—when they had had their last explanation. But now his face was marked by a complete absence of features.

Two and a half years ago Apollon Apollonovich had been an old man, but . . . there had been something ageless about him: he had looked a man. But now? Where was his iron will, his stony gaze? They had vanished. His dessication astonished her, and so did his stooped shoulders, trembling jaw, shaking fingers; and the color of his greatcoat—never while she was with him had he ordered a greatcoat of that color.

At last Apollon Apollonovich raised his head and falteringly said: "Anna Petrovna!"

Her features suddenly came to life; she made an impetuous movement to meet him, but did not stir from the spot.

Apollon Apollonovich however rushed toward her, still in his overcoat and hat in hand; his enormous skull, bare as a knee, and his projecting ears were familiar as his lips brushed her hand.

When he straightened up, she looked into his bulging eyes which did not seem hard to her.

Apollon Apollonovich tried to express his feelings.

"Do you know . . ." he began.

"Yes?"

"I've come to pay my respects . . ."

And Anna Petrovna noticed the distraught, soft, sympathetic look in the cornflower-blue eyes.

"We have. . . . There's a strike on . . ."

2

The door was suddenly thrown open.

Nikolai Apollonovich found himself in the entrance hall, and from there he sped upstairs in tremendous haste; as he ran past the ancient arms on the walls of the stairway, they seemed to be mere flashes. While still running, he tore the Italian hat off his head with an abrupt gesture. Panting, he reached the top landing; he shivered with ague. He still limped, and the trouser leg showed a rip; the cloth hung like a rag; moreover, the tear in his uniform had not been mended. With the torn tail of his uniform trailing behind him, Nikolai Apollonovich looked hunched and lame.

Beside himself, he flew into his multicolored room, startling the green parrots which desperately screeched in their cage and wildly flapped their wings. Their cry interrupted his flight; for an instant he paused, and his eyes fell on the spotted leopard skin with open maw at his feet. He groped in his pocket for the key to his writing table.

"Ah? . . . The devil take it. . . . Have I lost it?"

Helplessly, he floundered about the room, looking for the forgotten, treacherous key. He turned all the ornaments upside down, muttering to himself. He had his father's habit of talking to himself.

Then he dashed into the next room—to the writing table. He bumped into the Arabian tabouret and upset it. He was startled to find his desk open and the guilty drawer half pulled out. His heart sank: how could he have forgotten to lock it? He pulled out the entire drawer. . . . And . . . and . . .

It was not there!

All sorts of things lay in disorder in the drawer and on top was the cabinet-size portrait: the sardine tin was missing. His eyes darkened and dilated; he stood between the armchair and the bust—Kant's, of course.

He pulled out the drawer; the bundles of neatly tied letters and papers were in good order. He put everything on the table, but —no sardine tin. His legs gave way under him; still in his Italian mantle and galoshes, he fell to his knees, pillowing his burning head in his perspiring hands; breathless, he froze thus; in the half-twilight of the room, his shock of hair looked like a ghostly patch.

Then with startling suddenness, he sprang to his feet and rushed to the wardrobe. He threw open the door; all sorts of objects came flying out, landing on the rug; but there was still no sardine tin. Like a whirlwind, he swept around the room, his impatient gestures reminiscent of his esteemed father's. Fate was playing a joke on him. Having searched under the pillows, he crossed from the bed to the fireplace; he soiled his hands; then he went to the lower shelves of the bookcase, thrusting his hands in and out among the books. A host of volumes fell to the floor.

The sardine tin was not there.

His face, smudged by ashes and dust, senselessly rocked above the pile of objects. . . . He was interrupted in the middle of his search.

"Nikolai Apollonovich!"

Squatting, he turned and saw Semenich; quickly he spread his mantle over the pile of objects and, in this position, looked like a brood hen.

"I venture to report, sir . . ."

"Can't you see I'm busy! . . . You can see I'm sorting out books."

An absurd figure, he rose mechanically to his feet.

"You say my mother? Anna Petrovna?"

"Yes, sir. She's with Apollon Apollonovich . . . in the drawing room. They asked me to tell you."

"Tss! Semenich, Semenich—I want to ask you something!" —Nikolai Apollonovich dashed through the open door and, overtaking Semenich, seized him by the sleeve and made him stop. "You haven't seen, by any chance—you see, it's this way . . ." He became entangled in his words. "You see, I'd forgotten to. . . . There was a certain object in this room. You haven't seen it, have you? Here, in my study. . . . An object—a kind of toy . . ."

"A toy? . . ."

"Yes, a child's toy. . . . A sardine tin."

"A sardine tin?"

"Yes, a toy that looks like a sardine tin—very heavy, with a winder—it ticks like a watch. . . . I left it here . . . this toy . . ."

Semenich turned slowly, disengaging his sleeve from the clutching fingers, and for a moment his eyes fixed on the wall, on an African shield. Then he answered rather brusquely:

"No!"

Semenich was thinking of the Ableukhovs' reconciliation, of the new domestic happiness; he had not seen his master so happy in a long time. This was an event. . . . And here was the son fussing about a sardine tin, a toy; here he was in a torn uniform, distraught . . .

"What shall I say?"

"I'll come at once—at once!"

The door closed. Nikolai Apollonovich stood there, hardly realizing where he was. . . . Soon however he took off his torn suit and put on another; he washed the dust from his face and hands and, while dressing, murmured to himself:

"I simply cannot understand it. . . . Where could I have put it?"

Nikolai Apollonovich was not yet fully aware of the horror of the situation resulting from the disappearance of the sardine tin; it had not yet dawned on him that, in his absence, someone might have entered his room and, finding the sardine tin of terrible content, taken it away.

3

The same houses rose out of the mist, and the same gray human streams flowed on, and there was the same greenish-yellow fog. . . . Prospect after prospect ran to meet it, and the spherical surface of the planet seemed gripped in the coils of a serpent . . . and the net of parallel prospects, their surfaces intersected with squares and cubes, spread endlessly.

But Apollon Apollonovich was not contemplating his favorite figure: the square. He paid no senseless devotion to these stone parallelepipeds, these cubes. Cradled in the soft cushions of a hired carriage, he again and again cast sidelong glances at Anna

Petrovna, whom he was taking back to his lacquered house. Their conversation in the tiny hotel room remained an undivulged secret. But they had decided that Anna Petrovna was to move the very next day from the hotel to the house on the Embankment. And now Apollon Apollonovich was bringing her to see her son.

Anna Petrovna felt abashed.

Few words were exchanged in the carriage; Anna Petrovna stared out the window: for two and a half years she had not seen these gray prospects: now she could see the house numbers and the traffic. There—on a clear day, in the distance—one could see the dazzling gold needle, the clouds, and a ray of the red sunset. But on cloudy days one could see no one, nothing.

With unconcealed happiness, Apollon Apollonovich reclined against the back of the carriage and, from this confined cubicle, he cast sidelong glances at Anna Petrovna: sometimes she intercepted them—those distraught, perplexed, and yet gentle glances —then so blue and carefree, like an infant's. Had he fallen into dotage?

"I've heard, Apollon Apollonovich, that you're destined for the Ministry."

But Apollon Apollonovich interrupted her:

"Where have you come from, Anna Petrovna?"

"From Granada . . ."

"So-so, so-so . . ." He added, sniffling: "My days in the service have witnessed much unpleasantness lately . . ."

And—what was this? He suddenly felt the contact of a warm hand stroking his own. . . . H'm-h'm: Apollon Apollonovich was disturbed, confused, even a little frightened; he even experienced some discomfort. . . . For fifteen years he had not been shown such affection. She did it so simply. It must be admitted he had not expected this from her . . . h'm-h'm . . . (but two and a half years ago Apollon Apollonovich had regarded her as a woman of loose conduct).

"The fact is, I'm resigning . . ."

The lackeys were astonished!

Grishka, the youngest, who happened to be at the front door when the Ableukhovs arrived, described it to the others:

"I was sitting there when who should arrive but the *barin* and *barinya*. I opened the door and—heavens!—it was the *barin* himself in a hired carriage and with him the *barinya* in a cheap raincoat! . . . The *barin* jumped out of the carriage and gave his hand to the *barinya*. He was all attention, like . . ."

"Go on . . ."

"It's the truth . . ."

"I don't think they've seen each other in two years . . ." several voices said.

"Yes, there was the *barinya* getting out of the carriage—but not looking like herself at all. . . . And there were unmended holes in her gloves; maybe they don't mend them in Spain."

"Well, go on . . ."

"There was the *barin*, Apollon Apollonovich, standing before the carriage door humble-like, near a puddle and under the rain . . . so help me, God! And when the *barinya* gave him her hand and put her whole weight on him, he nearly toppled over—how could he hold such a heavy lady?"

"Now, don't be telling us stories!"

"It's the truth I'm telling. . . . Well, let Mitry Semenich tell the rest!"

"Well, then . . ."

"The *barinya* has aged. . . . At first I didn't know her, then I did . . ."

That was how it was.

Anna Petrovna and Apollon Apollonovich were both agitated by the reconciliation, but, after entering the house, they refrained from any further excesses of tenderness; Apollon Apollonovich blew his nose—under the rusty halberd—and stroked his side whiskers. Anna Petrovna responded to the servants' greetings; she embraced Semenich and seemed about to cry—but a handkerchief proved unnecessary. .

Apollon Apollonovich maintained an air of detachment; as if nothing had happened. All was well!

However, there were some servants left who remembered the lady's behavior before her departure from Russia: on the eve of her departure, she had shut herself away from the *barin*; with her was that same chap, the one with the mustache—what was his name? Oh yes, Mindalini, who used to sing at the house: "Tra-la-la . . ." And who never tipped.

Now husband and wife were in the grand salon which was rarely heated; Apollon Apollonovich spent most of his time in the study, but now he realized that he was no longer alone: so now he paced about the salon with Anna Petrovna, walking on the lacquered hollow parquet squares.

He had rarely walked on these squares with his son—almost never!

He took his wife by the arm and led her across the salon; she soon made him stop and pointed to a pale-colored fresco:

"Do you remember this fresco, Apollon Apollonovich?"

"Surely!"

"Where?"

The recollection came to him of a misty lagoon, of the enchanting aria that had sounded in the distance: that had been thirty years ago. Memories also overwhelmed Anna Petrovna; these memories divided and branched out; she thought of that night thirty years ago; and—of Nikolai, her son . . .

"Nikolai . . ."

Now the pair entered the drawing room: scattered about, bric-a-brac, incrustations of mother-of-pearl and bronze burst upon them.

"Oh, Nikolai! He manages to get along . . ."

"Why didn't he come to see me?"

"You see, Anna Petrovna . . . mme-emme . . . he's been very, very . . ." the Senator let the sentence hang. He drew a handkerchief from his pocket and kept blowing his nose.

"He was overjoyed . . . "

A silence followed. The bald head swayed under the long-legged bronze.

Semenich came in response to a ring.

"Is Nikolai Apollonovich at home?"

"Yes, sir."

"Mm . . . go tell him that Anna Petrovna is here!"

"Perhaps we ought to go to him," Anna Petrovna suggested with some perturbation, but Apollon Apollonovich, interrupting her, addressed Semenich.

"Me-eme . . . Semenich, go and tell him . . ."

"Very well, sir!"

"And Semenich . . . when the husband's a Turk, what is the wife?"

"Can't say, sir."

"A turkey, Semenich!"

Semenich left, laughing appreciatively.

"Nikolai's been behaving—now don't worry about it—rather strangely . . ."

"How so?"

"He's become rather secretive." Apollon Apollonovich coughed. Then, he drummed the tiny table with his fingers and, remembering something, frowned and began to rub the bridge of his nose; but he promptly recovered and, with unusual cheerfulness, exclaimed: "In any case, it's nothing. . . . Don't give it a thought!"

4

Nikolai Apollonovich, overcoming the intense pain in his knee joints, limped slightly as he ran the length of the corridor.

Whirlwinds of thoughts and notions stormed through his mind: the horror of his position had struck him. The sardine tin, that is, the bomb, had vanished. Someone had obviously taken it away. He would be arrested, but that was not the main problem: the bomb must have been taken by Apollon Apollonovich himself, taken at the very minute that he had closed his account with the bomb. So Apollon Apollonovich knew everything.

Everything—what was that? There was no such thing. There was no murder plan, Nikolai Apollonovich denied it resolutely. It was pure slander, that plan.

The fact of the bomb remained.

But since his father wished to see him, and his mother too —but he could not know, he could not have taken the bomb from the room. There were the servants—but they would have revealed everything long ago. So there was no one—nothing. They did not know about the bomb. But where was it then? Had he really put it in the drawer? Perhaps he had thrown it under the rug; he had often done things like that—mechanically, accidentally.

Within a week the bomb would doubtless be found. . . . No, that could not be. It would explode this very day with a terrific thunder (the Ableukhovs disliked thunder).

Perhaps it would explode under a rug, under a pillow, or on a shelf; he must find that bomb; and there was no time to search for it. Anna Petrovna was waiting to see him.

Everything had become confused: with inhuman rapidity, whirlwinds of thoughts spun and dinned in his ears: actually there were no thoughts.

With this senseless seething in his head Nikolai Apollonovich ran, limping on a leg that now ached intensely.

5

The first thing he saw was his mother's face: it had greatly aged, and her hands trembled visibly.

"Kolenka, my dear, my dear!"

He was unable to resist her: everything in him yearned for her.

"My little boy, my little boy . . ."

He was unable to resist her. Falling on his knees before her, he embraced her; he pressed against her knees; and he broke into feverish sobs—no one knew why. His broad shoulders shook (in the last few years he had not experienced an affectionate caress).

"Mamma—Mamma!"

He wept.

Apollon Apollonovich stood in the shadow of a recess; with his fingers he touched the tiny porcelain figure of a Chinaman; the Chinaman shook his head; Apollon Apollonovich left the dark recess. Taking short steps, he unexpectedly murmured:

"Be calm, my dears!"

It must be confessed he had not expected such emotion from his cold, secretive son: in the past two years he had seen nothing but wry grimaces on his face. His mouth had always been agape from ear to ear, his glance lowered. Distraught, Apollon Apollonovich left the room—with some purpose in mind.

"You—Mamma!"

"My own dear little boy."

The touch of fingers on his hand brought him to himself.

"Here, Kolenka, drink a little water."

When, still on his knees, he raised his eyes, he saw the infant-like gaze of the sixty-eight-year-old man: Apollon Apollonovich stood over him, holding out a glass of water; his fingers danced; he patted—or tried to pat—his son on the back, shoulders, cheeks; then suddenly he stroked his flaxen hair. Anna Petrovna was laughing and rearranging her collar.

Nikolai Apollonovich rose from his knees.

"Excuse me, mother. I'm not myself . . ."

He drank the water.

Apollon Apollonovich replaced the glass on the mother-of-pearl table. Suddenly he laughed senilely.

"So-so, so-so . . ."

Nikolai Apollonovich was standing by the pier-glass that was crowned by the wing of a golden cupid, when suddenly he remembered: the sardine tin!

His mood changed abruptly.

"I'll be back immediately . . . immediately . . ."

"What's the matter, my dear?"

"Don't bother him, Anna Petrovna. I advise you, Kolenka, to remain alone for a while . . . for five minutes. . . . Then come back."

Trying to conceal his emotional outburst, Nikolai Apollonovich reeled and dramatically hid his face in his hands: his shock of hair looked strangely lifeless. He walked out unsteadily.

"Yes, yes. . . . To tell the truth, I didn't recognize him. Such feelings . . ." Apollon Apollonovich began to pace the room: from the mirror to the window sill. "Such feelings . . ." and he stroked his side whiskers, ". . . reveal . . ." he resumed, "good qualities of nature . . ." He put his hands behind his back, under his frock coat, and, pacing the room, looked as if he were wagging a tail. "I never expected it of him."

A snuffbox on the little table attracted the attention of the eminent dignitary; to give the table a more symmetrical appearance in relation to the tray, he snatched a visiting card from the tray, turning it between his fingers; at that instant, unfolding in the receding labyrinth of external revelations, a profound thought occurred to him.

Anna Petrovna, sitting in the armchair, remarked:

"I've always said . . ."

Apollon Apollonovich suddenly crossed the room from the little table to the mirror.

"I . . . I . . ."

Then he turned from the mirror to the table.

"Kolenka astonished me and, I must admit, his conduct has reassured me . . ." he frowned, "concerning . . . concerning . . ."
He removed a hand from behind his back and drummed on the table. "Y-yes . . ."

He lapsed into thought.

6

Nikolai Apollonovich re-entered his room. He stared at the Arabian tabouret; he examined the incrustations of mother-of-pearl and ivory. Slowly he walked to the window that opened on vistas: there the river flowed, and a sailboat rocked. In the drawing room, in the distance, roulades broke the silence. It had been like that before: he had often fallen asleep to those sounds.

Nikolai Apollonovich, reflecting painfully, stood over a pile of objects:

"Where can it be? How could it be? Where, really, could it have gone?"

He simply could not remember.

Shadows began to fall upon the room—shadows and shadows. They cast a greenish hue over the chairs; and, out of the shadows, emerged a bust—of Kant, of course.

For the first time, he noticed a sheet of paper folded into four sections. Visitors, not finding him at home, often left notes for him. Mechanically, he picked up the paper and saw Likhutin's familiar handwriting. He had quite forgotten that Likhutin had been there, that he had rummaged among the things.

A sigh of relief broke from him. Everything was explained. It was Likhutin! Of course, of course! He had rummaged here; he had been looking for something and had found it. Having found what he was searching for, he had taken it away. He had seen the open desk, had looked in, and the sardine tin had caught his attention: its weight and appearance and its clock mechanism. The Lieutenant had taken it away. There was no doubt.

Greatly relieved, he sank into an armchair; the roulades thundered in the silence; it had been like that before—nine years ago. Now it seemed to him that nothing had happened—everything was so simply explained: Lieutenant Likhutin had taken the sardine tin. As for the rest, Alexander Ivanovich Doodkin would attend to it—indeed, at this moment, Alexander Ivanovich was having his discussion with Lippanchenko in the cottage at the shore. Nothing had occurred.

The roulades thundered.

7

After two and a half years the Ableukhovs had a family dinner.

The cuckoo sang, the steaming soup was brought in, Anna Petrovna shone with contentment. Apollon Apollonovich was unrecognizable in the ageless man who deftly snatched up his napkin. They were at soup when the side door creaked and Nikolai Apollonovich entered—clean-shaven, powdered, wearing a neat student uniform with an especially high collar rather reminiscent of the era of Alexander I. He took his place at the table.

"*Mon cher*," exclaimed Anna Petrovna, affectionately adjusting her pince-nez, "I see you're limping."

"Ah?" Apollon Apollonovich glanced toward Kolenka and seized the pepper shaker. "So he is . . ." He began to overpepper his soup.

"Ah, *mamman*, I stumbled over something. . . . And I sprained my knee."

"Shouldn't you put a compress on it?"

"Ah, Kolenka," Apollon Apollonovich interposed, lifting a spoon to his mouth and glancing curiously at his son, "you shouldn't make light of a sprain. It might lead to something worse . . ." He swallowed his soup.

"A mother's feelings," Anna Petrovna said, showing her large child-like eyes. "It is strange: he's already grown up, and I still worry about him."

She had forgotten that, for two and a half years, she had no concern about him; he had been obscured by a man with a long nose and eyes like plums; daily, in Spain, she had tied a stranger's silk necktie and called him a pet name.

After dinner father and son paced about the large unlighted salon; there was some light from the moon and the shaded lamp; both of them paced over the little parquet squares, crossing from the shadow into the light cast by the shaded lamp and back again. Apollon Apollonovich, his head lowered, spoke with unusual trusting softness to his son about various things.

"Do you know, it's hard to be a government official."

They veered around, passing from light into shadow.

"I told them that to encourage the import of American self-binders was no trivial thing; in this, indeed, there is more humaneness than in all their verbose speeches . . ."

They paced back across the hollow-sounding squares, crossing from shadow into moonlight.

"All the same, we need humanitarian foundations; humanism is a great affair, for which great minds like Bruno suffered much . . ."

For a long time they paced back and forth.

Apollon Apollonovich talked in a very shrill voice; sometimes his fingers seized a button of his son's coat, and then he spoke almost into his ear.

"They're babblers, Kolenka! Always talking of humanity, of humanity! I tell you, there's more humanity in self-binders than in all their talk: self-binders are needed!"

With his free arm he embraced his son's slender waist, leading him to the window—in the corner. He continued to murmur and shake his head: "they" no longer considered him, "they" no longer needed him.

"Do you know, they've passed me by!"

Nikolai Apollonovich could scarcely believe it; everything had happened so naturally—without explanation, without storm, without lectures. This murmuring in the corner was a caress. Then why, all these years . . . ?

"And so, Kolenka, my dear boy, I'll be frank with you . . ."

"What did you say? I can't hear you over that!"

The shrill, crazed siren of a small steamboat sounded just then; a red lantern disappeared into the mist, leaving broadening ruby circles on the water. Thus, with trusting softness, Apollon Apollonovich spoke to his son of this and that; and they continued to pass from shadow into light, and from light into shadow.

Apollon Apollonovich—small, old, bald, and scarcely revealed by the dying flare of the coal in the grate—began to set out the cards for a game of Patience on the tiny mother-of-pearl table. Two and a half years had passed since he had laid out cards for Patience; thus he had been imprinted on Anna Petrovna's memory. It had happened two and a half years ago, just before their decisive conversation, when he sat at this very table over a game of Patience.

"You need a ten . . ."

"No, my darling, it's hidden. . . . What do you say, Anna Petrovna, to the idea of going to Proletnoye in the spring? (Proletnoye was the name of the Ableukhov family estate in the country: Apollon Apollonovich had not visited it for twenty years.)

Fifty years before, in that region of snow and ice and forest, he had almost frozen to death accidentally; in that hour of almost freezing to death someone's cold fingers had stroked his heart; the icy hand had lured him on, while behind him the ages had sped into the immeasurable, and ahead, the icy hand had pointed into the immeasurable; it had flown to meet him. That icy hand!

And now the hand was thawing.

Liberated from service, Apollon Apollonovich remembered for the first time those desolate provincial expanses, the smoke of villages, and the jackdaws; he wanted to see the place once more: the smoke of the villages and the jackdaws.

"We'll go to Proletnoye: there are lots of flowers there."

Carried away by memories, Anna Petrovna spoke of the vivid colors of the Alhambra palaces, but in her rapture she forgot herself. Instead of speaking in the first person, again and again she had said "we"; that is, "I" plus Mindalini (or perhaps it was "Mantalini").

"*We* arrived in the morning in a fine carriage drawn by donkeys, and *our* harness, Kolenka, had such huge pompoms, and, do you know, Apollon Apollonovich, *we* got used to . . ."

Apollon Apollonovich listened, shifting cards. Then he gave up; he did not finish the game. He sat hunched in his chair, shown by the purple glare of the coals in the grate. Several times he gripped the arms of the Empire chair as if to leave, but each time he restrained himself—it would be tactless—and, yawning, sank back into it.

At last he said gently: "I must admit I'm tired."

And he moved over into a rocking chair.

Nikolai Apollonovich was called to take his mother back to the hotel. As he left the drawing room, he turned full face toward his father; seeing him in the rocking chair, Nikolai Apollonovich felt that his father, as he rocked, was gazing intently at him. This was his last conscious perception: strictly speaking, he never saw his father again. At sea, in the mountains and the cities, in the resplendent halls of great European museums, he remembered this gaze; in retrospect, he was to feel that his father's nodding head and rocking legs were a conscious salute of farewell—that aged face, the creaking of the chair, and that gaze!

8

Nikolai Apollonovich accompanied his mother to the hotel, and then turned toward the Moika. The windows of the familiar little flat revealed no light: the Likhutins were not home. There was nothing to be done. He returned home.

He stumbled into his bedroom, and stood for a while in the

darkness, amid the shadows and the lace-like light from the street lamp. From habit he removed his watch and glanced at the dial: it was three o'clock.

Then it all began again.

His fears rose to the surface again. The confidence that he had felt during the evening began to waver. He wanted to take a bromide, but there was no bromide; he wanted to read *The Apocalypse*, but there was no copy about; at this moment, a disturbing sound reached him, a ticking sound, not very loud––the sardine tin?

The thought grew stronger.

It was not this that tormented him, but rather some ancient delirium, something forgotten by day and only felt at night:

"Pépp Péppovich. . . . Pépp . . ."

Nikolai Apollonovich shivered; something blew against his forehead; something inside him threatened to explode . . .

He walked in the direction of the sound; he tried to find the place whence it issued. With creaking boots he stole up to the table from which this regular sound seemed to emanate, but here he lost his bearings.

The ticking continued.

The sound—very low—came from the shadowy corner; he tiptoed to the place again: from the table to the corner, but there were only shadows and shadows there, and sepulchral silence . . .

Weaving among the dancing shadows with a candle in his hand, Nikolai Apollonovich began to pant. He snatched at the fluttering sound—as children might chase a yellow butterfly.

Where, where, where?

Stubbornly persisting in his search for the source of the sound, he finally found it: he found it in his stomach. Standing at that moment over the night table, he suddenly saw on the table there, level with his stomach, the watch he had removed, ticking. Distraught, he looked at the dial: it was four o'clock.

He re-entered his former frame: Lieutenant Likhutin must have taken the cursed bomb away, of that he was convinced. His delirious mood was dissipated as was the terrible weight he had left in his stomach; he removed his trousers. Not without pleasure, he also pulled off his starched shirt. Taking off his shorts, he noticed his swollen knee, but thrust his legs beneath the snow-white linen sheets, and resting his head on his elbow, he fell into thought.

The candle had been blown out.

The watch continued to tick. Complete darkness enveloped him, and the ticking grew more insistent in the dark: now it seemed here, now there. And his thoughts ticked in rhythm with the sound. They throbbed in all the various places of his inflamed body: in his neck and throat, in his arms and head—an entire solar system.

Leaving his body, they remained outside the body; on all sides of him, they shaped a conscious outline, perhaps a half-yard or more away; he realized that he was not thinking; it was not his brain that thought, but something that had formed itself outside —this consciously pulsating shape; it had pulses, projections of pulses—they had all been transformed into autonomous thoughts . . .

"It's ticking, ticking . . ."

This thought confirmed a situation that his brain had rejected, that he had stubbornly resisted: the sardine tin was here, yes, here. A little hand inside it was moving in a circle, approaching the fatal point—indeed, was quite close to it. The pulsations of light scattered furiously, as sparks scatter when a new log hits the fire. . . . The trembling web of light held him with a grasp like that of a gigantic spider from another world, and it found a reflection in his brain. . . . With an involuntary movement Nikolai Apollonovich sprang from bed: in an instant his subconscious thoughts changed their orientation. His pulse began to beat rapidly —in his temples, in his throat, in his neck, in his arms . . . within the bounds of his organs.

He walked barefoot across the floor and found himself in a corner.

The light of dawn was beginning to appear.

He slipped into his shorts and walked into the corridor: but why, why? He was simply afraid. . . . The purely animal desire to live had gripped him; he had no wish to leave the corridor. He had not even the courage to glance into his room; he had no strength left to look for the bomb. Everything seemed in a tangle: he could not remember the hours and the minutes. Any instant might prove fatal.

Finding his way to a corner in the corridor, he squatted down.

Instants dragged slowly here; minutes seemed like hours; many hundreds of them passed in this way; the early blue light crept through the corridor; then it turned gray: daylight.

Nikolai Apollonovich was beginning to reassure himself of the absurdity of his fears; his brain seemed clearer. When he decided that sufficient time had elapsed, when his former belief that Likhutin had removed the sardine tin was reaffirmed, then, still squatting, he lost all fear; exhausted, he dozed off.

He wakened when something slippery touched his forehead. When he opened his eyes, he saw the damp muzzle of the bulldog, sniffing and wagging his tail. Indifferently, he pushed the dog from him, but he felt he must do something. Suddenly he wondered why he was squatting on the floor.

Why was he in the corridor?

He wandered back to his bedroom, thinking to fall asleep . . .

Suddenly there was a crash—now he understood everything.

In the future during long winter evenings Nikolai Apollonovich would remember over and over again that terrific crash: it was a special kind of crash, not comparable to anything else; it was dull and deafening, and had a bass, metallic, overwhelming quality; an immense stillness succeeded it.

Soon voices were heard, the tramping of naked feet, the low wail of the bulldog; and the telephone rang. He opened his door: streams of cold wind poured in, and lemon-yellow smoke filled his room. He ran in the direction of the wind and stumbled over a large splinter: a fragment of a shattered door.

Here was a pile of broken bricks, here running shadows visible through the smoke; here were charred pieces of rugs—how did they get here? One of the shadows shouted to him:

"What are you doing here? A terrible thing has happened!"

He heard cries:

"Oh, the swine! They ought to be slaughtered—the lot of them!"

"It's me," he tried to say, but he was interrupted:

"A bomb . . ."

"Oh!"

"Exploded—all by itself . . ."

"Oh?"

"In Apollon Apollonovich's study . . ."

"But? . . ."

"Thank heaven!"

Apollon Apollonovich had carried the sardine tin quietly into his study and had then forgotten all about it—he had no idea what it contained.

Nikolai Apollonovich ran to the spot where a door had been; now there was no door: only a large gap from which smoke poured. A crowd had gathered in the street, and a policeman was edging them away from the pavement as, with mouths open, they gaped at the black smoke billowing from the windows.

Nikolai Apollonovich ran from the smoking gap and found himself . . . he didn't know where . . .—

—There on the bed, on a pillow, sat Apollon Apollonovich in his undershirt, hugging his bare knees to his chest. Grasping his knees and groaning, he huddled there, forgotten in the general excitement. There was no one to comfort him; he sat there all alone, groaning loudly . . .—

—Nikolai Apollonovich ran toward the frail little body, ran toward it as a nurse might to a three-year-old infant, which had been intrusted to her care and whom she had forgotten; but at the sight of the intruder, the frail body sprang from the pillow and, in indescribable terror, sprinted with startling agility into the corridor.

Shouting "Stop!" Nikolai Apollonovich ran after his father to the other end of the corridor where the flames were being extinguished. "Wait!" he shouted. "Where are you going? Wait!"

Reaching the door of "the place like no other," the pursued, with inscrutable cunning, pulled open the door and then slammed it after him.

Nikolai Apollonovich desperately beat his fists against the door, imploring hoarsely:

"Let me in . . ."

"Aaa . . . aaa . . . aaa . . ." was the only response.

He fell in a faint before the door.

The servants came running. They carried him to his room.

We shall not attempt to describe how the flames were extinguished; how the Senator, suffering a severe heart attack, made his explanation to the police; that after this explanation, there was a consultation of physicians who discovered an enlarged aorta. Nonetheless, during those days of the strike which so worried the government offices, he was a mere ghost of himself. He did succeed in proving something to the police and, as a result, someone was arrested and later released. An investigation was started, but it was squashed and no one suffered.

During those days his son was in bed with a paroxysm of nervous fever: for a long time he did not regain consciousness. When he came to himself, he was alone with his mother in the lacquered house. Apollon Apollonovich was not there: he had retired to his country estate where he spent the whole winter. He requested an indefinite leave of absence and eventually passed into retirement; before his departure, he had prepared a passport and a letter of credit for his son. Anna Petrovna accompanied Kolenka. But she returned that summer. Nikolai Apollonovich came back to Russia only after his father's death.

EPILOGUE

The February sun was setting. Shaggy cactuses were scattered here and there. Soon, very soon, sails would come scudding from the gulf toward the sandy shore: here they were—sharp-winged and tilting. A tiny cupola vanished among the cactuses.

In light blue native dress and a bright red Arabian fez, Nikolai Apollonovich squatted. The long tassel of the fez dangled: his silhouette was clearly outlined from the flat roof. Below him was a village square, from which came the sounds of "tam-tam" with a dull, beguiling nuance.

Everywhere one could see the white cubes of houses; from beyond came the shouts of an olive-skinned Berber urging on a donkey.

Nikolai Apollonovich was oblivious to the "tam-tam" sounds and the Berber's shouts; in his mind's eye, he saw his father Apollon Apollonovich, small, frail, and bald, rocking in a swing, moving his head and legs in rhythm: he remembered that rocking motion . . .

In the distance an almond-tree flushed pink; beyond, a jagged summit of a luminous lilac-amber that was Zaghouan; and the promontory, that of Carthage.

Nikolai Apollonovich had rented this little house in this Tunisian village from an Arab.

Branches of fir trees bent low under the weight of the snow; they shaggily fronted a five-columned wooden structure; beyond the railings of the terrace the snowdrifts had piled into hillocks; upon them rested the tender rose reflection of the February sunset.

A small, stooping figure in felt boots and woolen mittens, supporting himself with a stick, passed by: his fur collar was raised, his cap pulled over his ears. The small figure, led by the arm, was threading his way through a cleared path; the person leading him held a warm plaid rug.

Since he had come to the country, Apollon Apollonovich had worn enormous eyeglasses; they frosted over in the cold air, and he could not see through them the distant jagged line of wooded hills or the smoke of village huts or the jackdaws. He saw only the moonlight on the parquet squares and at his side, his son Nikolai Apollonovich—gentle, attentive, receptive—with lowered head, crossing from shadow into light and back again from light into shadow.

In the evening the little old man sat at a table surrounded by round frames with portraits: an officer in kid gloves and an old woman in a head-dress. The officer was his father; and the woman was his mother, who had been born a Svargin. Apollon Apollonovich was writing his memoirs for posthumous publication.

They were eventually published the year after his death.

They sparkled with wit—Russia is well-acquainted with them.

The flame of the sun beat down unmercifully: one saw red before the eyes. If one turned away, the sun beat fiercely on the nape of the neck; in this light, the desert looked dull and green. In any case, life here was moribund; a fine thing it would be to remain here forever!

Nikolai Apollonovich, in a cork helmet with a gauze protector, sat on a sandpile; in front of him, an enormous head loomed from the ageless sands; Nikolai Apollonovich sat confronting the Sphinx.

He had already been here for two years, engaged in research at the local museum. There were many misinterpretations of *The Book of the Dead* and the writings of Manethon. Nikolai Apollonovich had burrowed beneath the Egyptian earth; in the twentieth century, he foresaw Egypt: this decrepit head was the end of a culture. With this head all had died, nothing remained. There would be an explosion—everything would be obliterated.

Ah, how good it was to be busy. Sometimes, tearing himself away from his *schema*, he would concentrate; not everything had died. There were sounds. There was a din in Cairo: a peculiar din, reminding him of a familiar sound—dull and deafening, with a bass, metallic, overwhelming quality. Nikolai Apollonovich would return to the mummies; "chance" had brought him to them. As for Kant? Kant was forgotten.

The evening was drawing down; the massive piles of Gizeh stretched grimly into the eyeless twilight. Yes, everything seemed to have expanded in them; something was expanding within them; and in the hovering dust one could see dark brown lights. The air was stifling.

He leaned meditatively against the side of the dead pyramid; he himself was a pyramid, the summit of culture, which would crumble.

In the full sunlight, the little old man sat immobile in a soft armchair; his eyes of cornflower-blue were fixed upon the old lady; his legs were wrapped in a plaid rug (they were useless now). Clusters of aromatic lilac were heaped on his knees. He leaned as far as he could toward the old lady:

"Did you say he's finished it? . . . He's coming?"

"He's putting his papers in order . . ."

Somewhere in Egypt Nikolai Apollonovich had completed his monograph.

"What is it called?"

"The monograph is called . . . me-emme . . . *Concerning the Letter of Dauphsekhrut,*" Apollon Apollonovich replied, beaming. His memory was failing him: he had forgotten the names of common objects, but he firmly remembered the word "Dauphsekhrut," about which his son had written him. When he looked up, he caught the gold of greening leaves. The wind was blowing furiously; the sky was blue and soft as lambs' wool; and a wagtail was scampering on the path before him.

"Did you say in Nazareth?"

What a field of bluebells! The bluebells opened their lilac mouths; among the tightly packed flowers a heavy movable armchair had been placed; in it, under a canvas umbrella, sat Apollon Apollonovich, his unshaven face wrinkled and covered with a silvery stubble.

In the year 1913, Nikolai Apollonovich roamed for days the meadows and woods of his estate, morosely and lazily observing the the tillers. He wore a cap and a native coat of a camel color; his boots creaked; a golden, spade-like beard had altered his appearance. A shock of hair falling from under his cap revealed a recent silver streak. The Egyptian sunlight had affected his eyes, and he now wore blue-tinted glasses. His voice had coarsened, and his face was weather-beaten. He had lost his former agility. He lived alone, never called on anyone, and no one ever visited him; he was often seen in church and, lately, he had been reading the philosophical works of Skovorod.

His parents had died.

Selected Grove Press Paperbacks

E573	KEENE, DONALD, ed. / Modern Japanese Literature / $7.95
E522	KEROUAC, JACK / Mexico City Blues / $3.95
B9	LAWRENCE, D. H. / Lady Chatterley's Lover / $1.95
B373	LUCAS, GEORGE / American Graffiti / $1.75
E716	MAMET, DAVID / The Water Engine and Mr. Happiness / $3.95
B10	MILLER, HENRY / Tropic of Cancer / $2.50
B59	MILLER, HENRY / Tropic of Capricorn / $1.95
E770	NELSON, PAUL / Rod Stewart: A Biography / $8.95
E636	NERUDA, PABLO / Five Decades: Poems 1925–1970. Bilingual ed. / $5.95
E687	OE, KENZABURO / Teach Us To Outgrow Our Madness / $4.95
E315	PINTER, HAROLD / The Birthday Party and The Room / $2.95
E411	PINTER, HAROLD / The Homecoming / $2.45
B438	REAGE, PAULINE / Story of O, Part II: Return to the Chateau / $2.25
B213	RECHY, JOHN / City of Night / $1.95
B69	ROBBE-GRILLET, ALAIN / Two Novels: Jealousy and In the Labyrinth / $4.95
E759	ROBERTS, RANDY / Jack Dempsey: The Manassa Mauler / $6.95
E741	ROSSET, BARNEY, ed. / Evergreen Review Reader: 1962–1967 / $10.00
B138	SADE, MARQUIS DE / The 120 Days of Sodom and Other Writings / $6.95
B323	SCHUTZ, WILLIAM C. / Joy: Expanding Human Awareness / $1.95
B313	SELBY, HUBERT, JR. / Last Exit to Brooklyn / $2.95
E618	SNOW, EDGAR / Red Star Over China / $4.95
E703	STOPPARD, TOM / Every Good Boy Deserves Favor and Professional Foul: Two Plays / $3.95
B319	STOPPARD, TOM / Rosencrantz and Guildenstern Are Dead / $1.95
B341	SUZUKI, D. T. / Introduction to Zen Buddhism / $1.95
E749	THELWELL, MICHAEL / The Harder They Come / $2.95
B395	TRUFFAUT, FRANCOIS / The Story of Adele H. Illus. / $2.45
B365	WARNER, SAMUEL J. / Self Realization and Self Defeat / $2.95
E219	WATTS, ALAN W. / The Spirit of Zen / $2.95

GROVE PRESS, INC., 196 West Houston St., New York, N.Y. 10014